The
Woman
in the
Photograph

'An **enchanting** read that will make you shed tears of **sadness and joy** in equal measure'
WOMAN'S OWN

'**Brave**, **intuitive**, incredibly grounded and funny . . . A clever book that is **unputdownable**'
CANDIS MAGAZINE

'An engaging read with a **relatable** and **realistic** heroine'
THE LADY

'**Oh, wow. Just . . . wow** . . . Butland has created such an unforgettable character . . . **Poignant**, heartwarming, and **totally unforgettable**; *Lost for Words* is the soul-searching, exceptional novel that I have been waiting for'
THE WRITING GARNET

'Brimming with **hope**, drama, **friendship**, love, and **new beginnings** and I read this book from cover to cover in one evening. This book is **stunning** and special and everyone should read it as soon as possible'
BOOKS OF ALL KINDS

'Oh how **I adored this book**. I loved everything about it . . . Simply **beautiful**'
FROM FIRST PAGE TO LAST

'*Lost for Words* is a compelling and lovely read that will warm your heart and leave you with a smile on your face . . . definitely do not miss out on this one!'
A SPOONFUL OF HAPPY ENDINGS

About the author

Stephanie Butland lives near the sea in the north-east of England. She writes in a studio at the bottom of her garden. Researching her novels has turned her into an occasional performance poet and tango dancer.

@under_blue_sky
/StephanieButlandAuthor
@StephanieButlandAuthor

Also by Stephanie Butland

Novels
Letters to My Husband
The Other Half of My Heart
Lost for Words
The Curious Heart of Ailsa Rae

Non-fiction
How I Said Bah! to cancer
Thrive: The Bah! Guide to Wellness After cancer

The
Woman
in the
Photograph

Stephanie Butland

ZAFFRE

First published in Great Britain in 2019 by
ZAFFRE
80–81 Wimpole St, London W1G 9RE

A CIP catalogue record for this book is
available from the British Library.

ISBN: 978-1-78576-896-5

Also available as an ebook

1 3 5 7 9 10 8 6 4 2

Typeset by IDSUK (Data Connection) Ltd
Printed and bound by Clays Ltd, Elcograf S.p.A

Zaffre is an imprint of Bonnier Books UK
www.bonnierbooks.co.uk

For Dad, who taught me about photography,
and that I can do anything

'What makes photography a strange invention is that its primary raw materials are light and time.'

Understanding a Photograph, John Berger

24 April 2018

The Photographers' Gallery, Ramillies Street, London

Seeing the photograph will be a shock.

It always is. Even though she is the one who took it.

Veronica leans against the wall opposite the gallery entrance, braces herself, and turns her eyes to the poster. The no-nonsense font declares: 'Women in their Power: Veronica Moon and Second Wave Feminism: 26 April—26 August 2018'. Two days from now. Vee reads the words until they cease any sense they were making, and then she makes herself look at the image. Doing it here, publicly, with cyclists skimming through her field of vision and grimy London noise all around, makes her feel half-disappeared already.

The feelings have never changed, even if the memory is long gone. Love and loss and ache and sheer flaming rage at everything that was taken from her in the moment that she pressed the button that opened and closed the shutter faster than a final blink. Vee is top-full of it all, still, even after all of these years.

Leonie, the woman she loved as she has loved no one else in her seventy years, glowers from the frame. Her heavy brow, half-closed eyes, great arc of a nose, all suit being enlarged to poster size. Leonie always knew that she deserved more space than the world gave her. The black and white image looks contemporary after thirty years, as the novelty of colour and fuss in photography has come into fashion and gone again.

Veronica can, if she tries, admire this as a photograph. All of her craft is here: the way she managed the light, chose the angle, created a portrait that is both greater than Leonie and the very essence of her, distilled to an almost unbearable likeness. But there are good reasons why she avoids it. It was the moment of the two greatest losses of her life.

Even now, when she should be facing everything, resolving everything, when her eyes should be taking in all that they can before it's too late, she cannot bear to look at this image for long.

Whether Vee likes it or not, it's what she will be remembered for. Though if she had been a war photographer, she would have been congratulated. If she had been a man, come to that. Unflinching, they would have said. Bold. Uncompromising. Veronica, by virtue of being a woman: heartless, ambitious, unfeeling, selfish. Career over.

Part 1: Subject

Part I: Subject

First, forget all you think you know about the camera being a neutral object, a benign, unlying eye, watching and capturing everything without judging or deciding. That's what the world wants you to think.

In the hands of a true photographer, a camera can be clever, wily, sharp, cutting; it can be consoling, healing or divisive; it can be smart. It should definitely be smart. At least as smart as the person who is holding it. And if that person is a woman, she will know already how to pay attention, to watch the world around her for signs and clues to what she needs to be careful of.

Every time you press the shutter, you are making a choice about where to look, and what you are choosing to show, or to remember. You are creating a history.

Veronica Moon, *Women in Photographs* (unpublished)

'Postman at the Picket Line'
Veronica Moon

Exhibition Section: Early Days

Camera: Nikon F1
Film: Kodak, 200 ASA
First published: *This Month* magazine, 1968

Welcome to Veronica Moon's world: quietly subversive, women-centred, and not afraid to allow the viewer to deduce the story behind the image.

This photograph was taken at the picket line at the Ford Dagenham strike of 1968. Female machinists had walked out in protest at being paid less than their male counterparts for equivalent skilled work. Moon had just arrived at the site when the postman came to deliver the mail; in this photograph, she captures the moment when he decides not to cross the picket line and turns back, cheered by the striking machinists. Notice how the focus of the photograph is not the postal worker himself, who is caught leaving the shot, only his shoulder and bag visible. Rather, Moon draws the watcher's eye to the three women in the foreground of the photograph, the interplay between their bodies, arms linked, and the tilt of their heads as they laugh. The image is reminiscent of Land Girl publicity posters and seaside holiday snaps, and connects to our ideas of women as sisters, united and formidable.

The women here are strong, good-humoured and full of purpose; the camera's view is steady and honest. Behind the trio of faces the photograph focuses on, you'll see another group of women; the one on the far right is the second wave feminist and writer Leonie Barratt, a long-term associate and close personal friend of Moon.

This early photograph bears many of the trademarks of Moon's later work. The focus is sharp: as with her later portraits, there is no desire to hide flaws or soften images. The photographer draws our attention to the faces of her subjects by positioning them a third of the way down the frame. And there is nothing static or posed about this photograph. It is a moment captured that would otherwise have been lost.

This is the first of Moon's images to have been published in the UK national press, when it appeared to accompany a column by Leonie Barratt in *This Month* magazine, in July 1968. *This Month* was published from 1962 to 1986 and published a range of reviews, features and columns, with a readership of 250,000 at its peak. It could be seen as the first photograph of Moon's feminist career. Many of the photographs that Moon took previously while working at the *Colchester Echo* do feature women, but these are in traditional roles – at coffee mornings and charity events. Moon was assigned these jobs while her male colleagues were given news and sports stories to cover; she went to Dagenham on her day off, having been refused permission to attend as an official photograph by the *Echo*'s editor.

In 1968:

- Harold Wilson was Prime Minister of Great Britain
- In the USA, Senator Robert (Bobby) F Kennedy and Martin Luther King were assassinated within three weeks of each other
- The Beatles had two number one chart singles in the UK with 'Lady Madonna' and 'Hey Jude'
- Enoch Powell made his notorious 'Rivers of Blood' speech

- The TV show *Dad's Army* was first screened
- A demonstration in London's Grosvenor Square against US involvement in the Vietnam War ended in violence and mass arrests
- the Abortion Act 1967 came into effect, legalising abortion on a number of grounds
- Agatha Christie's novel *By the Pricking of My Thumbs* was published
- The film *Rosemary's Baby* was released
- The iconic photograph 'Earthrise' was taken when the Apollo 8 spacecraft orbited the moon

And the female machinists at the Ford Dagenham car plant went on strike because they believed their skilled work should be appropriately rewarded, and they should be paid at the same rate as men doing equivalent grade jobs. Veronica Moon went to take a look.

15 June 1968

'WHAT ARE YOU SIGHING ABOUT now, Dad?' Veronica's father, Stanley, reads the *Daily Mirror* less for news and more as a starting point for discussion.

'I'm all for equal rights but this is going too far. Listen. "Thousands of car workers will be laid off next week unless 187 women sewing-machinists call off a strike for more pay."'

'You ain't really for equal rights, then, are you?' Vee has her kit spread out on the dining table, and she's checking and cleaning each part in turn: camera body, lenses, filters, strap, the case she carries it all in. When she presses the shutter and winds on, the sound always seems synchronised with the beat of her heart.

'I am. But it ain't an equal situation, now, is it, Veronica?' He leans forward in his armchair, crumpling the newspaper into his lap, and says, 'The women will only be working for pin money. The men who get laid off – they're the ones putting bread on the table. And their wives will have something to say if they come home with nothing.'

'I thought I might go down, later in the week. I've got my day off on Thursday.'

'Bob isn't sending you to cover it, then?'

'It's a bit out of our way, and anyway, Bob wouldn't send me. He'd send George. I just get the jobs George don't want.' A jumble sale to raise money for the Spastics' Society was the highlight of last week.

When Vee got a start as a junior photographer at the *Colchester Echo* she knew she was lucky, and she knew she would have to work her way up. (Not least because she suspected that her dad had probably twisted Bob's arm to get her the job in the first place. The two of them were at school together. Veronica hasn't asked if that swung it for her, because she really, really doesn't want to know.)

Stanley gets out of his chair. 'Well. That allotment ain't going to weed itself.'

'That's for sure,' Vee says.

'It's a nice day. But you'll be shutting yourself under the stairs, will you?'

Vee smiles. 'What else would I be doing?'

Stanley shakes his head. 'This will all have to change once you're married, you know, treasure. Barry won't want you sneaking round here every Saturday afternoon.'

'Barry doesn't mind, Dad. And anyway, the wedding won't be for a few years yet.'

'Your mother was only nineteen when we got married.' It's eleven years since she died, but the hollowness of loss is still great enough to make a short, hard moment for them both before they look at each other and sort of smile in acknowledgement that she is gone, they are not, and they are the only two people in the world who could ever understand, precisely, what that means.

'Will you bring some rhubarb? We can have it for afters, tomorrow.'

Stewed rhubarb and condensed milk is her dad's idea of heaven.

Stanley nods, takes his hat from the stand by the door, and he's gone.

Almost as soon as Vee had managed to get a camera of her own, when she was fifteen, thanks to savings and a birthday and Christmas present combined, she realised that she'd never be able to afford to have her films developed, so she set about learning how to do it herself. The novelty of her makeshift darkroom under the stairs, the sour/sharp smells and the eerie light, has yet to wear off.

Vee can still remember the first time she saw a photographer at work. It was at a cousin's wedding. Vee was a seven-year-old bridesmaid, in shell pink with a little white knitted cardigan, pink silk roses to hold, and borrowed satin shoes with scrunched-up handkerchiefs in the toes to make them fit. Every picture of her from that day shows her staring into the camera. She remembers how much she wanted to know what was happening under that cloth the photographer was hiding in. When she wasn't in the photographs she stood behind the tripod, listening to the clicks and winding sounds of the camera at work. When the photograph album was shown – cousin Betty had married up in the world, there was no one in the family who had had a proper album before – Veronica saw how the adults used the photos to relive the day. They commented on this hat and those flowers, what a shame it was about the weather and how handsome Betty's husband was. That man, under the cloth, with a button and a handle to wind, had quietly made the shape of their memories.

She didn't understand it in those terms at the time, of course. She just knew she wanted a camera like other children wanted a pogo-stick.

Now she and Barry are engaged, and he's keen for them to spend all of their spare time together, she still pleads for her Saturday afternoons. Once Dad started inviting him to the football, that got a bit easier. On match days, she can join them in their local pub afterwards, commiserate or celebrate, head on to the pictures or to Barry's mum and dad's for tea. She finds it easier to be polite, to talk about *Z-Cars* and Harold Wilson, and other things she isn't much interested in, if she has spent a few hours in her cramped, impossible-to-stand-upright-in darkroom, lit by its red light bulb, watching her images develop as they float below the surface of a chemical bath. Feeling her soul's happiness as she does what she has wanted, above everything, to do since cousin Betty's wedding day.

20 June 1968

VERONICA MOON HAS NEVER BEEN to a picket line before.

'Don't do anything I wouldn't do,' Dad said, as he waved her off this morning. He had checked the tyres on their shared Ford Anglia, as though the hour and a half from Colchester to Dagenham was some kind of epic journey. Still, it's probably the longest drive she has ever done on her own.

'Funny thing to do on your day off,' had been Barry's comment, but Barry's job isn't his hobby, so of course he wouldn't understand. Vee hates that he calls photography her 'hobby', but she can't think of a better word. It's her passion, really, but when she said that to him he laughed and said, no it wasn't, he was.

And now, here she is. Actually where the action is, for once.

The papers yesterday reported that Ford are losing more than a million pounds a day because of the strike. The Secretary of State is involved. All the way, in the car, Vee has been thinking about what she would find when she arrived. She thought she would be able to see the world changing, and that she could be the one to chronicle it. She's been drawn back, again and again, to Bill Eppridge's photograph of the dying Bobby Kennedy. She feels the shock of the event, of course she does: she's crowded round the papers, the television, with everyone else as the impact has been discussed, all over the world. But when she looks at the image of the man on the floor, the blood, the young man cradling his head, she feels something else, too. Or rather, she imagines – imagines she was the one in the Ambassador Hotel in LA when the bullets were fired. Would she have had the presence of mind to take those photographs? She thinks so. She just needs to get herself to places where history is happening.

The picket-line women are in flat shoes and mini-dresses, arms bare to the sun, tiny and bright against the metal gates, the grimy brick of the factory building glowering over them. Vee wishes she hadn't dressed the way she always does for work. Her knee-length skirt is sticky with static against her stockings. Her jacket, so handy with the pockets for film cases and spare lenses, is weighing her down, and she can't take it off because she knows she has sweated through the blouse beneath it. She feels old-fashioned, out of touch. Why doesn't she have a mini-dress? Why is she sleeping in rollers? And why on earth are hair and clothes what she is thinking of now?

Maybe this is what the world changing looks like. It's not as dramatic as what happened in Grosvenor Square or the protests in Paris, but it could still be part of a change. As her dad says, nothing lasts forever.

She takes a closer look at the banners. They are painted or coloured in, made with careful attention to detail, letters equal height and the spacing of the wording considered. 'No Deal Till You Recognise Our Skill' reads one banner. 'Unequal Pay Is Sex Discrimination', reads another. 'We Want Sexual Equality' says a third. These women are organised and they mean what they say. Vee inhales and straightens her spine. This is change, all right. She needs to teach herself to see it.

Behind the banners, women chatter and laugh. Someone is handing round sandwiches. Well, there isn't really any reason why something like this shouldn't feel like a picnic. However serious it is.

She looks around, for a leader to introduce herself to. There's no one obviously in charge; but then she recognises one of the women from the press coverage.

'Hello,' Vee says, 'I'm Veronica Moon. I wonder if you'd mind if I took some photographs? Of the picket line?'

'Be our guest,' the woman says, 'it's nice of you to ask. The blokes don't. Where you from?'

Vee takes the lens cap off the Nikon F1 that she still can't believe is hers, although technically, it isn't, until she's finished paying Dad back for it, out of her wages. 'Colchester. The *Echo*. But I'm not here officially. It's my day off. I came just to see, really.'

The woman nods. 'There's been a few of those. Especially women. Do you get paid the same as the blokes?'

Vee thinks about George, who behaves as though she should be paying him for the privilege of working under him, and the male journalists who barely tolerate her, the secretaries who've done their best to make her feel welcome. She's a fish out of water, really. No, it's not that. She's a fish that the other fish refuse to make a space for. She would swim as fast, if she could. 'I don't think so,' she says.

'No surprises there,' says someone else, and Vee nods – she doesn't trust herself to speak, suddenly, feeling the enormity of what she is up against and, at the same time, the possibility that is offered here, for all women. She takes photographs of the gathered strikers, the banners; drops to her knee and changes to a wide-angle lens so that she can capture the size of the factory behind them, how it both dwarfs them and creates a dull background to their light and power.

What if this isn't as simple as another strike, interesting because it has women at its heart this time? What if what is happening here is – connected? Part of the same power in the world that means she has to be grateful for being 'a woman in a man's world', that her married friends look down on her and talk about meals for their husbands as though housekeeping is a vocation? 'Women's lib' is an easy joke in Vee's world; she remembers Barry's dad laughing about it getting out of hand, when he did the washing up at Christmas. Barry's mum laughed back and said if that was the case she wouldn't bother washing her hair. But what if women's lib is more than men pulling their weight? What if it could be about genuine equality? What if Vee could be judged on her merit? What if no one cared whether she was a woman or a man and only cared about the work she did? The rhythm of her blood accelerates at the thought of it: she feels it in her temples and her wrists, at her throat. She nods her thanks to the women, stands, and takes a breath and she tells herself what she always tells herself when she feels overwhelmed or out of her depth: do your job, Veronica. Do your job and do your best.

She's changing back to a standard lens when she hears something behind her: a woman's voice raised in a catcall, laughter. She turns to see a postman.

'I go on holiday and miss all the action,' he says, 'this is the famous picket line, is it, girls?'

'Equal pay for equal work,' says a short, short-haired, bright-blonde woman, 'you ain't going to argue with that, are you?'

'Definitely not. My Sheila would have my guts for garters,' he says, to general laughter, and Vee, hardly realising she is doing so, raises the viewfinder to her eye and takes a photograph. She's not sure why, because she shouldn't be putting a man in the middle of this, really. Waste of a shot. Still, she's caught the moment. She winds the film on. 'Still not sorted, then?' the postman continues.

'Nah. They said we was irresponsible, and they said they'd have an inquiry. We said we'll come back to work when we're getting recognition for our skill.'

'Well, good for you, girls,' the postman says, 'so this is an official picket?'

'Course it is. We know how to do things proper. That's why your car seat never comes apart at the seams.' Everyone laughs at this, and Vee wants to drop her camera, to join in, but if there's one useful thing she's learned at the paper it's if you want to get a decent photo, keep your distance. 'You're not here to be one of them,' George, the senior photographer at the *Echo*, told her, the first time he took her out on a job, 'you're here to be the only one of you.'

'In that case, my fellow workers,' the postman says, 'it looks like these here letters won't be getting to your bosses today.' And he returns the bundle of envelopes to his bag and turns away. Vee clicks the shutter. She's got the shot that matters. It's not always obvious to the eye, but she feels it in her gut. And even though, if this image is ever published, the quality of it will be terrible – nothing looks good on newsprint – she will know that it's good. Really good.

'Oi.' It takes her a moment to realise that the woman striding along the road is calling to her. There is a solid fierceness in her walk that tells her to keep her camera lowered. Two other women are close behind.

'Hello,' Vee says, and holds out a hand. She's surprised to see it isn't shaking, 'Veronica Moon.'

The stranger's hands are in her dungaree pockets, so Vee drops her arm. Dungarees! She's never seen them in real life. Not on a woman, anyway. 'Does that mean anything? Am I supposed to know who you are?' Her voice has the confident sort of non-accent that Vee wishes for. It's not as posh as the radio but there's no trace of where she has come from in it. That has to be useful.

18

'Probably not,' Vee says. She's torn between continuing to do what she was doing – she knows she's within her rights, knows she has nothing to hide – and justifying herself. She's outnumbered, so, 'I'm a photographer with the *Colchester Echo*. But I'm really just here for my own' – what's the word? Not 'amusement', not 'satisfaction' – 'it's my day off, and I wanted to see for myself what was going on.'

And now the woman offers a hand to shake. Vee takes it, suddenly self-conscious about her bubble-gum nail polish. She doesn't wear her engagement ring to work, and she didn't put it on this morning. She tells Barry it's because she wouldn't want to lose it but she's not sure that's really the reason. It feels awkward, still, like the word 'fiancée' does.

'Leonie Barratt.'

'Veronica Moon,' Vee says again, 'Vee, for short.'

'Hello, Vee,' Leonie says, letting go of her hand and smiling. 'I'm writing this up for my column in *This Month*. Well, I might be. You came to have a look? What do you make of it?' The woman has clear skin, brown eyes, and her face, bare of makeup, is dominated by a large, bony nose. Vee becomes conscious of the half-hour she spent doing her hair and putting on foundation, blush and eyeshadow before she left the house. Putting a face on, her mum used to call it. Vee knows what she meant. She doesn't always feel as though her own face is enough. This woman – Leonie's not a name Vee has heard before – apparently has no such problem.

'Well,' Vee says, 'I'm all for it. Obviously.'

One of the women behind Leonie titters, but Leonie ignores her. 'Striking? Or equal pay?'

'Both.' Vee replaces the lens cap, and starts to turn away. If none of the Ford workers are questioning her motives, she doesn't really see why a journalist and her up-themselves mates should be. And she gets enough of that sort of thing at work, from the men.

'Do you want me to introduce you to some people? So you can get some photos?' Leonie asks.

'No thank you,' Vee says. She's not sure what will happen if she starts to look official and it gets back to Bob. For fear of sounding rude, she adds, 'I don't want to get in the way. I'm not really supposed to be here.'

The women with Leonie laugh, and one of them says, 'You're missing the point, sister,' in a tone that makes Vee squirm. She hoists her bag on to her shoulder, ready to make a circuit of the action, shoot the last half-dozen frames on her film, and then head back to the car.

Better to make a move, than stay to be laughed at.

But Leonie puts a hand on her arm, and then turns to her friends with the fierceness that was in her stride as she walked over. She says, 'Come on. We support our sisters. Everyone starts somewhere.' Looking back at Vee, she smiles, and her brown eyes grow warm, 'Why don't we split, and have a drink? I'll catch you up on a few things.'

Vee assumed that by 'drink' Leonie meant 'tea' – it was barely noon when they left the picket line – but ten minutes later she finds herself in the George and Dragon. One of the panes in the door is missing, the space covered with taped-on cardboard, and the carpet is tacky underfoot. The mirror behind the bar has a crack running down the centre, which warps the faces of people waiting to be served. Leonie's friends, who are called Bea and something beginning with F that Vee didn't quite catch, go to sit down. Vee follows Leonie to the bar.

Before Leonie can order, the barman says, 'We don't serve ladies at the bar, I'm afraid.'

'What?' Leonie says, her voice loudening with incredulity. 'Seriously, man? It's 1968! Women earn their own bread, and they spend it how they want to. Christ knows, they could do with a drink in this bloody world, so your landlord needs to shape up.'

If Vee ventured a 'bloody' at home, Dad would tell her off for bad language, but the barman shrugs. 'Not my rules' – he indicates two men sitting towards the other end of the horseshoe-shaped bar, one of whom is looking on with interest – 'but I'm sure one of these gentlemen will oblige you.'

'What if we don't want to be obliged?' Leonie asks. There's an imperious tone to her voice, now: she means business. She might be what her dad calls 'entitled'. Born with a silver spoon in her mouth. Or at least went to a posh school, the sort of place with a hat as part of the uniform, like they probably do in Epping. She's not backwards in coming forwards, that's for sure.

'I'd be happy to help you ladies out,' one of the men sitting at the bar says. 'You go and have a seat with your friends. What are you drinking? I'll bring them over.'

'Thank you,' Vee says, and she smiles towards the man who's just spoken. She's drowned out by Leonie.

'Have none of you heard of equal rights for women? Liberation?'

The barman has long hair, a lazy smile, and a Tyrannosaurus Rex T-shirt. He's probably quite the local attraction. 'Yeah, we have, but you're in Essex now, love. Not your fancy bits of London.'

Leonie stands up straighter. She's not that tall, but she seems it, and she knows how to take up space. She looks the barman in the eye, and says, 'It seems that a prick's a prick wherever you go.'

Vee hears her own intake of breath, and sees that Bea and someone-beginning-with-F have stopped talking and are getting to their feet, coming over to the bar. This could go either way. Vee has seen it before. She and Barry sometimes go for a bar meal at the King's Arms on a Friday night. If an argument starts, it can either flare to fists or diffuse into laughter. She doesn't think there'd be a fight here – men who won't serve women in a bar aren't going to hit them, not in public at least – but it's not comfortable. So she catches the eye of the man who offered to buy their drinks, and smiles at him again. He laughs. The fine thin membrane of tension dissolves, and it's an ordinary lunchtime once more. Ordinary if you go to the pub for lunch every day, anyway.

'All right, then,' says the barman. 'Quick. What do you want?'

Leonie looks at Vee, a question. 'Sweet martini and lemonade, please.'

'Really?'

'Yes. I like it.' At least Barry and her dad don't tell her what to drink.

'Suit yourself.' Leonie turns to the barman. 'Sweet martini and lemonade, and three pints of cider. Please.'

The barman's hand hesitates over the pint glasses, but he thinks better of saying whatever he might have said, and pulls the pints.

'There you go, ladies.'

'Thank you,' Vee says.

At the same time, Leonie answers, 'We're not ladies, we're women, but I really don't have the time to go into that now.'

When they get to their table and sit, Vee is more relieved than she would think it was possible to be, perched on a wobbly stool in a dingy pub with three strident women she barely knows. Then a gaggle of men arrives and fills the place with smoke and swearing, and attention moves away from the women. Vee feels herself exhale, long and slow, as though she's just got away with something, though she honestly couldn't say what.

From the way that some of the men greet Leonie and the others, and from their not-from-round-here accents, Vee gathers that they must be journalists covering the strike. Covering the strike *too*, she tells herself. She is a professional photographer and she got a great shot back there. Come on, Vee.

The others drink without comment; this must be normal for them. Leonie turns to Vee, and says, 'You shouldn't flirt men into buying drinks for you. You shouldn't appease them when they're being pricks like that. It doesn't help any of us, in the long run.'

Vee holds her gaze. She's impressed by this woman – the unapologetic way she goes about what she sees as her business, her bravado – but she's fought for her career, such as it is, and before that she fought for her place on a photography course where she was the only woman. 'So what do I do? What you tell me?'

Bea laughs, a wet splutter. 'She's got you there, Leonie.' Then, to Vee, 'You need to keep her in her place. Stand up for yourself. It's not just the men who are the oppressors.'

Leonie has the grace to laugh too, and then she looks at Bea, slides her hand under the table and squeezes her thigh. Vee feels herself blush as she realises what she's seeing. It took her a moment to recognise flirting out of its usual context. And then Leonie turns back to her, 'I didn't mean to sound patronising. What I was trying to say was that women have learned to get what they want from men by wheedling around them. But actually, we have the right to ask.'

Vee nods. 'It's easier, though. Ain't it?'

'It's easier to work for seventy per cent of what men get paid than to strike,' Leonie counters, 'but if we're satisfied with that – we're never going to get anywhere, are we?'

'No,' Vee agrees, and then she thinks about her dad, how he would order a drink at the bar for a woman if those were the rules, 'but those blokes just wanted to help us out, didn't they?' She's drinking too quickly, and she didn't have breakfast. The alcohol is going straight to her head. She feels as though this is an important conversation, but she can't hold on to the threads of it for long enough to work out why. It relates to the feeling she had, earlier, photographing the women on the picket line; that there's something else going on in the world, that she has a job greater than trying to be taken seriously.

Someone-beginning-with-F is tittering, saying something to Bea in a voice too low for Vee to catch. Leonie hears it, though. 'Shut it, Fen. Everyone needs to learn. It's hard to see how pervasive the patriarchy is when you've grown up in it.'

'I'm not Eliza Doolittle, you know,' Vee says. She wants to say, 'I'm not sodding Eliza Doolittle', but her dad doesn't like her swearing. And though that's probably patriarchist (that might not be the word, Vee thinks) of him, she loves him, and he's all she's got, apart from Barry. He might not be exactly on board with women's lib but he's always been on her side, always taught her things she wanted to know and encouraged her to follow her career.

'Quite right,' Bea says, 'you tell her.' Leonie and Bea grin and Fen gets up, returning a few minutes later with four pints of cider. By then Leonie's told her about the magazines she writes for, the stories that are coming up, the groups that are forming and the way that women are starting to make change happen for themselves, to organise, and Vee feels a fizz inside, something more than the martini and the cider she's adding to it.

Fen and Bea leave after the second round; Vee and Leonie stay for another. As Bea and Leonie arrange to meet up later, they kiss, lip to lip, Bea's hand, briefly, on Leonie's throat.

'You can stop staring,' Leonie says.

'Sorry,' Vee says, and the cider, helpfully, adds, 'it's just that I've never met lesbians before. I think you're my first lesbians.'

Leonie laughs, 'I doubt it,' she says, 'and anyway, I'm not a lesbian. I just go with women some of the time. The rest of the time, I go with men. But, on behalf of the lesbians, hello.' And Leonie leans forward and kisses Vee on the mouth. There's a chorus of whistling from the journalists at the bar; Leonie gives them a V-sign and they laugh. Vee doesn't know which is worse: the kiss, the odd soft buzz of it, or the feeling of being drunk, or the centre-of-attention discomfort that having a camera usually protects her from.

'I've got a fiancé,' she says, 'we've been going steady since we were fifteen.' Because one thing she is certain of: you can flirt (whatever Leonie says), but you don't want to be a tease. And that must apply to lesbians too.

'Good for you,' Leonie says, with a smile Vee doesn't really like. One of the crowd at the bar brings two more pints over. Leonie tells him to sod off, and he responds by telling her to sod off herself. From this, Vee gathers that they know each other. One of the strangest things about working at the paper is how rude everyone is to each other. Vee's dad is a great believer in good manners and the result of this, for Vee, is that she spends most of her working life being either mocked for her politeness or shocked into silence by the casual, inconsequential rudeness of her colleagues. She cannot imagine what would provoke her father into telling anyone to 'sod off'. And if he knew she was in a pub, talking to someone who uses the word 'prick' in public, he would not be happy.

'He wants us to get married next year,' Vee adds.

Leonie feels around in her pockets, pulls out a tin and starts to roll a cigarette. She, Bea and Fen had been smoking Bea's

Benson & Hedges before. Vee had declined. She has tried smoking, with some of the typists from work who gather around their pooled copies of *Marie Claire* and *My Weekly* at lunchtimes: she just doesn't like it. It makes the inside of her mouth hot, unpleasantly tingly. She can say the same thing about kissing women now. Maybe. Though everything, the first time, is more strange than anything else. 'What do you think about that?' Leonie asks.

Vee says, 'I don't know. I think we should wait a bit longer. He says I can keep working, and all that. At least until we have a baby. But he says we don't need to do that straightaway.'

'Does he? That's good of him.'

Vee knows that Leonie is being sarcastic, and she can see that, for a lot of women, that sort of situation would be sad; they would be wasting their capabilities. But Leonie doesn't know Barry. Barry's mother has never worked, and she's always making digs about Vee's 'little job', like it's a joke. But Barry takes Vee seriously. 'He wants me to have a career. He thinks it should be normal for women to have serious jobs, not just work for pin money.'

Leonie takes a drag on her cigarette. 'What do you want? Surely that's the question.'

'Me?' Before she got here, Vee had been thinking that she has all that she wants, really. Her job isn't perfect, but she can learn, and even if she is going to have to work her way up and earn respect, she'll get there. She has enough money coming in, and Dad's happy, and Barry's happy. But sitting here, in a pub where the same people have been sitting on the same barstools for what looks like fifty years, and where close by, women in short dresses are shouting for their rights, like they really believe they deserve it, she's no longer sure that what she has is happiness. If you see a wrong, right it, her dad says when he picks up other people's litter from the pavement outside their gate.

'Yes, you. There's no one else here that I'm talking to, honey.'

'I want . . .' Vee senses that only her most audacious dreaming will be good enough for Leonie. 'I want to take photographs that mean something to people.'

No, that's not it. All photographs mean something to someone. Her first efforts, blurred line-ups of family and a shaky shot of a birthday cake, are terrible attempts at capturing moments, but that didn't stop Dad from sticking them in an album.

She tries again.

'Women,' she says. As she speaks the word, she realises that that was why she got the feeling she did at the picket line when she pressed the shutter. It's what she's been feeling her way towards, at the paper, even though every time she tries something different she gets shot down. Her photos of women talking over a cup of tea at a coffee morning are not used. Her photographs of women in a line, one holding a wonky home-made cake on a plate, one with a teapot, are what Bob wants. Even though no one looks comfortable; even though there's nothing in these line-ups that isn't interchangeable with last week's church fair, tomorrow's get together at the Mothers' Union. 'I want to take photographs of women where they look like . . . themselves.'

Leonie doesn't take her gaze from Vee's face. Vee feels her intention forming as the words emerge. She has the feeling that she is waiting to see what she will say, as much as Leonie is. 'I mean – women are always meant to look like something, aren't they? Like their job. But most of them ain't good jobs, real jobs, like being a carpenter or a lawyer or something. So photos are usually being somebody's wife, or with something they've baked, and even if they're something like – like a singer, like Dusty Springfield, they still have to look – their looks still matter more than they would if they were a bloke. I mean, look at Pink Floyd. Women couldn't get away with that.'

27

Leonie nods. 'And how does all that fit with getting married?'

'I don't know.' The cider is going down quickly. 'Barry wouldn't mind. And anyway, why shouldn't I get married if I want to? What else are women supposed to do?'

Leonie lights her roll-up. 'Well, if they've got the guts, they could follow their heart. They could take their profession seriously. They could build a career. If they had a vision. And they recognised that the world was about to start taking women seriously. In all respects.'

Vee sits up straighter at the thought of herself as being someone with a vision. The room rocks. 'Is that really going to happen, though?'

'Well,' Leonie says, 'we've got Barbara Castle in our corner. That's one woman in the Cabinet. It's a drag that there's only one, but it's a start.'

'There are loads of MPs this time, though.' Vee's father had commented on it, after the 1966 election, with something like wonder.

'Twenty out of six hundred plus,' Leonie says, 'that's not what I'd call representative.'

'No.' Vee should have thought of that.

'We've got the women out there bringing Ford to a standstill, because for all their production lines and big swinging bollocks, those men can't make cars without seats – and the women are the only people who know how to do it. We're getting power. We deserve power.'

Vee feels her head nodding. 'Yes we do,' she says.

Leonie balances her roll-up on the ashtray, takes off her cardigan. The peace badge on it clatters against the edge of the table. Vee catches, unexpectedly, the scent of lavender; then a glimpse of unshaven armpit. There are jokes, of course, about women with hairy armpits, but Vee has always imagined they are an exaggeration, a cliché. Because surely having clean, smooth armpits is the same as having clean teeth or brushed hair? Vee feels something close to queasy, and at the same time she wants to put her finger in it, just to see how it feels. Her own armpits have been scraped smooth once a week for as long as she can remember. It's just what you do. Her friend Patty's mum had showed them both how, the summer they were fifteen. Leaning back against the wall behind her, Leonie asks, 'Why do you like taking photographs?'

She just does. She always has. After Betty's wedding, whenever her dad got out his precious Contax rangefinder on holidays and at Christmas, she asked and asked until she was allowed to use it, then she asked and asked until she got a camera of her own.

Leonie's gone back to smoking, and though she's watching Vee, she doesn't seem impatient for an answer. Oh, this is pleasure: not to feel compelled to say something clever, fast, not to have to dive into a silence, say anything, if there is to be any hope of being heard. If work were like this, she might get further, faster.

'I think,' she says, 'I like being able to control what I see. What other people see, when they look at my photos. I can tell the story how I see it. But nobody knows I'm doing it. Not really. They think the camera never lies, don't they?' The black box of the viewfinder that holds the whole world, in that instant: the way that, in moving the camera, or zooming in, just a little, she can change the story, make something else important – that's what Vee likes. Well, one of the things. Leonie nods, and then she seems to wait for more.

'And so it's—' Vee takes another gulp of her drink. 'Control. Yeah, control. I took photos at my little cousin's wedding last year. Her mother was a cow to me when my mum died. I was only eight. She told me I needed to grow up. And so I cropped a

29

little bit of her out of every photo I took. Top of her hat, end of her legs. She'd got these new shoes, went on and on about them beforehand, how pricey they were. Them shoes ain't in one single photo of that wedding.'

Leonie laughs, a throaty half-bark, head thrown back, shoulders rising. 'Woman, beware woman.'

'It was nothing to do with her being a woman,' Vee says. 'It was because she was a cow.'

'Well, good for you. So you like – control.' Leonie takes a drink. 'What else?'

'Hiding,' she says.

Leonie cocks an eyebrow.

'Nobody sees the photographer. I mean, they see you, but they ain't interested. They only really see the camera. So you're not the centre of attention. Not if you don't want to be.'

'Why wouldn't you want to be the centre of attention?'

She will never know what makes her say the next thing. Maybe it's that she's already mentioned her mother's death. 'I hated it when my mum died. There was just me and my dad. People came and they wanted to help but it was like – like the zoo. If you cried, they were all over you. If you were normal, they said you were in shock. If you made them a cup of tea you were brave and good. I couldn't stand it.'

'I don't blame you,' Leonie says. 'When my father died and me and my sister were the same. A friend of our parents' came to pick us up from boarding school. We barely knew him – he used to come to dinner parties, but we were always sent to bed – but he still told us that we had to pull ourselves together for our mother's sake. We didn't even know his name.' And everything that's intimidating about Leonie – the voice, the stride, the way she swears and doesn't seem to care, the kiss, the armpit, the general lack of apology that seems stitched into her – drops

30

away. It doesn't matter. Vee isn't out of her depth anymore. Because all she's doing is sitting at a table with a woman who looks as though she might understand. Leonie sighs, smiles, drinks, and then the bravado's back. 'So, you have power, and you have invisibility. And you like it. And you want to use it.'

'Yes.'

'Welcome to feminism,' Leonie says. 'We need sisters like you.'

'Thanks,' Vee says. She must be a feminist, then. Although at work the word feminist is usually followed by 'ball-breaker'. This might not go down well with Barry. She finishes her pint. He wouldn't like that either.

Leonie smiles a sideways smile, something that would look like flirting on a man, and asks, 'How about we get some food, soak this lot up a bit, and then you take my photo? That would be groovy.'

'Groovy,' Vee repeats. She's never heard anyone say that in real life before, only on the TV. Being with Leonie feels like being at the heart of something.

As she drives home, Vee thinks back to when she and Barry got engaged. They'd been boyfriend and girlfriend for four years, since they were fifteen, and he is good and kind, and they have a laugh. It was the logical next step, he said, and she agreed. The night they talked about money and planned for the future is nearly six months ago now but she's never forgotten how she felt. She'd slapped his hand away when it started to slide up her thigh, because she was tired, and it felt too much like he wanted a reward for telling her what his wages were. And after he'd gone she'd worked out what she might earn, before she had kids, what she could earn afterwards, if she went back to work part-time. And when she'd seen the difference between what she would be likely to achieve, and what Barry could take for granted as an estate agent, even without commission, she'd felt stupid for thinking of herself as a career woman. It had seemed that there was no such thing.

When she gets back, Barry is at the house. She'd forgotten they were supposed to be going to the pictures. 'Hello, love,' she says, and he looks at his watch before kissing her on her cheek. He's always prompt, is Barry. Reliable. That's one of the things Vee and Stanley like about him. He can be funny, too, and kind. 'You smell like a brewery. What have you been doing?'

'Really?' Stanley looks concerned. 'You know it's not a good idea to drink if you're driving, treasure. And now they've got breathalysers.'

'I'm not drunk. I had a drink at lunchtime, that's all. Just . . .' Vee thinks back, and subtracts the last round for the sake of peace, 'a sweet martini and a pint of cider.'

'A pint?' Ah, of course – these two won't be fans of women drinking pints.

Well, may as well be hung for a sheep as a lamb. 'Yeah. With some lesbians I met. Now come on, we don't want to be late for the film.'

July 1968

This Month magazine

Leonie Barratt: Letters from a Feminist

Our monthly column from the front line of the Battle of the Sexes

Dear John,

After three weeks out on strike, the Ford Dagenham machinists have gone back to work. I know you're relieved. You might not drive a Ford, but you respect a Ford. And I bet you respect Henry Ford. Because he was a man who knew how to put things in a good old-fashioned honest way, for other men to understand.

We might call his wisdom homespun, if that wasn't such a womanly expression. And wisdom from the hearth cannot possibly bring anything worth knowing to a factory, can it? Factories are for well-ordered pumping, hammering, and screwing. Factories are places of oil, toil and sweat. Women might have their places, on some production lines, packing or checking, doing the small unworthy tasks. But factories, like Mr Ford's, are run by men.

Yet Ford was brought to a halt by women. There's something to ponder, John.

I'd like to know what Mr Henry would make of what went on in Dagenham. He is, after all, the man who said, 'Coming together is a beginning; keeping together is progress; working together is success.' I'm not sure how paying your workers who wear bras less than the ones who don't constitutes working together. It could be that my hormones, or my breasts, are getting in the way of my understanding. Perhaps you can explain it to me. When I've finished sewing the buttons back on your shirt.

I know this won't be the first time you've read about the strike in the press. I know, us women, we do go on, don't we? I expect you'll write to me, to complain, once you've worked out whether I'm nagging or ball-breaking. Allow me to save you some time. I couldn't care less what you think of me.

The reason I'm going on about the strike? It's important. And it's always going to be important. I visited the picket line this week, and do you know what I saw? I saw determination. I saw a sense of what was right – certainty and conviction. And it's hard to keep that going when you're hungry. Three weeks on strike pay might not make much of a difference to your life, John, but if that's the money that goes in the electricity meter or pays the milkman, then believe me, you'd soon feel the lack of it. If there are no savings in your tin, because you only get paid three-quarters of what the men get paid, then striking is not something to be done lightly. It's something to respect.

Something else I saw on that picket line was support, from my sisters – and my brothers, too, like the postman turning back because he belongs to a union. I met people who had travelled, just to see, to find out what was happening. And now the strikers may have gone back to work, in victory, not defeat, but don't think for a minute, John, that that is the end of it.

What happened at Dagenham was about more than car seats and machinists getting too big for their bras. It is about more and more of the world waking up to what's right. You need to get on board, John. You need to see which way the wind is blowing. You need to pay the women who work for you the same as you pay the men doing equivalent jobs. Or stand with your sisters if they aren't being paid as well as you. That's all. We don't want favours. We don't want anything we don't deserve or we're not entitled to. I've told you this before, remember? The reason women wheedle things out of you, the reason some of us expect you to pay when we go out with you, or like to be 'treated' to meals or clothes – that's because we don't have as much money as you. Can you see what might happen if we were paid equally, for equal work?

The next time you get into your car – and the seat's probably been sewn by a woman, even if you do prefer a Hillman – remember something else Henry Ford said. 'If there is any one secret of success, it lies in the ability to get the other person's point of view and see things from that person's angle as well as from your own.' Go on. Give it a try. It's the manly thing to do.

Leonie

2 February 2018

Four days ago, stars at the Grammy awards carried white roses to draw attention to the Time's Up movement against sexual harassment in the music industry.

Eleven weeks and six days until exhibition opening

'Will you be home for dinner?' Marcus asks Erica. He's gathering up his keys and phone in readiness for leaving for work; she is rummaging in the fridge to make sure there's something in there for her mother-in-law's lunch. And Tom is in his highchair, playing with his cereal now rather than eating it. Marcus has managed to kiss him without getting smeared in anything, which is more than Erica ever achieves.

'I should think so. Your mother's coming at twelve. I need to go by half past.'

'You won't be late, though?'

'I'm meeting a seventy-year-old photographer to talk about her exhibition. It's not a hen party,' Erica says, more sharply than she probably should have. The timings are on the calendar on the wall, not that Marcus ever looks at it. She heads for Tom, to get the worst of the Weetabix off before it sets.

'Are you nervous?'

He asks in a way that suggests he cares, rather than having a dig at her for being sharp with him. So she answers accordingly. (When did their marriage become a protracted diplomatic negotiation?)

'Yes. No. I don't know.' She laughs at herself. 'I don't think nervous is the right word.'

He's still looking at her, inviting her to say more.

'I've worked so hard for this.' Veronica Moon hasn't been seen in public for decades – no exhibitions, no appearances, every invitation to lecture, to write or even to attend a party turned down. And yet she has agreed to this. Maybe she will talk about Leonie properly, at last. If she's going to tell anyone the truth, it should be Erica, who would have said, when she began this project, that her interest was ninety per cent academic, ten per cent personal. This morning, those percentages are the other way round.

'I know you have.' He puts an arm round her, and kisses her forehead. She leans in, puts her head against his chest, listens to his heart, muffled by shirt and jacket and coat but hers to hear, if she concentrates. It's as though they are twenty-five again, and nothing in the world could ever be as important as the love they found.

And for a moment – just a moment – it's lovely.

Then Marcus steps away and picks up his briefcase. 'Well, I can take over the babysitting from Mum if you're not back.'

Either he has moved away before he felt her body stiffen, or he's chosen to ignore it.

'It's not babysitting,' she says, loudly enough to make both Marcus and Tom look towards her; identical pairs of blue-grey eyes.

'What?'

'It's not babysitting. Tom is your child.'

Marcus puts a hand on the door handle, a clear sign that he doesn't have time for this. 'I know that. It's just a figure of speech.'

It doesn't feel like one, today. Erica was up twice during the night with Tom. Marcus says he will get up if she wakes him, but he always proves unwakeable. 'A figure of speech that suggests I'm the only one with responsibility for our child.'

Every morning she gets up and is determined to make an effort. And every day something like this happens, and she's sniping and carping. Sometimes it doesn't happen at breakfast, but at dinner, and she's started to count those days as wins. She has no idea when it changed. When Tom was born, they were joyful, delighted, united.

Marcus sighs, 'Maybe we made the wrong call, with you doing this exhibition. It's such a lot of work. And not a lot of money.'

'It's important to me,' Erica says. She's thirty-eight; if she ever wants to be more than a part-time, associate university lecturer she needs to start making a name, building a reputation that's more than 'turns up on time and does what she is contracted to do'. Consultancy on the occasional TV series is fun, and well paid, but confirming that the right sort of pans are being used and checking the Bakelite is the correct colour is hardly a stretch.

When she finished her PhD, she had such plans. And then she met Marcus. And then her mother became more ill. So now she teaches six hours per week during term time, delivering the modules on domestic changes that she taught before she had Tom. She really doesn't think she was forced or coerced into any of it. And yet.

She had wondered, for a while, if that would be her lot. But then she'd found the box of papers and photographs in her mother's loft, and started to see another side of her Aunt Leonie: the one who was a living feminist, way ahead of her time, rather than a woman whose death was more important than any other part of her story. When she put together Veronica Moon's work with Leonie Barratt's story, she knew she had a real chance to have the career she deserved, and rescue two women from obscurity as she did it. Acceptance of her exhibition proposal, and the funding to go with it, felt like a triumph. 'It's really important to me.'

'I know. And I'm supporting you, aren't I?'

'Yes, you are.' She hears how tired she is. This isn't the time to try to explain – again – why this grudging sharing doesn't feel like support. Marcus is checking his watch. If he misses his train then she'll have to give him a lift to Kingston so he can get a fast one. Erica washes Tom's face while he is still in the highchair. There's Weetabix on her coat, which she'd left within range. Great.

If she points out that it's not the work that makes her life hard, but the way their home life is organised, he'll be wounded, and then she'll definitely have to give him a lift. She doesn't have time for that. And anyway, she doesn't know if he will understand how, some days, she can feel her brain starting to atrophy. She has nothing in common with the women she is meeting at coffee mornings. They're not stupid, by any means, it's just that they are absorbed into motherhood as though they have worked for it, are entitled to it. Or as though it is their new job. Erica cannot find that in herself. Somewhere else she is failing. When she's at work she's tired. And at home, reviewing the exhibition, she's afraid that she's making mistakes, or missing her chances to make Vee's work shine, and to shine too. Motherhood has made her mediocre. And it shouldn't have to be that way

'You need to go,' she says, 'we can talk later.' And when he bends to kiss her she moves her head, just a fraction, so that he kisses the side of her cheek rather than her mouth. It's petty, but she doesn't care.

'Erica?' Vee frames it as a question, but the woman walking towards her could be no one else.

'Ms Moon? Veronica? It's an honour to meet you at last.'

Vee debates whether to stand, but it was work enough for her knees to get her to a sitting position on this bench.

'It's Vee, please. Good to meet you, Erica.'

Erica's hair is the colour of a milky morning coffee, and it hangs straight and fine. Her eyes are big, warm and wide, a dark complement to her hair. A narrow mouth, smiling, small teeth, white. High cheekbones, narrow chin, pink lipstick. Imagine her face rounder, without the makeup ... Only the nose is wrong. Vee hears herself inhale, a sharp shocked sound. She should have been prepared for the resemblance.

'It's an honour,' Erica says, again, 'and such a privilege to be trusted with this retrospective.'

Vee has never known what to do with compliments, so she just nods at them, as she does to dogs and children. She moves her bag to the floor by her feet, so that Erica can sit if she wants to. She does. No wonder, wearing ridiculous heels like that. 'Have you had a nose job?' she asks. She realises, as soon as she has said the words, that she shouldn't have; but she is truly out of practice at conversation, forgets that you don't just say what's come to mind.

Erica's hand goes to her face, and she traces the bridge of her straight, unassuming nose with her finger. 'Absolutely,' she says, making steady eye contact with Vee. There's a smile in her voice, a glint in her eye, and Vee feels a grudge of admiration for Erica's style, even if she doesn't approve of her actions. 'And you would have done too, if you had my aunt Leonie's nose.'

Vee nods, stops her tongue.

It's busier than she would have thought a gallery would be on a Tuesday afternoon. There's a constant stream of people interrupting Vee's view of the media wall. It's showing a piece about the nipple, how we hide it and eroticise it.

She still always arrives everywhere early, even though it's a long time since that mattered, much. She wished she'd waited somewhere else. She's not really likely to be recognised, now, but, if she was, the Photographer's Gallery would be the place it would happen. Strange, how she fears to be spotted, and at the same time burns for the recognition that should have been hers.

While Erica unwinds the long navy scarf from her neck, Vee takes a sideways look at her. She must be nearly forty. Though Vee finds it harder to tell how old people are, these days, because they all seem young. Erica is wearing boots with heels high enough to tip her off balance, jeans, and an emerald-green coat, new-looking, but with a crust of something spilled and dried near the hem.

'I'm sorry you had to wait,' Erica says.

'You're not late. We said two, and it's two.' This generation apologising for everything is something the sisterhood of Vee's younger days wouldn't have believed. Along with the heels. Women of 2018 still crippling themselves for the sake of a patriarchal notion of beauty? It beggars belief.

Vee looks at the boots again – Erica has stretched out her legs in front of her – and she must make a sound, a tut or a sigh, because Erica sees where her gaze is resting, and says, 'I like heels.' That stubbornness – the particular timbre of it, the tug and fall of the consonants against the vowels, each word a fight – runs deep into Vee. It lands in her brain and heart and gut, and strikes a note through her body that she never thought she'd hear again. She closes her eyes for a moment, against the memory. Opens them, and looks at the toes of her own boots. She's worn Doc Martens since 1972, when Leonie bought her her first pair, for her birthday. They only came in black, then. This latest pair, electric blue, must be five years old. They might be her last. She wonders how many there have been. It's such a pleasure to never have to think about your feet; just to let them take you where you want to go.

Erica pulls a notebook from her bag. 'I'd like to walk the space with you today, and tell you what I'm thinking. How the exhibition will be laid out, what I want to bring forward, and how I plan to use the ephemera and objects—'

'Ephemera?'

Erica smiles. 'Sorry. Jargon. Paper-based items that relate to the prints. So, a lot of Leonie's archive of your work. The contemporaneous things that she kept. Magazines, newspapers and so on. The objects are the equipment. I mentioned them in my initial email? And I sent you a breakdown.'

'I'm sure you did,' Vee says, 'I just need reminding sometimes.'

Erica accepts this – oh, she is young, and thinks she will never be old, and forget things in her turn – and continues, 'It's mostly the things I found in my mother's loft after her death. In a box with "Leonie" on the side. I don't think it can have been opened since my mother cleared Leonie's flat.'

'I do remember.' Vee does, now. Leonie had had very little good to say at the time about how newspapers reported stories, how women were portrayed in magazines, or the way Vee had sold out by working for them. Today, the thought of Leonie quietly buying and carefully keeping a record of Vee's work feels almost unbearably touching; like finding a lost love letter when the lover has died, Vee imagines, though she wouldn't really know.

Reading the first email from Erica about the exhibition had set off a series of explosions in Vee's body, from mines that had been buried deep. A shock of memory behind her eyes, showing Leonie at her shining, smiling best. A thud of pain low in her pelvis, grief making her heavy and slow. And in the space between her sternum and her heart, a fizzing burst of loss, relived as though it was yesterday that she took the final photograph of her friend. She could be overwhelmed again, if she allowed it to happen.

She takes a deep breath and focuses on the media wall. A bare breast fills the space, then the image is broken up as individual screens are replaced with text. They look to be quotes about identity. Vee closes her eyes. It's hard to believe that this still needs to be debated. Or that women are still wearing heels and having nose jobs.

'And an artefact is anything that isn't a print or an object, basically,' Erica continues. If she noticed how Vee was almost overcome, she doesn't show it. 'You said you thought you might have some other things? Cameras? Images from your own archive?'

'Did I? I remember you asked.'

Erica looks at her hands for a moment. Vee sees that she paints her nails, but it doesn't look as though she takes very good care of them – the polish is chipped, and the cuticles are red, rubbed or worried at. Hands, eyes, teeth, feet – they are the tools you need most in your life, and they need to be cared for the way Vee's father used to care for his carpentry tools, clean and sharp always. Erica will learn.

'Shall we go up?' Erica hands Vee a pass, and they take the lift to the second floor.

The current exhibit is a collection of photographs about crossdressing. It must be years since she's been to an exhibition that she hasn't been expressly invited to. And even then, if she's honest, she would only show up so that she could feel her own sense of injustice, rub the wound raw again at misogyny in action. She wonders who will come to one about her.

Erica says, 'I know a lot of curators frown on a purely chronological approach, but I think it makes sense for your work. We will trace your growing confidence as a photographer as we trace the growth of the women's movement.'

Vee takes a breath and looks around. The space is long and narrow, divided into sections and rooms. The light here is good: not natural, but neutral, plentiful, well directed.

'We'll start with your 1968 Dagenham photograph, and then we'll move through to the 1970 Miss World, then into the portraits, then Greenham,' Erica says. 'We'll have a different configuration of walls than this current show's, obviously, to demarcate the sections. And I'd like to have a single photograph to lead into each section, with text to contextualise, which I'm working on at the moment.'

Vee has never had a wall moved for her convenience. She's always worked with what she can see.

'I'll be giving a whole section to the Greenham archive. I'm going to put the artefacts from your darkroom there, too.'

'The darkroom ...' no, Vee cannot bring herself to say 'artefacts' '... kit is from when Leonie and I shared a flat. So it's a good five years before the Greenham peace camp started. Most of those photographs would have been developed at labs. I didn't have time to do much of my own developing by then.'

Erica nod-shrugs, stepping aside to let a group of chattering tourists pass. 'We'll date and label them correctly. And we'll end with the photograph of Leonie.'

'Must we? I mean ...' Vee knew this was coming, she's not a fool, 'I understand it needs to be there, somewhere. But at the end?'

'Well,' Erica says, and she presses her lips together, as Leonie used to when she was thinking, 'if we're being chronological, it's the obvious thing to do.' She turns away, walking to the other end of the gallery. Vee might own the photographs – it might be an honour for Erica to work with her – but there's no question of who is in charge in this space. Well, Vee's the one in charge of herself. She lets Erica walk away, and pretends to study the images on the wall, though she is thinking of her own work.

That final image of Leonie is another reason why this exhibition was a bad idea. Vee knew, even as she was typing the email to say she would go ahead, that she should just say no. And yet, she did it. She knows she has holes in her memory, and not just the usual spaces a woman of her age might expect. A surgeon carved years out of her brain when he took the tumour tissue back in 2007. She thinks sometimes that she has holes in her reasoning, too. No gaps in her feelings, though – oh, no. The lack of Leonie is raw, cut-flesh raw, whenever she comes up against it.

Maybe she wants to be remembered. She's been invited to one too many retrospectives, book launches and exhibitions of the male photographers who were her contemporaries. She has never gone. Why would she? Why spend an evening standing to one side with a warm glass of wine, knowing that even if she hasn't done anything to speak of since 1984, she's achieved easily as much as the men being admired left, right and centre? More. Taking photographs in a war zone is too easy. Point and click and you'll get something. The same with photographing beauty, or fashion. The work is done for you. Stylists, makeup, studio lighting, a digital camera that will take thousands of shots in an hour – any fool can shoot a *Vogue* cover. Natural light, real film, real people – that's where you see real skill.

And she had skill. Maybe has it, still, if she wasn't too afraid to pick up a camera.

Erica had been very clear in her proposal: she would manage everything, she would seek other permissions, track down materials, negotiate with the gallery. All that Vee would need to do would be to give written agreement for her images to be used, and clarify any areas where Erica might have questions.

So she had said yes to the exhibition of her work. Not recklessly. She'd read Erica's email and studied the attached CV. Erica had a doctorate in social history, and had lectured at several universities. Overall, she had seemed credible. She was Leonie's niece: that fact woke a protectiveness, a sense of duty, almost, in Vee that she could neither explain nor dismiss. And she wanted to exhibit Vee's work. She wanted to excavate the box of cuttings, prints and magazine portraits that Leonie had, apparently, kept, and turn them into an exhibition. At the point Vee was approached by Erica, she hadn't put herself in the public eye for more than thirty years. She had been retired from lecturing for fifteen. So the thought of fading into nothingness – the possibility that seemed so achingly desirable for so long – was becoming a reality. At the time her career ended, Vee was too absorbed by other griefs to care about how she and her work would be remembered. She wanted to be forgotten. But in the years since, she has wondered at the way her career was stopped rather than having the chance to end her way.

So she had said yes, with caveats. She wouldn't talk to the press, she wouldn't speak at the opening night. She would not give quotes, or be quoted, because that's something she has never done, and would not begin to do now. Words are not her medium. And she would not, under any circumstances, discuss her final photograph of Leonie Barratt. Once the caveats were explored and her worries assuaged, and the exhibition proposal agreed, submitted, and accepted, she'd left Erica to get on with it, until today.

Tap-tap-tap go Erica's heels in front of her, making a knocking at Vee's temples, a pressure waiting to turn into a headache.

Erica turns, in the end space, indicates the far wall. 'Here's the obvious place for the Leonie photograph. It's such a . . .' she hesitates, and Vee sees how she is choosing her words '. . . it's such a high-quality image that we'll be able to blow it up to a good size. I want people to be able to make up their own minds.' Her eye contact, which has been so unequivocal, falters: Erica is looking at Vee's hairline. Erica is not quite as impartial as she would like Vee to believe.

Vee's own focus is rising, falling, as pain starts to swell behind her eyes. She still dreams of Leonie's death sometimes, the sudden horrible blank of it: now I'm here, now I'm gone. In sleep is the only time she remembers it. Waking, there's just a space of missing memory, like a photograph taken when the lens cap was still in place.

The year after Leonie died is still the most terrible of her life. Not even dying, so far, is as bad – not so long as she can see. Many of Vee's memories from the years before that period are lost, her first brain tumour twined around them, it seems, plucking them from her mind when it was removed. The life of the Veronica Moon of the early 1980s exists in photographs only; parts of the 1970s are barely there, either. She'll never know whether her last photograph of her father – sleeves rolled up, checking the oil on her car before she set off to drive home, no doubt – was the last time she saw him. She imagines she would have told him that she knew how to check her oil. And he would have said, 'Just humour your old dad, treasure.' And she would have driven away. She has his death certificate, the paperwork from the sale of the house; she knows all that happened, can read her notes from her diaries, her own handwriting telling her she was there, she experienced it all. But there's no memory of it. No memory of those last years of Leonie, either. Or of that last day. A therapist she saw, later, suggested that Vee might be blocking painful memories, and the brain was using the surgery as a convenient way to hide what she didn't want to confront. She supposes that's possible. But she cannot believe that any memories, however difficult, however painful, can be as enduringly aching as the absence of them. Plus, her recollections crash back in the immediate aftermath of Leonie's death, during the worst time in her life she can remember. If she could block anything, it would be that.

'Obviously we can discuss anything you want to add to this section,' Erica adds. Vee refocuses on what Erica is saying. She cannot read anything into her expression. 'And we are going to have to talk about my aunt's death at some point. Not today.'

'No.' The word is sudden and loud. Even Vee is surprised. 'I believe I was clear,' Vee continues, and her voice is still loud but it's steady. No sign of the shaking she feels. 'Wasn't I?'

'Well, yes,' Erica says. Her eyes have become brighter – oh, that stubborn expression is so familiar to Vee, in the same way Erica's voice is Leonie refracted – 'but the exhibition visitor will need the facts—'

'I've given you access to private material. I said I wouldn't discuss anything related to your – to Leonie.' Vee needs to get used to hearing her name again. 'And there's nothing I could add to . . . to what happened to Leonie, if you have the articles. Visitors will have the photograph. They can make up their minds from that. They always have.'

Erica nods but Vee isn't fool enough to think that means agreement. 'There are so many questions around the photograph.'

'More fool anyone who thinks I have answers.'

Vee cannot have the truth: she cannot understand, or reconstruct, what happened that day with certainty. So why could she, would she, give anyone else an easy answer?

'All I want,' Erica speaks gently, quietly, as though she can coax Vee into line, 'is for you to tell me what you remember.'

'No. It's not up for discussion and it never will be.'

Vee walks slowly to the end of the gallery, her soles squeaking. After a few minutes she hears Erica tap-tap-tap to catch up. They look at each other, and Erica nods. It's a truce.

'You haven't mentioned a section of photographs of me.' There's a bench in this room and Vee lowers herself on to it, resentful and grateful at once. She used to spend hours on one knee or both, crouched or on tiptoe, all to make sure she got the best shot that she could. It's as though she used up her knees faster than the rest of her; faster than a normal person would.

Erica laughs, the relieved sound of someone back on safe ground. 'I wanted to talk to you about that. There aren't a lot of photos of you in the public domain. There's your official self-portrait, and by the look on your face you took that under duress. A couple of press ones, from when you won the Political Photograph of the Year in '84.'

Vee nods. 'I've got the trophy, somewhere. If that would do as an – as ephemera . . .' oh no, that's not right, it's not paper, 'an object.' She can't remember the night itself, but she has the evidence of it. Something about the thought of it scratches at her.

'That would be good,' Erica says, looking round the space. 'Do you have any other photographs of you?'

'I might have,' Vee says. Heaven knows what's in the loft. She was always meticulous about labelling and storing negatives, though. She must have something, somewhere, to change the way the end of the exhibition looks. She had hoped it might redeem her, but it looks as though its climax is going to be her greatest failure. 'And maybe more of Leonie.' Leonie alive. Leonie blazing and bright, 'We knew each other for a long time.'

'Her writing was . . . it was amazing. She was way ahead of her time.'

Sadness knots at the back of Vee's throat, pulling the pain from her temples downwards. 'That's what she used to say. She was very . . . she was unimpressed by the way she was treated.'

49

'I didn't know that. My mother never really talked about her much. Or you. Well, not in a . . .' she looks sideways at Vee, measuring, decides it's OK to say it, '. . . she wasn't kind about you.'

'That's understandable.' It all seems a long way away, now. Until Vee lets herself think about Leonie, properly, and then it's as immediate as the ache of the stitched flesh around a two-day wound. 'Truth be told, your mother and I never had a lot of time for each other. Even before.' What Vee remembers most about Ursula Woodhouse is the way that she smelled of flowers, wore pastel colours, as though she was trying to be all of the feminine that she thought Leonie was not. Though she could fight her corner as well as Leonie. Ursula and Vee could never, ever find anything to talk about. Even before it all went to hell. Vee puts her hands to her head. Her temples feel tender to the touch.

'I didn't know that.' Erica's tone tells Vee nothing about whether she wants to hear more. The noise in the gallery is growing, or maybe being amplified by the headache. Vee has painkillers in her bag, but no water to take them with. It's probably too late for them to stop it now. Though there hasn't been a headache as bad as this one threatens to be in years.

'Ursula had a low opinion of most of Leonie's friends.'

Erica laughs, something sour running beneath it. 'It was hard to square what my mother was like with what I knew about my aunt Leonie. It always seemed odd, that two sisters could be so different. I used to think of them as the feminist and the anti-feminist. But later' – Erica runs her hand through her hair, her fingers tracking from her forehead to the top of her spine – 'I realised my mother wasn't really anti-feminist. She was . . . I think she was anti-uncertainty. She didn't like anything that made life unclear.'

'No wonder she was so uptight,' Vee says – it's out before she can stop it, but she puts her hand to her mouth all the same – stable

50

door. 'Erica, I'm sorry. To me, your mother is someone very ...' oh, where are the words? 'Very abstract. We hardly saw each other. We didn't have much in common. I forgot that's not the same for you.'

'It doesn't matter.'

'It does. She was your mother.'

'She couldn't have done more for me,' Erica says.

'Neither could my mother.' Vee feels Erica's body tilt towards her, ever so slightly, and tilts her own away by the same degree.

Erica nods. 'She never went to university, you know, when she was young. She got a job as an administrator in a private junior school when she was eighteen. When I was studying GCSEs she started a degree at the Open University, so she could keep me company, she said.'

'That's really something,' Vee says. She can't square it with the Ursula she remembers, but being a mother changes people.

'It was,' Erica half-laughs, 'I didn't appreciate it at the time.'

Vee can't think of anything to say. She concentrates on her breath, making its way down to her belly and up again, and tries not to think about her headache.

Erica sighs, 'The generation that is coming up now – people younger than me, people I teach – they lack context for the past. The world is nuanced now. I think it's important to look back to when things were ... black and white. No pun intended.' She smiles. 'When men were the enemy, and—'

But Vee doesn't hear anything else. The headache, that has been licking at her temples since she entered the gallery, opens up its jaws and bites.

Part 2: Light

Part 2: Light

To be a photographer is to be a student of light. If you want to be a good photographer, all you need to do is learn to see the light. Study it, understand it, anticipate what it is going to do when you expose film to it. Light is equally accessible to all.

Veronica Moon, *Women in Photographs* (unpublished)

'Weeping Beauties'
Veronica Moon

Exhibition Section: Early Days

Camera: Nikon F1
Film: Kodak 400 ASA
First published: *Marie Claire* magazine, 1970

It is 1970. The paparazzi has yet to invent itself. Photo-calls are respectful. Beauty queens are seen in carefully orchestrated settings, where they are groomed, polished, always smiling.

Now, consider how radical this photograph is.

It was taken late in the evening following the Miss World contest in 1970, which was disrupted by feminist protesters opposing the objectification of women. After the demonstration and stage invasion at the Royal Albert Hall (see video, left), the protesters moved to the Café de Paris in the West End of London, where the after-party was being held.

Moon left this second demonstration, where she had been photographing her fellow protesters, and went around to the back of the building. There she came upon two of the beauty queens who had participated in the contest, still wearing their evening dresses. Moon captures the women in the harsh strip light coming from the fire escape, though she used fill-in flash to bring sharpness to the image. The faces of the subjects have a pale, flat quality that makes them appear ghostly. Both are crying, their heads tilted towards each other. Capturing contrast – the glamour of the gowns, the jewellery, and the makeup, against the backdrop of a fire escape and the distress and disappointment on the faces – is typical of Moon's emerging style. *Marie Claire* magazine (displayed to your right) ran this photograph in December

1970, with their article 'Woman Beware Woman: the new face of feminist protest?'. The photograph was passed on to a writer there by Leonie Barratt, who sought Moon's permission to use the image, and in doing so, reintroduced Moon's work to mainstream publishing. This time, unlike when the Dagenham protest photograph became an image used worldwide, Moon was in a position to capitalise on her exposure. She had established herself as an independent photographer, and grown in confidence in her own ability. Shortly after publication of this photograph, Moon moved from her family home in Essex to London.

At this time, Moon was the only female wedding photographer in Essex. A few of Moon's wedding photographs are displayed in this section, along with early independent journalistic work. Notice her impulse to capture the informal, at a time when traditional wedding portraits were the norm.

In 1970:

- The Equal Pay Act (a direct result of the 1968 action at Dagenham) came into law
- *The Female Eunuch* by Germaine Greer, *Sexual Politics* by Kate Millett and *Sisterhood is Powerful: An Anthology of Writings from the Women's Liberation Movement*, edited by Robin Morgan, were published
- The age of majority in the UK dropped from twenty-one to eighteen and a general election in June led to a surprise victory for the Conservative Party, led by Edward Heath
- The first jumbo jet landed in Britain
- The half crown ceased to be legal tender, in preparation for the introduction of decimal currency in 1971

- The Methodist church allowed female ministers to be ordained for the first time
- The first Glastonbury music festival was held in September
- The first Page Three girl was featured in the *Sun* newspaper in November
- 'In the Summertime' by Mungo Jerry was number one in the charts for seven weeks

And the newly formed Women's Liberation Front made a plan to disrupt the Miss World competition, held in London. Veronica Moon and Leonie Barratt, by now good friends, were there.

20 November 1970

Colchester

Vee is just getting into the car when Barry rounds the corner of the street. Even though it's three months since she called off their engagement, her body doesn't always remember, and she feels a little lurch of familiarity when she sees him, followed by another, of regret. Not that she wants him back. It's just that she's sorry.

Barry hadn't taken it well.

Vee had assumed he would have seen it coming. She'd been putting off setting a date for the wedding for two years. Her excuses were getting thinner and thinner, even to her own ears. First, she had said she wanted to wait until she got her business established. Her friends used her for their weddings, but couples she didn't know often seemed puzzled by her – 'So, who actually takes the photos?' – as she showed her portfolio. 'I do,' she would reply, and she would smile and hope for the work, and think of how Leonie would tell her off for reinforcing old ideas about women. 'What would Leonie think?' has become a guiding principle of her life, in the two and a half years since they met.

Building her business bought her some time. Then Barry was promoted, and she said she didn't want him to be worrying about helping her with planning a wedding while he was getting on with his new job. He'd looked puzzled, said he'd assumed she would do most of the planning, and then quickly added that he knew she was all for women's lib so actually he would like to be involved. She'd felt terrible.

In March, when he had brought it up again, she had almost said that she had changed her mind. But she hadn't changed it enough to be sure, and she was always sure that she did love Barry. Maybe not enough; maybe not in the right way. But she wasn't certain enough to say she didn't want to marry him. She'd got used to wearing her engagement ring, too; it kept a lot of pests away when she was working on her own. There was a tender circlet of white skin at the base of her finger when she took it off at night.

After another summer of watching brides and grooms, the looks on their faces and their steadfast conviction that they had chosen right for their whole lives, Vee was sure that she wasn't going to marry Barry. She wasn't sure how she would tell him, or tell her dad, who called Barry 'son' and had bought him a season ticket for the football. She was going to have to choose her moment.

But then the moment chose itself.

The final straw had been – well, straw-like. They argued about *Late Night Line Up* when Barry said Joan Bakewell, the presenter who had been called 'the thinking man's crumpet', was too clever by half and no one would ever marry her. Vee retorted no one would marry him if that was the way he thought, and anyway 'crumpet' was derogatory.

He'd sighed, in a long-suffering way that he'd been doing lately, and got right on Vee's nerves. There was no way she could put up with that for another fifty, sixty years. 'It's all changed since you met that friend of yours. Leanne. You never used to use words like "derogatory". You used to be a laugh.'

'Leonie. You know her name, don't pretend you don't.'

'Well yeah, I should, because I hear it often enough. She's turning you into a lesbian.' Every time she'd planned a trip with Leonie, Barry had opposed it, and when she told Leonie, all she'd done was raise an eyebrow, or say, 'do you think that's good enough for you?', or, 'do you think that's the way women deserve to be treated?'. That was all. And that had been enough to help Vee to – well, to wake up to what Barry was like.

'Barry's not a bad person, though,' she'd said to Leonie, once.

'He doesn't have to be,' Leonie had replied, 'he's grown up in a system that makes him think he's more important than you. Or any woman.'

The night her engagement ended, Vee decided against ignoring his dig at her friend, 'Don't be ignorant, Barry.'

'I'm no more ignorant than I've ever been. You're the one who's more la-di-da. If you're too good for me, you should just say so.'

There was never going to be a better time. Vee took a breath, found her balance, the way she does before she takes a photograph, 'I ain't a lesbian. And I ain't too good for you,' she'd been trying to talk more neutrally, more like Leonie, but when she was under stress her Essex came out. Breathe. Keep trying, 'I'm not right for you, though, Barry. Surely you can see that.'

But apparently he couldn't. He'd sat in silence, refusing to leave, until she went to bed. When she got up in the morning, he'd gone; she'd told her dad, and he'd been disappointed – 'Barry's a good lad' – but told her it was up to her who she married. She didn't feel up to explaining that she might decide not to get married at all.

Finally, Barry got the message. And it seems like no one in Colchester has time for Vee, or a good word to say about her new friends and her new interests, which is a bit much, as they haven't bothered to find anything out. She's stopped seeing most of her old school friends because she's sick of the snide comments about why she doesn't wear makeup any more, and of how she's 'talking posh'. Vee has given up trying to explain that if she wants to work more widely she needs to be more neutral. She is sick of being scoffed at, or being told that Michael Caine isn't too good for his accent. Yes, Vee says, but he wants to stand out. I want to blend in. 'Blend in here, then,' they say. She had tried photographing them, a few times, but it hasn't really worked; they try to look posed, different to their everyday selves, and that's the opposite of the images that Vee wants her camera to find. And now she doesn't seem to be invited to the regular get-togethers. She doesn't mind. Not really. But although she doesn't miss her old life anymore, she's lonely, sometimes, without it.

'Hello, Veronica,' says Barry. He doesn't call her Vee any more.

'Barry. How are you?'

'As well as can be expected,' he says, and then, his face trying to swallow a smile and failing, 'I'm going out with someone tonight.'

Vee waits long enough to check that she doesn't mind. She doesn't. That's a relief. 'Oh. That's good.'

'It's Cathy,' Barry adds, 'my sister's friend?'

Cathy. Cathy. It takes Vee a moment to place her. 'Works at the doctor's?'

'That's right,' Barry says.

'I hope you have a good time. She's always been lovely with Dad when he's been in.' You should help a sister out when you can, is what Leonie always says. She probably doesn't mean helping a sister to get herself married to Barry, but if that's what Cathy wants, more power to her, as far as Vee's concerned.

Barry nods. If he'd been looking for jealousy or disappointment in Vee, he hides it. 'Where are you off to?'

'London. To see Miss World.'

'I though you didn't approve of that sort of thing.' Last year, she had refused to watch it, even though Barry's mum had put on a buffet and invited everyone round to see it on their new colour TV.

'I don't,' Vee says, and she gets in to the car and drives away.

20 November 1970

London

It's a crisp day, cold air and quiet, dull sky, and Vee arrives early to the cafe where she's meeting Leonie, even though she knows Leonie will be late, because she always is. She had parked round the corner from Leonie's Chelsea flat, and taken the bus to Oxford Street.

It's cool to sit in a cafe in Carnaby Street – Carnaby Street! – and feel as though she's in the middle of where it's all happening, even though the coolest thing is that Leonie will soon be here. Vee is full of fizz at the thought of her friend, and their plans for today. And she's walked past boutiques that she wouldn't dare go into, places like 'Gear' and 'Pop', where the stars shop; just passing the doors makes her feel special.

She's not special. Not special-looking, anyway. She has taken the odd self-portrait, watched as her face emerges from the chemical bath in her darkroom under the stairs. (Dad says she can convert the spare room, if she likes, now that she's making a living from photography, but she sends her films away to be developed, most of the time, keeps the little darkroom for mucking about in. She likes the way it holds her younger selves, reminding her of how far she has come.) Looking at photographs of herself, she's come to the conclusion that she is utterly unremarkable. Nothing is odd or wonky or out of proportion. Nothing like Leonie's great, straight nose, her too-big eyes. Vee cannot wait to see her friend again.

Leonie showed her, from the beginning, what was possible. The week after they met in Dagenham, Vee sent her the contact sheet of the photographs she took there, after they left the pub. She'd circled the ones she thought were best. Leonie had returned the contact sheet with different images circled, and they were the ones in which she was at least a third profile, her nose not minimised or made smaller by angle or light.

Vee would love to snap the young women at the next table, one in a skirt that brushes the floor, the other in a mini-dress and knee-high boots, as they pour tea into brown mugs and talk in hushed tones about what they are planning for tomorrow night. She almost asks if they'd mind being photographed, but Leonie might arrive at any moment.

Vee will have to use flash tonight, and it's not her preferred approach. It never feels quite right to her. It's not so bad using it indoors, when she has time to set up, to place reflectors and bounce the sharp explosion of light from the flashbulb away from the subject, and back again: she can control for harshness. Tonight won't be like that. But the important thing is that she will be there and she will be making a record of what women can do. (Once you realise you're living in a world designed for white men, you see discrimination, assumption, everywhere. Leonie says she and the others don't see the half of it, either, because they're white women, and that protects them from a lot of what's going down for other sisters.)

The last time Leonie and Vee saw each other was three months ago, at the first Women's Liberation Movement meeting. Vee had felt for the first time as if she belonged among the women she saw around her. They were all so different – races, ages, colours, roles in the world. But what they had in common was that they all knew they deserved their places. None of them was better than the other. Each deserved a chance, equal with each other, equal with the men. It had been a buzz. A high.

She'd stayed over at Leonie's flat that night, gone home the next day with a sick hangover and a determination to do more photojournalism. (She'd said yes to the beer, passed on the joint.) But Leonie has been quiet since – no notes scribbled on the back of fliers, shoved in envelopes and posted to her – and Vee has not yet worked out how to do the job she wants to do without her friend. So it's been back to weddings and christenings, and wishing she had the courage to take smiling brides aside and say: remember you have power of your own.

The cafe door opens. Vee's heart gives a glad leap. It always does, when she sees Leonie.

'Hey, sister,' Leonie says, and hugs Vee, tight. She smells of lavender, as usual, and there is cold air coming off her. She sits, then puts her head in her hands for a moment before looking up with a smile. Only a small one. 'Meeting went on.'

Leonie never apologises. Vee isn't sure if it's personality, rudeness, posh-girl confidence, or being liberated. 'That's OK,' she says.

'How are you?'

'I'm fine.' Vee thinks about mentioning having seen Barry, but it really doesn't seem that important, now. Even if she did think about him most of the way on the drive. Or at least think about how her life would have been certain, if she had stayed with him. Unengaged, and with no real desire to find someone, life has become a nebulous, unlimited, and therefore frightening thing. She's never talked to Leonie much about Barry. It was as though part of her already knew that marrying him wasn't going to happen, so she didn't waste her breath on it.

'Was your meeting about your book? How did it go?' One of the best things about last year for Vee was when Leonie sent her the typed pages of the book she was writing, and asked her what she thought. Vee had thought, simply, that this was the most amazing thing she had ever read. It should have been hard going, because it was about complicated things – politics, the economy, history, all the reasons women are kept down. But Leonie's wit and sharpness had struck sparks in the air around her as she read. Vee had never been much of a reader, but she stayed up until she had finished the last page. She'd sent back a note, the next day, full of praise and enthusiasm, which Leonie hadn't replied to.

The waitress comes over; Leonie orders a cheese sandwich and coffee. Vee asks for a second coffee. 'It was – not cool,' she says, pulling a face that shows her bottom teeth, narrows her eyes, 'The lowdown is, I'm before my time. Which is a big fat no.'

'Is it really? Or do you just have to wait? Until time catches up?' One of the few things Vee and her father still agree on (now that marriage, careers and the women's movement cause disagreements every time they come up) is how you Never Give Up. And it's just not possible that people can't see how fantastic Leonie is.

Leonie makes a laugh-shaped noise. 'Oh, my little ray of sunshine. I wish. No, it really was a big fat no. The world isn't ready for me. I don't see why the world can't have a go. At least put it out there and see, you know? Someone took a punt on Betty Friedan. And on Kate Millett. They believed Robin Morgan when she said she could edit *Sisterhood is Powerful*.' She sighs. 'I should move to the States. Your best way of being a published feminist here is to be Sylvia fucking Plath. Or Stevie Smith.'

'Aren't they poets?'

'Exactly. You're not allowed a voice of your own, here. Not if you're trying to be factual. You have to be poetic. So the powers that be, the MEN, can write it all off as . . .' she twists her face into a simper, 'feelings. Which they can then ignore. Some of the sisters are talking about setting up a magazine, but—' She makes a gesture that encompasses despair and impatience.

'I'm sorry, Leonie.' Vee doesn't know how hard it is to get a book published but she knows for a fact that Leonie is good enough.

'I know you are.' There's a real smile, this time, and Vee feels her face light in return. Then Leonie remembers something else. 'Or Australia. There's a book you need to read by a sister called Germaine Greer. It's interesting. She's right about quite a lot of things. Maybe half of it.'

'Is that good? That she's getting some of it right?' The thought of Leonie in America or Australia – how much would a plane ticket be? – gives Vee a sort of indigestion of the heart.

'Yes and no,' Leonie says, 'good for consciousness raising. Bad because now the patriarchy can point at her and say, but we've published a book about woman and sexuality and how we men hold women back. Why do you need another one, darling? You keep writing your pretty words, by all means, but the position of the woman with unpalatable truths about female bodies is taken.'

'I see what you mean.'

'The thing is, the establishment holding me back – I'm used to that, you know? But the sisters should be behind me.' Leonie shakes her head. She looks as though she might cry. 'They should be willing to try. The editor I talked to today – she's a woman. She's a friend of Jo, you know Jo?'

'Yes.' Vee probably does. She hasn't spent enough time with the feminist crowd to be able to put all the names to all of the faces.

'So I hoped, y'know? I thought, an editor, a woman, one of us. But it looks like she only got there by playing it safe. Not drawing attention to the fact that she's a woman. Jeez! This is so not cool. If we only do what's safe—'

Leonie is getting louder. People are looking round. Vee knows she shouldn't feel as though there is anything wrong with making a noise. 'What didn't she like? This friend of Jo's?'

Leonie glares. 'That's the question I asked. Not that I would change it. But she just said it "wasn't right" and "wasn't for them". Coward.'

'Sounds like it,' Vee says, and adds, 'but you are the bravest person I know, you know, so . . .'

The glare is replaced by a smile, but not a nice one. 'Well, that's something. Braver than all the housewives in Essex.'

'Oh, come on, Leonie. That's not fair.' Leonie has taught her to stick up for herself, for the validity of her own experience. Well, time for her to see what a good job she has done.

Leonie, who has her head in her hands, looks at Vee from under her fringe, eyes tired, mouth a frown, and for a second it looks as though she is going to get up and leave. But instead she shakes her head – it looks as though she cut her hair using a bowl as a guide, and it doesn't suit her – and says, 'I need to get some bread of my own from somewhere. It's not cool to live off my trust fund. If I can make a living I can give more money away, to the sisters who need it.'

'What will you do?'

A sigh. 'I might teach a night class. Kiki was asking me if I wanted to do it. I don't, really, but beggars can't be choosers.'

Vee nods. Leonie has no idea of how lucky she is, how her life is full of possibility. Every time she doesn't get what she wants, she asks one of her posh friends for help – and she gets it. She has the trust fund, too, though Vee isn't completely clear on what that is. She does know that Leonie has a degree in something called PPE, and might do a 'doctorate', which is nothing to do with medicine. And that she spends a lot of her time – when she isn't writing – organising, volunteering, and helping women.

'Sounds good.'

When Leonie heard how Vee had left her job, after Dagenham, she had been that friend to Vee in her turn. Vee had written her a letter, tried to make the argument with her boss sound funny, and as though she hadn't minded being told to stay in her place. She'd left out the part about her dad going to see Bob behind her back and asking him to give her another chance, or Barry's 'maybe it's for the best' attitude. Leonie had seen through her bravado and written back to say she should come and have lunch with her and they would see what they could do. She had put money in the envelope for her train fare. Vee thinks the official word for this sort of thing is 'patronage'. Leonie says sisters help their sisters, and it's just what men have been doing for each other always, and that's how the patriarchy keeps itself strong. Vee's father calls it 'it's not what you know, it's who you know', which Vee thinks is unfair. Because Leonie wouldn't be much use to her – or she to Leonie – if she couldn't take a decent photograph. Leonie had introduced her around, and she's always the one who's invited to take photographs at protests, meetings and marches. She doesn't get paid for being there but she sometimes gets published: her photographs, grainy, in *The Times* and the *Daily Express*, make her the happiest she has been, and the fees puff her up with pride.

'I'm going to write my next column about makeup, perception of beauty, how we should be enough without being expected to slap all that on our faces,' Leonie says, and Vee thinks guiltily of the lipstick in the bottom of her bag. Old habits die hard, but she's learning, sometimes the hard way. She wore a skirt to one of the first marches Leonie took her to. Leonie didn't seem to notice, but another woman hissed at her. She always wears jeans now, when she's going to do something with the women. She's bought some dungarees but she doesn't feel brave enough – or maybe qualified enough – to go out in them yet. She nods. Leonie adds, 'So if you get any shots of anything I can use—'

'I'll give you first pick.' Vee holds up her camera, grins. She loves the thought that she is going to be here, for this, and has a shiver of anxiety that adds to the excitement. She indicates her camera bag. 'I'm ready.'

Leonie laughs. Her moods come and go, fast flares of misery and brightness. The trick is to take each one as it comes. 'You call that ready?' She opens her handbag – it's bigger than the one she usually carries, more old-fashioned, plain black leather with a metal zip across the top – and Vee peers inside.

'What is that?' There's a strange smell, half-sweet half-dead, that makes her pull back her head in a hurry.

'Probably the rotten tomatoes. The lettuce doesn't really smell, but it's slimy. I've had it in a plastic bag on the windowsill for two weeks.'

Vee approaches the bag again, more cautiously, and puts in a hand, picking up a small paper bag. 'And what are these?'

'Have you never seen a flour bomb?' Leonie laughs again, 'You should see the look on your face. I bet you've never even had detention, have you?'

Vee shakes her head. 'I was a proper goody-two-shoes,' she says, 'until I met you. You've led me astray.'

'That's what I like to hear,' Leonie says, 'that is cool.' She kisses Vee, corner of the mouth: she often does it, and Vee has learned that it means nothing to Leonie, though it cannot help but feel sexual to her. Leonie is the only person who kisses her, now, and she's ashamed by how much she treasures something Leonie does without thought.

Leonie feels around in the side pocket of the handbag, then slaps two tickets down on the table: *Miss World Pageant 1970*. 'We're near the front. The signal is a football rattle.'

For a moment Vee wants to get up, go home, put on some lipstick, knock on Barry's door. She reminds herself that this is important work. They need to get noticed. They need to make people see what's wrong with the world.

'I don't know if I'll be able to get any decent shots inside, especially if there's flour,' she says, 'but if not, we can look around outside, afterwards.'

Leonie nods. 'Bound to be a postman somewhere,' she says, with a smile, and Vee feels the pleasure of this friendship like a stab. 'There's the protest outside the Albert Hall, and then outside the Café de Paris afterwards.' She says it 'Par-ee', so it takes Vee a moment to work out where she means. Leonie is on the WLF committee, and always knows everything that's planned. 'And are you going to crash at mine?'

'If that's still . . . cool,' Vee says, the word unwieldy on her tongue. Her father tells her off for using what he calls 'hippie talk', but she wants to fit in. It's another way to move through the world without being noticed. And not being noticed is how you take a decent photograph. And taking decent photographs is what gets you noticed. Life is like taking photographs: to do it well, you have to understand it. Film, exposure and darkroom are easier to manage, and have more predictable results.

'Good,' Leonie says. The waitress brings her sandwich and she closes her handbag, puts it on the floor, 'I'll eat this, then we'll split. Let's see if we can get you arrested. It's about time you saw the inside of a cell.' She laughs, 'I wish you could see your face!'

73

At the Royal Albert Hall, a police officer looks at her twice as she goes up the steps, but a smile gets her through. And Leonie doesn't see her smiling, so that's good, because she hasn't got into trouble for appeasing the patriarchy.

There are a lot of other women with suspiciously large handbags, coats that swamp them, ill-fitting dresses. They have obviously all decided to try to look like the kind of women who would be interested in a beauty contest. She realises that her chances of being arrested are not high. She had tried to look amused at the prospect, but the thought of it scares her. Which is shameful of her, really. She voted for the first time in June, and she's been reading a book Leonie had given her about the suffragettes at the time. Standing in the polling booth, she'd tried to imagine what it was like to be imprisoned, force-fed, because of the strength of your principles. And she'd wondered whether she would ever really be brave enough to do the part that got the women arrested in the first place: civil disobedience, throwing bricks through windows, setting fires, resisting arrest. She hasn't even brought lettuce to throw, and she's terrified, her throat tight and her legs weak. But then again, there's nothing to say that the suffragettes weren't terrified. They did it anyway.

There's a chattering excitement filling the building as Vee and Leonie follow the curving corridor to their entrance. Of course, most of the people here have no thought of protest: they're excited about the pageant, and have probably never thought that a beauty contest could be exploitative and wrong. The crowd thickens at their door to the stalls, and Vee finds herself pressed up against a man in black tie who winks at her. She pretends not to see, and tries not to think of the suffragettes.

Vee has never been inside the Royal Albert Hall. The curves and detail of the interior of building, the sheer scale and beauty of it, from the red plush seats to the organ to the gilt on the carving on the ceiling, make her half-dizzy with awe. Leonie makes a joke about Albert's massive organ, and someone behind chips in about patriarchal archetypes; Vee pretends to laugh, and tries for nonchalance, but cannot stop herself from gazing at the beauty of the place. She wishes she could photograph it, but there's no point, not with this level of light. 'Have you been here before?' she asks Leonie.

'All the fucking time,' Leonie says, earning a tut from a different man, also in a tuxedo, sitting further along the row. 'My parents were really into classical music. My sister Ursula and me used to get dragged along to what felt like every prom. And the occasional opera in between. Ursula still comes, because she's a good girl, but I've got better things to do.'

'It's such a beautiful building, though.'

Leonie shrugs. 'If you like buildings designed for the wealthy to use to support the status quo, yeah, it's the bomb.'

Vee will never, ever get the hang of this. There's too much of it – there are too many invisible-until-pointed-out-and-then-they-are-obvious ways that women have been oppressed. When she's talking to her dad, in their mostly good-natured debates after watching *What the Papers Say*, or when she's writing out an invoice, she feels liberated, competent, strong. She's confident in marshalling her arguments for why she might not want to settle down and have children, and even if she does, that's no reason why she shouldn't have a career too. The Equal Pay Act, thanks to the Ford machinists, should make that easier.

More than that, among some of her old friends from school, who are starting to settle down, she can talk about ambition, her own and theirs, and she makes a point of being a good sister to those who are thinking beyond what's usual for them. She can point to Margaret Thatcher as one of many women doing important work and being taken seriously as they do it. Leonie would say one female Secretary of State is not enough, but to Vee's friends she's an object of speculation and strangeness. (What does her husband think? Surely her children suffer?) A Colchester local ~~counsellor~~ councillor has admitted publicly that she's a lesbian. Not 'admitted', that isn't the right word for it. But the point is, the world is changing, and Vee is on board with the changes, and will fight for them, and even be something of a small trailblazer in her neck of the woods. Being the only female wedding photographer in Essex might not be all she wants, but it's something. A start.

Except just when she thinks she's got a handle on it, she admires the architecture of a building, and discovers a whole new level of oppression that hadn't even occurred to her before. Leonie says she shouldn't be ashamed of that, because it's not her fault the patriarchy has normalised this shit. Vee loves the way Leonie talks, education and swearing in equal measure. And she loves that she says it's always OK to ask questions, but it's never OK to be deliberately ignorant.

'Leonie?' Her friend turns towards her; that face so photogenic. Vee is proud, every day, that one of her photographs is Leonie's publicity photograph, appearing small and slightly blurred next to her articles in *This Month* and as the main image in a piece she wrote for the *Telegraph* about the impact of the Equal Pay Act for all women. Leonie looks a little bit distant – she's probably still thinking about her meeting. Vee cannot imagine how disappointing it must be to have someone reject your book, especially such a book as Leonie is writing. And she knows that once the action starts, Leonie will be fullthroatedly alive – her disappointments put aside for the sake of the sisterhood.

'Uh-huh?'

'What do you call it ...' Vee makes sure not to drop her voice, because there's no shame in asking a question about sexuality '... what do you call it when a lesbian admits it? I mean, what's the expression?'

There's an unhidden titter from the women sitting behind them. Leonie doesn't turn around, but raises her right arm, lazily, rotates her hand, gives them the finger. 'Telling other people is "coming out". Admitting it to yourself doesn't really have an expression. I suppose you'd call it waking up. Like, sexual awakening.'

And then the lights go down, and there's a cheer and applause, and it begins. Vee tries to keep her critical faculties alive, remember why she's here. She knows with all of her heart that women are more than their measurements and have easily as much potential as the men who patronise them and, knowingly or unknowingly, exploit them.

Vee is not going to be drawn into this.

She is only here to protest.

But oh, it's captivating.

There are the lights, and the whole sparkle of it, and, when the women start to emerge, the sheer shining beauty of them. The audience, too – the way the people sound, gasps and applause, so thrilled, so excited. Plus – Vee hadn't thought about this, really, until now – beyond this dazzling room, full of thousands of people, there's a whole world watching.

Vee is holding her breath. She can't take her eyes from the stage. And then, because she can't help herself, she's joining in the collective coo of approval when another beauty – no, not beauty, 'woman who fits the conventional notion of beauty' – walks onto the stage.

And yes, it's artifice, and yes, it's conditioning, and yes, it's wrong. But how Vee would love to take to those faces with her camera, sculpt the angles with light and shade, turn conventional beauty into something powerful and stripped back and stunning. Whichever beauty queen is now centre stage is sim-pering and smiling and talking about how much she loves the colour of her gown. She's wearing high, strappy shoes which catch the light, and her hair is solidly in place in a pleat that looks as though it would survive the worst that the IRA could do. Vee imagines this woman barefoot, wearing a towelling bathrobe two sizes too big so that the only flesh on show is her face and neck, a triangle of throat, her hands and feet. Her hair would be wet – not damp, wet, hanging in rat tails around her face, the tops of her ears sticking out. The shape of her body – what-ever stupid measurements they are spouting on the stage now, as though they are her worth – would be hidden by the thick-ness of the fabric. And she would not be smiling. Or pouting. Or come-hithering. She would be staring into the lens, fierce, with a look that said: I have no time for your men-rule-the-world bullshit. This is what I look like. This is me.

There's a line-up of all the women on the stage, and then they file off, to applause and cooing from the audience. Some of the women around them are applauding, presumably to avoid suspicion, although it's hard – for Vee, at least – not to be pulled into genuine admiration. She remembers how her mother used to love to dress up, her one pair of high-heeled shoes always wrapped in their tissue and put back in their box after they were worn. Vee leans over to Leonie and says, 'I'd love to take their photographs. Without makeup. Just women.'

Leonie says, 'Not "just". And why not do it with other women? The ones that aren't meeting a patriarchal notion of beauty? It's a total waste.'

'Of beauty?'

'Don't be ridiculous. That's not beauty. That's patriarchy in action. Brains. It's a waste of brains. And time. How long does it take them to do whatever they do to their eyebrows? Or starve?

Worry about every damn thing they put in their mouths?' Vee thinks of the photographs she has already seen in the press, of a woman in a swimsuit smiling as a man with a tape measure wraps it around her hips, takes a reading. Leonie is right. Well, she's always right. But Vee is the one who can see a different way to portray beauty. Or perhaps, a different kind of beauty to portray.

She doesn't think the protest will really happen. There is something so impossible-seeming about disrupting a live television broadcast, and one with the word 'World' in it. Marching in the streets, yes. Going out on strike, yes. Invading a public space, or not doing something you were expected to do: Vee sees no reason why the fight should not take place on these battlegrounds. But there was something so audacious about this idea that she could barely believe it would happen. When Leonie had first told her about it, Vee had thought she was joking. They were at the opening of an exhibition of artwork made by a collective of women protesting against the Vietnam War. Vee was photographing the art, the artists, and the lighting in the gallery was a nightmare so she hadn't really paid attention to what Leonie was saying. The details had arrived in the post a week later, and Vee had copied them into her diary, but she still hadn't quite believed it. She had imagined it would be like those schoolgirl schemes, the ones where everyone is definitely going to stand up and walk out the next time they are given extra homework, or everyone was without question going to refuse to come to school the day after Amanda Johnson got the slipper for forgetting her PE kit three weeks running, when everyone knew she only did that because her mother didn't believe in bras and she was more afraid of the boys' laughter than she was of the teacher's ire.

And then it begins.

And she's part of it.

She is so angry when she hears what Bob Hope says at the beginning of his turn on stage – 'It's like a cattle market back there, I've been backstage checking out some calves' – that when the football rattle goes off, it feels like immediate and glorious justice to be on her feet, bellowing at the wrongness of it, and she wishes she had brought more than her camera. And then Leonie gives her a flour bomb, and she hurls it, joining in the chant of 'We're not beautiful! We're not ugly! We are angry!' For once, she is in the thick of it, and there is nowhere else in the world she would rather be. The air is full of fury and flour, shouting and screams; the security guards and police are there soon, but not soon enough. This is action. This is real. Vee and Leonie are part of a movement that is changing the world.

The man who tutted at Leonie's swearing earlier barks a sharp, 'I say! That's enough!' Vee, turning to glance at his purpling, indignant face, feels something else within her fall into place, lock, make her stronger. She's not just here to protest about the way women are portrayed. It's about the whole damn world. The beauty queens only parade because the men in bow-ties want to look at them. The women who are with the men in bow-ties have been made to think that this is OK. No one here believes they are doing anything wrong. Everyone is brainwashed. And among the confusion and the shouting, under the disapproving gaze of the people who came here to watch the show, and the blank eyes of the television cameras, Veronica Moon gets it. Really, properly. Not in words, but in feelings. She might not know everything, but she understands. She unclips her camera lens cap, puts the viewfinder to her eye.

Shoved and shunted from the building with the other shouting protestors a few minutes later, Vee finds herself next to a grinning Leonie, and because she cannot express, exactly, what it is that she has felt, she blurts, 'I love you.' Leonie seems not to hear.

Leonie drinks a lot, fast, as they stand in the street outside the Café de Paris two hours later. Hip-flasks filled with brandy and whisky are being passed from hand to hand. Vee sips – she likes the warmth the alcohol brings, but she wants to keep her wits about her, just in case she does get arrested. The police seem benign, good-humoured almost, chatting to some of the quieter protesters who are asking them about their wives, their sisters, talking about how beauty contests undermine the women in their lives. The police don't appear to be taking them seriously, but you never know. Some of it might sink in.

Vee feels overwhelmed, still, by her sudden understanding of how much work there is to do. Feeling around in her handbag for her hanky, her fingers find instead her lipstick, and she pulls it out and throws it in the gutter. She'll never wear makeup again.

Every time the protesters start to feel cold, or tired, more women arrive with more placards – 'Women Are People Too', 'Women Demand Liberation' – and the chanting finds new strength with new voices. There's euphoria everywhere at the disruption the action at the Royal Albert Hall has caused; speculation about how many millions of people might have seen the protest on television. Hundreds of thousands, maybe. Vee can't begin to imagine it. She can imagine Barry's mother's face, though.

What a thing to be part of. What a night to remember. Who'd have thought that she, Veronica Moon from Colchester, daughter of a carpenter and a part-time shop assistant, could be here, her voice one of many crying out for a new world? Yet here she is. Time to get to work, properly.

But now the first excitement is over, Leonie – much more used to this kind of thing than Vee, of course – is on a real downer about her book being rejected. Once alcohol hits her system, her disappointment starts to show. She is telling the others around them about her book, about how she has been let down by her sisters, her words oppressed. She gets unsteady and goes to sit on a step.

'You should take her home,' Jo says to Vee, 'she's an ugly drunk.' Vee looks across at Leonie, who is silent now, her head in her hands, probably not being hassled by the police because she looks like a tipsy old man in the half-hearted light from the street lamps. She's tempted, for a moment, to photograph her. She tells herself not to – it wouldn't be kind.

She scans the crowd for faces she knows, and faces that look like the faces she is thinking about: old faces, tired faces, faces with double chins. Leonie has given her a set of keys to the flat, in case they were separated at the demo, so why not just get absorbed into the crowd, seek out the people whose names she knows and start with them? Kiki's here, Fen and Jo too; they could be the place to begin. Leonie can fend for herself. Vee will catch up with her back at the flat.

She glances back at Leonie, who hasn't moved, her head still in her hands. She'll be fine here. She has sisters all around her.

But then Leonie looks up and around; as soon as she sees Vee, she smiles with unguarded relief. Vee smiles back. Nothing is more important than her friend. Help a sister out, Vee says to herself. Leonie first, photographs tomorrow.

Leonie is quiet in the taxi. They are back at her flat within ten minutes; almost as soon as they arrive, Leonie goes out again, saying she'll be back soon. It's almost eleven – not late, not really, but it's been a long day, and all Vee really wants to do is go to bed. But she does the washing-up and puts some things in the bin. She did the same the last time she was here. Leonie accused her of being indoctrinated by patriarchal values of what a woman's role should be, but it's really not that: it's just a desire for order. She had framed it to Leonie as a characteristic of a photographer, not a woman, and Leonie bought it, though she grumbled that her cleaner sorts it all on Mondays so it was a waste of Vee's energy.

Leonie comes back half an hour later, with a bottle of wine and a pizza on a plate from the restaurant around the corner.

'C'mon,' she says, ignoring the cleaned-up kitchen table, 'let's eat on the sofa.' Vee hasn't eaten pizza before. She watches as Leonie folds a triangular slice over and eats it like a sort of hot sandwich, and does the same. Her fingertips sing at the heat, but she doesn't mind – this doesn't seem like a knife-and-fork meal. It's delicious, tomato and cheese and slices of something black and round that is probably olive. Dad might like it. He likes cheese on toast.

'I was hungry,' Vee says, 'I didn't realise.'

Leonie grins, and puts the plate on the floor. 'I'll look after you.' She wraps her arms around Vee, who feels herself brace before she relaxes. Leonie feels it too: 'Be cool. I'm not going to kiss you.'

'It's not that, it's just . . .' Vee doesn't have the vocabulary to tell Leonie about the way she thinks about her, sometimes, a feeling like she used to get with Barry. Though Barry had to work a lot harder than Leonie to give her that warmth in her belly. And how strange it is, because up until that local coun<del>sel-</del>c̷i̷l̷l̷o̷r̷ came out recently, Essex has always appeared to be a lesbian-free zone, and she had never ever thought of herself as someone who could love a woman. Not like that.

Before she can even begin, though, Leonie says, 'I think I might like men best. There've been a few. I'm wondering. Not that I'll give up women altogether.'

Just when Vee thinks she's getting the hang of something, it changes. 'That's . . .' she begins, but the only word that comes to her tongue is 'good', which she knows won't do. So she switches to a question. 'Do you have to choose?'

Leonie slaps Vee on the knee. 'Your education is progressing, sister. Some people don't choose. If you were going to put a label on it' – her expression shows exactly how little she thinks of that – 'you'd call it bisexual. Swinging both ways. I've got enough on my mind without trying to work out if I want to shag every-one I meet, or only the ones with the pricks.'

Vee nods. She has wondered, quietly, whether not shagging anyone at all might be what she wants. When Barry touched her, she liked it; if Leonie kissed her she'd be . . . interested. But she can't seem to conjure up the hunger for sex that everyone else seems to have. And anyway, thinking about sex, and love, must cloud the vision. A clear eye is what a photographer needs, above all. 'Fair enough.'

Leonie begins to laugh, and every time she seems to have stopped, she starts again.

Vee doesn't like being laughed at, but in the end she can't help asking: 'What's so funny?' Vee can't help but to be pulled into the laughter, though she doesn't understand where it's coming from. This is Leonie's great power, it seems to Vee: not just her words, her cleverness, but the sheer force of her pulls you in.

'You wouldn't have said "fair enough" to that when I met you. And you wouldn't have said it in that voice either. You would have been much more "Cor blimey, Professor Higgins".' The remains of laughter make Leonie's voice warm.

Vee rolls her eyes. 'No I wouldn't. And anyway, Eliza Doolittle was from the East End. Not Essex. How would you feel if I mixed up . . .' Oh, if there was only an easy way to explain these things to Leonie. 'Fulham and – and – Wales?'

'I'd laugh myself stupid. Anyway, I was trying to be nice.' She pours the last of the wine into her own glass; Vee is only halfway through her first. It has a dark, harsh taste; she didn't really want it, but if she hadn't taken it, Leonie would have drunk the whole bottle herself.

'Were you? Trying to be nice?'

'No need to sound surprised.' Leonie is serious again, half-smiling, asking a question with her eyes. So Leonie wants to be liked, too, despite what she says. That's reassuring.

'It's just that you've always been . . . anti-nice. So it's weird when you are.'

Leonie fumbles in her pocket for her tobacco tin, takes out a roll-up, lights it, and shrugs. 'Trying to stop you from flirting with blokes in pubs so the landlord doesn't get challenged isn't about nice or not nice. It's about right.'

Vee nods. 'I know that.' She thinks of how she smiled at the security guard on their way into the Royal Albert Hall. After what she saw tonight, the insidiousness of it all, she won't be doing that again.

'Good.' Leonie's grin is back. 'Anyway. I'm not going to come on to you, baby, you can sleep easy in your bed.' She gets up, stretches, and kicks the pizza plate under the sofa. There are a few similar plates in the kitchen; Vee wonders if they ever make it back to the restaurant.

'What are you going to do?'

'I'm going to write some opinions.'

'Now? When you're—'

'What? Pissed? Horny?' Leonie's life may be cluttered but the desk beneath the window is neat. She switches on the anglepoise lamp, puts her hands flat against the desk and leans her weight down on them for a moment, head dropping. 'Write drunk, edit sober. That's what Hemingway said. But he was a know-nothing entitled prick so I say write any way you like, edit any way you like.'

She turns, waiting for a response.

'I say photograph sober, develop sober,' Vee says. She's entitled to her work ethic.

Leonie nods. 'Probably wise,' and she sits down at her desk.

Vee is woken by the smell of frying bacon and the sound of Leonie's loud, tuneless singing. It's almost 10 a.m. Whether it was the wine, the thrill, the cold on the streets last night, or the lulling rumble of London traffic, she has slept like a stone. Leonie greets her with a smile, pours tea for her, and puts a plate of bacon sandwiches down on the kitchen table.

'You were up early,' Vee says. There are copies of the *Telegraph*, the *Guardian* and the *Express* on the table, along with a paper bag spilling apples and a box of Mr Kipling's French Fancies. They've fast become one of Stanley's favourites, and Vee feels a sudden ache at the thought of her father, who will be well into his Sunday morning routine now, cleaning out the fireplace and relaying it ready for later.

'I haven't been to bed, yet,' Leonie says, 'I'll sleep later.'

Just the thought of working through the night makes Vee want to cry with a sort of empathetic tiredness. Leonie seems fine, though; there are bags under her eyes, and as usual, her hair could do with a wash. The tips of her ears poke through it, which Vee finds endearing. 'Good writing?'

'Best column yet,' Leonie says, biting into a sandwich, 'that bitch editor from yesterday is going to read it and weep.'

'Good.' They chink their mugs together, and Vee turns to the papers. One has a front-page image of the protest, the other a smiling Miss World, with only the briefest mention of the protest in the text. 'Look at that. And we were part of it.' The feeling she had yesterday, whatever it was, has stayed in her, moving from her gut to her backbone, making her straighter, stronger.

Vee reads the story, which includes the result, as they didn't see the end of the show. 'At least they let a black woman win it,' she says.

'There is so much wrong with that statement that I don't know where to start.' Leonie play-punches Vee's arm; bacon falls from her sandwich. Vee shakes her head, laughs at herself. She must get better at thinking before she speaks.

'Let me have a go. At all the things that are wrong.'

Leonie sits back in her chair, crosses her arms. 'I'm listening. Redeem yourself, my child.'

'OK.' Vee thinks back over what she said, 'No one should be letting a woman do anything because it takes away her power—'

Leonie nods. 'Or?'

'Or implies she doesn't have any.'

'Good. And?'

'And she didn't win because she was black, or she shouldn't have done, because skin colour shouldn't matter, just like sex shouldn't.'

'Gender.'

'Sorry. Gender.'

'And do you think it's OK for you to say skin colour shouldn't matter?'

'Well' – surely this is obvious – 'I would never say it should matter. Because that would be racist.'

87

'I mean,' Leonie says, 'do you think it's OK for you to make those judgements? You're white. There are things you can't comment on. Like, if I hit you I'm not entitled to say how much it hurts.'

Vee loves these conversations. She has the same feeling she used to when she was a little girl, watching her dad work, him explaining how he was dovetailing a joint. Later, at college, in her first darkroom sessions, she was bursting with that same sparkling sense of understanding how something works. And knowing that all she needs to do is pay attention to be able to do it too.

Leonie tops up their mugs. Her teapot has a knitted cosy. Vee can't imagine that she knitted it herself. It's the sort of thing that her uptight sister Ursula might do, from what Vee has heard about her. 'You said "at least" they let a black woman win. "At least" suggests we're happy with a minimum. And, winning a beauty contest is not good, because—'

Vee laughs, slaps her hand on the table as though she is throwing down a winning hand of poker, played for spent matches with her dad. 'Patriarchal notions of beauty!'

'Exactly, sister. We're getting there.'

'Thanks, Leonie. I still feel stupid a lot of the time.'

'We support our sisters. And sharing the knowledge is sharing the power. The education we get is through the patriarchy. Don't feel bad. Because . . . ?' Leonie tilts an eyebrow.

'Because feeling bad is an expectation placed on women, and it comes from outdated patriarchal notions of society?'

'Right on, sister.' Leonie has finished her bacon sandwich, and pulls a French Fancy from the box. 'Fen moved out a couple of weeks ago. Do you want to move in?'

Vee has imagined what it would be like to be Leonie's flatmate. Or her sister. Or, once – she doesn't know what got into her – her girlfriend. 'I'd love to!' If being with a woman who knows all the ways the world needs to change could be Vee's life, she would be ecstatic. And she'd be part of the fight. Properly, in the middle of it. But – 'What's the rent?'

Leonie shrugs. 'Just pay your half of the bills.'

'But that's – do you mean that?'

'Sure.' Leonie grins. 'That's what I do. It's a family place. My folks bought it when they used to live in Norwich. For when they were in London. Then they moved to London and bought a house, but they kept this.'

Vee nods as though people owning flats in cities they might visit is as everyday as Leonie makes it sound. 'I'd love to,' she says again.

And then the phone rings. Leonie goes to the hall to answer it and, after a brief conversation, comes back into the kitchen, face tight, running a hand through her hair, 'Still got film in your camera?'

'Always. Why?'

'We need to get over to Jo's. Kiki just arrived. Her husband cut up rough when she got back last night.'

'Kiki's husband? I thought he was OK. She said he was cool with her doing this.' Not that it's up to him, of course.

'So did she.' Leonie is pulling on her boots, the DMs Vee covets (although she's not sure she could carry them off). 'Seems he was horny when she got back. She said she didn't want it but he took it anyway. Jo's going to see about finding her a place to stay. I'm going to write her account. You can take photos of the damage. She's got cuts on her face and bruises on her thighs and her wrists.'

Vee swallows bile. Kiki is a kind of wonder-woman to her: clever, sparky, bright. The thought of her being hurt is almost too much. But, women help women and this is something useful she can do. 'Has anyone called the police?'

Leonie hesitates for long enough to look straight at Vee. 'Kiki's married. He hasn't done anything wrong, legally.'

'Right.' Except of course it's not right. 'I'll need to go back in a couple of days. When the bruises have come out more.'

Maybe Leonie hears something in her voice, because when she comes back from the living room with their coats, she holds Vee in a brief, tight embrace. 'Not everyone could do this, you know. Thanks, Vee.'

21 November 1970

'WHY ON EARTH WOULD YOU move out?' Vee was prepared for her father to be hurt, or angry. Confusion, she is finding more difficult to handle. It's always been obvious, to her, that this was going to happen at some point.

Stanley has been more strict about her paying half of the bills since she split up with Barry: it's obvious he thinks she is going to be alone forever, so he needs to make her self-sufficient. But she didn't really think that he assumed she would live here until – well, until he died. (Her body shrinks in on itself at the thought.) It seems she was wrong. He, apparently, thought she had two options: marry and leave home, or not leave home.

In fairness, he's never treated her like a girl; she can use a hacksaw and a lathe, light a fire, change a fuse, top up the oil in the car. But those were things he showed her because she asked, or because she was keeping him company in the garage while he worked on a chest of drawers for her bedroom, or mended a neighbour's bedside table. They were things that stopped both of them from being alone. Now he seems to be preparing her for the dry spinster life, although it's obvious from the way he drops Barry into the conversation whenever he can that he hopes she will see sense and settle down. 'Settle for', she had said, and she doesn't want to do that.

Your London friends won't be there when you're old, he had said. Your fancy feminists won't be able to build you a dining table or fix a faulty fuse box.

You don't know that, she had said, and anyway, I'm not sure Barry was much good with a screwdriver. Estate agents aren't, usually. She'd hoped that he would call her out for making assumptions, so she could point out that he was doing the same. But he'd just smiled and said, you know what I'm saying. And she had known: he was saying that he cared. She knew, too, that the only way to convince him that she could manage was to do it: move out, work, make a name.

'I just don't know what to make of this, Veronica,' he says, now. 'I know we have our differences, but I didn't think . . .'

Vee has photographed her father several times, usually when she's trying out a new piece of kit, and images of him are always compelling: there's something about the proportion of his face, the straightness of his brow, the angle that his nose makes to it. His earlobes are long and his left eyelid droops a little more than the right. And now he looks sad, weighed down by her decision, and she wants to do three things: photograph him like this, tell him that it doesn't matter, just to see him smile – and explain. She takes the hardest option. 'It's nothing to do with you, Dad. I just want to be independent. And I want to have a career. London's the best place.'

He shakes his head. 'You've changed, treasure. I don't know what to make of you.'

She puts her hand over his. She is so small, in comparison; she knows this is what he is seeing too. 'I'm still me, Dad. I'm just finding my way. Changing with the world. Isn't that what happens? Did Gran and Gramps never say they couldn't understand you?'

A smile; a chink.

'It's all different now. Women have more options. They don't have to get married and have babies anymore. There's the Pill. They can make choices.'

Fen says they should talk about sex and contraception in front of men, to 'normalise it', and Vee agrees. Plus, she and her dad have had to about to talk about things she would have normally discussed with her mum, periods and bras, so she thinks it should be all right.

'Is that so?'

'Yes,' she says, and then she looks into his face and realises what she's said. Her parents got married when they found out her mother was pregnant; her father sometimes says she was the best accident that ever happened, usually when he has drunk too much at Christmas, or on the anniversary of her mother's death. 'Oh, Dad. I didn't mean—'

He gets up, pushing his weight against the table, and she has no choice but to move her hand away. 'I know,' he says, but his face has become a blank and he won't look at her. 'I'll talk to Johnny at the allotments and see if I can borrow the van. It'll save you making a few trips. Just let me know what day.'

93

November 1970

This Month magazine

Leonie Barratt: Letters from a Feminist

Our monthly column from the front line of the Battle of the Sexes

Dear John,

Well, Miss World was quite a ride this year. Did you spot me, John? I was there. I didn't quite get to the stage, but one of my flour bombs did. In the excitement I forgot about the rotten lettuce in my handbag, but battles rarely go completely as planned.

I wonder, were you impressed by the way my sisters and I took action? That we variously lumpen, big-nosed, gap-toothed women wanted to show that we are all valid members of the human race? Or were you upset that your night of looking at 'perfect' women in swimsuits and evening dresses was disrupted? Did it make for even more excitement? Did you imagine yourself wiping away the tears of those poor, frightened 'beauty' 'queens'? In your dreams, did they look at you, pale but still beautiful, and whisper, 'I'm afraid, John. All I want, really, is a good man to love me. Will you hold me?'

John, we need to talk about beauty contests. We really do. Because they are not, in any way, shape or form, cool.

Whereas women themselves, in any way, shape or form, ARE cool.

It's not the way we look that matters.

I'd like to think I don't have to explain this to you, but I'm going to spell it out, just to be on the safe side. Then, next year, if you notice that Miss World is on TV, you can go and do something more useful with your evening. Something a bit less oppressive. Like, have a conversation with a woman you know and like. Maybe go out for a meal. Maybe split the bill, because a lot of us feel a little intimidated at being 'treated'. Listen as much as you talk. Just general equality in action, you know? (You don't have to wait until next year to do that, though. Do it tomorrow, if you like.)

Unlike some of my sisters, I don't think that you are automatically A Bad Thing, John, just because of the testosterone. I think you have been conditioned into thinking that women have a certain role to play in your life. Like: being beautiful. Wearing swimsuits and turning around so you can get a good look at their behind. Tricking, cajoling or nagging you into marrying them. And then doing all they can to not lose their looks, because we all know that if they put on a couple of pounds and realise lipstick is just another tool of oppression, you will be entirely justified in going back to the Royal Albert Hall and picking yourself a better beauty queen, next year. That's the patriarchy. That's how it works. If you have something that shape-shifts that you keep in your Y-fronts, you can just cruise on through your life, doing exactly what you like, surrounded by women doing what they've been trained to do. Please you, make you comfortable, do all they can so that you never, ever question your entitlement to taking anything you like from the world.

This is not OK, John. I've been reading the newspapers (yes, I can read) and watching the news (yes, I can afford a television, which I bought with money I earned) and I see that the sisterhood has been getting a bit of stick. I see we, the protesters, have been accused of being jealous. If we had legs that long, or hair that glossy, or could make an impression on the world just by standing on a stage and letting people look at us, you say, we would do it. But we can't. So we behave exactly the way you would expect silly, envious girls to behave. Sour grapes, you say.

This commentary (and I know it doesn't all come from you, personally, but I also suspect that, when the men in your office or at the golf club have muttered about the way we 'bloody feminists' behaved, you haven't stood up for us, which makes you part of the problem) presupposes that the best thing a woman can be is beautiful in the crippled, doll-like way the women at the stage on the Royal Albert Hall appeared. Men objecting to the protest on these grounds assume that women with cleverness, or curiosity, wit or bravery, would all willingly exchange those characteristics for a pert nose and a cute smile. Do you see how deep this all runs? Because that's patriarchal thought in action, right there, and it's wrong.

We did not throw rotten tomatoes at our sisters, we threw them at the man who was belittling them. We did not cover them in flour or shout at them. We object to the idea of being judged on our looks. We object to a man making jokes about cattle markets. We wish, with all of our hearts, that women did not think that their value is in their looks. That's why we were protesting.

John, if there are women in your life that you love, next time you spend time with them, watch them. Do they eat less than you, or talk about the Grapefruit Diet? Do they always put on makeup before they go out? Do they ask you if they look OK?

If the answer to those questions is yes, I'm afraid that you're a part of the problem.

Have you any idea how much time a Miss World competitor spends on her looks? (And make no mistake, she is a competitor, and it is a competition, woman against woman. Which is clever, because it stops women from seeing where the real battle is.) She will spend time every day moisturising and anointing different parts of her body with different potions, to make her skin softer or paler or sleeker. She will spend a long time in front of the mirror, trying to find flaws, not understanding that she is exactly as flawed, and flawless, as the rest of her sisters.

She will think about each and every damn thing she puts in her mouth before she eats it, because – consider this – because someone is going to measure her, and look at her, and judge whether she is the right shape or not. (She is never the right shape. If she is 36-26-36, that's all well and good, but if everyone is 36-26-36, there is going to be a part of her wondering if it would be better if she was 36.5-25.5-36.5 or 35-24-35.) She probably never gets filthy drunk. Do you know how many calories there are in a sweet martini and lemonade, John? You can bet a beauty queen does, I bet she never eats candyfloss at the beach and licks the sticky residue off her fingers. I bet she doesn't open the door without having put all of her makeup on. There's probably a mirror in the hallway, so she can check that her hair is glossy enough before she goes anywhere.

There's a good chance that your beauty queen practises walking, John. If you are any shade of a decent man you must be able to see that that is not cool.

She probably goes for days and days without anyone asking her what she thinks about the Vietnam War. If they ever have. But she probably has a view. Because she is more than her looks, and she deserves to be treated as such. Just like we – the feminists, the protesters, the ones who don't get leered at in the street because we reject the game of prettiness – deserve to be credited with more than jealousy for our actions at Miss World.

So, why not stick up for us, John? Why not admit – to yourself, to your colleagues, to the women in your life – that we had a point, and we made it, and we did it because the world needs to change? And don't expect me to thank you for it. Because being grateful to men is a whole different area of wrongness that we need to talk about, some other time.

Leonie

98

19 February 2018

In Dapchi, Nigeria, 110 schoolgirls are kidnapped by the extremist group Boko Haram. On 25 March, the BBC will report that most were released, after having been warned not to return to school. Five did not survive.

HRH Queen Elizabeth II attends London Fashion Week.

Model Eunice Olumide tells a BBC reporter, 'We're not able to represent reality in the industry ... There's no minimum wage for models, no requirement to make clothes in different sizes.'

Nine weeks and three days to exhibition opening

'Cheer up, love,' says the man at the ticket barrier.

Vee can tell from his face that he means no harm, but that's not the point. Never miss a chance to educate, as Leonie used to say. 'I appreciate that you're trying to be friendly,' she says, 'but you have no idea what's going on in my life, so telling me to "cheer up" isn't appropriate. And neither is calling me "love".' She walks on, before she can see his reaction, but she imagines it: rolled eyes, the person behind her at the barrier saying something like 'that's what you get for trying to be pleasant'. Well, Vee might not be able to do a lot for the movement these days, but she can stop it going backwards when she sees the opportunity.

She should have thought today through better. For years her life has been quiet. She knows that she is ill and her emergency appointment with Dr Wilding after meeting Erica for the first time only confirmed it. And still she's agreed to spend the afternoon with Erica, despite having spent this morning at hospital, being scanned and tested, questioned and touched. Every now and then Vee gets drawn into something, a meeting of old colleagues or a fundraiser, and she thinks it will be OK, because, she says to herself, how difficult, really, how trying, can spending a couple of hours with other people be? And then she does it, and she remembers. There are so many places where it's such hard work. So many ways that you need to be thoughtful, and she just doesn't think that way anymore. She used to. She used to do it too much, and Leonie helped her to see why she was allowed to put her own needs first, because that was her right. Not her right as a woman, but her right as a person, equally as important (and unimportant) as the next person. 'Except you,' Vee had said, walking home to their flat after a Woman's Liberation Front meeting in the month after she moved in. Leonie had laughed, and looked straight into her – those eyes, sepia, so clever and so bright. If Leonie had kissed her, properly, then, Vee would have kissed back.

What Vee hadn't known, of course, when she agreed to Erica's exhibition, was that Erica would be so very Leonie-like, or that that resemblance, from eyes to tilt of head to timbre of voice and the way her stride lopes, would make Vee think about all the things she has banished from her mind for so many years. If only her memory was better, or more of it had remained after the surgery. Though knowing for certain might not really help.

She steps on to the train and takes a seat, takes off her coat, and rubs at the crook of her elbow, where cotton wool is taped over the place where a needle went in. Vee is unused to touch. (Apart from Marja, who comes to her house to massage her pain away.) Even though she knows what she has endured this morning are objective medical processes, that the concentrated pressing of fingertips was exploration, quest, she still felt them as unwanted intimacy. And she knows, more or less, what the tests will show. Mr Wilding had said as much. He'd looked through her notes, listened to her description of headaches and moods, odd appetites and new blanks in her memory, the way she is grasping for words. And he'd said, 'Well, we knew this was a possibility, Ms Moon. There are other things that it could be, but a recurrence is, I'm afraid, the most likely. Let's do some tests and then we can see exactly where we are.'

Two hours of hospital, tests and questions but no conclusions yet, is horribly uncertain. Especially when she is so horribly certain, herself, and confirmation will be something like relief. It's just a question of how many steps to the grave. A decade's survival of glioblastoma is such a best-case scenario that she should almost be pleased.

In two days she'll go back to Harley Street and talk practicalities and likelihoods.

Between now and then, she needs to wait.

At least this afternoon is filled up. Even if she shouldn't have agreed to go to Erica's. ('Any lapses in judgement?' one of the nurses today had asked. 'How am I supposed to know?' Vee had bitten back. 'Everything makes sense to me.')

Vee doesn't usually mind the overground lines out of London – she used to know them as well as she now knows the names of all the pills in her bathroom cabinet – but today, it's hard work. Two families gaggle onto the carriage at the last minute at Waterloo, and Vee is not far enough away to tune them out, so she has to listen all the way to Hampton, where they get off. The mothers are talking to their offspring in that quasi-educational way that people do now: *yes I see the bus, what colour is the bus? Do you see what the number is on the front? Yes, it's a bit like a 45, but have a look at the second number again* . . . The two fathers (or uncles, or brothers, or friends) sit in seats across the aisle from their families. One is on his phone, and the other slouches, hands in pockets, looking out of the window, as though the children squawking less than five feet away are nothing to do with him. Maybe he will hoist one of them on to his shoulders, later, when they are tired, and expect the mother to be grateful. Vee is composing the photograph of it in her head, now, the man with the child held aloft, smiling, talking, the woman carrying bags, her body partly cut out of the image by his, her tiredness clear in the way her shoulders drop, her switched-off face.

Bloody men.

Oh, she's tired.

She hires a cab from Hampton station, even though it's not far to Erica's house. She is driven through streets of stately, semi-detached houses, most with loft conversions, two cars on the drive, tidy front gardens and shining windows cleaned, in all likelihood, by someone who isn't the owner. They scream middle-class convention. Erica has ended up in a life that is surely not the one Leonie would have wanted for her, though Ursula no doubt would have been perfectly content. Well, it was ever so. Parents want safety for their children. Vee's father would much rather she had settled down with a man, after all.

Marja, a masseuse Vee has used since her last illness, came to the house and worked her magic yesterday. The gripe of the headache was driven away, and Vee slept for ten hours without the trace of a dream or the shadow of a pain. It was bliss. But today, she feels worse, and it's partly because of the hospital, of course, its synthetic light and lack of air, all of the people she has never met touching her and calling her by her first name. But it also feels though her brain is punishing her for the respite that a long sleep brought. Maybe this is how it's going to go: a back and forth of headache and rest from it, with the balance shifting, day by day, until there is never peace but only pain and lesser pain. Maybe it's already happening; maybe her perception is shifting, and her head always hurts. That might explain the towering impatience she is feeling this afternoon.

'Here you go,' says the cab driver, 'visiting your grandkids, are you? I've got a dozen of 'em. It's all my wife ever does, go to see them. It's a new lease of life.'

'I'm going to work,' Vee says, 'and you're making a lot of assumptions.' She gives him the exact money.

It is all, still, such a great effort.

Vee takes in the silence and the space, walks down the path to the house, steps slow and quiet. Although the day isn't warm there's something gentle and soothing in it. Spring, perhaps.

Air and light. She hasn't had enough of them today. Her daily walks along the river, from Battersea Park to Putney and back, have been part of her routine for years, but lately she hasn't had the energy, or her sleep has been so bad that she hasn't been able to face it. And morning, early, is really the only time: everyone is doing their walk or run or dog-exercising before the day begins, so there are nods of recognition but no risk of conversation. It suits her perfectly. Suited.

She rubs at the place on her arm again. Her scalp is itchy with the aftermath of sweat and scrutiny. Straightening her shoulders, she rings the doorbell. She's exactly on time.

Erica opens the door with a smile. 'Come through!' she says, and turns, leading Vee through a hallway into a kitchen-diner that must run the length of the back of the house. It's a bright

103

room, with deep windows the length of one wall, and skylights too. It would be great for a photoshoot; Vee never stopped being anti-flash and a space like this would be a dream. A good quarter of it is given over to a great dining table, solid and dark, which has files and folders stacked along one side. There's a pile of family detritus at the other edge – letters, opened and unopened, mugs, a plastic bowl with cereal in it, a cuddly animal of some sort. Erica, who is barefoot, hair in a pony-tail, wearing jeans and a shirt but still madeup, sees where Vee is looking, 'I'm so sorry about the chaos. Marcus's mother arrived late to collect Tom and I'm behind with everything. I'm nearly there.'

'Take your time,' Vee says. She could so easily be annoyed. But she knows how to wait. She likes it. Patience was her technique, really, the way she got her best photographs. Watch, wait, let the artifice fall away; wait for the people to be the people.

'Thanks.' Erica clears the table, bowl into sink and toy lobbed into a basket, everything else added to a pile of papers on the kitchen worktop. It looks as though it might be made of granite. Vee wants to rest her forehead on it, feel the coolness, the uncompromising hardness.

'Coffee?' Erica asks. There's an elaborate red-and-chrome machine, which doubtless makes coffee a thousand times better than the stuff Vee boredom-drank at the hospital this morning, but caffeine isn't exactly known for being the headache's friend. She shakes her head.

'Right, let's get started.' But Erica pauses and takes the lid from a slow cooker, stirs it. Seeing Vee look, she says, 'Marcus is more of a child than Tom. If I don't feed him within twenty minutes of him getting home, he's a nightmare. But he doesn't always know when he's going to arrive. So – slow cooker.'

'Well,' Vee says, because – where to begin? She reminds herself that she has not had a child, a husband, has never had anyone to please but herself. It's depressing, though, that this woman should think this is OK. She is curating an exhibition about the second wave of feminism. She is a university lecturer, and an expert in a corner of modern history in her own right. 'Do you think of yourself as a feminist, Erica?'

'Of course,' Erica says, replacing the slow-cooker lid, wiping her hands on a cloth, and walking across to the table, 'but the meaning has changed, hasn't it? It's not the . . . blunt instrument it was. In your day.'

'Better a blunt instrument than a feather duster.'

'Maybe.' Erica looks like Leonie but she doesn't have the scrappiness. No way would Leonie have let Vee get away with a comment like that.

Erica spreads the folders around the table. There are seven, each with a photograph on the front – the prints Erica has chosen to be the focal part of each section of the exhibition. She'd sent Vee an email about framing and sizing last week. Vee had been desperate to go to bed – it wasn't just her head that ached that day, but her whole body, in a way that was more than the aches of being an old woman – and, though it wouldn't be fair to say she didn't care at all how the work was framed, she has reasonable confidence in Erica to do a reasonable job. So she hadn't read the email properly, and hadn't therefore seen which images Erica was leading with. And now, here they are, laid out in front of her in manila folders, each with a poorly reproduced print on the front, apart from the last one, on which Erica has written '*Self-Portraits (?)*'.

Her work can all be boiled down to this, then. Veronica Redux.

Vee pulls the Miss World one towards her, for no reason other than that she hasn't thought about it in a long time.

'This was not long after the Women's Liberation Front started, wasn't it?' Erica asks.

'It must have been,' Vee says.

'Did my aunt Leonie get you involved?'

Vee feels herself smile, 'Leonie got me involved in everything. She was the first active, unapologetic feminist I met. She pulled me in. My life wouldn't have been what it was without her.'

She's just used the past tense about herself. Well, may as well start now.

'She was a kind of a mentor to you, then?'

'I suppose she was. Though I wouldn't have called it that then. It's one of the words I wouldn't have known. Leonie helped me in a very – basic – way.'

'Mmm.' Erica is sorting papers; it seems that she's looking for something. Vee looks back at the photograph and thinks of all the things she didn't know in 1970. She didn't even know the words. She had started looking them up in her old school dictionary: 'patriarchy', 'misogyny', 'eunuch' when she read Greer. She once went to a meeting where people were talking about a new lexicon for an equal world. She didn't know what 'lexicon' meant.

'I hadn't been educated in the way that a lot of the women in the movement had. The ones I was mixing with, anyway, through Leonie. I felt quite honoured that she had taken me under her wing and I didn't want her to think I was so ignorant that I wasn't worth the bother. So I looked words up and I started reading the news. There was a programme called *What the Papers Say* on TV, so I would watch that, and listen to discussions on the radio. And I asked your aunt a lot of questions, too. She always took me seriously. Some of her friends weren't so nice to me. She saw herself as a writer but really I think her gift was for education.'

'My mother was a teacher.'

'Ursula? Oh yes, of course, I remember.'

'What do you remember?'

Go carefully, Vee. 'Ursula would come to the flat, sometimes, but I don't think she was sure what to make of us. She was working in a school, I remember, and she was married, so she had quite a settled lifestyle.'

Erica has stood still at last. 'What was it like? Living in the flat?'

'It was . . .' Where are the words? 'It seemed very – free – to me. Leonie wrote and went to groups and did some teaching. And she helped women she heard about through the . . . through the—'

'Grapevine?' Erica supplies. She doesn't seem to register that Vee couldn't find the word. Maybe having a toddler does that to you.

'Yes. No.' Ah, here it is. 'Network. It was organised. It had to be because not everyone had a phone. There was a list of people you called, for different things.'

'What did people call you and Leonie for?'

'Leonie, when they needed power. Straight talking. Clear thinking. Me to take photographs.'

'Of what?'

Vee remembers these vividly. 'Injuries. Beaten women. So there was a record.'

Erica pales. 'Of course.' She's paying full attention now. The slow cooker could catch fire and she wouldn't notice. 'I didn't know about this.'

'There's no record – I took them, developed them, but they were private. They belonged to the women, not to me.'

'Could we include some?'

Vee thinks of the women she visited, sitting silently in spare corners of their friends' houses, how she had to coax them into the light. 'I gave them to the women.'

'Not the police?'

107

'Things were different. It was a brave woman who went to the police. If they did, there was a good chance the police would ring their husbands to come and get them.'

Erica shakes her head. 'That's awful,' she says.

'It still is. It's different, that's all.'

Erica looks away and Vee wonders, for the first time in years, who got out from under and who didn't. She remembers Kiki didn't go back; she got a divorce, started over. Most women didn't.

'We should include some of these in the exhibition. Do you have any at all?'

'I might,' Vee says, 'but they would need to be ones where people couldn't be identified.'

'Of course.' Erica nods. 'So, would you look for them?'

'I'll see.' There are some boxes that she really needs to go through: the private photographs, the family and the moments she doesn't want to share with the world. She's left them because she doesn't want to look at them again.

'Thank you,' Erica says, and then, after the smallest hesitation, adds, 'I know you don't want to talk about when Leonie died—'

'There's nothing to say.' Vee makes a point of not knocking determined women but oh, this is hard.

Erica nods. 'I'm not asking anything. Except – if you're look-ing for photographs, would you see if you have the contact sheet for the first film you took that day?'

'What?' Vee has given her the contact sheet and film of the final photographs. She hasn't even mentioned that there was a first film.

'Your contact sheets. I've studied them. You usually take a few shots while the subject settles in, from a few angles, then you stick with one place or one pose. The contact sheet of – of my aunt's death – it doesn't feel like that. It looks as though there was a film before that one.'

Vee shrugs. It hurts her head. Which serves her right. 'I don't know,' she says. It's an outright lie. She does know.

Erica's expression flickers, just for a second, something like pain; she can recognise a lie. She looks back at the Miss World photograph. 'You were close, around that time? When you shared a flat?'

'Yes.' Once she started to live with Leonie, see more of her private self, she saw more of what would normally be hidden. Vee's married friends back in Essex went to great lengths to keep what they considered unfeminine from their husbands; they hid razors, plucked eyebrows behind locked bathroom doors, talked about keeping romance alive with lace negligees and euphemisms for menstruation. Leonie broke wind at will, left greying bras hanging over the shower curtain, and ate cereal from packets with her hands. She teased Vee for her occasional skirts and the way she left a hairbrush by the mirror in the hall; she never let her forget the time she said she wanted to be 'pre-sentable'. And, if anything, all of these things made Vee love Leonie more than she had before she moved into her flat, tak-ing the spare bedroom and, later, converting the box room to a darkroom. Vee's father had been big on privacy, scant on touch, and so living with Leonie was the most physically intimate that Vee had ever been with another human being, before or since. From this distance – and with her punctured memories – she has to wonder whether she was in love.

'Do you think people still remember the Miss World protest?' Erica asks, when it's clear Vee isn't going to say any more. 'Or are aware of it, if they weren't born? It's so important to get the level of detail right.'

Vee can see, from where Erica has opened another of the fold-ers, just how much Erica has been putting into this exhibition. Well, good. People talk about talent and luck, but as Dad used to say, it's graft that makes things happen. There's tightness across the top of Vee's chest at the thought of what Leonie kept, the skin around old scars flexing. 'I don't know. Does it matter? It was about what the protest achieved, as much as anything else.' Vee thinks of the humming of excitement in her gut for days afterwards, the way the disruption was all over the papers, reported on the news.

'But,' Erica says, 'I think I need to find a way to context-ualise that. From this distance, it looks . . . it's difficult. It was still women attacking women. Not that that's stopped. But it's different. The protest looks – brutal.'

It's so hard to explain what it was like to people who weren't there, who take so much for granted now. 'We were working things out, then. We were trying to break the world down to make it again, and this was one of the obvious ways to do it. We saw women in heels and lipstick as . . . as bonded, trapped.'

Erica shifts from foot to foot, and presses her lips together as if to hide the coral stain on her mouth. 'You would never pick that fight now, though? Haven't we understood that as feminists, as women, we respect each other's choices?'

This would be the time to mention Erica's nose job, and the way she has lost something distinctive and strong for the sake of what the male gaze considers acceptable. But she hasn't the energy. Instead she says, 'If we're feminists by making choices, instead of being limited by the patriarchy at every turn, then that's a thin kind of feminism. It's not what we were really about. We wanted a better world for women. Not one where we respected each other's right to be oppressed.'

Erica seems to flinch, but Vee can't be sure. 'From what I've read, women were hard on each other in the seventies, too. At least there's a bit more live and let live now.'

Vee sits in silence for a moment, leafing through the maga-zines that Erica has laid on the table, recognising her photographs on covers. 'Leonie teased me for wearing dresses when I went to see my dad.'

Erica laughs, 'Really? I don't think of her as teasing anyone. Listening to my mother talk, you'd think Leonie did nothing but . . .' she casts around for the right expression, a precision that Vee likes in her, 'verbal assassinations and scorn.'

Vee tips her head, smiles, to show that Ursula had a point. The movement makes something in her head prick and sting. 'In the early days, we weren't worse to each other than men were to us, but we weren't always better. And that was hard, because we expected better from each other. And I don't think we grasped that – that if someone had spent years thinking about their appearance, if they believed their value was in their beauty, then they didn't see Miss World as exploitation. They saw it as achievement. We weren't trying to undermine that, but of course women who had invested that way felt undermined.'

Erica nods too. 'I really want the exhibition to make people think about the way women are seen today. Miss World looks tame in comparison.'

Vee thinks back to what she remembers of that time. 'I think we hoped that the way women looked could become irrelevant.'

Erica nods. 'Do you think you were naive?'

'Well, probably. And idealistic. But if you're changing the world you need to start with the ideal you want, don't you? Not begin by aiming for a compromise?' It's strange to be talking as though she had been an activist when she was really a hanger-on, at the beginning at least, horrified by Leonie and her friends and drawn to them, like a ten-year-old tagging along with shoplifting teenagers. 'My generation did what we could. Your generation needs to take this fight further, I think. We gave you enough for it to be possible for you to do that. Not . . .'

Erica's face is interested but there's something hard in it too, a Leonie look. 'Not what?'

Vee shakes her head. She feels shaky, and her soul is exhausted by this conversation, and the memories it brings back. 'I don't know, Erica. I think we imagined that your generation would be – free. More free than we were. Sometimes I think you have it worse.'

'Maybe,' she replies, and Vee wonders whether, if she were a people person, if she was Leonie, or Ursula, she would put all talk of the exhibition aside and ask Erica how she was.

Erica nods, and then, laying out the contents of the Miss World folder – handwritten notes, printed notes, permission forms, newspaper clippings – says, 'I haven't got a contact sheet for this one. I wondered if you still have it? If you're looking through them anyway. For the other photos we talked about.'

'I should have that one.' Vee always kept good records, unlike most of the newsrooms of the 1970s and 80s, which were uninterested in anything once it was yesterday's copy. Once she started working for the newspapers directly, she always made friends with the lab technicians in the hope that she would be able to get her original films and contact sheets back. It worked until she was doing well and getting the good jobs. Then her films and contact sheets were filed more carefully, according to the celebrity she'd photographed. Even her most established contacts in the lab, the closest people she had to friends at the papers and magazines, didn't dare return them to her after that.

Apart from that one time.

'Did you know, the lab technicians used to go through the films at the end of the year, pull out the ones they thought no one would want again, and strip off the silver to sell, to pay for the Christmas party?'

'Mmm.' Erica's not listening, not really; she's scrutinising the images Vee took outside the Café de Paris: blurred faces, greyscale banners, but a sense of purpose all the same. After a moment she says, as though it's nothing, 'I've never actually been on a march.'

'What?' Vee hears that her voice is a bark. Making allowances for the world changing is one thing. This is another, 'You're not serious? Nothing?'

'I write letters,' Erica says, holding a file to her chest in defence. 'I go to see my MP and I sign petitions. I do a lot of sharing on Facebook. I'm active.'

'You haven't been on a march? Never?' Vee searches through recent memory. 'Not even Trump? Stop the War? Me Too?' Jesus.'

'Was Jesus a march?' It's nice that she and Erica are relaxing around each other a bit, enough to make jokes, but—

'Do not be flippant about this, Erica.' Vee is half-here, half in a memory she cannot quite hold on to, Leonie livid about her sister's way of ignoring anything inconvenient, difficult, not immediately personal or threatening. And if you lived like Ursula did, cushioned and not exactly ignorant, but in a well-ordered, well-off world, nothing felt personal or threatening. Well, nothing except Leonie.

'You're making a lot of assumptions about my beliefs and my life.' Erica's not making eye contact, and her tone seems too mild for the conversation, as though she's placating her child, or her child-husband.

'Maybe,' Vee says, 'but you're clever. And clever people usually care about the world.'

'You think because I didn't make a placard I don't care?'

'That's not what I'm saying.' Well, not exactly. 'But I can't imagine living without protesting.'

'You see? This is what I mean.' Erica's hands are on her hips and her voice is still quiet, but it's angry now, and a little sad, too. 'I did a PhD and worked part-time through most of my twenties. Then as soon as I got my first university teaching job, my mother became ill. I did what I could for her. She died. I was dealing with her estate and clearing her house while I was planning my wedding. I was pregnant while I was putting the proposal together for this. It seems like a long time since there was one thing that needs my attention. So no, I have never been on a march. Neither has Marcus. But he's on the PTA and we give money to charity and we are really, really trying to be good people in the world. Doesn't that matter more?'

'More than equality for half of the world's population?'

Erica looks up to the ceiling. 'Of course we need feminism, I wouldn't have proposed this exhibition otherwise. We need to look back to look forward. We need to understand. But we need compassion, too. And, if it makes you feel any better, things are hard.'

Vee feels something twist in her. It's a relief, almost, to feel emotional instead of physical pain. She nods. 'I'm sorry, Erica. I shouldn't judge.' She has patience; she should try for compassion. It's not as though she's never been misunderstood.

'You do, though. I'm fighting. You might not see it. I'm trying to make Marcus see that it's not my job to be in charge of every damn thing.' Erica sags. 'But you're right. I've never been on a march.'

'Would you like to?'

Leonie will never forgive her – from wherever she is now, the place where Vee will be before long – if she doesn't show Erica what she's missed.

Marcus has brought flowers home: a bouquet of roses and gypsophila, red blooms against a gauzy white background, wrapped in brown paper; Erica panics for a second, not knowing why, and then remembers how her mother thought that red and white flowers together were unlucky. It's a good thing she isn't superstitious. Even if she does feel as though she's been ambushed by Ursula's ghost, shaking her head in the corner. Marcus brought flowers, though. Erica feels something in her unlace, so that she can breathe a little more easily.

'Thank you.' She pushes her nose into them, even though she knows that, at this time of year, hothouse roses will smell of nothing much.

'How did it go today?'

Lovelier than the flowers is the fact that Marcus remembered Vee was coming today; they'd barely spoken this morning, and he was home late and drunk last night after a work night out, so he slept in the spare room so as not to disturb her. That's what he said, anyway. When did she start looking for other motives in kindness? 'She can be a bit ...' she considers '... sharp. Unpredictable. But today was useful. I think.' Every time she spends time with Vee, she is left with more things to think about. That's good though. It gives her more choices when it comes to creating the story she will tell at the exhibition. With eight weeks until the opening, and less than six weeks until everything needs to be signed off, she needs to start firming her thoughts up. She'll book Marcus's mum for a couple of days next week. (Why, even in her own head, does she never call her Sarah? And why does she never ask Marcus's father to help with childcare? He's retired too.)

'That's really good.' Marcus tousles her hair, and she tries not think of a dog who came straight back when called. 'Where's Tom?'

'He's asleep.' So asleep that Erica took him out of the car seat, out of his zip-up suit, and carried him up to his cot without him even flickering an eyelid. 'Sarah let him drop off in the car on the way back. She was very apologetic. I told her it didn't matter.' They have always tried to have 'adult evenings' – having agreed, when they decided to have a baby, that they wouldn't become one of those couples who do nothing but talk about, and think about, their child. They would still go to the cinema. They would strap the baby on and walk along the Thames for a lazy weekend lunch as they often did when it was just the two of them. Their sex life might enter a new phase, of course it might, but they would keep on pleasing each other.

In reality, 'adult evenings' usually mean falling asleep on the sofa in front of the TV.

Erica secretly likes it when Tom has a nap late in the afternoon, because Marcus will happily entertain him while she takes a glass of wine and a book and has a long bath, as though she has no needs but her own to consider.

'Ah well,' Marcus says, and he pulls her in, 'us time.' He still smells a little like the morning after, under the last traces of his aftershave and the commuter-train sweat. 'How about we go to bed for an hour? Then I'll order us a pizza.'

He takes off his jacket and drops it onto the chair where Vee was sitting, just a couple of hours ago. Erica looks at his back, the broadness of his ribs and the way his shoulders knuckle as they move under his shirt. She asks herself if she feels like sex. She doesn't really know. But if they have pizza tonight they can eat what's in the slow cooker tomorrow, and that makes it worth trying to work up some enthusiasm.

Part 3: Focus

Part 3. Focus

The photographer must know what she is trying to create. The act of photographing is the act of placing a three-dimensional object into a two-dimensional space, in a way that will have meaning for the person observing the finished image. It's a complex task. You won't achieve it unless you have some sense of what it is you are aiming to portray.

Veronica Moon, *Women in Photographs* (unpublished)

'Alison as Beverly in *Abigail's Party*'
Veronica Moon

Exhibition Section: Portrait Power

Camera: OM-1
Film: 400 ASA
First published: *This Month*, 1977

[Technical note: Moon switched to using an Olympus OM-1 camera in 1976. It is smaller and lighter, but has many of the same technical specifications as her previous Nikon F1. Although newer models did come out in subsequent years, Moon never upgraded again.]

If you've seen a photographic portrait of an important female figure of the 1970s, there's a good chance Veronica Moon took it. She was one of the most active and in-demand British photographers of the late 1970s and early 1980s. This is the section of the exhibition where you'll see her really hitting her stride. She was part of the movement taking photography to a more naturalistic style: you can look at the work of Antony Armstrong-Jones (later Lord Snowdon) and Annie Liebovitz for photographers pioneering a similar approach.

This portrait of Alison Steadman in her role as Beverly in Mike Leigh's play *Abigail's Party* was Moon's first cover shot, taken for the May 1977 issue of British magazine *This Month*, which ran from 1962 to 1986. Leonie Barratt, who introduced Moon's work to the magazine, wrote her famous 'Dear John' column for it from 1966 to 1981.

Alongside this portrait you'll see the magazine in which the Steadman profile appeared, and Moon's ticket to the press night, as well as the contact sheet from which this photograph was selected. Note how Moon has taken very few shots in which Steadman is looking at the camera.

Moon took this photograph at the first night of *Abigail's Party* at the Hampstead Theatre in April 1977. She photographs Steadman next to the stage door. The actor's face is in profile, head tilting slightly downward, face calm and still – the opposite of the character she plays. There's a smudge of makeup under one eye and she has let down her hair. The twilight lends a slightly flattened quality to the image, and the brickwork behind the actor makes the calmness and clearness of her face seem almost eerie. This is a good example of what was by then Moon's signature style: unguarded, subject seemingly unaware of the camera, natural light doing most of the work.

You'll find a selection of her portraits in this section of the exhibition. Some are photographs commissioned by national newspapers and magazines. Others are from private collections – Moon often photographed friends and fellow members of the women's groups to which she belonged. She also took portraits of well-known activists and feminists, which they used as publicity shots.

Moon was sometimes criticised because she also photographed women who did not identify as feminists, and men. As the women's movement has broadened in scope, the idea of men being automatically excluded from identifying as feminists seems arcane; however, in the 1970s, men were often perceived by feminists as enemy figures who couldn't possibly understand what women were up against. Men were, by definition, part of the problem.

In 1977:

- It was a year since Susie Orbach and Luise Eichenbaum set up the Women's Therapy Centre in London
- It was a year since the Domestic Violence and Matrimonial Proceedings Act enabled married women to obtain a court order against violent husbands, independently of divorce or separation proceedings. (The first recorded use of the term 'domestic violence' in the context of the home was in 1973 in an address to Parliament by Jack Ashley, MP.)
- It was four years since Virago Press, committed to publishing women's writing and books on feminism, was founded
- *The Women's Room* by Marilyn French was published
- The United Nations formalised International Women's Day
- The first *Star Wars* film was released
- *Saturday Night Fever* was a box office hit
- Fleetwood Mac's album *Rumours* was a global hit
- Greenpeace UK was founded, in a borrowed office in London, with four members and £800
- The first series of TV's *Top Gear*, presented by Angela Rippon and Tom Coyne, aired in the UK
- Edinburgh women held the first 'Reclaim the Night' march in Britain
- The Women's Liberation Movement held a national conference in London, where Sheila Jeffreys presented a paper called 'The Need for Revolutionary Feminism'

And, in a Chelsea flat, Veronica Moon and Leonie Barratt are having a difficult time.

123

15 April 1977

Chelsea

Vee is transferring the last of her London Street Project films from the safety of their black plastic cylinders to the safety of the developing tank. It's the trickiest part of the developing process, because if a film is flooded with light now then whatever carefully exposed image is on it is gone forever. If light gets in later, then it's a print that's ruined, and though it's a pain to develop another, it's possible. But open the darkroom door when the film is being transferred and there is absolutely nothing to be done to save it. You are exposing a light-sensitive material to more light. You are bludgeoning it. Vee finds that she is holding her breath. She is working via the eerie red glow of the darkroom bulb.

There are five films, thirty-six frames on each: one hundred and eighty images altogether, and a year's work.

Once the transfer is done, she will add the developer, look at the negatives, and develop the first round of prints, maybe twenty or so from throughout the sequence, to see what's there, what the theme of this work might be. It's exciting. And now that most of her films are developed by newspaper and magazine labs, it's good to get back to basics in the darkroom like this. There's nothing quite like the thrill of being the first person to see what you took, and whether it matches up with the shots you think you have.

This project had all come about because of a late-night conversation with Leonie and Bea, when they'd been talking about how the world was, or wasn't, changing. Neither Leonie nor Bea were sanguine. They were worried about schisms in the sisterhood, and in the never-ending impossibility of getting the patriarchy to stay dismantled, when they did manage change.

But Vee felt – feels – differently. She sees herself as an example of change as it's happening – a woman in a man's world, and she might not exactly be accepted in all quarters, but she's here. Vee looks back at that year at the *Colchester Echo* now and can't believe what she put up with.

Look at her now. Look at the world.

Women are rising up. They are shouting for equality – real equality, no more being underpaid or struggling into ridiculous clothes or feeling as though getting married is anything other than an outdated patriarchal notion that nobody needs. Equality, true equality is coming. It's in the legislation, it's in the literature, it's in *Spare Rib* and the flares and ponchos that feel like freedom. It's in the air at the Women's Liberation Front meetings, where more and more sisters come, with more and more stories of what they are protesting, what they are refusing to put up with. It's thrilling, and too many people are missing it.

Leonie and Bea had been sceptical of her view. They still see Vee as a junior, beginner feminist, a little sister. Vee had cited the Sex Discrimination Act and the Equal Opportunities Commission, but Leonie and Bea had looked at each other, smiled, and then explained, rather too patiently, that it wasn't enough; that it might even stop the sisters from rising up the way they should because they think equal rights for women is all taken care of.

But Vee had known she is better qualified because she's closer to reality than her privately educated, clever friends. So she had set out to change their perspective with photographs. And the more photographs she took, the more she stopped thinking about making an argument against what Leonie and

Bea thought. They would always run rings around her, intellectually. But she could show what she meant. She could track change, show the broadness of women's lives, the scope of them, their power.

Since then, whenever she's had a spare daylight hour, she has stopped women in the streets near their flat. There are always people passing: workers in a rush in the mornings, pram-pushers, afternoon drinkers, evening strollers. After her first afternoon of loitering, nervously and indecisively, Vee made a rule that she would stop the first woman she saw. Otherwise she'd only have photographs of the approachable-looking, the friendly, and she may as well not bother. Most have agreed to being photographed when she has promised to take no more than five minutes. Vee has not given any of them time to tidy their hair, put fresh lipstick on.

She had a feeling there might be an exhibition in it, eventually: a year in the life. This morning she is taking a first look, thanks to a shoot being delayed: Fleetwood Mac are flying in from the US a day later than planned, so she can't photograph Stevie Nicks until tomorrow. Stevie Nicks! Vee still can't get over the fact that she is the photographer on these shoots – but this unexpected darkroom time is exciting, too. So exciting that she forgot to lock the door from the inside.

She's about to put the lid on the developing tank, and exhale, when the door doesn't so much open, as crash through its maximum arc, bouncing off the wall behind.

Vee crams the lid on the developing tank but she knows it's too late.

'NO!' she shouts, as though sheer volume will wind back the light, unruin her work. If she was melodramatic she would sink to her knees. She isn't. She takes a step towards the man in the doorway. 'What the hell do you think you're doing? You've just ruined a year of my work, you bloody idiot.'

'I'm bursting for a piss,' the man says. He's clearly just woken up; he's disorientated, still drunk, maybe. He's wearing Leonie's red dressing gown, though Vee isn't sure why he bothered to put it on, because it's not fastened. He smiles; it's probably meant to be charming, 'I'll just do that and then – and then I'll come and help you.' He looks around, blinks, in the hope, presumably, of seeing the damage he has clearly done. 'I'll come and help you . . . fix it. What I broke.'

'You cannot,' Veronica says, 'wind back the light.' And she looks away because she truly has never had a genuinely violent thought until now, when she could, happily, throw whatever liquid comes to hand at his crotch and hope to see his pathetic cock shrivel up and drop off. Not that anything in the darkroom is especially caustic. But for a second she wishes it was.

'I'm sorry,' the man says.

'That doesn't help.' Vee leans a shoulder against the door, presses the space between her eyes with the pad of her thumb. 'There's nothing you can do. Get out.' She cannot bear to look at him, his unshaven face and smell of sweat and garlic, his hairy paunch and bony knees – he has, at least, pulled the dressing gown around him, maybe sensing her intent to do him damage.

He walks backwards from the room, looking aggrieved, just as Leonie emerges from her bedroom, sleep-faced and confused. Vee slams the darkroom door, locking it behind her this time. It's a futile gesture but it feels good, and it means that no one can interrupt her with apologies or offers of help.

Of course, she should have locked the damn thing anyway. But Leonie rarely surfaces before eleven. Lesson learned.

18 April 1977

'ARE YOU STILL SULKING?' Leonie asks as she lumbers into the kitchen, where Vee is washing up. She may be being unnecessarily clattering about it, banging crockery onto the draining board. Maybe she is half-hoping something will break, to give her something else to be annoyed about.

'I'm not sulking. I'm angry. And we need clean plates.' She thinks about turning to face her flatmate, but instead she starts to blot at the water that pools on the Formica of the worktop between the wall and the back of the sink, and adds, 'I think I'm entitled to be annoyed that months of work was ruined. You went mad at me that one time I forgot my key.'

'It was 2 a.m. You ruined my flow.'

'And you got it back. I won't get those photographs back.'

'It's not like you needed them. They weren't *for* anything.'

Vee takes a deep breath, but it's not really to calm herself down, it's to fuel her fury. She had hung about in the darkroom until she was sure the idiot man had gone, then taken a bath, then gone out with her camera for the rest of the day. She missed her Nikon's familiarity for a long time, but the OM-1 feels as though it's really right for her, a good fit in her hands, and so light that carrying a spare over her shoulder is barely noticeable. She'd intended to start photographing women again, but her heart wasn't in it. And the more she thought about what she'd lost the angrier, the sadder, she got. An essential part of living with Leonie has always been to let her selfishness flow over and round Vee, like water, like wind. But this, Vee can't let go. 'They were for me. They were my work. I don't belittle your writing, even though—'

'Even though . . . ?'

'Nothing.' She could say, 'Even though most of what you write is rejected', but that wouldn't be fair. Especially as Vee's success is due, in a great part, to either taking up the early introductions Leonie made, or adopting her approach, by simply asking for the jobs she wants.

Not long after Vee moved in to the Chelsea flat, Leonie sat her down with a pile of newspapers and said, 'Read. Make a list of female journos and a list of people you'd like to photograph. Write to the journos. Ring up the newsdesks. Tell them if they're going to do a piece on people you're interested in, you'd like to photograph them.'

'Will that work?'

Leonie had shrugged. 'I don't know. It's worth a try, though, isn't it? I think Germaine Greer's got something else coming out. Start by saying you could photograph her.'

'Yes,' Vee said, 'I could do that, couldn't I?' As her dad says: you don't ask, you don't get.

'You could,' Leonie says, and then adds, 'Why don't you send' – she pauses for a minute while she thinks – 'I don't know what you call them. When you make a sheet with all the images on the film, in rows? With the edges of the negatives showing?'

'Contact sheets?'

'Contact sheets.' Leonie grins. She's always been fascinated by them, ever since Vee sent her that first one, the week after they met at Dagenham. 'That's got to be more interesting.'

And Vee had done just that. It had been cheap, too – she had contact sheets already, and it showed her technique and range better than a single photograph did. After all, anyone can get lucky with one good shot. A contact sheet shows the way your photographer's eye works, what your camera noses out about your subject. Within three weeks she had her first commission, thanks to Eve Pollard, a journalist Leonie knew at the *Daily Mirror*, putting a word in for her. By the time April 1971 came she was doing a shoot a week. It wasn't a lot but it was more than nothing. She spent a long summer schlepping out to Essex at the weekends to photograph weddings, but it meant she could see her dad regularly. By September, she had decided to take no more bookings for portraits, weddings, or family photographs: she was a press photographer. Her savings paid her bills; her earnings paid for living, and travelling, and – after a year when the commissions were coming faster – a new camera, lenses, and a proper bag to go with them. She had started to feel like a real photographer at last.

Vee knows she owes Leonie a lot. And she feels bad, watching her struggle for exposure for her writing, for an audience. The monthly column was meant to be a starting point, but it's all Leonie has. Vee cannot imagine why. Plus, there was the abortion. Leonie insists that an abortion is – should be – nothing, but Vee isn't so sure.

So Vee has done her best to be helpful, patient, sympathetic, within the bounds of what Leonie will allow. But that doesn't mean she can't stand up for herself when she needs to. And it doesn't mean that she can't be hurt, furious, in her turn.

Leonie sits down at the kitchen table. Without turning round, Vee can visualise the movements that go with the sounds: the scrape of the chair pulled out, the thump of sitting down, the sigh. 'They weren't that important, though, were they? I mean, the brilliant Veronica Moon doesn't develop her own photos these days, does she?'

Breathe, Vee, don't take the bait. 'Just because the photographs I develop here are non-commissioned, it doesn't mean they don't matter. You of all people should know that.'

Leonie makes a half grunt of agreement. Her continuing failure to get her more radical work published has worn her down. Though she doesn't see it a failure of her own, but of the establishment, and Vee thinks she is probably right. She reads everything Leonie writes, before she sends it off to wherever it's going. She rarely makes suggestions. She mostly admires. But she does it sincerely. And she knows that's what Leonie wants. Not as an ego trip – just confirmation that her words work. They call it the Doolittle test. Vee doesn't mind. Sometimes her test for photographs is, 'Would Barry recognise this subject if he saw this shot?'

The sink cannot be any cleaner. And it's too tiring to keep this argument going, because what's done is done. It's seven years – longer than some marriages – since she moved in and they know how arguments end. Leonie never backs down. So Vee changes the subject.

She turns and smiles, pulls out the chair opposite Leonie's. 'Who was he, anyway?'

'Who?' Something else Vee has learned: Leonie is not graceful in victory.

'The idiot who opened the darkroom door.'

Leonie shrugs. 'Paul. I met him at Fen's last year. You missed it, because you were selling your soul to the patriarchy, again.'

Ignore, ignore. 'I think I was photographing David Steel.'

'Like I said.'

Oh, for crying out loud. 'He's the new leader of the Liberal Party and he got the Abortion Act through Parliament. He's hardly Hugh Hefner.'

'Would you actually turn that job down? Or just put your bunny ears on and take the shot?'

'Leonie,' Vee says, and then just to get the conversation away, onto different ground, 'Paul. Is he the . . .' She pauses, to choose the right word, and Leonie jumps in, primed for annoyance, 'The what?'

'It doesn't matter.'

'It did a minute ago.'

And this is why people leave marriages, Vee supposes. It's easier than it used to be, to get out of a miserable relationship. It's acceptable to be divorced (at least in London, though she wouldn't fancy the chances of her friends back home), and though the sisters are claiming this as a victory for women taking their power, taking control, Vee suspects that many splits are nothing to do with women realising how oppressed they are. Divorce is surely more likely to be born of one too many conversations like this, bickering and unkind. It's so strange, the way you get to know someone well enough to antagonise them, and at some point, you choose to do that. Whereas you used to choose to support them, because you know them well enough to do that, too. 'Is he the what? Go on, ask.'

Vee sighs, 'Is he the father?'

'Of who?'

'Oh, come on, Leonie.' Vee gets up. 'I don't have time for this.'

'No, because your fucking career takes up all your time.'

'OK.' Vee holds up her hands, an 'anything for peace' gesture. 'Is Paul the father of the baby you—'

The hesitation is tiny but Leonie's on it. 'Come on, Miss Unflinching Lens. Say the a-word.'

'Ms. Not "Miss",' Vee says. It's worth a try – Leonie can sometimes be diffused this way – but she doesn't laugh. She's paler than usual, her hair greasy. Left to herself she eats badly, and Vee hasn't been around to cook, much. She always makes sure the fruit bowl is full even though she knows that's a pretty redundant exercise. Leonie likes pizza from the restaurant round the corner, rice pudding eaten from the tin with a spoon, French Fancies, cheese. She eats bananas, sometimes, and the occasional apple, though she says they are too much work.

Leonie glares. 'Don't change the subject.'

'Is Paul the father of the baby you got rid of?'

'Can you do it less judgementally?'

'What have I got wrong? *Baby*? *Got rid of*?' Vee slides a look at her watch. They need to leave in an hour, at the most. It's going to be a long evening in more ways than one. Leonie is bound to want to go to the after-party. Vee's not a great one for the theatre, or parties, come to that, but this will be her first cover shoot and she feels as though she should make the most of the evening. She'd like there to be time for photographs outside the theatre, before it gets too busy. She doesn't really know how famous Alison Steadman is. She's well known enough to be on the cover of a magazine. Hopefully, anonymous enough still to stand in the street, the corner of a poster for the show in shot.

'Paul might be the genetic father of the foetus I aborted. He might not. I don't know and I don't care.'

'Well,' Vee says, and then doesn't really know what to add. She stands up, thinks about wiping the table down, but the mood Leonie's in, she'd probably get a lecture on not subjugating herself.

'It was only an abortion. And mine. You'd think it had been you, the way you've gone on about it. I couldn't care less.'

Leonie had cared, very much, on the day of the abortion, holding tight to Vee's hand, tears in her eyes. It could have just been the physical pain. Leonie would say she has no right to assume anything else. But the not washing, the constant eating, in the three weeks since would suggest a deeper misery.

'We need to leave at six. Do you want to have a shower before I use the bathroom?'

'Where are we going?'

Vee sighs. She knows Leonie knows this. 'Hampstead Theatre. A play. *Abigail's Party.*' Leonie hates public transport with a passion, so she adds, 'I'm driving. I'm photographing one of the actresses for *This Month.*'

A sigh, out-of-proportion deep. 'That's tonight?'

'Yes.'

That shake of the head that Vee is so familiar with. 'I don't think I can, Vee. I'm not up to it. You know.'

If Vee doesn't say something there's a risk she will bite through her tongue. 'You said you'd come. I could have asked someone else but you said you wanted to come.'

Leonie shrugs. 'I have to read this,' she says, putting her hand on a book that's been sitting on the kitchen table for a week, a proof copy of something called *The Women's Room.* 'I'm reviewing it for *Spare Rib.*'

'You can take a couple of hours off.' Vee doesn't feel like letting this go, tonight. Even after this almost-decade of being part of the movement, she's still more comfortable with Leonie by her side. Plus, she's wretched with jet-lag from last week and flying to India to photograph Mother Teresa, and being with someone else will make this evening better than a chore. 'Come on, Leonie. It will be a laugh.'

'Did a woman write it?'

Vee unpins the tickets from the corkboard on the wall and looks at the detail. 'No. Mike Leigh?'

'Well, a woman wrote this' – Leonie waves the book – 'so she wins. Anyway. I'm really not up to it.'

And Vee just can't be bothered, anymore. Almost seven years of living with someone who bends the rules to suit themselves is, all of a sudden, too much. 'You're well enough to shag some idiot who can't read a DO NOT OPEN sign on my darkroom door.

Take some responsibility, Leonie. You're not ill. You just can't be bothered.'

'I'm not well,' Leonie says, in a voice on the edge of whining, 'and you have no right to say what's going on in my body—'

For once, Vee interrupts. 'I think I have the right to call you on the bullshit you talk so you never have to do anything you don't want to do. Do you think I want to do this tonight when I've been at a shoot since eleven and I've got another one that starts at eight in the morning? Do you think I never get sick of being "that bird photographer", like I'm a freak show? Do you think I like ironing my clothes? Do you think I never get tired of the endlessness of this stupid fight?'

'You've been a feminist for, what, less than ten years and you're tired of it? Tired of being able to work a camera without your tits getting in the way? Well, sorry making a living off the back of the rest of us isn't enough for you.' Vee has seen this malice in Leonie before, directed at men who talk over the top of her, women who think feminism might be complicated, or different, to the way Leonie sees it. This is the first time it's been hurled in her direction, and it stings.

Especially because, 'I didn't mean that fight, Leonie. I meant this fight. The one we're having. Me selling out, you being keeper of the flame or whatever it is that you think only you can do.'

'I'm what?' Leonie's gaze is focused, hard.

May as well say it. 'The rest of us are – getting on. Finding ways to work in the world. You sit in here and you judge us and tell us where we're going wrong. Especially the ones who are successful.'

Leonie makes a sound, something like a hiss, 'I'm not successful? By whose standards?'

Vee forces herself not to look away. 'I mean you've retreated, because you haven't got what you want. You should keep saying what you're saying, and I think we need someone like you. But you seem to be giving up. On your book—'

'I'm not giving up on that,' but even the way she says it is half-hearted. 'It's just that every fucking idea I have, someone beats me to it. Germaine, so bloody cutting that people say she's witty, she screwed my chances of getting the first one published, even though it was about so much more than sex. Now Orbach, diet book for pleasing yourself instead of the patriarchy, but she still wants us all to be thin. So nobody wants a feminist book on women's bodies or sexuality now because Germaine and Susie have written theirs. Like they are the only ones we need. Because, one woman's voice, or two, and we're done. One woman Secretary of State at a time, one newspaper editor, a couple of QCs. Well done, feminism.'

Vee thinks of the shelf of books they have, written by their sisters, talking about women and their lives in essays, polemics, poems and prose. She decides against mentioning them. She needs to leave soon. 'The column – you're a voice, Leonie. You should be proud of that.'

'Yeah. You of all people know that what I always wanted to be was the acceptable voice of feminism. Come on, Vee. I deserve better.'

They usually have this argument drunk, jokingly. Now, in the sober late-afternoon light, it feels different. Vee wants nothing more than to smile, apologise, and have them settle in to their happy old roles of mentor and student. But those days have gone, and anyway, Vee deserves better too. 'You're cutting off your nose to spite your face. You won't compromise and that means you can think of yourself as a glorious failure, beaten down by the patriarchy, whereas actually . . .' Leonie's gaze doesn't flinch, daring her to go on, and this time, she is damn well going to dare. 'Whereas actually you just can't get off your arse and get on with it, like the rest of us do.'

'Yeah, the sisters thank you for those photos you took of Richard Burton and Elizabeth Taylor, and George Best.'

'I haven't got the luxury of a family flat and a trust fund. I have to work.'

'That's right, poor you. You were forced to sell out.'

'It makes sense for some of us to be on the inside.'

'Pissing out on the rest of us?'

Vee's camera bag isn't packed, she needs to change; she hasn't got time for this. 'I need to go and get ready, Leonie.'

'That's it, you walk away.' Leonie's sneering has become her default position. The friend Vee moved in with – nurturing, helpful, inspiring – is someone she rarely sees, these days. And she misses her.

'I'm doing my job.'

'You're letting everyone down. And we trusted you. We let you in.'

'For crying out loud, Leonie.' Actually, she is not taking this, not this time. 'You never used to be so . . . elitist. You made me feel like your equal. There were plenty of women who would have laughed me away because I didn't know how to be a feminist, but you didn't laugh. You knew what I needed.' Vee rarely cries, and yet here are tears. 'I know everything you did for me. And now it's – it's this? Just because I don't do what you're doing? Just because I'm not—' the word is out before she can make it stop, 'failing?'

There have even been times when Vee has wondered whether Leonie is trying to sabotage her. Yesterday was not the first time her darkroom door has been opened by accident. She almost missed the chance to photograph Judi Dench last month, because Leonie didn't pass a message on. Sometimes her keys are in places where she knows she didn't leave them. It is starting to look like sabotage, at worst; at best, a plea for the kind of help that Vee isn't qualified to give and Leonie isn't prepared to accept.

But Leonie says nothing. After a moment, she gets up, goes to the fridge, and takes out the cheese that Vee bought.

Vee doesn't comment. She steps round Leonie, towards the door, and asks, 'You're definitely not coming?'

'I'm not up to it,' Leonie says, 'whether you believe me or not.'

There's a cue here for Vee, and she knows it. Sit, talk, reassure. Make Leonie feel better. It's what a friend should do. What a sister should do. But this time she's not going to do it. She has her camera bag to pack, rush-hour to negotiate. 'Suit yourself,' she says. And she locks the darkroom from the outside before she leaves.

15 May 1977

'LEAVE THEM, TREASURE,' STANLEY SAYS, as Vee gets up and goes to the kitchen with the plates, 'I'll clear up when you've gone. You've got better things to do than washing up now, anyway.'

He doesn't mean it to sound the way it does, Vee knows. He's proud of her. 'I can do it, Dad,' she says.

'I know you can,' he replies, and then he picks up the magazine she brought to show him, with her latest shoot in it. 'Mother Teresa. Who'd have thought. My girl going all the way to India to take a photo.'

'I can't really believe it, either,' Vee says. There's always a slight shock when she meets anyone famous, and another when she realises that she is there to photograph them, and for the length of time that takes, the two of them will be something like equal. (Some people do as she asks; others ignore her. The best subjects are the ones between, who have their own sense of what they should be, but can respect a different opinion.) Every job – even the tricky ones, too little time or not enough light, an assistant or a journalist hurrying things along or interrupting – seems too good to be true. Part of Veronica thinks her luck will run out, one day, and each job will be her last. Her diary is filling up with commitments for the next three months, though. All she has to do it keep at it. Keep doing a good job. Just like her father always says: do your best and keep doing it.

'She's a saint, for sure,' he says, now, looking at the photograph, again. Vee caught her mid-yawn, hand midway to her mouth, eyes looking downwards, brow furrowed, as though she is puzzled by this most human reaction, as though she has never known tiredness before. Vee had asked her if she needed to rest. She'd shaken her head, smiling, as if to say, what does it matter what I feel. The images Veronica caught then, three in quick succession, were her favourites, and the picture editor had liked them too, printing them in a column down the side of the text of the interview. The yawn is on the facing page, between headline and byline. Vee's name, in tiny capitals, runs up the side of the photograph.

'Not everyone thinks a lot of her.' Leonie had been scathing: people like Mother Teresa are only called saints by the world because they tidy up the mess the world – by which she means men – makes.

'I'm very proud of you, you know,' Stanley adds, 'people said all sorts when you moved away, that you'd be back when you got sick of London, that you thought you were too good for us, but I knew you would do what you'd set your mind to. And I knew you wouldn't forget your roots.'

Vee looks away, thinking of how she's worked to make her voice neutral, and how it's been a month since she last drove out to Colchester, probably the longest time she's ever not seen her dad. And she's only really here because she needs something. She had meant to come three weeks ago but it was the weekend after *Abigail's Party*, and Leonie had needed a lot of attention. Then, at 4 a.m., while Vee was aching with tiredness and Leonie was pouring another glass of Beaujolais, Vee had realised that what they both needed, really, was for Vee to move out. They were becoming – what was the word Kiki used to describe Jo and Bernard? – co-dependent. The next morning, long before Leonie would wake, Vee had been to see an estate agent. She'd had the presence of mind to bring a bank statement, so they did take her seriously. Now she's seen a place, near the river in Battersea, which apparently is 'up-and-coming'. Vee doesn't really care whether it is or not. She has the knack of not being noticed, so her chances of getting home in one piece are pretty good. And if she can afford to buy the tiny mews house she's seen, she's not going to be able to do it up for a while, so it's not going to look like much of a prospect to burglars. It's been empty for eight months. It could be hers by the end of summer.

She's more or less made up her mind to it. She just needs one thing.

'OK.' She puts the bowls down, and sits. Her father's repertoire is limited, in shopping, as well as in cooking, so they have the same meals, over and over. Tinned peaches and custard on Sundays always makes her feel like a child again. She's been eating it most Sundays for as long as she can remember. (Except in summer, when it's fruit from the allotment, and evaporated milk.) The question she's about to ask seems absurd, given that being here makes her feel eleven years old, inside. Still, if there's one thing she's learned from Leonie, it's that if you don't ask, you don't get. And you're entitled to ask. 'Dad, I need a favour.'

'Of course, Veronica.' It's painful, to see how his face lights at the prospect. Vee knows that he's lonely, without her at home, even though he fills his days well enough, 'What do you need, treasure?'

'I've seen a little place I want to buy,' she says, 'and I'm earning good money. I've got enough for a deposit and I can pay the mortgage. But I can't get a mortgage, without a man to guarantee it.' She hears her voice waver, almost tearful, and she knows it's not because of anything except the ridiculousness of the situation, that women are put in this position. But her father is bound to misinterpret the shake in her voice.

Stanley pats her hand. 'What's the hurry? You still might meet someone, you know.'

Please, Vee thinks, don't tell me about Barry and his nice wife and his lovely kids, not again. In case he starts, she cuts in, 'No, Dad, I really want to buy this place. As an investment.'

'Investment, eh?' He smiles, and then considers. 'I thought you might come back here, one day. Live in this house. It will be yours when I go. You know that, girl. I won't go on forever, and those sisters of your mother's will get nothing from me.'

'Dad, you're not even sixty,' Vee says, 'and I'm working in London now. And all over. It's not practical for me to be here.' She thinks about saying that she would if she could, but her father isn't stupid.

'I suppose,' he says, 'you could always sell it. If you did meet someone. Or if you did decide to move back here.'

Vee nods. She can't bring herself to agree out loud.

'And you're sure you can pay the mortgage? It's a big step.'

'I'm sure, Dad.'

Stanley rises, and before he picks up the bowls to take through to the kitchen, he rests one hand on his daughter's head in absent-minded blessing, 'Then you just bring me what you need signed, Veronica, and I'll sign it.'

'Thanks, Dad.'

Only Leonie to tell, now.

July 1977

This Month magazine

Leonie Barratt: Letters from a Feminist

Our monthly column from the front line of the Battle of the Sexes

Dear John,

I've had an abortion.

I didn't tell you before I went because I had a feeling you would make it all about you. Or all about the squatting, breeding group of cells that you would doubtless call 'the baby', as though it already had a favourite spoon and a bike with stabilisers.

And I didn't tell you because the baby might have been yours and it might not. And I didn't need to put up with the conversation that would follow, as surely as Black Forest gateau follows steak Diane in a Berni Inn on a Friday night.

I know what we say – that it's fine, it's good, for us to be uncommitted and casual, it's the 1970s, we don't need the old rules. You often say, as you're leaving, that, 'You know this is nothing serious, right, darling?' (And don't think I haven't noticed how rarely you bother to use my name, honey.) But I suspect that, when it came to it, you would not like the fact that I was playing that game, too.

John, you're a lot like a lot of men I know, or know of. You're all for liberation and being open so long as you're the one who's being casual. But you like to think that the women you're casual with are just waiting for your call. And I don't think it occurs to you that if you did want to be more than casual, and you wanted us to have stickers with our names across the top of your car windscreen, and meet each other's families, I would run a mile. We're trying to make a new world but, man, those old assumptions, about what women want: they cling on. They will not die.

Unwanted foetuses are another matter. I didn't tell you about it because I didn't have the time, or inclination, to argue with you about your rights and your desires. Throwing up your guts takes time, and so does going to your doctor and letting him think you're too fragile for motherhood so he and his colleague will sign you off to get that squatter hoovered out of there.

My body. My abortion.

It wasn't very nice, but it was better than a rusty coat-hanger and septicaemia, or a punctured uterus. It was better than gin and a hot bath or a well-meaning hairdresser that a sister told me about sluicing me out with bleach on her kitchen table, and hoping no one reports her to the police. It was better than having a kid, for that matter. But up until a decade ago, those would have been the only options I had.

I imagine, John, that you think I'm writing this letter because I want you to come round with flowers, and tell me I am brave, and I didn't have to do this alone, and you're here for me. I expect, if you did, you'd feel like a hero.

Well, you're wrong. (I wish you'd learn, John. I've been trying to educate you for years now. I know we have many centuries of patriarchal bullshit to scrape away, but I'll be honest. I'd hoped we might be making a dent in it at this point. Maybe if you start working on it from your end, we'll make a new way faster.)

I'm writing this letter because I want you to know that I'm fine. I didn't want to have a baby and now I'm not having one. I got rid of it in a clean, legal way and I feel no shame. No regret. No anything, except relief. And a bit of sadness for the sisters who just ten years ago couldn't abort safely, and risked their lives to get out of an unwanted pregnancy, or the unwanted marriage that was likely if they didn't have the money or the contacts to help them to get rid of what they didn't want. I'm glad we've changed this. And yes, I know you'll point out that it took more than the women to do this, so credit to David Steel for getting the act through Parliament in the first place. I've never said all men are bastards, have I? If you were, I wouldn't be bothering to write you these letters, month in, month out. But it only had to be a man because we don't have enough female MPs. Don't think I haven't noticed. Don't think the sisterhood isn't on it. But that's a big conversation. We are going to have to save that whole topic for another letter.

We are getting some sort of equality for women, with safe abortions on the NHS, even if we do have to jump through a couple of hoops to get there. (The sisters are working on getting rid of the hoops. We are not satisfied with things as they are. Not yet. Imagine if you could only have a vasectomy if two doctors said that your mental health wasn't strong enough to handle fathering a child.) What we need now is for everyone to stop being so sentimental about it all.

I had an abortion, John. I'm glad. If you have some feelings to feel, then don't let me stop you. I'm all for men having feelings, admitting them and expressing them and not being ashamed of them. But if you have feelings about the abortion that I chose to have, I'd like you to go and have them a long way away from me. I've got better things to do than dry your tears, and I have none for you to dry. I can't be distraught in the way you want me to be. I'm relieved. That's all.

Until next time,

Leonie

26 February 2018

'IT'S NOT GOOD NEWS, MS MOON.'

'Of course it isn't,' Veronica says.

It's a week since the tests, and Vee is back in Mr Wilding's office. The top of his desk is clear, save for a laptop which sits a little to his right, a vase of scentless, out-of-season roses and a box of tissues to his left. The tissues are within Vee's easy reach. Of course they are.

She tried, briefly, in the waiting room, to talk herself into being a silly old woman worrying unnecessarily about a migraine or two. After all, she's seventy years old. Parts of her ache that never used to. The small of her back, her hips, her knees all complain when she asks them for the slightest out-of-the-ordinary effort.

But as soon as her name was called, and she rose to walk through to the consultant's office, she stopped all of her attempts at pretence as simply as other patients put down magazines when it was their turn to be seen. She's been lucky to have a decade; the surgery last time was successful in a running-repair sort of a way, but it was always just a matter of time until the tumour in her brain started to grow again. The only thing that would stop it, really, would be death from another direction: heart attack, cancer somewhere else, wrong-place-wrong-time putting her in the path of terrorist action or car crash. Those fates have not come her way. It looks as though she has this one.

Mr Wilding swings his laptop towards her, 'Here's an image of your latest scan. You'll see the scarring from the previous operation, here.'

Vee nods. The thick white line is the barrier between being able to remember the best part of two years, and a scattering of other memories. It blocks the taste of sweetness, the confidence to drive a car.

'And, as was always a possibility, you'll notice this cluster of marks here—'

'Where are they?'

The consultant's finger moves across the screen. It's blunt-ended and far too normal-seeming for the delicate use he puts it to, coaxing out the interloping growths that have rooted themselves into brains. 'Here,' he says.

'I meant' – Vee shakes her head as though that will arrange her words into something clearer, closer to her thoughts – 'I mean, which parts of the brain? What do those bits do?'

'Ah.' Mr Wilding sits back in his chair. 'Well, as you know, the brain is complicated, and we don't fully understand, for example, where and how memory is made and stored, how—'

'Yes,' Vee says, 'I do know.' She's never had any tolerance for mansplaining, even before one of her younger sisters invented a word for it.

If Mr Wilding is annoyed by her interruption he doesn't show it. 'You'll know, then, that we can't say anything with certainty. The tumour will have roots in many other parts of the brain. Are you vomiting?'

'Not yet.'

'Seizures? Slurring?'

'Not yet. Really just the headaches. And . . .'

'Yes?' He looks straight at her, waiting. And it doesn't feel as though there's anything significant enough to offer up to that clinical gaze. She's exhausted, out of proportion to what-ever she's been doing. And impatient. She looks at Erica's face and sometimes she thinks she sees Leonie's, trying to tell her something. 'Anything you can tell me will help, Ms Moon.'

'Nothing major. It's – tiny things. I'm tired. I ache.' Vee has a sudden memory: Leonard Cohen. She hadn't heard of him, when she was asked to photograph him in 1974. She bought a record, afterwards, and every one since. There was a lyric about aching in the places where you used to play. 'I just remembered a song I haven't listened to in twenty years. I keep finding my keys in strange places. I'm not hungry, and nothing tastes of anything.'

'It must be very disorienting.'

Yes. It is. And she doesn't want to die disoriented. She wants to die sure of the world she is leaving, of her place in it. She wants the last things that she sees to be real enough to photograph. She wants to keep whatever it is that she has that means she can compute the subject, the light, the film, the background and the story, and produce an image that feels true to the people who look at it, afterwards. And suddenly, she's crying, 'I don't cry. I don't usually cry.'

'You aren't usually in this position. Any disruption to your sight?'

'What?' She heard. Of course she did. She just didn't want to. The tears gather, grow, spill.

'Your sight. Anything unusual?'

No, no, no, no, no. 'Only when a headache is coming on. I get pinpricks. And the light hurts.'

Mr Wilding nods, waits.

Vee feels a patch of damp on her front; tears have fallen on to her collarbone, slid under her shirt, and the silk is sticking to her skin. 'That's normal, though. For headaches. Migraines.' If she states it, as a fact, she might make it true.

She is rewarded with a nod. 'It is. But you should be aware of the possibility that your sight will be affected.'

'Affected or lost?'

'Well—'

'Mr Wilding, please' – she hates that her voice sounds pleading – 'I really do not have time for this. Just tell me.'

She's rewarded with a nod. 'As time goes on, loss of vision becomes more likely. In some patients it can be an earlier symptom of tumour growth.' He looks back to the scan, then at Vee, who is aware that she is sitting very straight, now, as though keeping her head balanced will improve things. 'This cluster, here, is closer to the occipital lobe than we'd like.'

'I'm not losing my sight.' Vee had thought there was nothing worse than losing her memories – being unable to recall any details about her father's death, about Leonie's, looking back through her photographs desperate for clues to her life and her happiness. But it could be that something worse is waiting for her.

Mr Wilding leans back in his chair, watches her, and waits.

She won't be pitied. And she won't be blind, either. It's just not possible. She refuses.

She blows her nose, then inhales; forces her shoulders down from where they are hunching. 'What happens now?'

'Here's what I suggest you do. Put things in order. Take plenty of rest. Don't put yourself under undue stress—'

'Why not?'

'I'm sorry?' Mr Wilding is clearly not used to being interrupted. And at whatever he costs a minute, Vee is not surprised. But she does not have time for this. She needs to go out and look at everything, fill what remains of her mind with the colours of the world.

'What will happen if I don't rest? If I am under stress?'

'Well . . .' Oh, Vee loathes it when people steeple their fingers, prides herself on never having taken that photograph, even though there is a certain class of (usually male) expert who considers it the only way to be portrayed. 'Well, the disease could be speeded up.'

'So if I enjoy myself, I might die sooner?'

'Well . . .' Mr Wilding says again.

Vee nods, because that's her answer. 'What now?'

'We can give you painkillers, and we'll ask you to let us know of any changes. We can't really predict how the disease will progress from here, I'm afraid. We know the possibilities—'

'And the end,' Vee says.

He nods. 'Sadly, yes. We know the end. That's mandatory for all of us.'

'Mandatory. Bloody men,' Vee says, and laughs, and Mr Wilding joins in, though Vee isn't sure that either of them think what she said is funny.

8 March 2018

International Women's Day

Five million Spanish women mark International Women's Day by taking part in the country's first 'feminist strike', demonstrating against sexual discrimination, domestic violence and the wage gap.

Seven weeks until exhibition opening

The light of a March dawn is hardly strident, but still Vee winces as it starts to leak in around the edges of the blinds in her living room. It has been a long night. She went to bed at eleven, but the headache had come before she could sleep. The medication did nothing for her. At three she got up and groped her way downstairs, bore the bright light of the fridge-freezer for long enough to take out an ice pack and pour herself a glass of spiced rum. Her painkillers are not compatible with alcohol but they weren't touching the pain, so Vee was damn well going to do all she could to get some relief.

She lay on the sofa. Perhaps she dozed. Now morning is coming and the night has exhausted her: the headache has neither attacked nor vanished, but is skulking in her jaw, across her forehead, round the back of her skull. This is new. It's never hung around like this before. If Vee was one for prayer, she would pray to have the old headaches back. Even if she found religion, she thinks, she would like to believe she would still be a pragmatist.

She wouldn't ask for a miracle. Just a lessening of the pain; a return to familiar landscape, where she will know where and how the light falls. And her sight. She would beg and wail for her sight. She would have got down on her knees to Mr Wilding last week, if she though he had the power to save it.

She could cope with being a photographer who didn't take pictures, but not with being a photographer (even a long-retired one) who could not see.

Still, her time is nearly done. So long as her sight holds fast for as long as her breath does, she will manage.

Vee thinks of Erica, so much life ahead of her, and feels almost glad her own time is nearly done.

Of course, that could be the tumour affecting her brain, making her think that dying is something worth having. She keeps waiting to care more about it. After the clinic she walked, then sat in Regent's Park until the light faded, feeling old and cheated and bereft. Since then she's felt very little. 'I am dying,' she says to herself in the bathroom mirror, and she watches her reflection for clues to how she's feeling. It doesn't help.

She could ring the clinic, about the pain. Calling an ambulance would be melodramatic. She isn't an emergency, she's a painful inevitability. And until she has a seizure, there's really nothing else to be done.

Vee watches the light at the edges of her window, tries to see it thickening and growing. But its creeping is too clever, like the creeping of the growth in her brain, too easily dismissed as nothing until it was undeniably and irrevocably something. Something unstoppable. While she waits, she tries to remember what it is about today. She is doing something today. Something for Leonie. Except it can't be, because Leonie's dead. Is it too much to hope for headaches then death, without the blindness or the jumbling of past and present? Vee has got used to living without what she lost after the surgery a decade ago. The older she gets, the less relevant those memories feel, though at the time she had mourned for every lost one of them, and their lack had made her feel unstable, uncertain, shaky on her feet.

The knock comes at nine-thirty.

'Morning,' Erica says, with a broad, lipsticked smile and a coiled up energy that makes Vee almost glad she has lived alone for all of these years. Other people are just so tiring, closeup. Even if you aren't ill. They always want something: conversation, help, company, praise. Compromise. 'All set?'

'For what?'

The smile pauses. 'The march?'

Oh, Christ on a bike. This is what today was about. Vee sits down on the sofa, the small warm space that she made in the night. 'I'm not well.'

'A headache, again?'

'Yes, a headache.'

And there's a new sort of pain, too. Missing Leonie has become visceral, again, with Erica so close by.

'I've got painkillers in the car.' Erica sighs, as though trying not quite as hard as she should to hide her annoyance; letting the edges of it glisten. (Was it always this much of an effort, with people? It's so trying, to interpret, to interact.) Then she adds, 'I had to arrange childcare.'

Vee considers letting this go, but then she imagines what Leonie would say: 'Why does that make it worse? Couldn't you just be angry on your own behalf? You're a person. You're enti-tled to feel—' Oh, if only the words would come, more easily than they do. 'Pissed.' No, that's not quite right. '. . . off. Pissed off.'

Erica acts as though she hasn't heard, 'I don't want to go on my own. I want to see what you see. Your perspective?'

'That is not my problem.' Vee is becoming fond of the emerald coat: the colour is good against Erica's skin, just warm enough, just bold enough. Looking at Erica's straight shining hair, the whiteness of her teeth, the gloss of her shoes (patent pewter brogues today, not heels), she feels coated in sweat and the grime of the night's pain, illness clogging her pores. She could have a shower when there's someone within earshot. That presence would make the rest of it – the undressing-dressing, the rinsing of shampoo from her hair, the first hot sting of water on her skin – bearable. It would be worth it to feel at least a little bit renewed.

'I'm going to have a shower, and then I'll see how I feel. I've been sorting through some boxes and I found photographs that you might like.' She pauses, amends, 'Might like to see. They're on the table.'

Erica looks at the box the way a dog would look at a bone. But she pulls her gaze back to Vee as she stands, and asks, 'Can I do anything? For you? You look . . . you don't look well at all.'

'Just be quiet,' Vee says, and she sets off up the stairs, every step an effort.

Just be quiet? How much noise is one woman looking through one box of photographs likely to make? Vee should try living in a house with a toddler who has discovered what his toy hammer is for, and loves above all things his talking teddy bear.

Erica boils the kettle – that can't be considered noisy – and takes one of four plain, bone-white, bone-china mugs from a plain white cupboard. She spoons loose-leaf tea into a glass teapot. Vee seems to live the way magazines make you believe everyone lives: her house is pale, her possessions spare and beautiful. The fridge hums as though it has been tuned. Erica thinks of her own fridge, the door covered with invitations, newsletters, bin-day and recycling reminders and Tom's works of art, and inside crammed with half-used jars of this and that, out-of-date fruit and salad leaves turning to slime. Vee's fridge has a carton of milk and a bottle of rum in the door; on the shelves are tomatoes, pears, fresh pasta, and a carton of clam chowder. Erica wants to worship the simplicity of it, and the lifestyle it implies. She loves her family, she really does. But oh, for the time to taste the food on your tongue. When she goes home she will get rid of all of their chipped mugs.

But now it's time for the box. Erica tries not to think of the treasure she might find. She's an academic. She's an adult. She'll wait and see.

The contact sheets, roughly A4 size, are on the bottom, and individual prints on top, the four-inch by six-inch ones on top of the five by eight. They aren't in date order, then: that doesn't seem like Vee. But when Erica turns over the top photograph – an unremarkable image, a line of women linking arms, no distinguishing features, but her aunt Leonie second from left – she sees a date pencilled lightly on the back, along with an abbreviation that she assumes will make sense to Vee. ('WLFC'. Women's Liberation Front Conference? Probably. She'll check.)

Erica begins by looking at the dates on the back of the images and trying to put them into sequence, but soon she is overtaken by the need to look at the photographs, every one, as fast as she can, her gaze gobbling through them, knowing that she can slow down, later, go back through and examine them properly. But first there is the rush of noticing something in each image, letting her eye lead. Here, she is startled by her aunt's scowl, her raised hand, as she was obviously being photographed when she didn't want to be. She understands why people use words like 'formidable' with reference to Leonie: here, she seems terrifying. In another – there's a heart-shock as Erica recognises her mother with her aunt – the sisters are standing in a doorway. Ursula looks as though she's in charge, Vee having captured the moment where she is talking, Leonie listening, head dropped, meek. There may well be a photograph in Erica's grandmother's album of the two girls in childhood, where the same dynamic is visible.

Here is Leonie, in her dungarees, hair tied back with a scarf, jabbing her finger at a man who seems to be confronting her; there are out-of-focus placards in the background. Here, Leonie stands on a table, with a raffia-wrapped bulbous bottle of wine raised high in one hand, mouth open in what has to be a victory cry. In another image, Leonie is slumped in a chair, eyes half closed, mouth half a smile, making a V-sign at the camera. Here, she's marching: here, her face is caught among others, all looking in the same direction, all listening, focused, waiting. It's the sort of photograph that makes you hold your breath, and wish you were there, hearing what those women were hearing.

Erica lays the photographs of her aunt side by side, imagines them in the same section of the exhibition as the moment of death photograph. They will make the exhibition visitor feel the loss of Leonie all the more. To see her so very alive, next to the image of her so newly dead. Erica feels sadness rising in her, bloating her heart and making her vision soften and shake; she wipes her tears, quickly, so they cannot fall on the photographs. Though Erica doesn't recall much about Leonie or her death, she lived with her mother's grief for all of her remembered life. Grief wakes in Erica now, a slow low keening in her guts, as she lets herself think of all she will not have again. No mother. No answers to the question of Leonie's death. She was a fool to think that Vee could be persuaded to talk to her about Leonie. She is more of a fool to keep hoping for it.

Erica walks away from the table, stands at the window and looks at the beginning of spring in the budding of the trees. She breathes deep. She would cancel the exhibition tomorrow, throw all of her work away, just to know what happened that day. Her own scant memories don't feel right. Veronica could help. but she won't. She won't.

And Erica could cry her heart out now, but she won't. She goes back to the table, looks at her aunt with her academic's eye. Leonie could be cold and clear. So can she.

It would be possible to date the photographs, roughly, without looking at the back, or at least put them into chronological order: flares narrow and hair shortens as the 1970s wear on, slogans become more consistent and placards more sophisticated. Vee, too, changes where she focuses. She moves from taking groups, vistas, gatherings, to focusing on faces and exchanges. Often, in these photographs, Leonie is arguing with someone. Sometimes it seems good-humoured but very often it clearly isn't, with Leonie's bulk pushing forward, her face thrusting close, her hand in a fist by her side or raised and flattened in the air, telling the other person to stop. Stop talking, her body language says, stop resisting, stop disagreeing.

Erica could also date the photographs, she realises, from Leonie's size. She's solid in the 1960s, and then in the early 1970s she's starting to be – well, it would be called obese now. And still she grows: more chins, more girth, her fingers plump and then fat, the joints disappearing. She looks like Andrea Dworkin, though she came later, Erica is sure, becoming famous after Leonie died. Or is it wrong to equate the two so easily? Not all overweight women look the same, just as all thin women are different. If only it were simple. It should be, by now. That's clearly what Veronica thinks. She's right. But saying it should be sorted doesn't make it so.

There are other things to notice in the photographs: Leonie's transition from dungarees to men's shirts and loose trousers; the way Vee rarely took photographs when the subject was looking directly into the lens, preferring to watch them as they watched something else, or were absorbed in action. Erica could write another PhD on Veronica's photographic decisions. Maybe a book.

'I think that's a bit better,' Vee says, behind her.

Erica wipes her eyes, just to make sure there are no traces of tears, before she turns around.

Vee has dressed – jeans, a white shirt beneath a navy sweater, not very new but made of something (cashmere?) that isn't meant to ever wear out. She's wearing socks; her boots are next to a bag at the door, so she must have been planning to come. Despite all this, it seems as though she has not yet put her skin back on. She's like Tom is in the mornings, when he wants to cuddle, before he sets off to conquer his toddler world. Or Marcus, after sex, when he pulls her in, kisses the top of her head, says something like, *it's not so bad, is it, darling? We're lucky to have each other, aren't we?* It's the only time he sounds uncertain; the only time, if she's honest, that she really actively feels she loves him still. Oh, she knows she does. But feeling it is different.

'Can I get you anything? Make you some tea?'

Vee closes her eyes, longer than a blink. 'Water, please,' she says, then, 'Damn. I forgot to bring my tablets down. They're in the bathroom cabinet. Top shelf, white box. Would you mind?'

The cabinet is as neat and tidy as the fridge. There are three boxes of medication on the top shelf, all different. Erica isn't an expert, but she knows a serious health problem when she sees it. One of the packs is steroids, the other two both prescription painkillers, or at least she thinks they are. A shocked, roiling nausea rises in Erica: she had assumed that Vee was difficult, because – well, because she was that kind of woman.

Erica puts the medication boxes down next to Vee, and goes to the kitchen and pours a glass of water. Vee nods her thanks, takes the glass with a slightly shaking hand, and swallows some tablets with a practised jerk of the head. She steadies herself with a palm on the back of a dining chair, closes her eyes. 'I don't know whether my headaches ever go,' she says, 'or whether I'm just so used to them that I stop noticing.'

'This one doesn't seem as bad as the day we went to the gallery,' Erica offers.

There's almost a smile from Vee. 'That wasn't a headache. That was – an assault.' The first assault of her last war. She puts a finger to her temple, gently, as though the very skin of her face is tender.

Erica is still standing; she isn't sure what will happen now. She could go to the march on her own, of course she could. She's not a child. But she doesn't want to do it without Vee. She says, 'Thank you for letting me look at the photos.'

'What did you think of them?'

Maybe because Vee sounds as though she doesn't care, or because her eyes are still closed, it's easy for Erica to be honest. 'I thought my aunt looks hostile in a lot of them. She seems to be spoiling for a fight.'

The fraction of a nod from Vee, the foreshadowing of a smile. 'And does that surprise you?'

'Not really. Like I said, I know her mainly by reputation. And her writing. Which was – is – pretty uncompromising.'

'Hmm.' It's half-sigh, half-question.

In the peace of this room, talking becomes irresistible. Plus, Erica doesn't really want to think about what those pills mean. 'Her essay on abortion, in particular. Not the column, the piece in her book. That made me think. She was very clear. That it's only a transaction. No more important than having a tooth out.'

Vee doesn't give any sign that she's listening. She doesn't speak. And Erica can't stop. 'I remember when I was first pregnant. My mother died eighteen months before and it was only a year after we got married. It was so emotional. Leonie wrote rationally about abortion. It made me see how irrationally we think about babies. I can see why people wouldn't like that kind of – of forthrightness.' Erica herself had put down the iPad she was reading Leonie's book on, her hand shaking, and looked across at Tom, who was sleeping on the sofa, battened in by cushions so he didn't roll off and hurt himself, his perfect shells of ears sticking through the straight, soft hair that she cannot bear to have cut. She'd wondered whether, if she hadn't had him, she might be less unhappy.

There's a pause. Vee opens her eyes, looks towards the window, the light. When she speaks, her mouth hardly moves, as though she is trying to keep her jaw still. 'That's depressing. Women of your age, your education and means getting swept up. It's the opposite of what the movement was fighting for.'

This again. If Erica doesn't start to confront it, she will be trampled. She won't be able to look Tom or Marcus in the eye when she gets home, as it is. 'Weren't you fighting for the right not to be judged? It sometimes seems to me that you only wanted that in theory. I get judged every which way, and much more by women than by men.' She thinks of Marcus's mother, Sarah, who considers it shocking that she employs a weekly cleaner. An older former colleague told her that she was letting the side down by having a baby. Whereas most of the men she works with couldn't give a toss about her childcare arrangements or

161

the moral compromises she has made, so long as she turns up when she's supposed to. 'You would say you spent the seventies fighting for women's freedom but that only seems to be true if we are the right sort of free.'

'That's probably a fair point,' Vee says, after a pause so long Erica thought she was ignoring her.

Erica can't help but nod, with a kind of 'ha!' abruptness.

They stand in silence for a moment, then another. Erica goes to the table and leafs through the photographs again. It's the first time in a long time that her aunt has seemed more than an abstract figure, the family icon/tragedy. 'She looks . . . dynamic. And angry, a lot of the time. My aunt.'

Vee half-laughs, an affectionate, remembering sound. 'She was. We all were, to an extent, in that we were all trying to make changes, and we were aware of how unjust the world was, and we couldn't believe it wasn't changing faster. If you'd told me then that I was going on this march today, I'd have written you off as a pessimist. Leonie would have hauled you over the coals for not believing in the power of the sisterhood.' She smiles, looking straight at Erica for the first time today. 'Do you want to call a cab while I put my boots on?'

'Are you up to it?'

'I have no idea,' Vee says, 'but I sorted out my camera last night, so I'll give it a try.'

'You're going to take photographs?' Erica must have misheard. Vee doesn't photograph. In an early email about the exhibition, she'd written: 'I haven't taken a photograph in more than twenty years, and I won't again. You may not quote me on that, as you may not quote me – directly – on anything.' She'd read the email out to Marcus. 'You've a heart like a lion to be doing this,' he'd said.

'Yes. I am a photographer.'

'I thought you didn't photograph anymore.' There's a thrum of excitement in Erica, where grief was a few minutes ago.

'I've changed my mind.'

It would be more accurate to say that her mind has changed. More accurate yet to say that disease has changed it. There is no reason for her to be doing this. But as she sorted through her equipment yesterday she had thought, *why not?* She won't get the chance again. No one is going to notice her, or care about her, at a march. They'll have bigger, better things to care about than what Veronica Moon is doing. And press photographers now won't recognise her. They might have heard of her, studied her, but she looks like just another old woman. So, she's going to take some photographs today. If the tumour is making her do it, squashing her memories and blocking her fear, well, she's going to let it.

The trouble with having a tumour chewing through your brain, Vee thinks – putting aside impending death, for a moment, and worse, the threat of blindness – is that you know you cannot trust anything you think. At home, as Erica talked, Vee had seen, so clearly, so simply, that she was lonely, she was afraid, she needed someone the way Vee had once needed Leonie. And so coming to the march seemed more important than anything else. She'd had an odd thought, floating in from nowhere, that perhaps she owed Leonie this.

But then, in the cab, she'd become certain that the rattle and swerve of motion was doing sudden, terrible damage to her ailing brain. She holds on, hard fists and closed eyes, until the taxi driver drops them on Great George Street.

As soon as her feet hit solid ground again, and she begins to walk, her camera bag bouncing on her hip, she knows she can do this. They cut across to Parliament Street, walking with it just as it is changing form, turning from a flowing, street-bound river to a sprawling, square-edged pool of women.

The patches of song, the laughter and the chants taken up, shifting and swelling and quelling, work like a balm as she and Erica make their way towards them. There is nothing in the world like the sound of women protesting.

The air grumbles and sings under the weight of noise in it: there's so much energy that Vee feels circled, surrounded, her steps easy. The rhythm of her pace next to Erica's settles into a steady harmony. Vee feels her breath deepen, her spine straighten. She's forgotten exactly how good it is to march: how important, how scary, how real. Her edges dissolve into the sound and light around her. She tastes petrol fumes, breathes in the shouted-out breaths of the women around her. 'The women, u-ni-ted, will ne-ver be de-feat-ed.' How long since she was in the midst of the sisterhood like this? When the chant starts again, she opens her throat and lets her voice join it.

The pain in her own head is there, all right, and it's not nothing, but it's as though it has moved to the other side of her skull, taken up by shouts and jeers, chants and drums, and is nothing to her anymore. Erica is next to her, silent but wide-eyed as they join the women making their way into Trafalgar Square. It's time to yell and shout for justice and autonomy and the right to not be ogled, harassed, spoken down to, blackmailed or abused. She should be bellowing for every damn thing that should be hers by right, like the women around them. Vee reaches out an arm to touch Erica's, smiles when the younger woman looks around and smiles back.

The police presence thickens as they approach the entrance to Trafalgar Square: horses in pairs, vans watching darkly from side streets, uniformed officers in clumps, alert, attentive groups.

The world knows women can be dangerous. Vee's smile spreads wider – her face is probably aching, but she can't feel it, can't feel anything. She sees how Erica glances at the police, then back to her, for reassurance. 'We're the ones with the power here,' she shouts, close to Erica's ear, 'we don't need what they have.' She hopes she's right.

The marchers spread around Trafalgar Square, pooling into the space at the front of the stage and washing out. Vee puts a hand on Erica's arm – touch is easy, once you start. 'I'm going to stand at the side,' she says, 'where I can get a bit of height. If we get separated, don't worry about me. I'll be fine. Email me tomorrow.' Erica nods, and looks around – Vee sees her taking in the scale of this, the seriousness of it, with more police lining the space as it fills, and TV cameras in place, recording it all. And she thinks of what Erica's day to day life is. She does whatever you do with a child, and she lectures, and researches. She is a library-dweller, an only child, and probably a solitary soul, even if she is married. Vee knows what some parts of that are like. 'Enjoy it,' she says, with the hope that she sounds reassuring. And then the noise starts to build and build as the first speaker strides onto the stage.

This woman is an actor, well known, who refused to be paid off after being sexually harassed by a director. Even though everyone knows her story – it's one of the ones that kicked the #MeToo and #TimesUp movements into orbits the world could no longer ignore – something akin to silence rustles over the crowd as she tells her story. The speaker is good – she has the confidence to pause, to let the crowd absorb her words. And they do. More than the noise and the shouts, this is Vee's favourite part of any event, and it always has been. Her own first march, with Leonie, was smaller in scale than this one – she thinks again of how overwhelmed she would be, if she was Erica right now – and the world was different. But some things haven't changed. The listening women are focused, still, and their faces show so much power and intelligence, still, and her desire to capture, to record, seems as strong again as it was fifty years ago.

Vee steps up onto a low wall, unzips her camera bag, and takes out her beloved old Olympus OM-1. Once she started using this model – in '75, maybe – she didn't see that she ever needed anything fancier, better, or more sophisticated. Instead she bought another body, then another, all the same, and she went out into the world with one round her neck and a spare slung over her shoulder. This is her implement and her weapon, and they have been through enough together to work as one. Vee loops the worn, warm strap around her neck, clips off the lens cap – she loves the tension then give of the movement – then palms it into her pocket. When she does this, she isn't seventy and dying. She's twenty and anxious, thirty and assertive, forty and confident, fifty and at the top of her game. She's sixty and learning herself all over again. She's Veronica Moon: photographer, observer, force.

She lifts the camera to her face and her left eye finds the viewfinder, relaxes into the way of seeing it invites. Her right eye closes, and the place between her eyebrows rests against the top of the camera. Vee's left eye is, has always been, the one that wants to do the looking – a camera has never felt right to her when she tries to use her right eye – so when she takes a shot she has to move her head away to wind the film on, with the lever at the top right. She used to envy photographers who took shot after shot without needing to take the camera from their right eye, winding on as they looked, but now she realises that that second of grace and refocus gives her the chance to find something a fraction better than what she had in the last frame.

Erica glances around, looking for her, and Vee smiles, then makes a shooing motion with her free hand; Erica does not need her, here, and she definitely does not need Erica. A photographer is a solitary thing, half-person, half-camera. Her feet are solid and her hands are steady, as serious as they have always been when they are working.

Vee scans through and over the crowd, waits for something to snag her eye. First it's a woman with a child of five or six on her shoulders, the woman reaching a hand up and the child reaching for it, both of them smiling, neither able to see the other's face. She presses the shutter, winds on, settles in again, looking for another image. A better one, this time.

She looks for Erica. It takes a couple of seconds to find her. She is shifting further into the crowd the way that people do, without ever noticing. There's no photograph worth taking there; just the green of the coat, the straight brown of her hair, nothing much to see. She'll take a photograph later, a record for Erica that she was here.

Vee crouches – her vision tilts for a second, but soon finds equilibrium again – and from this angle, placards form a new skyline against the cold March blue; in the bottom of the shot, the hats of the women in the crowd make a bumping horizon. That's more like it. Click.

Now she's started she can't stop. Was she always compelled like this? Maybe she was. She ought to be cold but she doesn't feel it. She photographs an older woman, hair dyed purple, pussy hat, blowing on her hands, and the cloud of coldness in the air makes the boldness of her stare all the greater. It's a good photograph. In Vee's heyday, that would have made a cover shot for a picture editor worth their salt: mauve hair, pink hat, blue sky, grey air, questioning bright eyes, demanding to know why Vee is pointing her camera in that direction. The cover line would be something like: '*Women's Rights: coming in from the cold*'.

Looking around the crowd, she picks out other faces, captures their expressions of outrage, unity, sadness with a series of shutter clicks. The crowd is more multi-coloured than it once would have been, more nuanced, too. As though there are more kinds of woman than there used to be.

Leonie once wrote that feminism would only succeed when it was made up of more than white women and dykes. Well, here you are, Leonie, Vee thinks: here is your crowd, my friend. Black, brown, white, gay, straight, bi, cis, trans. Vee takes shot after shot. She would photograph every woman here, if she could. If there was any film left over she'd photograph the men, too.

Oh, this is a good feeling. If Vee aches, she doesn't know it. Her old self is back. She might be missing a part of her brain, but with her camera in her hands she is very nearly whole.

She is months from death and yet she is happier than she has been in a long time.

Being here, in the noise and the fury and the overwhelming goodwill from sister to sister, is something like being young, and very likely to be the last time she experiences this. Oh, what they could have done, in the 1970s, with mobile phones and a media shaped and called out by any woman with a hashtag and a sense of outraged self: Leonie would have loved it. (Once she had vented her outrage at media still owned, governed and run by men.) The sisterhood of the 1970s would have won, properly, thoroughly, if they had only had what women today have, and think nothing of. Surely.

Leonie would have loved to see Erica here, too. (There's something about Erica's name that bugs Vee, at the edges of what she has forgotten.) And been horrified that it was her first demo.

Although, of course, if Leonie was here Erica would have been to plenty of protests, whether Ursula liked it or not. Vee lets the camera search for Erica again, finds her further forward now, her small green back standing out. She's talking to the woman next to her, pointing at the stage, earnest. The sight of her makes Vee lower her camera and close her eyes, let the pain be in her head, instead of outside it, joined to and drowned by this noisy, fierce crowd, whooping their support for the actor who is calling for more action, for persistence and resistance and never giving up. Erica looks around, in the lull, looking for Vee, who raises a hand. Erica looks brighter than Vee has yet seen her. 'Thank you', she mouths, and then she is pushing a fist into the air with everyone else, as the actor leaves the stage, her own fist raised.

Vee doesn't recognise the next speaker, but from the shape of her, the poise, she must be an athlete.

The athlete is holding up a medal, letting the crowd praise her – how strange it is to see a woman taking credit, still – and when the noise dies down she starts to tell a story. It's about abuse and fear, about so many men in authority taking what they shouldn't, and that quiet sneaks over them all again, as they listen. Vee hears enough to be horrified – so many of these stories, and yet instead of becoming inured to them, hearing each makes all the others sharper, more bitter and more sad. But at the same time she is watching, capturing a face with tears running down it here, two women with their arms around each other there, a woman who has put her placard down and is leaning against it a little way behind her. It says, in haphazard capitals, 'PROTESTING THIS SHIT SINCE THE 1960s'. Vee takes a photograph which includes the placard, the slump of the woman's spine as she rests, the concentrated look on her face as she looks towards the stage. They might have known each other, back then.

Even though she's only watching, at a fraction of a distance, not bellowing and showing her fury like the women she sees in front of her, still she is part of this purpose, less conscious of her body, mind full of now. She assumes that she has a headache, still, but she really cannot tell. As speaker after speaker takes the stage, she focuses, winds on, watches, waits, and feels outrage and sorrow and strength seep into her. Her own preoccupations seem like nothing, here. The chants are getting more ragged edged and sustained, the noise level creeping up and up. The police horses seem more restless, one in the corner of Vee's field of vision stepping from foot to foot, stretching its neck and raising its head as though trying, also, to get free. Vee turns the camera to see if she can find a shot. There is tension starting to string its way through the air now, binding everyone in the space. This is how it goes, sometimes. The protesters are primed, ready for action: that's how it needs to be. But it is best if they go home primed, and start to take that energy out into the world, making changes. Leonie called it 'delayed amplification' and she was the queen of it. When she used to speak at meetings, in the early days, she could send their sisters home bursting with purpose and intention. They would come to the next meetings full of reports of what they had done: bosses challenged, legs unshaven, MPs questioned, dinner dishes left, unapologetically, for someone else to wash.

Here, though, there's too much energy, anger, connection for everyone to simply go home. It might be that today really is just one march too many, for people like Vee who have been doing it since the 1970s and for those who first took to the streets when Trump came to power, thinking it was a question of months, not years, until the world changed for the better. It might be that there needs to be a moment like the one Vee can feel coming: the women running amok, for once, tearing down shop signs instead of Instagramming their fury. Vee stretches her shoulders, deliberately feeling the blades pull apart. She might be getting ready to run. Or to throw something. The thought of it makes her smile. How long is it since she has felt that Leonie would be proud of her?

Erica is making her way towards her; except this is a spotlit Erica, lighter, brighter. She starts talking when she's three metres away, even though Vee has no hope of hearing her. '... Amazing! I had no idea that it would be like this!' she is saying as she comes to stand next to Vee.

'Good.' Vee sees herself at the Miss World protest, when she first fully understood that she was not alone in feeling that, for all of her ambition and her work, the world was holding her back, pushing her down.

'I'm done with sitting back,' Erica says, 'I'm going to do more. I need to see this stuff. I haven't always seen it.' She looks at her shoes, then up at Vee, shading her eyes from a sudden spear of low sun. 'I haven't always looked. I'm going to see it and I'm going to challenge it.' The light in Erica's eyes, the way she is tense and excited, suggest that she would be the first to throw a brick, given half the chance.

'Good,' Vee says again, stepping down from the wall, 'I'm glad.' And then she does something she would never normally do. She reaches out an arm to Erica, high and wide, and Erica, without hesitation, steps in, embraces her and says, 'Thank you.' Her hair feels exactly the same as Leonie's against Vee's face. Vee cannot remember the last time she was held, or wanted to be. Maybe it's the tumour. She is supposed to be aware that there may be 'behavioural changes' as her disease progresses. But is the desire to be close to someone as she gets closer to death really an oddity? Is the fact that there are things she cannot remember about Leonie, about Erica, so unusual for a woman of her years?

'How's your head? Do you need to go?' Erica asks.

Vee probably does. There will be consequences from this day, for sure, pain and exhaustion, and maybe another section of her brain dying from the sheer effort of being here. But right now – and what does it matter if it is the tumour talking? – the thought of her flat is as appealing as the thought of her grave.

Before she can say anything, though, it begins.

There's a sharp spike of sound; a cry, a shout. She swings her body around, bringing the camera to her eye, an ingrained habit. There's some sort of argument between a woman holding a placard and a police officer. Vee takes a photograph, another, moving closer and closer.

The police officer sees them and walks over. 'Were you taking photographs of me?'

'Yes,' Vee says. She reaches into her pocket for the lens cap and pushes it back into place.

'Can I ask why?'

'I don't believe there's any reason why I shouldn't.'

'Are you a journalist?'

'No.'

'She used to be,' Erica says, 'and a bloody good one.'

'Could you show me, please?'

'I can't,' Vee says, 'it's a film camera.'

'And why should she?' Erica chips in. 'She's within her rights to take photographs.'

Vee smiles at Erica; it's good to see fire in her, to know it's there.

And Erica takes the smile and uses it as fuel, as some sort of encouragement. 'Fucking police,' she says to Vee, as though the officer can't hear them. 'Fucking typical entitled men who think they can harass women. Bastards.' Vee has never heard her swear. She's never seen her spoiling for a fight, either.

On the other side of Trafalgar Square there's the sound of something breaking, a different kind of fury in the shouts; the chants have got ragged, moved to outraged yelling. It's as though the air has got sharper and dropped five degrees in the space of two breaths. A collective tensing of muscles runs through the crowd, police and protestors both.

Vee knows what this means.

To her left, the camera crews are paying attention again, focusing on the confrontations that are breaking out here and there. They will soon expand, she knows: the riot police will move in, and the protesters will get angrier, and there will be no chance of going home quietly.

The officer looks Erica up and down. 'Could I search your bag, please, madam?'

'Why do you want to search my bag?' She sticks out her chin, her lip. Vee can see what is about to happen. She removes the lens cap from her camera, raises it to her eye.

8 March 2018

Hampton, four hours later

'Oh, thank goodness,' Marcus says, getting to his feet, fast, when Erica walks through the door. In his arms, Tom shifts but doesn't wake. Erica has always envied her husband's ability to keep Tom sleeping. Her slightest move always seems to rouse him to restlessness. 'Where have you been? Why didn't you call? I was worried about you. I left you messages.'

'My phone battery died.' Erica hangs up her coat, then takes off her shoes and leaves them on the floor next to the shoe rack. She's too tired to bend down to put them in place. Marcus will no doubt mention it when he notices, because she always points out when he doesn't put his shoes away.

Every part of her is worn out: feet, voice, back, eyes, ears, throat. And at the same time there's an adrenaline fizz at the solar plexus that tells her she's a long way from sleep. She's hungry; thirsty; thrilled; horny. 'Wait till I tell you what I've been doing.'

There's no wine in the fridge. No clean glasses, either. They had friends over last night, and of course, because Marcus has been Doing Childcare, he won't have unloaded the dishwasher. She pours white wine from the rack into a melamine tumbler with a lion on the side of it, plonks in the last ice cube from the tray in the freezer, and goes to kiss Tom's fluffy, warm cleansmelling head. Marcus turns his face away when she tries to kiss him, too.

'I was worried about you.'

'You should be glad I'm home, then.' She sits down next to him, puts her head against his shoulder, ignoring the way his body stiffens at her touch.

'Of course I am. I thought you would be back hours ago. You said five at the latest.'

'Well, events overtook.' Logic, good sense, everything she knows about Marcus tells her to say nothing more, to go and take a bath and curl her body into his when he comes to bed, put a hand on his chest and let him know that despite everything she is not too tired for him. But there is nothing circumspect in the remains of the adrenaline. 'Don't you want to know what happened?'

He sighs, and smiles, and frees an arm to put around her shoulders. 'Stage dive? Tattoo? Joined the Foreign Legion?'

'I got arrested!' she blurts. Then, 'Well, detained. By the police.'

'You did what?' Tom shifts and murmurs against the sudden tension in his father's body.

'A policeman tried to search my bag and I told him to fuck off. He'd been bothering Veronica about taking photographs. I didn't think that was right. Next thing I knew I was in a police van.'

'You're not serious?' Marcus turns to face her; Tom barely moves.

'Yes! I had to wait ages at the station. They took my stuff away and searched me and I got my fingerprints taken.' Erica holds her fingers towards him, making wriggling stars of her hands, as though they are proof, although it was done on a screen, not with ink, so there's no trace. 'And my DNA. I asked if that was standard and they said it was. Then I rang a solicitor they gave me the number for, and she said she didn't need to come in and the police wouldn't do anything. Then I sat in an interview room for a bit.'

175

'Wow.' It's not an admiring 'wow', but she pretends not to notice. She smiles. He doesn't smile. His face is a sky of hurt with a brow of coming thunder.

'Erica, I was worried before you came back. I'm even more worried now.'

And the bravado rushes out of her as suddenly as it rushed in. 'I was scared.' And she was, just for a few minutes, scared that being in the police station would stop being an adventure, a misunderstanding, a case of pissing off someone who didn't, in that moment, need to be pissed off, and had the power to show it. She'd thought about miscarriages of justice, and whether she had to declare this on job applications. Wondered about the women who didn't have the luxury of all the things that protected her, however much she didn't want to believe that they did: money, skin colour, education.

Marcus half-smiles. 'I would have been too,' he says, 'why didn't you phone me? Tom and I would have broken you out.'

'A woman came to talk to me, asked me what my involvement was, and I told her, and then she let me go.'

Marcus lays Tom on the sofa next to him and barricades him in place with a cushion. Erica scoots along the sofa to make room, crosses her legs. She can smell the fustiness of her sweated-in socks.

'And what did Veronica do?' he asks. 'While all this was going on?'

'She took my photograph. What else was she going to do?'

'So it was a good day, huh?'

Erica thinks of the speakers she heard. Some had stories of blatant male abuse, but others spoke of the creeping insidiousness that made women subjugated, self-censoring, wondering whether it was worth making a big deal of a hand on a knee. She'd thought about how she and Marcus, good people who believed in equality – of course they did! – had slumped into him-going-to-work-her-mostly-staying-at-home because of the mathematics of it. He earned more, and his career paid the mortgage while hers was their frittering money, for meals out and holidays and covering the cost of the we've-rented-out-a-country-house-for-the-weekend fortieth birthday parties that their friends were starting to invite them to. They'd made a decision about this; it wasn't because she was the woman, it was because it made practical sense. And now Erica could kick herself, because the only reason it makes practical sense is because the world is so skewed in Marcus's favour. And she has, in her acceptance, been complicit.

'I thought about the world that Tom is growing up into,' she says, 'I thought about what I was doing to make it a place that's safe for everyone.'

Marcus nods, and then, before she can say more, says, 'I'll put Tom to bed.'

Erica knows Marcus is expecting her to do it, because he has been in sole charge of their child for all of ten hours. But she lets him go, and then she tops up her wine, ignores the dishwasher, and goes to run herself a bath. It's not much, but it's a start.

Part 4: Distance

The distance between photographer and subject may not need to be great. You don't need to show the whole. You can trust the viewer to fill in the spaces behind, around and between. A photograph of head and shoulders won't make a viewer wonder whether the subject has legs. Get as close as you need to to show what it is you want to show. Remember, the most interesting part of anyone is likely to be their face.

Veronica Moon, *Women in Photographs* (unpublished)

'Margaret Thatcher on Parliament Hill'
Political Photograph of the Year, 1979
Veronica Moon

Exhibition section: High Profile

Camera: OM-1
Film: 200 ASA
First published: *Observer*, 1979

You probably recognise Margaret Thatcher here – but can you think of another image that is quite so relaxed, or informal?

Margaret (later Baroness) Thatcher was already one of the most recognisable women of the late twentieth century when Veronica Moon photographed her. She had recently become Prime Minister of Great Britain and the first female head of state in Europe, Moon was commissioned to take a cover for the *Observer* magazine.

The photograph was taken on Parliament Hill, close to Thatcher's constituency of Finchley. At this stage in her career, Moon was sufficiently well known and well respected to be able to state her preferences. She always worked in black and white, although from this period onwards other photographers were experimenting with colour news photography, and *The Times* newspaper started to publish a colour supplement from 1982.

Here, Thatcher is shown half-laughing, looking slightly to the side of the camera, as a scarf knotted at her throat flutters upwards in the wind. When this image was published, it was with the cover line *Margaret Thatcher: which way is the wind blowing for the first woman in charge?* Gossip at the time suggested that Thatcher did not like the portrait and dismissed it as being 'unstatesmanlike'. The other photographs that accompany the article, also taken by Moon, are much more unremarkable: the Prime Minister is seen standing straight-backed looking out over London; in conversation with a passing dog-walker, head slightly to one side. These other photographs are still tellingly Moon, though; you'll notice the dog that the Prime Minister has not seen, appearing into the side of one shot, and the fact that the focus of the dog-walker is not, apparently, Thatcher. Rather, he is staring over her shoulder, as though waiting for the encounter to end. Moon never photographed Thatcher again.

In this section of the exhibition you'll find more of Moon's high-profile work – during the early 1980s it was rare for her to be commissioned for anything less than a cover shoot.

In 1979:

- It was the United Nations' International Year of the Child
- The early part of the year was known as 'The Winter of Discontent': high inflation and a weak economy led to shortages, strikes and unrest
- Politician Airey Neave was killed by an IRA bomb in March
- The Yorkshire Ripper murders continued. In 1981, Peter Sutcliffe would be tried and found guilty of murdering thirteen female sex workers and attempting to murder seven more. He claimed that the voice of God had told him to kill the women
- Dame Josephine Barnes became the first woman president of the British Medical Association
- Sebastian Coe set a new world record for running a mile

- Britain's first nudist beach, in Brighton, was given the go-ahead
- TV shows *Question Time*, *The Antiques Roadshow*, *Terry and June* and *To the Manor Born* were broadcast for the first time
- Southall Black Sisters was formed, to support all black and Asian women living in the UK
- Ridley Scott's film *Alien*, starring Sigourney Weaver, was released, as was Monty Python's *Life of Brian*
- Six women were acquitted in the 'Reclaim the Night' trials
- Angela Carter's *The Bloody Chamber* was published, as was *A Woman of Substance* by Barbara Taylor Bradford, *Kane and Abel* by Jeffrey Archer and *The Hitchhiker's Guide to the Galaxy* by Douglas Adams
- Following a vote of no confidence in James Callaghan's Labour government, the Conservative Party won the election and Margaret Thatcher became Prime Minister

And, much to Leonie Barratt's disgust, Veronica Moon is commissioned by the *Observer* magazine to photograph her.

15 May 1979

'HEY, LEE.' KENNETH IS A head taller than Leonie, wide as well as tall, and when he embraces her she feels, for a moment, small. She doesn't like it; she shakes him off.

'Hey. Long time no see.'

He grins and throws himself onto the sofa in the corner of the magazine office where he works. 'Have a seat,' he says. 'You should have said you were coming in, I could have skived. But I've got things to do.'

She did wonder about letting him know in advance, but in and out is probably best, 'I'm going to meet Veronica Moon after this,' she says.

Ken makes an impressed face. 'You're mixing in grand circles.'

Nobody remembers, or cares, that Leonie was the one who got Vee started. 'Sod off,' she says. She should get this over with but it's harder than she thought it would be, now she's here.

'What can I do for you? Last time was – a blast. As I remember . . .' He smiles, just the right side of lechery. It gives Leonie both the warm remembrance of one of the rare nights she actually let a bloke stay over – she learned from that time some idiot trashed Vee's photos – and the way to start the conversation.

'That's why I'm here,' she says, 'there were . . . consequences.'

Another nice thing about Ken: you can see exactly what he's thinking in his face. He goes from puzzlement to surprise to worry to calculation, and skims his gaze over her body – breasts, belly. 'Lee. I'm sorry. That was months ago, wasn't it?'

'Six,' she says, 'I didn't realise until a couple of weeks ago.'

He nods. 'Sure,' he says, 'you wouldn't.' Translation: someone your size wouldn't notice a pregnancy unless you were looking for it. He leans back on the sofa, letting out a long exhale. 'Christ. I'm sorry.'

'Hey. It happens.' Come on, Leonie. Talk. But this is a conversation that she isn't up for, all of a sudden. She wants to be with Vee. Sisters are always better at this sort of thing.

'I assumed you were on the Pill.'

'You assumed wrong.' Leonie's never bought into another way of making women be responsible for everything in the world except money, but she doesn't have the energy to explain that right now.

'What do you want to do? Is it too late to—' He makes a sweeping motion with his arms, waist to knee.

'Abort it? Yeah.'

'Right.' He gives her a nervous smile. 'I'm assuming you don't want to – like – get together. Get married, or anything?'

God, this is painful. Suddenly, talking is easier than playing this tortured game of pauses and sighs. 'Christ, Ken, it's 1979. I'm not marrying you because I'm pregnant. Or for any other reason.'

He knows her well enough to laugh, 'Well, good. So . . . ?'

'I suppose I'll get it adopted. Just thought I should check if you wanted it first.'

'Wow.' He sits forward, rakes his hands through his hair, which is longer than Leonie's, falling to a ragged line at his jaw. 'Wow. I feel like I should, but . . . I don't feel like I can. The job, you know? And the flat's not exactly . . . I mean, I would if I could, but it's just not . . . it's not feasible.'

Leonie shrugs. 'Thought I'd ask.'

'But hey.' Ken pulls his wallet from his back pocket. 'I can help you out. If you need money for – until it's . . . done.'

'I'm fine, thanks,' Leonie says, and she hauls herself to her feet. Even the good guys can get out of these things with three minutes of looking pained and an offer of cash. Time to go and see Vee, and then she's got a meeting about the shelters. Real work. She's wasted enough time on Ken.

15 May 1979

1 p.m.

'I'm sorry I'm late.' And Vee is. It's not like her to keep people waiting; she makes a point of her promptness – earliness, even. But this morning has been different, to say the least. She just photographed her first world leader.

'You're too important to remember your appointments with the little people now, I suppose?' There's a half-drunk pint of cider on the table in front of Leonie, a whisky chaser.

'It's not that,' Vee says, 'it's just you're normally late. So I thought I'd be on time, if I was late.'

Leonie laughs, and gets to her feet. She embraces Vee with what feels like a hard, clinging need. 'I had an appointment. It didn't take as long as it might have. I'm on time by chance. You can stay cool and comfortable in your world view, baby.'

'Thanks. I think. I'll get us some drinks, and then I'll tell you what I've been doing this morning. You'll laugh.'

At the bar, Vee orders two pints of cider, bags of crisps and sausage rolls; her work for the day is done, but she doesn't want to lose the afternoon, so one drink and some food to absorb it should be OK. She'll take the film to the lab, and talk to the guys there about how she wants it developed. They know her well enough by now to make sure they don't over-expose on the light, and they won't try anything fancy. By and large, Vee shoots exactly what she wants. Occasionally – dark days, unpredictable indoor lighting, a flash bulb blown – she needs some tinkering done. There's talk of colour magazines, not too far into the future, but Vee cannot imagine ever needing more than the tools she has: black and white film and natural light, flash when she must, and patience.

When she gets back to the table, Leonie is shoving something back in her bag.

'So, what were you doing that was so funny, sister?'

Vee leans close. 'Photographing Margaret Thatcher on Parliament Hill.' She waits for the smile, but it doesn't come. Instead, Leonie looks sad. The way her dad does when he waves her off on a Sunday.

'You've been taking photos of Thatcher? You're such a sell-out.' Leonie isn't wearing her customary outrage. Vee looks at her friend properly: she seems tired, and she's different, somehow. Not bigger, or smaller, but there's something that wasn't there last time they saw each other. Or it could be that something is missing.

Vee shrugs. 'Yes, I'm a sell-out. Or maybe I'm a role model for girls who want to be photographers.' She takes a drink. 'Do you want to know what happened?'

Leonie, shrugs, smiles. This is weird. Leonie is the least non-committal person Vee knows, has ever known, will ever know. She won't be able to resist. She has always loved whatever the non-sexist, non-judgemental word for 'gossip' is.

Leonie opens the crisps, starts on the fresh pint. 'Go on, then,' she says, then, before Vee can say anything, 'I've heard all the male MPs think she fancies them.'

'That tells you a lot about what they think of themselves.'

'And about how she operates.'

Vee has never, ever heard anything like this from Leonie before. 'I know we don't like her politics, Leonie, but what happened to sisterhood?'

Lately Vee has been fighting off a bit of male attention, and she knows for a fact that she does nothing to invite it. When she says no, she's often accused of 'sending out signals'. She doesn't want any more love, of any kind. She's come to the conclusion that, apart from her father and Leonie, there isn't really anyone in the world that she's that bothered about.

Leonie sighs. 'Tell me about Thatcher. If it really is funny. I could do with a laugh. Then I'll tell you my news.'

'Are you sure?' Leonie doesn't usually opt to go second, either. But she nods, and picks up the sausage roll.

'We were on Parliament Hill. They chose the location. Good light, but it's windy up there this morning. And Thatcher was – well, like a lot of these people—' Leonie raises an eyebrow. 'Famous people. Polite, but a bit distant. They've had their photo taken a lot and they just want to get it over with. Anyway, I started taking photos, but she was worried about her hair, kept putting her hand up to her head.'

Leonie laughs, 'I'd have thought you'd need a gale to shift it.'

'I'd already got her to take her hat off.' Vee had suggested to the Prime Minister that it was going to blow away, so it was a good idea to remove it. But Vee hadn't wanted it in the shot – it was an ugly thing, a sort of pillbox but a bit too tall. 'She gave it to one of her security people, and he stood there holding it as though it was a cake.' Vee holds out her hands in a mime, straightens her spine, and Leonie laughs again. It's such a pleasure to Vee to hear it. Being with Leonie is still one of the best things in her life. She is like an old cat that scratches and bites, but is worth suffering for the memory of her warmth. Not that she is old. But she seems to be ageing faster than anyone else Vee knows.

'I thought she might relax after that, but she still looked ... it wasn't right. I was shooting but I knew that what I was getting was the same as every other official photograph of her. You know.'

Leonie nods. 'Constipated headmistress.'

'Yes,' Vee says, 'exactly. And when she smiled it was worse. Constipated headmistress pretending to enjoy a school pantomime.' Leonie splutters cider. 'And then the wind caught a bit of her hair – a chunk of it, really, because it was sprayed solid – and she said, "I don't want to look unkempt." So I took the scarf you gave me out of my hair—'

'My scarf?'

'That's right. From Dagenham.' It's been in Vee's camera bag ever since then, as much as a part of her kit as her light meter.

'You still have that?'

Vee nods. 'Of course,' she says, 'I use it to keep my hair off my face when it's windy.'

'Are you going to tell me you gave it to Thatcher?' Leonie's smile is getting wider by the second.

Vee nods, starting to laugh at the memory. 'She looked at me as though I was mad – if she had had tongs she would have taken it with those – so I said, if you tie this round your neck, it will blow in the wind, and people who look at the photograph will understand that it's windy, and that will explain why your hair might look different to the way it usually does. She looked at the scarf, and at the man holding the hat, as if she was thinking, *well, this is not at all what I expected to happen here*. And then she tied it round her neck. About two seconds later, the wind blew it up into her face, and I thought, that's it. She's going to walk off and I'm going to have to use one of the earlier shots. But she laughed, and she pulled the scarf down, away from her face, and when she let go, the wind pulled it out sideways, and that's when I took the shot.'

'So my scarf was trying to strangle Thatcher? And that's the money shot?'

'Absolutely,' Vee says. She had taken a few more photos, for appearances' sake and to use the rest of the frames on the film, but she'd known that she had it. And then she realises something. 'I didn't get it back. She didn't give the scarf back to me.'

'Typical bloody Thatcher,' Leonie says, 'I've always said she's only out for herself. Bloody cow.'

'You'd hope for better from a woman,' Vee laughs back, knowing as she says it that it's not as simple as that, and that Leonie is about to tell her so.

But all Leonie says is, 'I told you, you can't trust the patriarchy. And she's as much a part of it as every man in the House of Lords.'

Last time Leonie and Vee were together, in the run-up to the election, Vee had, foolishly, attempted to argue that a female PM could only be a good thing, even if she was a Tory. Things has got heated. Leonie doesn't look as though she has a lot of heat in her today, though.

'How's it going with the new book?' Neither Leonie's book about women's lives and sexuality, nor the next – about their relationship with food – have been published. And Leonie keeps writing.

Leonie knocks back her chaser. 'A publisher I've been talking to really likes it.'

'That's fantastic! This is the one about what beauty is?' Vee still reads everything Leonie writes. Even when they don't see each other much, the envelopes come. Vee reads the photocopied typewritten pages, writes Leonie a letter about what she thinks, and posts it back. So she has read this latest of Leonie's books about why all of women's thinking about their looks, and their bodies, is wrong. Her friend is passionate about how everyone has got so used to seeing everything from the male perspective that there is almost no way to get away from it. So women who dress in order not to be sexualised are just as oppressed as those who wear pencil skirts and kitten heels, in Leonie's view:

no makeup is as bad as a full face of the stuff because it is a reaction against the way patriarchal society expects women to look. Therefore, it is just as dictated by the way men think women should look. And as for weight, ideas of fat and thin, sexy and overweight-therefore-unsexy – Leonie sees oppression in this, the time it takes to consider food, to decide whether to eat it, to label it 'good' or 'bad'. Ursula, Leonie's sister, goes to Weight Watchers and is always trying to persuade Leonie to join her. After these conversations, Leonie does an impression of her sister, weighing carrots and writing down calories in a notebook, that makes Vee feel sorry for them both.

Leonie's outrage, her vision, her fury with the world in which she lives and with her sisters who don't seem to see what she sees – these things blister the page. But somehow without Leonie there in person to make it all make sense, without her wit and her quick, clever eyes, the words feel like too much, the argument too uncompromising, and Leonie's advice – to refuse the choices on offer to women, to refute them, to find a new way – doesn't actually help her when she needs to buy some new trousers.

But Leonie has been told, time and again, that this is why even the readers who want to love her work struggle with it. Even her articles for *Spare Rib* have been poorly received. Fen had suggested, tentatively, that women might interpret her writing as Leonie telling them how to look instead of the patriarchy dictating to them. The only place where she seems accessible is in her 'Dear John' columns for *This Month* magazine, which began as a three-month trial and have run without a break for more than a decade. Leonie has refused to listen to anyone who has tried to tell her that the tone she adopts in those articles is what will get her message across much more effectively than her more strident writing. She says she doesn't see why she should sugar the pill.

And then, last year, *Fat is a Feminist Issue* came out, and the putative interest that there had been from a publisher in Leonie's work on the body disappeared. Vee had argued that it was only a question of time and finding someone who wasn't afraid of her words. Leonie had, grudgingly, agreed to keep trying. And now, here they are. Vee really couldn't be more pleased. She wants the world to have access to Leonie's mind. And, more than that, she wants Leonie to be happy. 'You're going to be published! That's such good news, Leonie.'

'I'm not going to be published,' Leonie says. 'They said no.'

'Why?'

Leonie shrugs, chins wobbling and shoulders sagging. 'I'm a polemicist. Not an apologist.'

Vee nods. She's just about to try to point out that there might be another way, an in-between, when Leonie adds, 'Or I might not be good enough.'

'Leonie! No! You know you deserve this. It's like you said. They publish a few women and then they think they've done. But—'

Leonie cuts across her with a shrug, 'I even tried Virago. They don't want me.'

'What? Why?'

'They don't like me. I'm not their kind of feminist.'

Vee has a shelf of Virago books. She hasn't read all of them, admittedly, but what Leonie says seems unlikely. There seems to be room for all voices. Surely that's the point.

'Did they say that?'

Leonie gives another shrug, one that Vee recognises as meaning 'I decline to answer', then says, 'Anyway. I'm pregnant.'

Vee feels her face struggle to hide her shock, mask it with something closer to surprise. 'You're having a baby?' Oh, Christ. 'I mean – are you going to keep it?'

'I am,' Leonie says.

'That's—' Vee cannot stop her gaze from landing on the empty glasses. 'That's surprising.'

'I found out too late to do anything else,' Leonie says, 'which means there's no point in stopping now.' Vee notices the cigarette ends in the ashtray. She hopes they aren't Leonie's, but they probably are. Still, women need to respect women in their choices. And the pack on the table are menthol cigarettes, at least.

'I suppose you don't want to commit to a book until you know how it all works out.'

Leonie shakes her head. 'When I said I was keeping it,' she says, 'I just meant, I was too late to get rid of it. I would have done, but I realised too late. My periods are, like, crazy.'

A man who has just sat down at the next table double-takes as he overhears this, and raises a disapproving/amused eyebrow at his friend. Leonie tips back her chair, flicks his pint over and says in a voice that's a growl, 'Women bleed. Be grateful.'

'Bitch,' the man says, jumping out of the way of the beer pouring onto the floor, then, as it hits his shoes, 'Fat cow.'

'You betcha,' Leonie says. This is why Vee should never, ever put her camera away. The man's face, outraged and, beneath, perplexed as to how he is powerless in this moment, is a picture, except it isn't, because she's missed it.

'So, are you thinking of putting it up for adoption?'

Leonie rubs at her eyes, then yawns. Vee suspects she's hiding tears, and makes sure not to look. If Leonie is going to talk to her about this, she needs to keep things cool, steady; if her friend suspects her of being emotional she'll shut the conversation down as swiftly as she knocked over that pint.

Leonie concentrates on folding up the empty crisp packet. 'I suppose. It's a faff. I might leave it on a step somewhere.' Oh, no. This can't be happening. Leonie might be right about there being too many children in the world, but—

Leonie puts a hand over Vee's. 'Your face! Of course I wouldn't leave it on a step. Just because I don't want a baby doesn't make me—' she pauses, 'subhuman.'

'You might feel differently about it when it's here,' Vee offers. Even as she's saying it, she knows these are the wrong words. But she doesn't know how to be helpful. Leonie does everything differently.

'Why would I?'

'Well, people do.' Any other conversation like this would be about maternal instinct, hormones, bonds, but Leonie wouldn't accept that, and Vee is not sure that she does, either. She closes her mouth again but it's too late. Leonie has read her thoughts, or seen the M for 'motherhood' her mouth had been beginning to make, and extrapolated from there. Photographers have to be ordinary, uninteresting, if they are to fade far enough from the subject's notice to get them to be their true selves. But Vee would like to say one surprising thing, sometime.

'Maternal instinct? Which makes women no longer want to leave the home or do anything except serve their families? Fuck that,' Leonie says.

'I didn't say anything!'

'You were going to.' There really is no point in arguing with Leonie, because – well, because she is Leonie, but also, because she's right. 'There's no such thing as maternal instinct. It's just another bullshit construct designed to keep women down and I'm not buying it.'

Vee nods and takes a drink. She has no desire for a child, certainly, or for the relationship she would have assumed would go with it.

Leonie adds, 'There are some primitive tribes where people don't know who children belong to. They are born and then they're fed by whichever tit is closest. Nobody can tell you who came out of who else.'

Vee sometimes wonders whether there's a tribe to fit every argument. She doesn't say so, though. She doesn't want to talk about hypothetical babies. She needs to know more about the one at the table, midway through its second pint of cider.

'When's it due?'

'In three months. I just found out last week. I can't get a late abortion. Don't fancy throwing myself down the stairs.'

This has to be, at least partly, bravado. 'But—'

'But what?'

'I don't know, Leonie. Would the father want it?'

'No. And why would I give it to a man?'

'If there's no such thing as maternal instinct, why wouldn't you?'

Leonie smiles, such a broad warm smile, and Vee wishes that she saw it more often. 'I always forget you can be fun to be with, Ms Big-Shot Photographer.'

'Thank you.' Vee bobs her head, to show she knows this is well meant, and Leonie sits back in her chair. She's definitely pink around the eyes. Vee squeezes her arm, smiles into her face. But Leonie looks away.

'Would you want it?' she asks, a moment later.

'Want what?'

'The baby. If you want it, you can have it.'

'Are you serious?' Leonie looks serious. This can't be how it works, legally, Vee thinks, but that's hardly the point.

'Why not?' Leonie lights a cigarette. 'You're my friend. When we first met, you were all set to marry whatshisname. Don't tell me you wouldn't have been up the stick within a year of the wedding.'

'I don't think that's fair.' Leonie doesn't mean it. It's just her way of dealing with a world that she feels is unfair to her. 'I didn't know any better. I'd only just met you.'

Leonie nods. After a moment of silence she asks, 'So, do you?'

Vee was up late last night sorting out her invoices, up early this morning to get ready for the Thatcher shoot. She must be misunderstanding. Leonie can't mean . . . 'Do I what?'

Leonie takes a breath, says slowly, 'Do you want the baby? You can afford it. Nannies and whatever. Or you can just take it to work with you. It wouldn't really make an impact on your life.'

No, she does mean it. This conversation really is happening. Vee takes a breath, a drink, a bite of sausage roll, just for the sake of making some space in her head and her heart. Does she want a baby? Need one? Her dad sometimes talks about how she'll be 'all on her own when I've gone'. She doesn't think she minds. But she closes her eyes and thinks about the space in her body where, theoretically, her child could grow. It feels the same as it always does: a blank, rather than a yearning. Vee opted out of relationships somewhere around 1975, when the man she was seeing said that she loved her camera more than she loved him. She'd protested, but he was right. Darkrooms were better than dinner. Publication was better than sex. Being able to buy her own house with money she had earned was the proudest moment of her life. And, then, she had Leonie to love.

Vee has a vision of herself on a shoot, baby strapped to her front in one of those sling things, or maybe in a pram next to her, wailing and waving its arms as she tries to get a CEO to drop their professional guard, or a woman famous for her looks to stop posing and just be. It wouldn't work. And anyway, if she did want a baby, she'd decide. Not hope that someone would give her a child the way her dad loads her car with the extra potatoes from the allotment. She says, gently, 'I'm like you, Leonie. I don't want – I've never really wanted a child. I just assumed that I would because that's what the world told me.' Thinks: you're the one who showed me how to think differently about all that. She almost says so, but she doesn't trust her voice to keep steady if she tries. And what they really need to talk about is Leonie. 'You're really serious? About giving it away?'

'Oh, I'm serious, sister. What would I do with this?' She puts a hand on her belly, briefly, and then takes it away, as though the child within has shaken her off.

'And you'd give it to me?'

'If you wanted it. So long as you promised not to give it to fucking Thatcher.' Vee laughs, despite herself. But another feeling follows. In three months from now she could be responsible for another human being. If she wanted to be.

The old, gentle smile appears on Leonie's face. She's the woman Vee met at Dagenham, less scary than she is now, less unpredictable. 'What is it, Vee?'

'I don't know.' Vee is flooded with something. It's definitely not need; she has never wanted a child. This feeling is more a spinning sense of the magnitude of all she has so casually declined. No relationship, and therefore no child, because she has photographs to take. And here she is: photographing the Prime Minister, known and respected in her industry, working to support her sisters, going home alone, and not minding. Society wants her to think that she is lonely, but she isn't. She's solitary. She's an observer. She's stepping outside the assumptions that the patriarchy makes about what women need. It's not the same as being lonely.

Best to point the lens away from this. 'You'd give me your child? Really?'

'Isn't it better to decide myself where it should go? Instead of leaving it on a hospital step?' Leonie indicates her belly, which

Vee can see now is a different shape, even under her friend's shapeless, too-big top, the fat that she seems to have deliberately cultivated, over the years, to make a point.

'Leonie. Those are not the choices! Adoption agencies would match—'

Leonie starts to laugh, a great shaking sound: 'Your face. I'm not an idiot. I have heard of adoption agencies. I'll give it to one of them. They can sort it out.' Leonie sighs, and looks straight into Vee's eyes for the first time since she told her she was pregnant. Her gaze has been not quite direct, up until then. 'I just didn't want it to go to a complete fucking idiot.'

Tread gently, Vee. 'You do care then? A bit?'

'I care about the world. And the world doesn't need another kid brought up to be an entitled patriarchal idiot. I should be able to stop that from happening. If I can find a non-entitled, non-patriarchal, non-idiot.'

'I can see the sense in that.' But, as far as Vee can tell, Leonie thinks most of the people on the planet are in thrall to the patriarchy. And she must feel something for this baby. There might be no such thing as maternity, but surely there is human-ness?

'You really don't fancy it?'

'No.' Vee is sure of herself this time. 'No, I definitely don't. But I'm glad you don't think I'm a tool of the patriarchy.'

'Not all of the time. Do you want another drink?' Leonie hauls herself to standing.

Vee can leave dropping off the films until tomorrow. Leonie needs her more. When her friend comes back from the bar – more crisps, more cider – she asks, 'Did you ever read *Fear of Flying*?'

'I'm not sure. I've read *The Women's Room*.' Vee starts to search her memory for what she thought about it. She remembers it was a fat book, and she read it on a flight to Kuala Lumpur, when she was on the way to Australia to photograph Barry Humphreys as

Dame Edna Everage for the *Spectator*. She thinks she might have got bored somewhere in the middle of the story. It had definitely made her glad to be single.

But Leonie doesn't want to talk about *The Women's Room*. 'Well, if this' – she nods downwards – 'is a girl, I'm going to call her Erica. After Erica Jong.'

'Who?' Vee definitely knows the name. Leonie narrows her lips, her eyes, somewhere between impatience and disappointment in Vee's failure to keep up. 'She wrote *Fear of Flying*. Which I gave to you when it came out in 1973. And you definitely didn't read it, because I found it in the flat when you moved out. It hadn't been opened.'

'Sorry.'

'Sure you are.' Leonie leans back, and says, as though she's delivering a great punchline, 'If you'd read it you'd know I'm calling this kid Erica because she is a result of a zipless fuck.'

Vee almost asks whether she knows who the father is, but she doesn't trust herself to do it without sounding prim. Instead, she offers, 'I can help you to find an adoption agency. If you like.'

'Thanks. But there's no hurry. I'm going to talk to my sister. She might be useful for once in her life.' Ursula, organised and serene, seems to Vee to be exactly the sort of person to deal with adoption agencies on Leonie's behalf. The responsibility for Leonie that was starting to descend on her dissolves.

16 May 1979

Pimlico, London

Vic Whistler asked for the shoot to be at his home, and Vee agreed, not least because she's been asked to shoot DJs at work before and the lighting in a radio studio is not impossible, but it's not easy. Small, sealed, dark-ish spaces are a pain to light, even if you like using flash, and there's never enough room for the kit. So she's done shoots outside the buildings, with the signs in the background, and there have been interruptions and distractions, plenty of them, not least from the young women who see DJs as some sort of accessible pop star. It's taken twice as long as it needs to, and she's gone home feeling ragged and unsure about what she's got. There's always been a good photograph in there, but she likes to feel more certain.

Vic opens the door in a shirt open to the waist; a medallion sits mid-chest, nestling among curling hair. He's tall. His smile is white as bones. 'The famous Veronica Moon,' he says, and reaches out a hand to shake hers, 'a delight to meet you. I see you even made my friend Squires look presentable, and he's got a face like a baboon's rear end.'

Vee has listened to Whistler's show twice this week, to get a sense of what to expect. He's the next big thing, hence the profile in *Smash Hits* and the cover shot she's been sent to take. She can't see it, personally – his sense of humour seems quite puerile to her, and the music too much of a mix to make comfortable background listening, but maybe that's the point. (Surely, at thirty, she isn't old enough to be unable to understand the young?)

'Could I have a look around?' she asks.

'Be my guest.' He follows her down the hall of his Pimlico flat. There's a balcony, overlooking the river. If she positions him right, London will swell and fade behind him; nothing too dominant, but a sense of the city he has, apparently, won over. She's pulled her hair back in a bandanna, seeing as Thatcher has her scarf. It could be that a crew-cut is the way to go. Or something a bit less extreme. Chrissie Hynde, who she photographed for *Melody Maker* not so long ago, had something good going on – gamine and unfussy.

He's still right behind her. 'You've a great view here,' she says. 'Shall we make the most of it?'

'Is that what your boyfriends say?' Vee turns away, pretending not to hear – Leonie is good at confrontation, at flicking over pints and giving fingers, but Vee can never quite dare and anyway, she's at work and she has a job to do. She gets out her camera, removes the lens cap, palms it into the back pocket of her jeans.

'Could you stand with your back to the river, and square on to the door?'

'Sure,' he says, and moves onto the balcony, sliding his arms along the top rail behind him, shoulders back, pelvis out. Vee retreats into the doorway, drops to one knee – she's expecting a blow-job joke, is already braced to not react, but he surprises her by keeping his mouth shut. When she looks through the viewfinder she sees why. He's nailed a smile to his face, a toothy and meant-to-be-seductive leer which he's clearly going to hold until he hears the shutter click. She takes the shot. The difficulty here is going to be getting him not to pose.

She takes half a dozen frames to let him get it out of his system, and then she really gets to work. She asks him about the view and he explains what's visible; every time he glances towards her, to see that she's listening, she takes another photograph, catches his face both animated and relaxed. She thinks the finished shots will have him looking like the sort of person he probably was, once, before he found the persona he's living. He'll almost certainly complain when he sees the magazine cover.

She shoots a film, then they move into his living room, where she needs to stand on a dining chair so that she can tuck the dark velvet curtains up and out of the way. Under the pretence of steadying her – 'Be careful, darling, you've got precious equipment there and I couldn't stand for it to be damaged!' – he holds her by the hips, hard, then, when she's stepped down from the chair, puts one of his hands on her buttocks. She steps, forward, away, and asks him to sit down; stands on a chair above him, looking down, and shoots a few more frames. There's nothing good about these photographs – he looks terrible, squat and leeringly foreshortened, but that's precisely why she enjoys taking them. A couple of seated shots – he opens his shirt a little more, and she realises it's because he has a nipple pierced, and wants it to be noticed, recorded. And suddenly she's sick of him, of this whole stupid game, but still she thanks him and compliments him on being a good sitter, because she needs to keep the calls from the picture editors coming in.

She drops the films at the lab. And then she goes home, takes a good, hot shower, and thinks about calling Leonie. But she doesn't have the energy, tonight; and if she tells her about the DJ, although Leonie will make no excuses for him, she'll have no patience with Vee's behaviour, either. Plus, Vee is totally out of her depth with the pregnancy and the adoption. She's certain

that she did the right thing. Being a parent feels like too important a job to take place on the fly, around the edges, although of
course every parent had a life before. Vee is not a person who is
capable of that.

She'll leave it for another couple of days to call. Just until
she's got a little more to give. Just until she's sure she's thought
everything through, and there's nothing else she can suggest.

Just in case she changes her mind, and decides she does want
Leonie's baby, after all.

June 1979

This Month magazine

Leonie Barratt: Letters from a Feminist

Our monthly column from the front line of the Battle of the Sexes

Dear John,

I know what you're thinking.

And not because I'm a witch, or have that 'feminine intuition' that is one of the many crocks of crap that is talked about women, who have been socialised to notice everything in order to be compliant and stay out of trouble.

I know what you're thinking because you and I have been in touch for many years, now, and I know how your mind works.

You're thinking: 'A female prime minister! Finally, something that will please Leonie Barratt! She's been nagging and moaning about equality of opportunity for all these years and now she's got it. Even Leonie cannot argue with a female prime minister.'

Well, John, you're wrong. You don't know my mind as well as I know yours.

I'm not pleased.

Except in one respect. We do have a woman representing the country. That's a good thing, even if it is way overdue.

But really, that's all I can get excited about.

Let's put aside the fact that this is worthy of comment – that 'female PM' is being trumpeted left, right and centre, because it's an exception (a first in Europe, too), and that's the opposite of how it should be. Prime Minister is a job in which what you're keeping in your underwear is irrelevant.

Let's ignore the symbolism and talk about the person.

We already know the cut of Mrs Thatcher's jib. We know she is a Milk Snatcher. (Although I do wonder, if she was a man, whether she would have a more manly soubriquet. Plot Hatcher? Cash Catcher?) She talks about economics in the guise of a humble housewife. I've heard she flirts her way to getting what she wants. She can only be a female PM by making sure no one forgets she's a woman. And that's the opposite of equality.

I'm seeing magazine articles about her being a mother and 'juggling' career and family life. I'm seeing questions in interviews about the dynamics of her marriage. Did we have those articles about Ted Heath? Funnily enough, we didn't. I'm going to stick my neck out and guess that, if the next PM is a man, he won't be bothered by these questions, either.

So although a female prime minister may, at first sight, be a good thing, John, let's not forget: while we spend time talking about what she wears, how she manages her family, and any other damn thing we did not discuss about Heath and don't consider when it comes to Jimmy Carter, we do not have equality.

While a woman in power has to coerce, cajole and flirt behind the scenes to get her way, we do not have equality.

While women are expected to show their power by behaving like men in public, we do not have equality.

And while we're on the subject of how men behave, John – do you never get tired of all of the things your conditioning compels you to do? I know, individually, men can be respectful and human, and not feel they have to swing their balls round everywhere. But put you together, or put you on the TV or the radio, or put you in any position of authority, and you cannot help yourselves.

In the last week I've had meetings with a doctor (male), an MP (male), and a solicitor (male). Every one of them has interrupted me or talked over the top of me. I've been to a family meal at which two men and three women were present. Guess whose voices dominated the conversation. Do you never think: I might listen, for a change? Do you never wonder why it is that you discount what a woman is saying before she's even finished saying it?

I'm going to empathise, now, John, even though I don't see why I should have to. Women only need empathy because it's the only weapon they have for staying out of the way of fists and fury, or getting what they want from men who don't think they need to pay attention to her indoors.

If I were you, I might not always enjoy the way I'm expected to be. I might not want to cry only at sporting events; I might be anxious about neighbours assuming I know how to help them jump-start their cars. There could be mornings when a day of shouting my opinions louder than other men's opinions might not be what I want to do.

But if I were you, I'd probably think that was a price worth paying for all the other advantages I get from having a penis in a patriarchal society. I'd square my shoulders, clear my throat, and wiggle my Adam's apple around for the sake of the extra wages and the right to be deferred to in most situations.

I can't blame you, although it drives me crazy – sometimes, I think, literally insane. I feel like the only person who sees not only the mountain of bullshit but the fact that it is being produced by a great big bull. My sisters shovel the bullshit out of their way, valiantly, every damn day, and I feel as though I am the only one who sees the bull and thinks we should deal with that. No bull, no shit. That's what I'm trying so hard to make you see.

Our problem is: there's no reason for you to change, because life is pretty sweet for you.

And it just got sweeter, because the next time a woman talks to you about our sexist society (you will probably think she is complaining, and if you have had a very hard day of shouting and swinging your balls around, you might even accuse her of nagging – in which case, shame on you, John), you have a new card to play.

You can say, 'What are you talking about? We have a woman prime minister.'

And actually, Margaret Thatcher has done nothing to make things better for women, and there's no sign that she will.

So no, I'm not pleased that we have a female PM. She does nothing for feminism. But she is probably going to do quite a lot for you.

Until next time,

Leonie

29 March 2018

It's ten days since Mississippi introduced the US's strictest abortion laws: no termination after fifteen weeks.

Four weeks until exhibition opening

'I've packed Tom's bag,' Marcus says, 'I think everything he needs is in there.'

'I'm sure.' Erica smiles, but she won't thank him, won't praise him. Why should she? They have agreed to be equal.

But Marcus looks hurt. Erica's determination to be a more active feminist has, in the weeks since the march, and despite her best intentions, involved a lot of carping at him. She needs time. Time and space to think. And the weeks are going by and she still she has neither, because she is so busy marking, writing and rewriting exhibition notes, and enabling other people to look after her child. And reassuring Marcus. Change takes time, she reminds herself.

'Are you OK?' Marcus asks, and his tone tells her that he's finding this shift in the balance of their marriage as hard as she is. 'You have to talk to me.'

Erica takes a breath. 'I thought I could be a mother without having to be' – she gestures around her, at the endlessly messy kitchen and the failings she cannot help but feel it implies – 'all this. I thought it would be . . . different.'

'Are you ready for today? Is there anything I can do for you?' He's working from home, once he's handed Tom over to his mother. Erica knows that he'll disappear into the den with his laptop without giving the washing a thought. She envies him as much as it makes her angry.

'I'm set,' she says.

'But?'

'I keep thinking, the day of the march, Vee had a headache before we went, and she asked me to bring her some painkillers. They were fairly serious prescription drugs. I want to ask her about them.' Erica has tried to remember the name on the box so she could look them up, but so much happened that day – the last time she saw Vee – that she can't recall it.

'She's old, though, isn't she?'

'Well, yes—'

'So something's got to give at some point. It's probably nothing major.'

'I suppose.'

Marcus takes breakfast dishes from the table and starts to load them into the dishwasher. Erica would have rinsed them first. She doesn't say so.

It seems to Erica, more and more, that while for her, little Tom has made her think of all the places life is vulnerable, all the ways she is dying, Marc seems to have taken fatherhood and used it to make himself taller, straighter, more sure of himself.

He looks up, smiles. 'If you go now, you'll catch the 9.15.'

29 March 2018

THERE ISN'T A HEADACHE TODAY. Not much of one, anyway. The medication that Vee is on isn't pleasant, but the reflexology she had yesterday brought her some rest. She is looking forward to Erica's arrival. She's been through all of the photographs now, everything either passed onto Erica, filed with her agency, or thrown away. Everything except the most private photographs, anyway. There are two boxes of documents but she can't face them: small type, faded printing, make her worry that she will use up her eyes, somehow.

So she goes to her bookshelves. She'll divide the contents into piles for the charity shop, Erica, and – well, maybe the university where she used to teach might want some of her books.

When she takes *Fear of Flying* from the shelf she feels instantly vertiginous. She would have put her reaction down to the power of suggestion, had she not loved every single plane journey that she ever took, nose to glass like a child. So that can't be why Jong's novel is making her queasy. Strange. She can't remember whether she ever read it. On the inside front cover, in Leonie's neat, sloping hand, is written 'To V, from L, with love'. Leonie gave her so many books. Leonie gave her so much. She thought she was grateful at the time, but she is so much more grateful now that she looks back on her life and sees Leonie so large in it. Oh, everything is sad.

And then Erica knocks.

She is so nearly the image of Leonie. Remembering hurts, but it's different to the griping, unsettled ache of the medication.

This is a blazing pain, as though Leonie had died yesterday, as though Vee had been the one who killed her. She hears herself inhale, the noise a warm rush in her head, and then she opens the door.

Erica looks up, waves her phone: 'I've been re-reading my aunt's "Dear John" columns,' she says.

Vee smiles. 'Come in. What do you think of them?'

Erica walks through to the living room, puts a folder on the table, and turns to look at Vee. Her face says she's filtering through words, finding the best one. Vee always liked this, about academics. 'She's quite – brutal.'

That's disappointing. 'Really? She was sharp, which is different. We said what we meant, in those days.'

Erica laughs – Leonie's laugh, from the days before she only laughed in sarcasm or in spite – and the pain of loss crackles bright in Vee again. 'And you don't say what you mean now?'

And now there is a sudden jab in Vee's head, a reminder maybe. 'Not always.' She adds, 'Thank you for taking care of me, before the march. I appreciate it.'

There's the slightest flicker of shock in the muscles in Erica's face. Her eyebrows rise and fall, her head moves backwards, just a fraction, and Vee thinks: *when did I become the person who shocks people when she thanks them?* This change could be due to the tumour, of course, but her heart – and she has always trusted her heart, and has no reason not to now – says, quietly, that she became rude long before she became ill. 'Manners and a smile cost nothing,' her dad used to say. He'd be unimpressed by what she has become, retrospective exhibition at the Photographers' Gallery or not. She closes her eyes, sees him loading her possessions into a borrowed van to help her move to London, even though he would rather she stay in Colchester with him. She needs to do better by Erica. That will be something.

'I was glad I could help,' Erica says.

'I'm sorry I couldn't do more, at the march.' She'd watched as Erica was taken away, but experience told her that there was nothing to be done but wait for news. She'd emailed Erica that evening, saying she hoped that she was OK, and then she'd gone to bed, unable to do anything else with her worn-out body and the steadily expanding pain in her head. The distance from action to consequence is ever shortening. The march was too much for her, and she paid for it, the next day lost in painkillers and half-sleep, cold rum and hot toast. But she didn't care. It was worth it, to be back on the battleground. And to take someone to their first march.

'It sounds selfish, but I quite enjoyed being arrested. Well, detained. Marcus wasn't impressed.'

Vee is seeing her mind as a roll of film, full of a lifetime's worth of photographs, now overexposed to light, the images it held eaten away. And yet, however much of her brain the disease has destroyed, there are things that she is still sure of. And one of them is that Erica is not happy. There's something brittle about the way she talks about her family, and her emails arrive late at night, when any sane person would be asleep, or with their loved ones, if their loved ones are nearby. Help a sister out, Leonie says, as clearly as if she was here. Vee will try to be kind.

Erica puts her hand on the file. 'These are the latest versions of the introductory texts for the exhibition sections, and the updated layout. I've got a week before they are submitted to the gallery for sign-off, and at that point we won't be able to make any more changes, so I thought we should go through, and—' She looks tired, the skin under her eyes a little blue, the way a child's would be.

'Or,' Vee interrupts, 'I could sign them off right now, and we could go and have a coffee.'

'You want to read them now? There's quite a lot—'

'No, Erica, I don't want to read them. I've seen enough of what you've already done with them. You ask intelligent questions and you listen to the answers. I—' She hesitates before the next word, because she's not sure that she's ever said it, to anyone, before. 'I trust you.'

Erica nods then exhales. 'But – don't you care?'

'I don't matter,' Vee says. She realises as soon as the words are out that it's the wrong way to put it, because Erica looks crushed. 'I mean . . . the point of photography isn't that the camera tells the truth, but that people look at images and interpret them. You've looked at me and you've interpreted me. You've done a good job.'

Vee thinks of all she's done, quietly, that she hopes no one will ever know about. That's her real legacy. She touches Erica on the shoulder. (Why does she keep touching people? She's never wanted to before.) 'Let's go out for a coffee. There's a cafe on the corner.'

She moves to get her coat – it wasn't actually a question – but Erica hesitates. 'Before we go, I want to know about your headaches, Vee. Your medication looks as though they're something serious.'

Vee inhales, exhales, and something starts to throb, behind her ear. She should probably be honest, even if she doesn't want to say it. 'Well, I have a glioblastoma. It's a brain cancer. The prognosis isn't good. I had it first in 2007. I was lucky then, because it was possible to remove it.' Her fingertips go to her skull, as if magnetised, feel along the scarline behind her left ear where her hair grows in kinks. 'It was always going to come back. It was only ever a question of time.' She hears how her voice gets caught on the words 'come back' and 'time'.

'I'm sorry.' Erica looks upset, so Vee looks away. She's not sure which of them she's sparing. 'You can't have surgery again?'

Vee shakes her head, not sure if it hurts. 'Not this time. It's inoperable.' She shrugs. 'I got an extra ten years.' This time she manages to make it sound more matter-of-fact than it feels.

'That's something,' Erica sounds unsure. 'Did you – has it been a good ten years?'

Vee laughs. (Is she laughing more? Is that a change? Does it matter? No. So long as her eyes keep working, nothing matters.) 'I didn't find a new gratitude for life. I tried. I travelled again. I got into . . .' Oh, what's the word, what's the word? Stupid, stupid tumour. 'Philosophy. No. Not that. I gave money to things. Set up some funds, some prizes.'

'Philanthropy,' Erica offers.

'Yes.' Her tongue doesn't want to go around the word; she doesn't make it try. If she has to lose something before she dies, let it be words.

'I haven't read anything about that.'

'It's all anonymous,' Vee says. At least she has still got some vocabulary.

Erica nods. 'I'm sorry, Vee.' She is wiping tears from her eyes, in that ridiculous way that women wearing mascara do, looking up and sliding her finger along the skin under her bottom lashes.

Erica had suspected, of course she had. The headaches, the swinging moods, the drugs, the objections to noise and light – they were always going to add up to this, if she had chosen to do the maths.

And yet Vee seems so calm, holding it all in or dealing with it or whatever she is doing. She is striding ahead down the street, looking for all the world like – well, like someone who doesn't have a brain tumour. Although, close up, there's a sallowness to her skin that Erica should have noticed, a dullness in her eyes that doesn't speak to health. If Tom looked like that, Erica would be torn between putting him to bed and taking him to the doctor. A cold shudder runs through her at the very thought of her baby with a brain tumour.

Vee walks much faster than Erica. Maybe Erica needs DMs instead of these stupid boots, which she had thought might make her feel like a woman again, rather than a chewed-up mother. She could probably do with being more like Vee.

The cafe is noisy: a hissing, bean-rattling coffee machine, chatter, a baby half-crying, and wood floor bouncing the sound around.

'You sit down,' Erica says.

Vee nods. 'I'd like a coffee and a cheese scone. I can't remember when I last had a cheese scone.'

'What sort of coffee?'

'Coffee.'

Erica orders two flat whites and two cheese scones. Three weeks ago she would have been worried about eating a scone, because there's still half a stone of baby weight she hasn't lost. But the march changed her. Vee is changing her, Leonie's words are changing her. She's done with worrying about the calories in a cheese scone.

Vee has found a table in the corner. At the next table along sits a couple, hands joined, a copy of *Love's Labour's Lost* between them; Erica can only see the back of his head, but she is animated, laughing, saying something about apples. It's cheering and depressing in equal measure. When did Erica last see a play, or hold Marcus's hand over a table? (When did she want to?) And why is she even thinking about such things – such trivial things – when the woman opposite her is dying?

'Your photographs,' she says, because she needs to say something about them, 'they are so important. To everyone.' Not least because Vee pointed her camera, when she could, at the unnoticed, and the unimportant. That's what makes her Greenham archive so special. Everyone who was there knew that they were all changing the world: Vee captured that like no one else. And those women in the shelters, beaten by their husbands, had no recourse to the law, but they had a record of what had happened to them with Vee's unflinching images. Erica had almost cried when she'd unpacked the envelopes Vee had couriered over to her: contact sheets of unidentified women, photographed with bruises flowering across their faces. And more, from later, when Vee returned and took photographs when these victims were happy and whole again.

Vee makes a gesture that Erica has learned means 'I choose not to engage with that': a slight pushing out of the lower lip, a dip of the head a fraction to her left. Instead of replying, she asks, 'And what did you think of your first taste of activism?'

'It was – I can't believe I did it. I'm the most law-abiding person there is.'

'You look more cheerful than you have done all morning,' Vee says, with a smile that tells Erica that it's OK to not talk about dying.

Erica laughs, a release of tension as much as anything else. 'It was weird. I was so angry when I thought that policeman was having a go. And the next thing I knew I was in handcuffs.'

'They didn't charge you, though?'

'No.' She often thinks of those few hours, the fear and the excitement, the waiting with the other women and the smell of old sweat and industrial cleaning fluid, but it's nothing, really, in the scheme of what people like Vee and Leonie did. 'It must all seem tame to you,' she says.

'I never got arrested,' Vee says, 'at least, I don't think I did. There are – holes, I suppose you would call them, in my memories.'

'Holes? That must be awful.'

'Well, you don't know what you don't know,' Vee says, her hand going to her head again, the same place as before, where the scar must be, 'and it's been a long time, so I'm used to it. But there are things that I just have absolutely no recollection of. My father's death. I know he died, and when, because I've got the certificate. It was a few months before – before Leonie. And I miss him, the way I would if I remembered his dying. But there's just . . . a space.'

'That is—' but there's no word significant enough. Weird/ awful/terrible are words that Erica probably uses most days, when talking about things that are nowhere near as bad as that.

'Yes.' Vee nods, slowly; it seems she's treating her head with caution. 'It is.'

'You might not have been arrested,' Erica says, 'but you were definitely more of an activist than me.' As soon as that 'were' is in the air she wants to snatch it, swallow it, turn it into 'are'. 'You are—'

'I talked a good game,' Vee says, showing no sign of caring about Erica mixing her tenses up and really, why should she? '. . . once Leonie had taught me the words. And I marched and shouted. Really, though, taking photographs was my activism, and then it became my career. Your aunt called me a pimp, once. Or it could have been a whore. Or both.' She laughs, 'I was furious at the time but she was right.'

'Those are awful things to say, though.'

'Leonie said a lot of awful things.'

'That's what my mother always said. She said Aunt Leonie never thought before she opened her mouth, and the things that came out were never kind.'

'I don't remember it being like that,' Vee says. 'They didn't have a lot in common. And your mother didn't buy into a lot of Leonie's views.'

Erica laughs, 'I can't imagine Leonie let that go.'

'No. and I think Ursula was pretty determined, too. Leonie walked all over me – she was always late, she cancelled things – but she did as Ursula told her.' Vee puts her cup down, and half-misses; it sits awry in the saucer. The expression on her face changes, from sure to hesitant.

'Vee? Are you OK?'

Vee looks straight at her – she has such wise eyes – 'I'd forgotten. Ursula once came to give Leonie a lift somewhere. They might have been going to their mother's. Leonie tried to get out of it. Ursula looked at her and said, "I spent yesterday afternoon getting twenty-one seven-year-olds to their swimming lesson and back. Do you really think you're going to get out of this?" I thought Leonie was going to flip, but the two of them just started laughing. And Leonie did what she was told.'

Erica laughs, 'That sound plausible. From my mother, I mean.'

'It drove Leonie crazy, that her own sister wasn't a feminist. We thought we could change everything. We didn't understand why all women wouldn't get on board. Not just women like Ursula. We had no idea of how privileged we were. Women working two jobs can't come on marches. Single parents can't always afford babysitters so they can come to meetings. Women who weren't white might not have wanted to be the only different face. We made a lot of assumptions. And we definitely didn't see what a long road we were on. We didn't imagine we would ever end up with people like you.'

She doesn't say it like an insult, but Erica feels it as one. She thinks of the 'Doctor' title she doesn't insist on, the fact that she is the one with babysitters' numbers in her phone. She would apologise, if she didn't know that Vee would tell her off for it.

Vee picks up her cup and sets it carefully in the centre of the saucer. 'I miss Leonie,' she says quietly, and she looks straight at Erica, as if to tell her that she knows what she is saying, that she is breaking her own rule by offering to talk about her friend like this.

'I don't remember much about her.' Erica speaks quietly, too, as though loudness might scare Vee away from this conversation. Oh, how she longs to know what really happened, on the day Leonie died.

'She really wasn't part of your life?'

'Not really. She and my mother argued a lot. My mother said that for someone who had no maternal instinct, she definitely had a lot of advice for her about all the ways that she was going wrong.'

Vee laughs, a sudden, sweet sound. 'Leonie was never afraid of having opinions.'

'I never used to understand why my mother got so annoyed with her. I do now.' Erica thinks of her mother-in-law's interventions, kindly meant, no doubt, and how they make her both furious and desolate with the loss of her own mother, over and over.

Vee looks straight at her again, and Erica feels as though her photograph is being taken, her image held, just by the older woman's gaze. The cafe around them gets louder. Erica is as self-conscious as she would be if she was actually being photographed. She sips at her coffee, for something to do, although she doesn't want the rest of it; it's got too cold and there's a bitterness in the flavour that doesn't taste quite right to her.

'You know people thought you had died? Or committed suicide?' she says, because she has often thought about this, and there might never be a better time to mention it. 'After the photograph of Leonie's death was published, I mean, and it all came out.'

Vee laughs, harsh and quick. 'They might have thought it. They didn't consider it. I still live in the same house I did when Leonie died. I was never hiding. I was just – private.'

'No one tried to contact you?'

'I wouldn't say that. I unplugged the phone for weeks, and my neighbours complained about the noise of the knocking at the door. But I didn't answer and they stopped trying, soon enough. Went away and speculated about suicide.'

Vee puts her hand to the side of her head, a sharp action that suggests a sudden pain.

'Are you OK? Do you need anything?'

'I'm – I'm fine,' Vee says, but her smile is odd, dislocated. Her skin has gone a pantone paler in the last two minutes. Erica should get her home.

'Let's go,' she says, and Vee rises without a word.

27 March 2018

Late afternoon

Vee is walking along the Thames Path. When days are limited, a morning walk may as well take place in the evening. She can't afford to be fussy about time of day anymore.

She hasn't got far, though, when the dizziness hits, sudden as lightning. She gropes for balance, grabbing for a fence, and closes her eyes.

But that makes it worse. She feels sick, scared, as though the world is flipping her over and over, and she cannot tell if she is standing or falling, standing or falling. Is this how it will be, if she does go blind? And is it normal to be more afraid of blindness than death, or is it the tumour that makes her think so? Surely any life should be better than none?

She opens her eyes, slowly, and almost cries out with relief when she sees the river, the sky, her boots on the path and the sun on the water. And the couple hurrying towards her. She must look like a heart attack in action. The man, slightly ahead of the woman, takes her under the arm. 'What's happened?' he asks.

'I'm just dizzy,' Vee says, 'I'll be fine in a minute. Thank you.'

'Are you sure?' the woman asks.

'I just need a minute.'

'I'm calling an ambulance.' The man is speaking to the woman with him, not to Vee. He pulls out his phone.

Vee collects all of her breath. She is not sure of many things but she knows there are plenty of times when she has felt worse over the last few weeks. And if she isn't OK, the last place she wants to be is in the company of a man with straining shirt buttons and hot beer breath.

'No,' she says, 'I don't need an ambulance. Thank you. I only live five minutes from here.' If she stares at the same spot on the ground the world steadies a little.

'I think we had better walk you home,' the man says. The pressure of his hand on her arm increases. 'Which way?'

Vee takes as deep a breath as she dares to keep her in equilibrium, and looks into the man's face. 'Please take your hand off me.'

'We were only trying to help,' the man says, and turns to walk away, saying to the woman with him, 'You'd think an old woman would be grateful for help.'

The woman says nothing, and looks back towards Vee, apology on her face.

Vee ignores her. She's done appeasing. She's channelling Leonie, who feels closer and closer as the days spin, aching, by.

Part 5: Movement

When you photograph movement, you will have both sharpness and blur. A photograph of a runner, for example, will show intensity of effort in her face, a sense of movement from the lack of sharpness in her arms and legs, and a blurred background. Movement on film requires that some things are sharp and some are lost.

Veronica Moon, *Women in Photographs* (unpublished)

'Greenham Common Salute'
Veronica Moon

Exhibition Section: A Protest in Pictures

Camera: OM-1
Film: 200 ASA
First published: *Guardian* magazine, October 1981

The words 'Greenham Common' are now synonymous with the anti-war, anti-nuclear and women's liberation movements of the late twentieth century. For almost two decades, from 1981 to 2000, women camped, blockaded and protested at the US Army base in Berkshire where nuclear missiles were sited.

This photograph was taken within weeks of the protest beginning, on Moon's first visit to the peace camp. This was the cover shot of the *Guardian Weekend* magazine on Saturday 31 October 1981, with the strapline, '*Greenham Common: A New Generation is Angry*'. It was her only official collaboration with author and journalist Leonie Barratt.

The now-iconic image shows a group of women in deep discussion: one has a clipboard, one is pointing; their faces are intent and focused. One woman is holding a sleeping toddler, another carries a baby in a sling. In the background, the chain-link fence to which the women took it in turns to be chained is visible. Only one person has noticed Moon: a girl of around eight years standing next to her mother. She looks directly into the lens, giving a V-sign to the camera. Her face is serious and staring.

The photograph spawned cartoons and comment among the right-wing press which was part of the mockery of the early protest at Greenham Common. However, the peace camp lasted for almost twenty years and claimed victory when the

American air base was decommissioned and demolished. Moon returned often and took many photographs, some to form part of the protesters' official record and some for her own archive. Even when she stepped back from her career, she kept coming back to Greenham Common.

In 1981:

- Baroness Young became the first female leader of the House of Lords
- The SDP (Social Democratic Party) was formed, with Shirley Williams one of the four founding members
- The first London Marathon was held
- Prince Charles and Lady Diana Spencer were married
- Bucks Fizz won the Eurovision Song Contest
- *Brideshead Revisited* was a TV hit
- *Cats* opened in London's West End
- Susan Brown was the first female cox in the Oxford–Cambridge boat race – and her team won
- There were riots in Brixton and Toxteth, fuelled by social and racial discord. Prime Minister Margaret Thatcher authorised the use of rubber bullets, water cannon and armoured vehicles against protestors.
- *Men Possessing Women* by Andrea Dworkin was published in America

And the Greenham Common Peace Camp was established to protest the siting of American nuclear weapons on UK soil. Leonie Barratt and Veronica Moon, commissioned by a national newspaper, went to report on it.

232

18 October 1981

Leonie

'There it is,' Vee says, unnecessarily. Leonie isn't blind. Against the grey-brown late autumn trees, the squared-off cement of the air base, the protest site is bright with colour and sound, banners and purpose. You could miss it like you could miss a circus. 'Do you want me to drop you here?'

When Vee proposed this job, she was half cautious and half-up herself, all 'It's my turn to help you out, now'. So Leonie had been half minded to tell her to stuff it, making like she's a sister when she's only out for herself. But she could use the work, and if she's going to keep thinking, keep the ideas coming, she needs to be out there in the world, seeing what's going wrong. She's been writing something about motherhood and she knows it's good, but if the world can't understand that women need to escape male expectation and let their bodies be, there's no way they are going to buy her ideas about why making mothering sacred is just another way of keeping women under control and out of the way. Friedan tried with *The Feminine Mystique,* so did Marilyn French with *The Woman's Room,* and look what impact that's had. Sod all. A lot of women talk like feminism has changed the direction of their lives, but then they meet a man with a better car than theirs, and they have a baby, and everything they used to believe comes out with the fucking placenta.

It's more than a year since Leonie made that phone call and Vee didn't come. She obviously felt bad afterwards. There were flowers, a phone call the next day that Leonie ignored, a dog-eared letter that arrived, weeks later, having been posted somewhere way out east, where Vee had been sent for some assignment straight afterwards. But she wasn't there when she needed to be there. OK, so it was all done, then – the baby handed over, life back to normal – but maybe that's why Leonie had needed her friend so badly. Vee chose prizes. She chose herself. And Leonie hasn't seen her since. When Vee called and asked if she'd like to work on this article together, the discomfort in her voice was priceless.

She'd almost said no, but her column is coming to an end, so she needs to keep her name out there. The occasional piece for *Spare Rib* isn't enough for her, and anyway, Leonie is sick of preaching to the choir.

The journey has been an hour and a half of Vee chattering about anything and everything except that night. Leonie sat in silence, letting her talk, giving her nothing. She was going to explain to Vee that there is a difference between being ambitious and being blatantly, hurtfully selfish – say what you like about Vee, she would always listen, learn. But first Vee talked and talked about all the things she's been doing. ('I took a bunch of photos' would have been enough, and anyway, Leonie knows, because she collects everything Vee has published. One day, she will tell her friend how proud she is of all that she's achieved. Even the photographs of the fucking idiot entitled men, and the women who are only famous because they let men think women are only about tits and arse, because she manages to make them look a little less confident and up themselves than they usually do.)

And Leonie is fine, now – has been fine all the time, really, that night was a glitch, a little moment where the patriarchy got under her skin with all of its ridiculous messages, and she was too tired to stop it. Vee isn't to know that, though. And that still hurts.

Vee pulls over and switches off the engine, turns to face her. Although Leonie is secure in all of her choices – although she believes, absolutely, that she should fill her body, stretch its boundaries with food and thought and pleasure – the ease with which Vee moves makes her envious.

Vee has tears in her eyes. 'Look,' she says, 'I know I was wrong, Leonie. I made the wrong call.'

'Oh yeah?' She doesn't get away with it that easily.

'Yeah,' Vee says. When she's upset or under stress, her Essex accent comes out, and it reminds Leonie of when she first met her, with her skirt and her heels and her forelock-tugging, 'am I allowed' attitude. She's come a long way, that's for sure. 'I just . . .' She raises her hands, drops them. 'I didn't think you were as upset as you were. It didn't – it didn't fit with what I knew about you. When I saw you in the pub that day—' she pauses, a question.

'I remember,' Leonie says. Vee reacted to the offer of the kid like it was nothing. She must have realised that Leonie meant it, but she just shrugged it off, like Leonie was trying to give her some old shirt she knew she would never wear. It had seemed like a good option – Vee must be loaded these days, and she was never really as cool with rejecting the conventional as she makes out. There was another life where she would have married some Essex welder and had a girl and a boy, and named the girl after her mother and the boy after his father. Leonie had thought that a kid might appeal to that part of her. But no, Vee had turned her down without blinking. She'd made more of a drama when her fucking darkroom door was opened that time.

Ursula, on the other hand, made it some kind of honour, with the tears and the 'are you sure's and the 'we'll never be able to thank you enough's. Funny how fast that got forgotten, too, and Aunt Leonie became an interfering pain who had no idea how hard it was to be a real parent. Well, that might be true, but Leonie is pretty fucking sure that it's not that hard to buy clothes for girls that aren't pink, and give them Lego as well as dolls. But Ursula and Alec are doing their thing, and Leonie has to let them get on with it. She doesn't think she really cares about Erica, except in the way that she cares about all of the children – abstractedly, because they matter, as part of the fight. Everything will get fixed a lot faster if kids learn that they are the same, from the beginning. It's so bloody obvious, but nobody gets it. Not properly. Even the ones who are trying to raise their kids equally walk round like they need a medal for it.

It had all gone exactly as planned. Ursula and Vee had gone to the Norfolk house as soon as they'd agreed that Ursula would take the baby. Leonie had assumed they would do a private adoption, but her sister had surprised her with a plan that took her back to the mischievousness of their childhoods, made the whole thing feel like a game. What clever sisters they were, fooling the adults. They had registered Leonie with a local Norfolk GP using Ursula's name. She'd been referred to the local maternity unit straight away and given a strict talking-to about not seeing the doctor earlier in her pregnancy. And then they'd waited two and a half months out. That time in Norfolk was when Leonie had written the beginnings of her book on why everything women believe about motherhood is wrong, lumbering from desk to loo to bed and wondering, before she fell asleep at night, whether she would be looking back at this version of herself when the thing was born, laughing at her ignorance, brain turned to mush and her whole world centred on a baby attached to her nipple. Manuscript in the bin. She may as well have done. No one has wanted the other three.

But it didn't happen that way, thank goodness.

It had actually all been easy enough. Well, apart from pushing the little slimy squib of a thing out. That had hurt. But the drugs were good, and after she told them to fuck right off when they tried to shave her and give her an enema, she got all the drugs she wanted. Ursula had been reading something about how they might not be good for the baby but she had told her to fuck right off, too.

In an ideal world, she would have never looked at the kid when it was born, and let Ursula take it away straight away and get on with raising it. But there was a pretence to keep up, so the baby was wrapped in a towel and given to Leonie to hold. She looked into its face and felt – relief, that she felt nothing. She had never understood the cooing that went on over babies – had never played with a doll, come to that – so she had first assumed, and then, as the pregnancy progressed, hoped that she would feel nothing. And she didn't. She kept her gaze on its hairline to begin with, in case its eyes held an ambush. But when she looked, cautiously, at them, as brown as her own, she felt nothing more than interest. It was a baby. It looked like one. The bits of it – fingernails, ears – she could admire the way she admired anything intricate and thoughtfully made or grown: a Frida Kahlo painting, or the reading room at the British Library, which she likes to think of as a tribute to a clitoris.

'What are you going to call her?' the midwife had asked.

'Erica,' Leonie said, with the sort of smile she imagined most new mothers would have on answering the question, but looking Ursula straight in the eye. The name had been the chip that she exchanged for agreeing to go along with pretending to be her sister. That gave Ursula absolute, irrefutable ownership of the kid.

'With Bella for a middle name,' Ursula-masquerading-as-Leonie added, in her guise of doting sister/aunt, 'our mother's name is Isabella. So she could go by that, if she chose to.' Leonie suspects that Bella is also an up-yours to her, an assertion that Ursula may be grateful but she will give no ground. Because what name would gall Leonie more than 'beauty', when women judged by their bodies – how they look, what they can do – is everything that she has set her life up to fight against? And that's leaving aside the 'Ursula is the pretty one and Leonie is the clever one' that has dogged and limited them both from the very beginning. The pretty one had been clever enough to get herself out of childlessness and Leonie out of a corner. The clever one hadn't worked out she was pregnant until it was too late to do anything about it.

Leonie was tired and thoroughly sick of her aching, leaking body. Her breasts were bound, and she had stitches in her peri-neum, and piles. She'd like to think she would otherwise have the energy to argue with the 'Bella'. But maybe it was best that she didn't. She wouldn't be surprised if Ursula is testing her, making sure that she is going to be as good as her word as far as interfering is concerned.

The midwife had nodded. 'Erica Bella Woodhouse,' she said, as though she was approving. Although actually it was none of her business, and neither of them cared at all what a midwife they would never see again thought of the child's name, at that moment both Ursula and Leonie knew they'd got away with it, smiling at each other in a way that no doubt looked like simple gladness at this new baby.

For the few days Leonie stayed in hospital, she kept up the pretence of being interested in Erica, but she really, truly wasn't. She imitated the faces that others made when they looked at their babies, and she never refused to hold her, just in case she was suspected of not loving her. But the only moment where she felt a tug of anything more than indifference was one morn-ing when Erica was put into her arms, and instead of a sleeping baby or a wailing one, she found herself looking at those eyes just like her own, and putting her finger on the nose that had the makings of being just like hers. The baby looked at her, then yawned, and Leonie, much to her own amazement, laughed and kissed the top of Erica's head. Yes, she did. A moment of the purest affection for the result of one of her zipless fucks. It soon passed.

Her body recovered. She got on with her life.

But Vee does not know any of this. She pretty much abandoned Leonie to her fate. There's no way Leonie is going to make it easy for her now.

10 April 2018

Vee

'You're not serious?' Vee looks at the child strapped into a car seat in the back of Erica's estate car. It's an hour and a half's drive to Greenham Common. Erica called and suggested this trip after she had been looking through Vee's photographs of the Peace Camp. That's what she said, anyway. Vee suspects that Erica feels sorry for her – she can't want any more information for the exhibition now, it's all gone to be printed and framed and it would be too late to change anything. But she had been overcome by a desire to see the place again, as acute and almost-sublime as the moment of out-of-body panic that wakes her most mornings. Those memories that remain of the place are good ones.

So Vee had agreed. She hadn't thought there would be a child involved. She's never been good with children, even before she was in the vice of a headache for most of every day.

'My childcare fell through,' Erica says. 'So I thought, is it worse to cancel at almost no notice, or to bring Tom along? He'll sleep.'

Vee laughs, although it hurts her head and she's nauseous, as she has been non-stop for the last three days. 'He's going to sleep? All the way in the car, all the time we're there, the drive back? I don't know much about children but I do know that's not likely.' She looks at the child through the window. It's chilly, standing in the street, but she doesn't want to get into the passenger seat because that will be a commitment. Tom looks back at her, his expression somewhere between boredom and contempt. It doesn't look as though he fancies this road trip much, either. Well, that's something.

'Vee,' Erica says. She looks not unlike Tom, the tiredness/ frustration on her face forming much the same expression as the boredom/contempt on his.

'I wish your generation didn't feel they had to apologise all the time,' Vee says, and she gets in and tries not to slam the door. Erica's not an idiot, and so she hopes that she wouldn't have suggested this if she couldn't make it work. And Vee likes her, for herself, as well as for the Leonie in her. Still, she doesn't want to think about what might happen to her head if the child starts crying.

Since the riverside dizziness, which wiped her out for forty-eight hours, she has barely left the house, and seen only Erica and Marja. She's been sorting through papers and books, clearing out old clothes, taking painkillers whether she thinks she needs them or not. Marja is coming, early this evening, to coax her body to sleepfulness.

Erica gets in to the driver's seat and slams her door. 'I'm apologising because your generation thinks working mothers have so much to apologise for.'

It's raining, only spits and spots, but Erica switches the wipers on to what must be the highest speed, and they thwack back and forth. Vee winces. If Erica notices, she ignores it. Vee thinks of where they are headed: Greenham, the women, the children. 'You're right,' she says, and then, even though twisting around in her seat makes her ache, she looks at the child and says, 'Good morning.' Erica starts the engine, and it's too late for Vee to change her mind.

It's not too late for her to try to do a bit better, though. 'Not long now. Until the exhibition,' she says. 'Are you pleased with it?' There was a flurry of last-minute emails a week ago, and now it's all fixed, finalised, whatever the word is.

Erica smiles, shrugs, sighs, all in one movement. 'Advance sales are good. They're going to timed tickets at the weekend. The gallery is happy, everything has gone to the printer, the installation plan's agreed.'

'Do you have to do much more?'

'I go in the Friday before the opening. By then they'll have built the new walls and painted everything. We'll make sure the layout is right, the technicians will hang the prints, install the vitrines . . .' Erica might be annoyed with Vee, she might be tired, but excitement is bubbling through her voice as she talks.

'You've worked so hard.' Vee used to work like this, but with only one job, not the two Erica is juggling, and without the complication of a family.

'I have,' Erica says, and just as Vee is thinking that she's not sure she's heard her take credit for herself before, Erica adds, 'and I'll take you round, a couple of days before, to see it all. If you're sure you don't want to come to the opening.'

'I'm sure.' It occurs to Vee that Erica has also had to manage Vee. 'I suppose exhibitions are easier to curate when the photographer is dead,' she says.

'Vee!' Erica sounds pained.

Oh. She should have thought of how Erica would interpret that. 'I didn't mean me! I was just thinking generally. If you'd been able to do this without—' What is she trying to say? That once people are dead, their history is fixed, in that nothing can be added to it, they cannot try to skew it or protect it or take things away from it. Dead photographers don't need to be looked after; they don't need day trips to Greenham Common, they don't refuse to come to opening nights. That's all she meant. But Erica has taken it differently, is thinking, no doubt, of how much time

Vee does not have, how close her own death might be. Vee doubts her own ability to explain this, though, so she says, 'I'm sorry.'

Erica laughs, 'You're sorry?'

She deserved that. 'For upsetting you. I didn't mean—'

'I know. But for what it's worth, I wouldn't have prepared for this exhibition any other way.'

The tumour is definitely making Vee more emotional. 'That means a great deal.'

Vee looks out of the window, and watches the landscape get gradually greener. She might never leave London again. She looks and looks. She has come to terms with a lot, these last weeks, but she cannot bear the thought of even a single day in an enforced darkness, not knowing who is near her, and maybe in pain.

The wheels eat the miles and Erica is quiet beside her. Vee is lulled into a sleepful waking by the movement, and the sound of three sets of breathing. She could easily have slept, if she had been willing to close her eyes.

When the car pulls to a stop, and Erica says, 'We're here!', Tom laughs and Vee feels herself smile, surprised by her own pleasure at the sound.

18 October 1981

Leonie

Vee says, 'You just seemed so – OK with it all. It was like being with you in the old days, at the beginning, when you knew everything and I knew nothing.' She says it as though life is the opposite now, Vee the authority and Leonie the learner. Leonie would challenge her, but her mouth has, without her noticing, become dry with tears that would fall if she let them. So she waits for Vee to continue. 'I thought about what you said, afterwards. I thought about it a lot. And about how if I got pregnant I would want to be as—' Leonie sees Vee's mouth hesitate, start to form one sound, then make another, 'detached.'

'Right,' is all Leonie can get out. Wow, she must be tired, if she's as emotional as this. She needs to get a grip. She clears her throat, hoping it sounds more like a cough than a cry, raises an eyebrow. She didn't know how deeply she felt Vee's abandonment, until now.

Vee is still looking straight ahead. 'What I'm saying is, what you thought – felt – about the baby, that was something I needed to think about. But I did, and I understood it, and I – I admired you for it. So that phone call – I didn't think it was as serious as it obviously was. I didn't know that I was letting you down so badly.' Vee looks as though she might cry. Well, good.

'And what would you have done? If you had realised how serious it was? Would you have given up your precious prizegiving night?'

Vee turns to Leonie so she can look her in the eye, sighs, and asks, 'Honestly?'

'Honestly.'

'I've thought about it, a lot, and I still don't know,' she sighs. 'I keep thinking – would we ask a man not to go to something like that? And would we be surprised, would we mind, if he refused?'

And Leonie, caught in her own trap, feels the tears she's holding in vanish, and finds that she can only laugh. Vee is right. It was only one night, unimportant then and unimportant now.

'What happened? With the baby?'

'Fuck off, Veronica. You're too late.'

'Please, Leonie.'

Oh, life's too short. 'My sister helped me out,' she says, and then, because she really doesn't need to talk about this anymore, 'Come on. Let's go and see what's happening out there. Let's work.'

10 April 2018

Vee

There's a sign at the gate of the Peace Garden, saying that it is on the site of the first of the women's protest camps. So this must have been where Vee took the first photographs. And the gates to the air base, the fences that women chained themselves to, were here. But you wouldn't know it, now. The boundaries and the buildings have been replaced by a Land Rover garage and an auction house. There are signposts to other businesses, selling cars and kitchens. It's as soulless as any other business park. It's hard to believe that so much emotion had its home here, for so long: such struggle, such fear and hope and determination. Now it's a blank.

It seems impossible, too, that it is so long since she came here for the first time. Thirty-seven years. But of course, that's what all old people think. Is it wrong of Vee to envy Leonie her death, just for a second? To die so suddenly and so young seems like a gift. She has achieved almost nothing in the years since Leonie died. She may as well have gone then, too. (Is that the sort of thought that only a diseased brain would have?)

Towards the bottom of the sign are the words: '. . . We hope the time you spend here will refresh your spirit.' Vee hopes so too. It feels like a lot to ask.

Erica is trailing behind with the pushchair, fussing over Tom with chatter and toys. Vee pushes the gate open, walks down a small scrubby path, and finds herself in a circle of half a dozen standing stones and a central sculpture which is made up of women-forms, flexing and curving like flames. Further on is a fountain, although it's not working: it's a stone spiral, and the words 'You can't kill the spirit' are carved into it. And then there's the memorial to Helen Wyn Thomas, who was killed on the site when she was run over a military vehicle during a protest. That was 1989. Vee remembers reading about it. She was away at the time, in Canada, still trying to fall in love with landscape photography. She had felt a long way away: she missed her sisters, her country, Leonie. She'd looked at the photographs in the days-old newspaper that had found its way to her Quebec hotel, and thought about how much better they could be, if the photographer had thought more about the framing of the shot. There had been too much sky, not enough detail of the shocked, grieving faces. The camera should not be shy of showing the detail of hard things.

The memorial is part of a flowerbed, which even on this drab March day has enough plants, in enough shades of green, to make the place feel alive and at least partly protected from the world without.

Erica has caught up, and parked the buggy by the central sculpture. She comes over to join Vee.

'The first time you came – were they happy to see you?'

'Who?'

'The women. The camp. The newspaper hadn't sent just anyone to photograph them. They had sent Veronica Moon.'

'They were probably glad I was a woman. But they had more important things than me to think about.'

Much of her Greenham memory has gone, but Vee smiles at one of the few memories she has of her and Leonie here. It's more of a photograph itself, really, the resurfacing of only a second or two of the hours they would have spent together that day. Vee with her camera bag, one camera in her hand, another over her shoulder, so she never missed anything; Leonie asking her if she had a pen. But Leonie's article was excellent, of course it was. And Vee is sure something else happened. When she thinks about their friendship, here, in this place, it feels as though something was saved.

'I think your work does such a lot to make people see the reality of this place. Rather than the idea of it.'

'I hope so.'

'So many female voices – and faces – have been written out of history. I want this exhibition to put them back.'

'That's good.' It is. Vee is glad, most of the time, that so much of what she has forgotten is still available to her, through the photographs she took.

'Your voice too, Vee,' Erica adds.

'Yes.'

They walk in silence, slowly, tracing the perimeter of the circle, Erica glancing towards the parked pushchair every few steps. There is no one else here.

'What do you remember about my mother?' Erica asks.

Something in Vee's mind awakes, whispers to her to be careful, oh, be careful.

She never saw that much of Ursula, really only when she came to the flat, which was always to collect Leonie, never to stay. But she must have something better than that to offer Erica. (Something safe, her mind whispers, something safe.) Ah, 'I remember offering to take Ursula's photograph, once. She was waiting for Leonie to get ready, and we were . . . well, we were trying to talk, you know, but neither of us were very chatty people and we didn't have a lot in common. So I said, shall I take your photo while you're waiting?'

Erica looks almost hungry. 'I don't think I've seen those.'

Vee laughs, then wonders if she's misjudged this, because now she's going to disappoint. 'She turned me down. Flat. She said, "I've seen your work, Veronica, and you're very good, but you're not for me."'

'Not for me.' When Erica repeats it, it's like an incantation. 'She said that all the time. About everything. Cake? Not for me, I'm watching my weight. Watch a film? Richard Gere's not for me.'

Erica smiles, and Vee does too. You never know what you're giving people when you offer them a memory. Or a photograph. 'They weren't as different as they thought.'

Erica's laugh has a taste of sadness to it. 'Yes. My mother said Leonie was strident.' She says the word in a tone that shows Ursula didn't mean it as a compliment. 'But it never occurred to her that she was, too.' She sighs, then, with a movement that makes her an inch taller, and a woman rather than a bereaved daughter, asks, 'Tell me about when you were here with Leonie. How did you see yourselves?'

There's a second – a mind-trick's worth of time – where Vee can almost see Leonie here, on that day, hugging an old friend she didn't expect to see, easing herself down onto the ground, straight into conversation, making a note or two but making it seem as though the interview part of what she was doing was secondary. Later, holding forth, laughing. Leonie was always best with a crowd of other women. If it was a performance, she didn't know it. She's sure there was something – something unpleasant – but right now she can't bring it to mind. 'She saw herself as right.'

'Like you?'

'Me? No, I was just looking.' Always looking.

Vee's hands seem colder, these days. But Erica is dressed for spring rather than winter. She hasn't done up her coat; her blouse is open at the neck. She's wearing a necklace Vee has seen her in before, an open heart with a chain passing through it. It's spring, of course. But Vee feels permanently on the cusp of winter. She pulls on her gloves, wondering whether her hands really are cold.

Maybe this is how people come to terms with their deaths. If you cannot trust your senses, if your memory is like your own shadow under a clouded sky, life is all but over. Funny how attached to it it turns out you've become, though. Even after thirty-odd years of self-sufficient solitude and a who-cares-anyway attitude.

Erica is looking around, taking everything in as though it's all happening around her right now. Which it still is, really. 'Was this place happy? I know it sounds strange, but it feels happy.'

'There was singing and hugging, if that's what you mean. But it wasn't all campfires and tie-dye. And anyway, the women who came weren't here to enjoy themselves. Feminism then was about liberty and justice, not the right to be happy.'

Erica glances towards the silent pushchair. It seems as though she's going to say something, challenge what Vee has said, but she doesn't. Of course she doesn't. To her, Vee is a dying woman, to be coddled and humoured. Probably slightly more trouble than a child.

18 October 1981

Leonie

It was good to get it all said. And the pain of that night had long since washed away, anyway, in the river of blood and time that being a woman entails. Leonie takes out her notebook and the pen she bummed from Vee. Even Vee's pens are expensive these days. '*River of blood and time: how motherhood washes women's lives away.*' It won't help this article but it could work in the book. That would put the cat among the sisters.

Vee has got leaner since they last saw each other, more muscular, and the cropped hair suits her. A few times during the drive Leonie had wanted to put her hand on Vee's head, rub her palm along the grain of the stubble then against it. Her friend has always had the body of a skinny pre-pubescent boy, and the non-threatening presence to go with it. Maybe that's why she's gone so far, slipping through the gaps in the status quo with her flat chest and straight hips, hiding in plain sight, an acceptable woman-man for success within the patriarchy. She carries that camera bag as though it's nothing, whereas Leonie knows it isn't – she moved it off the front seat of the car this morning, and it weighed a ton. (Vee had said she thought Leonie would be 'more comfortable in the back'. A euphemism for 'too fat for the front', so Leonie sat in the front just to show her. The car is ridiculously small, though, her thighs shoved by the door on one side and the gear stick on the other.)

Vee has seen that Leonie is watching her, and she grins, the way she used to when they were first friends, and Vee had saved up all her stories of the male chauvinist pigs she'd met and couldn't wait to talk to Leonie about. Leonie smiles back – it's good that Vee is here, that she wanted to come, that she invited her. It's good to be in the thick of it, to be reporting from the front line for a change. Leonie knows the movement needs her; it needs people who strategise, and look at the big picture rather than reacting. But living in her head can be lonely, especially when the world won't read her words.

The sunshine is feeble but it's here, halfway to warm. She turns away from Vee and looks at the sprawl of tents, the banners flapping and snapping in the breeze, and the people everywhere, purposeful and vivid. Tanya, a friend from the old days, is coming towards her. 'Leonie?'

She opens her arms. 'Who else?'

The next hour is a madness of old faces and new, bits of news and catching up. She barely has time to give the finger to a watching squaddie. She's aware of Vee, lurking and clicking like she does, but she ignores her. Because what could be better than women protecting the planet, women against bombs, women being a fucking force in the world? There are a few men, hangers-on, but they keep out of the way. They know their places. Leonie can see a time, in the future, when it's all equitable, but what she is hoping for is that the see-saw tips the other way first. Just give them a taste of what it's like to be second-class citizens. When one of them brings some tea for her, she takes it without saying thank you.

It must be a while since she's seen Tanya, because she has two children now. She points out the older one, who's running around with the pack of kids that was always going to come with a camp like this. Well, they may as well be activists. The younger one is a baby still. Tanya and Leonie are soon joined by others, and it's almost like the old days, when they would sit in the pub after meetings, talking about all that was wrong with the world, all they would do to fix it. Except now it's fennel tea and what they have done: some things they've surprised themselves with, some compromises, progress and a way to go. Leonie has stories from the women's shelters where she volunteers that make the others wince. They talk about the riots in Toxteth, and the hunger strikes in Northern Ireland. Plus, of course, the possibility of nuclear fucking war, and nobody with a cock seems to want to stop it. 'That's unfair,' a woman Leonie doesn't know says, 'my husband's just as active as I am. And there's Bruce Kent at CND. He's doing great things.'

Leonie sighs, because it's better than snarling. 'And that's the argument men use for everything. "Women have come so far. Look, you've got Thatcher and Shirley Williams and Esther Rantzen, and the barristers must be in double figures by now. You've done it."'

'Leonie,' Tanya says, 'I think Jacqui is right. We need to accept men as part of our movement.'

Leonie glances towards Tanya, which is a mistake, because she's breastfeeding, exuberantly, indiscreetly, shirt open to her waist, and of course, why shouldn't she? But it makes Leonie's guts squirm. She focuses on her old friend's face, or tries to, but Tanya is gazing down at the child now, like it's the new fucking Jesus. Leonie hates how babies do this to women. It's not necessary. She's proved it. She makes a non-committal noise, in her throat, and Tanya looks up then, and laughs. 'We need the uncompromising too,' she says, 'to keep us true.'

That might be so, but Jacqui still looks pissed off. Maybe it was her husband who brought the tea, or it could be that she's just the pissed-off sort. Well, Leonie has nothing against that.

'How old's the kid?' she asks Tanya. Not that she cares, but she really hasn't the energy to put Jacqui right – she looks a lot less likely to listen than Vee – and anyway her leg has gone to sleep under her and she couldn't get up and walk away. She stretches both legs straight out in front of her.

'Three months,' Tanya says. She's unattached it now and is holding it over her shoulder: it burps, she smiles. Then, with a movement Leonie didn't see coming or she'd have deflected it, her friend is on her feet and the baby is being dangled at her, so she can do nothing but take it. 'Hold him, will you? I just need to check how Saffron's doing.'

The others have gathered into another conversation, so Leonie sits with the baby lying along her legs, contained in the valley made where her thighs are pressed together. She pulls her knees up a fraction and puts the soles of her feet flat on the ground, leaning the weight of her upper body back on her hands, so that the baby is contained and secure but she doesn't need to actually touch it. It's a fist-faced thing, still, doesn't look like anything much.

She looks away, and spots Vee, who is circling with her camera. When she sees Leonie, she raises it to her eye. Leonie sends her a look that says, *I will actually kill you if you take this shot.* Vee doesn't. Well, it doesn't look as though she does. She lowers her camera and turns away.

Last time she held a baby was when she gave Erica to Ursula. They'd managed the whole deception pretty well, staying in Norfolk for the six weeks after the birth, so the health visitor could do her thing, and Leonie-as-Ursula could have her check-ups. Leonie wrote, and Ursula looked after the baby, and kept her out of Leonie's way most of the time. Alec came down at weekends, and apart from one awkward thank-you to Leonie, was soon behaving as though he had forgotten that the child wasn't, technically, his. (When the sisters had first talked about Ursula taking the baby, Leonie had asked what Alec would think. Ursula had responded with a tart, 'Since when did you care what a man thinks?' Which was both unfair and true. So she never asked again, and she never really found out. She assumed that he would be happy if Ursula was happy. And he was probably sick of being prodded to hell in Harley Street, too, as the campaign against their childlessness gained pace but no ground under Ursula's command.) After the six-week checks, they had moved back to a London readying itself for Christmas. Ursula registered with a new GP and showed up with her daughter, and that was it. Ursula's pregnancy after a history of apparent infertility was easily explained, it seemed, thanks to the still unsolved mysteries of the female body, and the fact that pregnancy after giving up on ever having a baby was a frequent anecdote in fertility circles.

When they returned to London, Ursula had surprised Leonie by insisting on a physical handover of the baby, so that symbolically, as well as legally, Erica was Ursula's child. Feeling slightly awkward, Leonie picked Erica up from the Moses basket in Ursula's front room – it was in the bay window, as though Erica was an aspidistra, and required light to grow – and stood opposite her sister, whose tired face was solemn, as though waiting for sentence to be pronounced. Like Leonie was going to suddenly decide she wanted a kid, now.

Erica's head had sat in the crook of her elbow and her backside had been in her hand. She hadn't even wanted to look at her, not really, but it had seemed as though she must. There had to be a bit of pretence for the sake of what Ursula believed her sister was giving up. She made the face she used to use at the hospital, after the birth, in front of the nurses. Ursula had watched her closely in those few days, anxious for any signs of attachment.

But Leonie really hadn't felt a thing. Just looked at the funny squishy mass of person-waiting-to-happen and felt a bit sorry for her. Better if she'd been born with a cock. She'd be having an easier life. She had stepped towards Ursula, whose arms were crooked, ready. 'Thank you,' she said, and Leonie nodded. Ursula left the room, carrying Erica. Leonie looked at the empty Moses basket, and then she left the house and went back to her own flat. She drank a bottle of wine. And then she called Vee. In retrospect, the tears, and the need, were probably nothing more than relief. But Vee didn't know that.

10 April 2018

Vee

Ah, here comes the rain. The traffic is heavy, and now there's the sound of the water on the roads as well as the engines. The Peace Garden sits in a corner created by two roads that come off the access roundabout; every vehicle is braking, accelerating, braking as it goes. Together with the noise from the roundabout and the wind in the trees, Vee feels something like claustrophobic. It's only weather, and traffic, she tells herself, you know what weather and traffic are. They won't hurt you. Ignore what the tumour says.

Erica fetches an umbrella from the tray on the bottom of Tom's pushchair. He is well protected from the rain, between the buggy hood and the plastic cover Erica pulls down over it. She hesitates before handing it over. 'It's pink, I'm afraid.'

'Pink is only a colour.' It's a good strong colour, too, this one, throaty and vivid against the green-black of trees, grey of the sky. 'This would look good. On camera.' She remembers a woman in a photograph she took, the first time she came here. She wore yellow dungarees; how bright and sharp she seemed, even against the tie-dye and boldness of the others around her. It was one of the few times Vee thought seriously about switching to colour photography. She had begun her career in the days when black and white was stock-in-trade; even when colour photography started to be seen more widely, from the early eighties, she wasn't interested. Instinctively, she knew that the way she had learned to work was the best way for her, and she could do pretty much anything with natural light. But she would have liked to have captured the yellow of those dungarees.

'Some feminists don't like pink,' Erica says, pulling up her hood.

'I think you'll find that what feminists don't like is the infant-ilisation of women,' Vee replies. She wonders if the yellow sou'wester-style coat and cream knitted hat that Tom is wearing were chosen deliberately because they were not blue.

Vee strolls the perimeter of the garden under her pink shelter. It's chilly, it's bleak, she's spent hours in a car, and yet today she is – not unhappy. Erica, pushing the pushchair now, joins her.

'What was it like? The first time you came?'

This is a part of her past that Vee has always remembered. 'The gates were huge, there were trucks going in and out all the time, a lot of soldiers and' – she pauses, feeling the backwards pull of remembered happiness – 'I liked the feeling of it. A lot of the women's movement at the time was getting very discursive. There was still activism but there was a lot of debate. And I sup-pose that was important, but it was good to come here and see purpose and drive. It reminded me of the early days.'

'And you were here at the beginning. That photograph.' Erica pauses, and Vee knows the one she means; if Leonie hadn't died the way she did, it probably would have defined her. 'There's just something about it. It's iconic.'

'I only pointed the lens in what seemed the most relevant direction. History made the story, afterwards.'

18 October 1981

Leonie

'Thanks,' Tanya says when she comes back from wherever she's been. She scoops the child up, sits, and puts him in the crook of her crossed legs. She's been absent long enough for the feeling to return to Leonie's pins-and-needles calf. Leonie has never wanted to conform to patriarchal notions of beauty and what a woman should be – in fact, she has set herself against them, on purpose, her body her field of action. But when she watches people move the way that Tanya or Vee do, with no thought for getting up or sitting down, no sense of hauling more than their bones can bear, she envies them their ease. She's been reading Andrea Dworkin, admiring the way she is showing the patriarchy that it has no agency over her. Dworkin wouldn't be sitting easily on the grass, either. It could be that she has found an intellectual ally at last.

'So, what's new with you?' Tanya asks.

'I'm busy with the shelters. And I'm always writing.'

'Cool.'

'Kind of.' Leonie resents every hour she spends working with the women's shelters. Not because she doesn't want to help the sisters. She knows she's in such a privileged position, and can't imagine having nowhere to go, not a penny, not even the certainty that you are drawing a safe breath. But she wants to fix things from the other end. No one would need to help these women if the world was equal.

'Haven't found anyone to shackle yourself to?'

This is why you should never have kids. Your brain goes to shit. She shakes her head. 'Why is that even a question? I've no desire to. I never have had, and I don't think I ever will, now. I'm forty-three, for chrissakes. Fuck settling.'

'I respect that,' Tanya says, then, instantly disrespecting, 'I never would have thought that I would find someone. Not really. But Trev is something special. Not all men are bastards. And the babies . . .'

Don't do the smile, Leonie thinks, please don't do the smile. But Tanya does. Leonie has seen it on Ursula's face, ever since she took Erica. It's one-third serenity, one-third sanctimoniousness, and one-third genuine happiness. Leonie doesn't need to look at it. At least Vee has earned her happiness through her own efforts, instead of letting her hormones do it for her.

She gets to her feet. Sweat sits in the small of her back; her arse is damp from the ground. Indoors is better. 'I need to get on with the job,' she says, and looks around for Vee. She's probably got enough material to work with, from what she's seen and what she's been told; she'll keep her views to herself, and quote the stuff that's been said about solidarity and women needing to protect the planet because no fucker else is going to. (She won't say fucker.) And what she hasn't actually heard she can make up. It's not like she doesn't know what these conversations are. Christ knows she's been part of them for long enough.

Vee's nowhere in sight and Leonie is thinking of heading back to the car. She spends so much time on her own these days that even an hour of this sort of sociability tires her, makes her shoulders ache with the effort of not curling in around herself. But then another voice calls her name, and she turns to see Bea.

In the Dagenham days, when they had their little fling, Bea had always given the impression of playing at being a feminist, and Leonie wouldn't have been surprised if she'd married her own trust fund to another and gone off to the country, limiting her Good Works to local charities, if she bothered at all. But no, Bea had surprised her. She'd done a PhD on the feminist movement as a reaction to poverty, rather than patriarchy; spent a few years teaching in the US; come back and is running a department at a London university, where she gets her way with a combination of charm and refusing to listen to anyone who disagrees with her. Bea hugs her; Leonie clings to the embrace.

'Hey,' Bea says. 'What brings you here?'

'An article. Veronica Moon is doing the photos.'

'Oh yes.' Bea looks around. 'She took some at the meeting we were having. I'm just down for a couple of days.'

'Were you there at Dagenham? When we met her?' Leonie doesn't know why she's talking about Vee, unless it's that she doesn't want to talk about herself. Not to the towering feminist achievement that is Bea, anyway.

'Oh God, yes, I'd forgotten! She was very – new, wasn't she?' Bea says. 'What else is happening? What have you been doing? It's been – how long has it been? I feel like I hit thirty-five and everything just accelerated.'

Leonie shrugs. 'I wrote some books. Nobody wants them.'

'Why not?' Bea looks concentrated, all of a sudden. She was always the one with Sellotape, a spanner and a spare pair of knickers in her handbag. She mostly used the spanner to break things. She could do a lot of damage to a porn shop.

'Too radical. Too much. Nobody wants to hear my ideas about why there's no such thing as a mother.' She wants it to sound casual, joking, but there's thinness in her voice that Bea doesn't miss.

'They should.' Bea offers Leonie a Marlboro, takes one from the pack herself, and lights them both with an old Zippo that might have belonged to Fen, originally. Those were happy days. Fen was a good woman, too. She's abroad now – South America, maybe – working in a jungle. Or something. She didn't last long in publishing; it was too tame for her. Leonie should pay more attention.

Leonie inhales. It's been three years since she smoked. Ursula made her give up when she told her about the baby; she tried to make her lay off the wine too. The taste of the smoke in her mouth is as warm as the words of a half-forgotten song. 'I know.'

They stand in silence for a minute, looking back at the camp. Bea gives the finger to three men in a passing car; there doesn't seem to be any reason for the gesture. Seeing Leonie notice, she says, 'I'm trying out the male experience. See something, react to it however I like, assume I'll get away with it.' She stubs out her cigarette, and adds, 'I'm setting up a women's studies degree. You interested?'

'I might be.' If there's one thing Leonie's learned this morning – apart from the fact that she was right to give the baby away – it's that she's a bit out of the action. And though she has no desire to sleep next to a campfire or dig a hole to shit in, she needs to find a way to keep being part of the movement. It's made the shape of her adult life.

'You're a great teacher, Leonie.'

At the edge of the camp there's a circle of sitting children, a woman leading them in a song about counting. 'My mother wanted me to be a teacher,' she says, nodding towards the woman, 'that sort.' By the time Erica was born, Leonie and Ursula's mother had barely a finger's grip on reality, so accepted a granddaughter without question or thought, calling Erica by the names of either of her daughters.

'Well, come and subvert her expectations,' Bea says. 'Call me.' She kisses Leonie and walks back towards the camp, something darkly floral in her wake.

10 April 2018

Erica

Tom has a look in his eye that tells her he isn't going to settle. So she takes him in her arms – he's getting heavy, she feels her body 'oof' at the effort – and holds his still-small form, dense with half-sleep, against her own. His body moulds against hers, his forehead against her cheek when she tilts her head towards him. It is not easy to hold this softness within her, for her child, when there is so much in the world that expects her to be hard.

Erica watches Vee as she walks from standing stone to standing stone, the umbrella a press of hard colour against the drab day. The older woman looks calm, meditative. And so, so ill. She seems thinner even than she was two weeks ago, when they last saw each other; greyer, too. Watching Ursula die taught Erica that death is cruellest as a fading.

The traffic is getting heavier, but at least the rain has stopped. Erica holds Tom a little closer and walks towards Vee, who has made her way back to the central sculpture, and is folding the umbrella, shaking raindrops from it. 'I don't think he's going to go back to sleep,' Erica says, and Tom confirms this with a yawn and three steady blinks before looking around. 'What would you like to do?' She braces for some sort of ticking-off: organisation, having a child, bringing it with her, even though the women who lived at the camps raised families here.

But Vee just smiles and indicates her bag. 'Why don't I take your photograph?'

10 April 2018

Vee

The look on Erica's face is priceless; surprise/shock/delight/puzzlement in a flickering slideshow. In the old days, she would have been ready, and she would have caught it on film.

'Really?'

'Yes, really.' Vee almost laughs at the surprise in Erica's voice. 'I am a photographer.'

'Wow,' Erica says, looking at Tom, licking her finger and wiping something from his face, then tucking her own hair behind her ear. 'OK. What do you want me to do?'

'Just do what you're doing.' Vee looks through the viewfinder, takes a shot just to see how Erica reacts. The protest photographs from a couple of weeks ago were nothing special, but she had enjoyed being in the darkroom again.

The sight of the camera has Erica standing as though she is in a queue for something unpleasant: unsure, anxious, straight-spined. Vee plants her feet, balances her body with her breath. 'Tell me what you remember about Leonie.'

'Not much,' Erica says, and as soon as she speaks her face finds its usual shape, chin slightly up, the slightest of tilts to the angle of her head. Vee presses the shutter. It's not a keeper, but Erica didn't so much as flinch at the sound of it, which is good. And Tom is looking around, half asleep still probably, but obviously used to being photographed. 'Leonie always seemed a bit scary. I mean, she was big – she was physically big, the biggest person

I knew, probably. But . . .' She glances towards Vee, as though she is forming a question. Vee presses the shutter again, and she's getting closer to the image she wants to take; there's something of Leonie in the expression, but there's Erica's own intelligence there too, softer than her aunt's but no less formidable.

'But?' Vee prompts.

'But I used to feel she watched me all the time. Then when I looked at her, she would pretend to be doing something else.'

Vee moves to the side, and somewhere above and behind her the clouds shift and the light is brighter, warmer. Erica turns her head to Vee. 'I suppose it was because she hated children so much.' She kisses the top of Tom's head, as though in apology. 'She couldn't be seen to be interested in one.'

'Did you see much of her?'

'Not really. Not that I remember. Most of my memories of her must be from the few weeks before she died. She was staying with us while she was back from America. She'd let her own flat. Years afterwards, my mother told me how much she'd missed Leonie when she was teaching in the States, so she insisted she stay with us when she came back. She said she regretted it almost straight away, because it was easier to love Leonie when she was on the other side of the world than when she was in the spare room.'

Erica tries to put Tom down, but he mews and clings. She shifts him to her other hip. He wriggles, and Erica is starting to tense up, so Vee asks, 'Look at the sculpture?' Erica does so, a faster move than Vee expected, and there's the shot: a strand of hair has stuck to her lipgloss, making a dark trail on her cheek, and something about looking at the flame-forms has sharpened her attention, the muscles at the corners of her eyes contracting and her expression both focused and faraway. Vee exhales; her body remembers this feeling, the washing of her senses in relief because there it is, the shot you want, there it always is, but until you find it you are never quite sure that it's going to show up for you this time. You might have taken your last good photograph. Except you never have.

Well, maybe this time.

It's such a shame Erica had a nose job. But of course – Vee hears herself sigh – she's within her rights to do so. Her body, her choices, her pain.

Erica has become silent, deeply so, it seems; Vee takes another photograph, another, and she lets her think. Heaven knows the woman must get little enough quietness in her life. Oh, it's always so good to hold this camera, to feel the chafe of the strap at the back of her neck as she moves. It always has been.

And then Erica looks directly at Vee's lens. The click is pure instinct, because the shape of her face and the play of the light, a hard dark something in her eyes and a mouth ripe with words not yet said – actually, that's the shot. Never presuppose, Vee says to herself, you forgot that. Don't think you've got it. Don't go home too soon.

'Meeting you has made me think differently,' Erica says, then adds, 'you've changed my life, Vee.'

Vee lowers the camera, 'Good,' she says, then, as a feeling of relief she doesn't understand brings tears to her eyes, 'you've changed mine, too.'

18 October 1981

Vee

When Vee gets back to the car Leonie is waiting, sitting on the verge. 'I couldn't find you,' she says.

'Until now.' Leonie squints a smile up at her, holds out a hand, and Vee takes it and pulls her to her feet, her other hand braced against the car behind her.

'Did you get everything you need?' As soon as she's said it, she wishes she hadn't, because Leonie was sensitive enough about getting this job via Vee as it was.

But her friend just smiles. 'Did you?'

Vee smiles back. 'Time will tell.'

'Are you going to go and bolt yourself into your darkroom?'

Vee declines the bait. 'The *Guardian* will develop it. My assistant comes in tomorrow. She'll take them.'

'Assistant, eh?' Leonie actually sounds impressed.

'Of course. I need to make sure I have time for the important things. Like reading your manuscripts.' Leonie doesn't speak, but Vee can feel that she's pleased. They've known each other for so long. 'Thank you,' she says into the silence.

'What for?'

'I thought you might stop sending me your work. After—'

She's gone too far. Leonie looks away, stiffens. 'The only thing my books have got going for them is that they've been read by the award-winning Veronica Moon.'

Vee unlocks the car, and they get in and drive off in silence.

After about five miles, Leonie asks, 'You didn't take a photo of me when I got stuck with that baby, did you?'

'I don't think so.' She did, but she went close up, so the baby wasn't part of the shot. Leonie had looked thoughtful, serene, when she framed the shot, but by the time Vee pressed the shutter she had realised she was being watched and was glaring straight into the lens. Some you catch, some get away. Leonie will never see the photo, so she doesn't need to know.

'Good,' Leonie says, with a slightly disbelieving look in her eyes that Vee knows she deserves.

'I saw Bea. It's been years.'

'She said the same about you,' Leonie says, 'we were saying how you'd changed.'

Vee knows this is a dig but she doesn't need to let it touch her. 'Well, haven't we all? But yes, I probably had further to come than the rest of you.' She runs her hand over her head, feeling the hair so short and sharp against her hand, and thinks of how when she came to see the strike at Dagenham she still slept in rollers, and sprayed the waves in her hair solid every morning. A willing party to her own oppression, in those days. She was sleepwalking, really, apart from that little curious corner of her heart that was sufficiently awake to want to see what was going on at the Ford machinists' strike. 'I wasn't exactly assertive.'

Leonie laughs, but it's a kind sound, a recognition. 'You weren't the only one. There are thousands of women, now, still, not asserting themselves' – she winds down the window, lights a cigarette from the remains of the pack Bea gave her – 'but the fact is, you can't be a woman in this world and not be assertive. Unless you're going to just accept your oppression and go and lie down under some man, have his baby and give up on yourself.'

Dagenham-Vee would have eaten this up, but Greenham-Vee ponders before replying, 'You're presupposing a lot about men, there.'

'I just spent half an hour talking to Tanya. She used to be all for slashing tyres. Now she's leaking milk from both tits and talking about peaceful protest.'

Vee laughs, 'That's not a man's fault, though, is it? That's Tanya. She once told me I was letting myself down because I didn't want to go to some workshop she was running. I think it was about masturbation.'

'Probably. She's always been all about the cunt. Which is great, you know. You have to choose your . . . battleground.'

Vee winces. 'True. But I'd rather think of it as an area of interest than a battleground.' She glances to her left, just as Leonie looks towards her, and smiles; they spend a mile or two in silence, the happy kind that reminds her of Sunday mornings in the flat, reading the papers, drinking tea, listening to London's church bells and, as Leonie always said, steadfastly ignoring the call to prayer.

'You'd be happy enough to call it a battleground if you'd pushed a baby out of it,' Leonie says.

'How are you feeling now? About—' Vee begins, even though she knows what will happen.

'You don't get to ask,' Leonie says, 'you know that.'

Vee nods, eyes on the road. 'I know.' She doesn't blame Leonie for refusing to talk to her; she let her down. Leonie is punishing her by not telling her what happened to the baby. That hurts. And she feels an odd responsibility to the child that might have been given into her care, and to that fine, bright spark of Leonie that is out there in the world, now, somewhere.

10 April 2018

Erica

This is not the Vee Erica first encountered, in the Photographers' Gallery two months ago. She looked up glioblastoma and she knows personality changes are likely as the disease grips. She knows the survival rates, too. She's amazed that Vee can walk through her life, day to day, with such hurt and care in her. But then again, she thought the same thing about herself, once. She didn't believe she would live through losing her mother. And here she is. 'It must have been amazing, to be here,' she says. 'When all that was happening.'

'We were just getting on with things, Erica,' Vee says, and then, indicating Tom, 'like you are. We didn't really know. We just—' she pauses. 'Everyone I met in the movement was there because she couldn't not do anything. Your aunt too.'

'And you.' Tom grabs for her ear, rubs the lobe between his fingers. This is what he does when he's tired, whether going to sleep or waking. Any ear will do. Erica cannot help but smile.

'I was just – here,' Vee says, and the way she says it, wistful and only half-believing, makes Erica wants to cry. Then Vee points downwards, towards one of the rocks that forms the base of the central sculpture. 'Look.'

It takes a second for Erica to see what Vee is pointing at, but then she spots them; stacks of smaller stones, carefully balanced on top of another. She imagines the women who come here – perhaps the daughters of the ones who formed part of the human chain around the fence – selecting a pebble. They must choose it with care from the land around the garden, then place it on top of one of the piles that are already here, hand pausing in the air, a millimetre away, to see that the balance is kept. Erica feels her own emotional equilibrium teeter at the thought of it. 'Cairns,' she says.

'Of course.' Vee is bending, searching for a stone. 'I couldn't remember the word.' She takes off a glove in order to pick up a small, sharp flat piece of flint, or maybe slate, and she looks at it for a moment, turns it over, before squatting to put it in place, on top of one of the smallest cairns there. Her hand is shaking. When she stands again, she says, 'I was here.' This time, though, it's something more like a prayer than a statement of fact. There is power in this place.

Vee steps back, and then holds out her arms. It takes Erica a moment to understand: why would Vee take Tom from her? But then she sees the space that Vee is offering her, and why she's done so. She hands the now sleeping child over, feeling how Vee is braced for his weight, then relaxes when she has sensed the perimeters of his body, its density. Half-woken by the move-ment, Tom looks between the two of them – both women hold their breath – and then he smiles and finds the space at Vee's shoulder that will best cradle him, settling his head there. He reaches for Vee's earlobe.

Erica squats and looks for a stone of her own. After a moment of searching she finds a smooth, tiny oblong, slightly tapering at one end. She places it, gently, on Vee's flint.

And now she wants to cry again, which is not like her at all. Marcus laughed at her when they got married, because he cried and she didn't. The only time she's ever been this emotional was when she was first expecting Tom.

Oh, shit.

October 1981

This Month magazine

Leonie Barratt: Letters from a Feminist

Our monthly column from the front line of the Battle of the Sexes

Dear John,

I'm not going to lie. My relationship with you has been the longest constructive relationship with a man there's ever been in my adult life. I mean, my dad's fine, but he's – he's over there, you know? On the right wing, with the money to send his daughters to boarding school. So when we do spend time together, as adults, it's nothing meaningful. Matching eyes mean don't mean a lot.

I've never married, and I don't intend to. I don't have a boy-friend or girlfriend, and I never have, for long. (I'm only telling you this because I choose to. To give you credit, you haven't asked, which is just as well, because no one has any right to.) I get bored, especially with people who can't keep up with a decent debate. I need intellectual stimulation. I haven't found enough of it in one person to make it worth making space in the wardrobe for them. And why should I? I'm happy. I don't buy the 'one is lonely' narrative. One is enough. Enough for me, anyway.

So you, John, are my long-term meaningful man. I think you've listened and I hope you've learned. Talking to you has been interesting. It's helped me to think about the world we live in, me and you, and how it's the same world, although we experience it oh, so differently.

But all good things must come to an end. Times change and things move on. It's time for us to part.

I bet you're feeling pretty pleased with yourself right now, John. I know what you're thinking. Yeah, I really can read your mind. You're thinking – *well, we must have done it*. They must be equal, the women. It must be sorted. Because there's no way Leonie Barratt would give up before she's got what she wants. If she isn't writing to me anymore, it's because I know everything there is to know about women and equality.

And you've helped, haven't you?

You've read this column, right to the end, most of the time.

You've defended your wife's right to go back to work to your parents and hers, when they pulled faces about it.

You can go to the supermarket with the best of them, and there was that time you tried to sew a button on.

We've won. We can share a victory lap, hand in hand, you and I, completely equally.

I see you, John, pointing at all the women in power. Thatcher, ruling over her nest of fawning, subservient men. Billie Jean King, who came out and the sky hasn't fallen in. We've even got a black woman newsreader.

I'm not saying we've achieved nothing. We've got a sort of veneer of decency when it comes to equal rights for women. We're like a couple who were fighting before their party. We're conspicuously civil, but that doesn't mean everything is peachy. Yes, there's legislation about equal opportunity, and equal pay. But the fight hasn't gone away. It's just moved. Equality is being achieved in some places – equality of a sort, at least – but, like any good opponent, the patriarchy has regrouped. Misogyny is mutating. You don't rule the world for millennia without learning a few survival tricks.

The fight has gone to greater places, and smaller ones.

At Greenham Common women are saving the world because none of you penis-wielding lot seem much interested. Either that or you're too invested, in all senses, in those giant phallic symbols your American buddies want to parade all over the countryside. We're fighting for women to be recognised as a force in their own right, but we're doing it WHILE WE'RE DOING SOMETHING ELSE – getting rid of nuclear weapons. Women doing more than one thing at a time, John – does that sound familiar to you? Let me let you into a secret. You don't actually live in a self-cleaning house.

Women have taken the fight deep into their own lives, too. Not all women. But enough of us. There's only so much a sister can do to shift that thinking, no matter how hard she tries. And the ones who haven't – well, that's patriarchal indoctrination in action for you, John. That and *Some Mothers Do 'Ave 'Em* trying to make everyone believe that incompetent men-children are a hilarious, harmless good thing. Let's hope this decade does better on the light entertainment front.

Women are seeking equality in their relationships and their homes, expecting and assuming that there will be help from the men they choose to share their lives with. And by help, I mean hands-on, dinner-cooking, bed-making, nappy-changing help. Not the I-earn-the-money-you-do-the-work arrangement that's been masquerading as an equation for all these years.

You should be benefiting from this too, John. Because equality really is what we seek, not a reversal in dominance, with men scrubbing floors and snivelling for scraps while women subjugate them in their turn. So you should be finding life better, these days. Maybe in private you're not afraid to say you don't feel like sex, or that you're worried about work. Rather than spending a Saturday on football or gardening, you read a book or go for a walk. It could be that in your house both washing the car and cooking the dinner have become shared activities. If you have a son, you might tell him it's all right to cry. If you have a daughter, I hope you're dressing her in trousers and encouraging her to ride her bike just as fast and recklessly as her brother does.

I hope that, if you feel like crying, you feel that you can cry.

Everyone should be benefiting from a changing world. Not that I much care what happens to men – you've had things your way for most of evolution, and a bit of emotional repression doesn't seem like that high a price to pay. But life should be fair.

So, here we are. We're moving on. This column is going and it's going to be replaced by something else.

But don't think feminism has gone, John. Don't think for a moment that all of the angry women who are left have taken themselves to Greenham Common, or that the world has reached some sort of manageable, workable compromise. We might have pockets of legislation and workplaces and homes where we're getting there. That doesn't mean everything is fixed.

My sisters and I are still here. We're in all shapes and sizes, because women come in all shapes and sizes. We have crew-cuts or plaits, six kids or no desire whatsoever to add more to the population of the world. We work in cafes and we're called to the bar. We're going nowhere and we're not going to forget that we are equal to you.

I'll see you around, John. Remember, wherever you are, a woman is watching.

Leonie x

Part 6: Exposure

To take a portrait is, in its simplest terms, to capture the essence of a person, using film and light. To go beyond the idea of how a woman thinks she should look takes time and patience, and the subject must have confidence in you. If a relative of the subject looks at a portrait and says, 'wow', then you know you've done it.

Veronica Moon, *Women in Photographs* (unpublished)

'Leonie Barratt'
Veronica Moon

Exhibition Section: Moment of Death

Camera: OM-1
Film: 200 ASA
First published: *Observer* magazine, October 1984

If you've only seen one photograph taken by Veronica Moon, it's probably this one.

It's the image that Veronica Moon is both most famous for and the one that, in effect, ended her career.

Leonie Barratt is sitting in a chair; her eyes are half closed, and her mouth is half smiling. The camera captures her from the waist up, and a bookcase is visible, blurred, in the background. In contrast, Barratt's face is sharp, with lines around her mouth clearly visible, and shadows beneath her brows and chin. It's an honest portrait; there's no soft focus, no flattering light. To the casual glance it looks as though she is lost in thought. But actually, she has died, seconds before the photograph was taken.

This image could be considered as a lesson in how photography works. We often say that 'the camera never lies' but at the same time, we see how much the viewer's perspective brings to an image. If you don't know that Barratt has just died, she seems at rest. The moment you are told that she passed away moments before, it's all you can see.

The *Observer*, the publication which had commissioned the portrait from Moon, used this image on the cover with the line *'The Death of Radical Feminism?'* At the time, the magazine's editors insisted that they did not know the photograph was taken post-mortem, although the news of Barratt's death was, by then, public. Moon was vilified in the press and within the women's movement for what was seen as a betrayal – in 1984, the world was much less used to the frank images of death that we now encounter so frequently, and without comment, more than thirty years on.

Moon disappeared completely for a time after the publication of this image. When she did reappear, in 1989, it was as a lecturer in photography at Roehampton College (now University). She taught there until she retired in 2005, but she never published a photograph again.

You can also view the contact sheet from which the cover image was taken. This has never been made available to the public before. The cover image is the third-to-last image; in the next frame Barratt's head is slumping to the side, and the final shot on the roll is a skewed image of a doorway.

Barratt's sister was vociferous about the lack of life-saving help that Leonie received, at the time.

Veronica Moon has never spoken publicly about what happened.

In 1984:

- The halfpenny was withdrawn from circulation
- It was a year since the appointment of the first female Lord Mayor of London
- Torvill and Dean won a gold medal for ice skating at the Winter Olympics
- The Miners' Strike began, and Women Against Pit Closures was formed
- The Thames Barrier was opened

- The Provisional IRA bombed the Brighton hotel where the Conservative Cabinet was staying, resulting in five deaths and several serious injuries
- Margaret Thatcher was still Prime Minister
- 'Do They Know It's Christmas?' by Band Aid was number one in the singles chart for five weeks
- The first episodes of *Crimewatch* and *The Bill* were shown on television
- Anita Brookner's novel, *Hotel du Lac*, was published
- *The Wasp Factory* by Iain Banks was published
- *Sisterhood is Global: The International Women's Movement Anthology* edited by Robin Morgan, was published

And it's a big year for Leonie Barratt, who is finally getting the recognition she deserves.

July 1984

Colchester

'You'll find, Miss Moon, that your father left everything in excellent order for you.' Derek Davison is her father's solicitor and the son of an old friend of his, and Vee hasn't met him in person before now. It's been easier to do all of the paperwork related to Stanley's death by post. But she's come back to Colchester to deal with the loose ends. (She doesn't like to think of them as loose ends. She will never tidy her father away.)

She has made sure the house has been cleared properly. She's taken all she wanted after the funeral and employed a house clearance company to do the rest. Once she's finished here she's going to meet Barry, who had come to the funeral and been more than decent afterwards, showing her photographs of his kids and joking that the photographs she took of him back in the day must be worth a fortune. He's the manager of a branch of an estate agent now, and he's going to sell the house for her. She knows she can trust him to do it properly, and to treat her like a human, rather than a woman. Though she still feels animal, really. Raw at being in a world without her steadfast father in it.

She doesn't like Derek Davison very much. He didn't thank his secretary, who brought in a tray with teapot, teacups, sugar in a bowl and milk in a jug, and left it on a table close to the end of his desk. If he's waiting for Vee to pour it, he'll wait a long time. He's reading through the papers; Vee would have expected him to have done so already. She doesn't turn up to a shoot and then start loading film into her camera.

'It's Ms, not Miss,' Vee says. 'We had discussed what would happen, when he died, and I was aware of what was in his will.'

The solicitor nods. 'Of course, there is only you. As a beneficiary. Which makes things simple, from a legal point of view. Will you be selling the house?'

Vee notes how he's sidestepped her correction to 'Ms'. 'Do you need to know that?'

'I'm sorry?' He looks up at her, surprised, and Vee almost smiles. It's as though the existence of her father in the world was the last thing that tethered her to tolerance. Since Stanley's instantly fatal heart attack three months ago, she's challenged everyone who's made assumptions, from her aunts who lamented her single status at the funeral, to the bank manager who had asked if she would need anything explained to her when she had gone in to close his accounts. ('Would you ask a man that?' she'd asked, and when he'd apologised she'd turned away and started reading. She was too deep in sadness, in trying to balance on a world without ballast, to bother to listen.)

'I don't think it's your business what I do next,' she says. 'And I suspect that if I was a son, not a daughter, you wouldn't have felt the need to check.' Is she a daughter, though, now that she has no parents at all? She doesn't dare wonder. She's on a narrow track, one foot in front of the other, not looking left or right, not daring even a full, deep breath or a glance towards the sky. Grief must be accepted. This is the knowledge that shaped hers and Stanley's lives.

'I apologise.' She can see he's panicking at the thought of calling her Ms. It's amazing how many men can't – won't – get it, saying '*Muzzzz*' in an exaggerated way, as though the word is a joke. This prick tries to sidestep it altogether. 'Veronica. If we can do anything else for you, please let me know.'

'I'll be using my London solicitors in future,' Vee replies. Fen's niece, newly qualified, is setting up a practice out of her mother's spare room and the sisters are bringing her their wills, powers of attorney, divorces, house purchases, and anything they can to help their sister out. 'And it's Ms Moon.'

5 September 1984

'VERONICA. EARLY AS EVER.' Ursula, who opens the door to Vee in leggings and a sweater with a stain down the front, has mascara smudged under one eye. She wears an expression that reads 'I could really do without this'. She looks like a woman who has fought five battles this morning, and won three.

Vee thinks about her own morning: a shower, coffee, putting on a white shirt, a grey V-neck, black jeans, DMs. All without the radio, or music, because she likes quiet in the mornings, and all achieved in a relaxed half an hour. Ursula must have children by now; she was never the kind of woman who would do anything else. Each to their own.

'Come through.'

Vee follows. She starts to form a question about how long it's been since they've seen each other, but decides not to bother. To Ursula, she has always been one of Leonie's feminist friends, a separate category, presumably, to merely 'friends', who must be the ones who don't upset the status quo. Though all of Leonie's friends are feminists, because Leonie wouldn't waste her energy on anyone who wasn't. Ursula steps aside so Vee can make her way in to the kitchen-diner at the back of the house. 'Let me know if you need anything,' she says, and then she makes for the stairs.

Her old friend is sitting in a chair by the window; she raises a hand, but doesn't get up. Vee is filled by an undamed hot rush of love for the woman who put her on the path to where she is now. Leonie is all she has left.

'Leonie.' She bends and embraces her; the familiar warm eyes, bright and quick, have never changed, and neither has the smell of lavender, clean and a little antiseptic, which Vee associates not just with Leonie but with the years they spent together in that flat. It's hard to remember how infuriating Leonie was, now; she remembers only her friend's generosity, her need to make the world understand how urgently women must be freed, not only from the patriarchal structures they inhabited, but from the ones in their minds.

'Hey, sister.' Leonie puts a hand to Vee's shoulder. 'It's good to see you.'

'It's good to see you too.' Vee straightens. It's strange, to tower over Leonie. 'And I'm so glad about – about how it's all worked out.'

'Yeah, well,' Leonie says, but there's a smile there. Vee's glad. It seems that America has been good for her friend.

'Yeah well nothing,' Vee replies, 'you deserve this.' She's looped the camera around her neck now – she's never seen any reason to move on from her trusty OM-1 – and she's going to take a few shots just to get Leonie relaxed. There's a blotch of colour on the side of her neck which suggests she's embarrassed; sweat on her lip, though it's anything but warm in here. Vee's assistant, Annabel, had scouted the location earlier in the week, and come back with a sketched plan of the kitchen-conservatory, and light readings. It looked good on paper and it looks good in person.

'Does that chair swivel? If you can move so you're facing the window, we should have everything we need.'

Leonie laughs, 'From your mouth to God's ear. Not that she exists.' She shuffles her feet so the chair is facing towards the window. Spring light and enough cloud to soften the sun: Vee can work with this.

'When's publication?'

'Fifteenth.'

'How's it going to go?'

Leonie sent her drafts, still, airmail from the American university where she now teaches. In April, Vee had received a proof, and seen herself in the acknowledgements: 'Thank you to VM, my sister and my friend, who sees everything.' She'd sat down and read the book, there and then, even though she'd seen its earlier version. But printed like this, it was different. Real. Vee understood, now, what her father meant when he said he was proud of her. She remembers his face, when she told him she'd been approached by a publisher to write a book about photography, a guide for people with their first real camera. ('I'll write a book for women with their first real camera', she'd said.) This winter, her own book has absorbed her free time, and a lot of time she should have given to Stanley. And so when she held Leonie's book, she knew, more than before, what had gone in to it.

And it's a feast of a book for anyone who is a Leonie fan, knows her work and her views. Vee can't say how it will read to someone who has never had the experience of sitting in a room with this clever, uncompromising force of intelligence, felt something like seduced by her words. *This Is What You Need To Know About Women (Especially if You Are a Woman)* is an abrasive, uncomfortable, unapologetic take on where women should be by now, and all the reasons they are not. Thatcher gets a pasting, which is fair enough, but so does almost everyone else. Women who work, women who don't, lipstick wearers, closeted lesbians, men who don't yet understand the whole thing, men who do. And as for feminists: Leonie is unimpressed by them, too, mostly for supporting the patriarchal structure, instead of razing it to the ground, but also for excluding the experience of their sisters of other colours and cultures. Vee enjoyed every word, but Vee knows that Leonie is a blast of cold shower that you know isn't going to last forever. Anyone who stays under there too long is going to hurt.

A lazy, rippling shrug, but the makings of a smile, too. Leonie can't hide how pleased she is, and Vee loves her all the more for it. 'How do polemics ever go? The people who like it are the only ones you don't need to reach. It's preaching to the fucking choir.'

'That's a shame,' Vee says. She wishes more people understood the sparkling, bracing humour of Leonie. If you don't, she could sound vicious.

'Why?' Leonie looks half-curious, half-hostile; that means it's safe to proceed. And it's a great photo. Click.

'If people are put off because they feel under attack, they might not understand your message, might not read it—'

'Then they're not ready.'

Leonie sits forward, eyes a little narrower, but brighter too, bird-of-prey readiness. Click.

'Are you saying my work means nothing? Because it will do nothing? In your terms, anyway, which seem to be how famous they make you—'

Vee ignores the last bit. She's not going to get sidelined into a debate about whether she should be photographing people who aren't out-and-out sisters: they've done that one to death. 'I didn't say either of those things. But—' she hears herself sigh. This isn't what she's here to do, today. And Leonie's book is what it was always going to be: clever, correct, and sometimes hard to stomach. Just like Leonie.

'But what?'

Vee puts the camera down, and it lies against her body, weight held by the strap. 'I don't see the point of giving people things they can't relate to. It's just a waste—'

'Not all of us sold out.'

Vee holds up a hand. She would never usually dare to stop Leonie: maybe that's why Leonie stops. 'I mean,' she says, and she didn't realise that her voice was going to sound so soft, that there might even be tears in it, somewhere deep, 'it's a waste of you.'

Leonie glances away. 'Like I said. It's a polemic. I'm ahead of my time. That's my job. I'm in front. I don't see that as a waste.'

The light from the window against Leonie's face is sharp, suddenly; a cloud has shifted on this blowy September day. The side of her forehead, the bridge of that mighty nose, the top of her cheek are warmed by the light. Click. It's time to make her subject laugh. 'I'm not sure that you're going to have much of a choir for this. I can't think of a single person you think is doing it right.'

'Well.' There's something borderline flirtatious in Leonie's look, and Vee thinks she's caught it: the cupid's bow, the fuck-me eyes. 'I'm pretty cool.'

And now they're both laughing, and the years have slid away from them. They're in the Fulham flat, the windows open to the blazing summer of '76, and Leonie is taking the mickey out of some hapless man who tried to explain economics to her. They're in Vee's first car, driving back from a demo in Leeds, and Leonie is drinking but not drunk and they have the radio on, and they're trying to count all the sexist references in songs and it should be depressing but it's funny, so funny, because they are repeating them in deepened voices. They're friends, again, and for all the places where it hurts and goes wrong and they have let each other down, they cannot, in this moment, argue with the fact that they chose each other, keep on choosing. When the picture editor called to book Vee for this shoot, she let slip that Leonie asked for Vee to do it. Vee moved two other jobs to be here. She's never stood in this room before and yet she's home.

291

'What's so funny?' The voice makes them both jump. There's a child standing in the doorway. She is looking from Leonie to Vee, ready to smile, ready to frown, depending on what the grown-ups do next. She has the stance of someone who does not want to be sent away.

Leonie's laughter barely falters: she can't seem to stop it. But Vee straightens up, as though it's not a child but a teacher who has walked into the room and caught her misbehaving.

Maybe if she had met Erica's father, she would see his contours in the face of this kid. But it's all Leonie, writ small, in this child's eyes, that nose, the jut of the chin.

Vee's first thought is that Leonie kept her baby after all – it wouldn't be the first time a plan for adoption had fallen through, and a mother had changed her mind. And it would be typical of Leonie to try to keep it quiet if that had happened, because it didn't exactly go with her 'maternal instinct as product of the patriarchy' line.

But this is not a child mothered by Leonie Barratt. That child wouldn't be wearing a pink ra-ra skirt, or have her hair held back with hair-slides, her feet in cherry-red patent-leather shoes. Leonie's child would be one step up from feral, wild-haired, sharp-eyed, and more than a match for anyone who put her down.

Of course. This kid must be Ursula's. Vee hopes that this child has cars as well as dolls to play with. She cannot begin to imagine how seeing this conditioning happening, in her family, under her nose, must gall Leonie. 'Who's this?'

'This is Erica,' Leonie says, then adds, 'did you ever read *Fear of Flying*?'

'I did.' Vee only got around to it recently, and it made her laugh. Oh. OH.

Erica Jong.

Zipless fuck.

'How old are you, Erica?' Leonie asks. Erica holds up a hand, fingers spread, thumb against palm, 'I'm four. I'll be five on the seventeenth of November.'

Leonie tilts an eyebrow at Vee, nods. 'There you go. Straight from the horse's mouth.'

Vee scrabbles back through her memory, to the conversations she had with Leonie at Greenham Common. 'So, Ursula? Why didn't you say?'

'I did say.'

'I'd have remembered.' Erica is watching them, gaze tick-tocking from face to face. Leonie is waiting, watching Vee too. It's uncanny, the two of them. 'I asked and you told me to fuck off.'

'Don't swear in front of my niece,' Leonie says, with a not-quite-smile, and Vee glances towards the child, who is standing there with three shocked rounds where her eyes and mouth were a moment ago.

Do you apologise to a child? Vee doesn't remember anyone ever apologising to her, except to say they were sorry her mother had died.

'And then I said?' Leonie asks.

'You said a sister helped you out.'

'I said *my* sister helped me out.'

'Oh.' Vee looks at Erica, her fists on her hips, now, her shock at Vee's swearing dissipated and her original curiosity, apparently, returned.

'What were you laughing about?' the child asks. 'I could hear you from upstairs. You disturbed me when I was playing.' And Vee can't help it, but she starts laughing again, because Erica looks so outraged. And because her mind is trying to absorb this apparent living, breathing truth, in front of her: Ursula helped her sister out, by taking her baby. And Leonie helped her sister out. Ursula must have wanted a baby.

293

'So, Ursula is your sister's—' how to phrase the question, 'only child?'

'Yes.' Leonie nods. 'There were problems, so—'

'What problems?' Erica asks.

'The adults are talking,' Leonie says. The sharpness in her tone would have most children running for cover, but Erica, it seems, really is her mother's daughter.

'Yes,' she says, feet unmoving, hands on hips, 'but you're talking about me.'

Then, the most unexpected thing from Leonie, who holds out her arms in awkward invitation. There's a second when birth-mother and birth-daughter are eye to eye, but Vee isn't quite quick enough with her camera to catch it. Erica goes across to Leonie, and rather than climbing into her lap, turns and waits to be lifted. Leonie puts her hands under Erica's armpits and hauls; Vee takes a photograph then. It's not going to be a good shot – she really just does it to see if Leonie objects. Leonie doesn't. Over Erica's head, Leonie says, 'I should have thought about putting a clause in the agreement. About pink. And all that goes with it.'

Click. 'I'm surprised you didn't.'

'I thought about it. But I wasn't at my best.'

Erica looks from one woman to the other. 'What are you two talking about? How does your camera work?'

'Nothing important,' Leonie says.

At the same time, Vee offers, 'I can show you, after I've taken Leonie's photograph.'

Erica nods. 'Are you going to take a picture right now?'

Vee drops to one knee, so her lens can be level with Erica's face. 'Yes, I am.'

So Erica – that precious only, that child whose every move is special, who must hardly spend a day unphotographed, judging by the studio portraits on the walls, the clusters of framed family images on shelves and tables – does what she knows to do. She poses. First there's a grin, wide and fake, and then she turns to Leonie and kisses her on the cheek. Vee thinks she has caught the second before Leonie looks startled/horrified, pulls away. She definitely gets the next, where Leonie wipes her cheek and Erica laughs, and Leonie smiles too, though it's directed towards Vee, not her daughter: a rueful, 'what can you do' smile, an expression Vee has never seen on Leonie before. Click.

'Erica!' Ursula's voice makes them all jump. It's followed by the tap of her shoes down the stairs, through the house, coming closer.

'I'm in here, Mamma. They won't tell me why they were laughing.'

Vee gets to her feet, waiting for Leonie to let go of Erica, and for Erica to run to her mother, whose footsteps are speeding up, the way they would to a forgotten pan left on the hob.

But Leonie pulls Erica closer, tickles her at her waist, and Erica squeals, laughs. 'Vee and I were laughing because we were tickling,' Leonie says to Erica in the kind of voice that she obviously imagines women use towards children they love, high-pitched and wheedling, 'like this!'

Click, click, click. Vee can never resist unexpected movement smudged across a photograph, the way it plays across an image and gives it life and light.

Erica gets a hand free, and tickles Leonie at her neck. Leonie moves her head to the side and takes Erica's fingers in her mouth, a play-snarl. She looks as though she is actually enjoying herself; Erica's whole body shouts out its laughter, its unexpected pleasure from an aunt she obviously doesn't know that well. Her legs are flailing and her baby-toothed mouth is wide, her eyes bright, a hairclip working loose. And then Leonie puts her hand on Erica's face, cups it, and the two look into each other's eyes with – with what? Vee can't identify it; it's more complicated than love, both more and less than affection. She can't identify it, but she can capture it. Click.

Ursula, standing in the doorway, hesitates for half of a heart-beat before saying, 'I think that will do.' She's changed out of her leggings and sweater into jeans, heels and a batwing top.

Leonie gives another tickle, but Erica has stopped laughing as suddenly as she started, her face its resting small and sober shape once more. Vee risks a final photograph but Ursula notices and holds out a hand, one finger pointing, towards Vee, without even looking at her. There's enough authority in the gesture to make Vee rest her camera on her chest. Ursula hasn't taken her eyes away from her sister and her daughter.

'We're just playing,' Leonie says. Erica makes a move to get down – Vee can see her legs wiggling – but Leonie is holding her on her lap as though she is a shield.

'Really?' Ursula says. The sisters are looking intently at each other now, Leonie defiant, Ursula furious.

'Really. I don't see anything like enough of my . . .' and Leonie plays the pause to perfection – 'niece.'

'Well, whose fault is that?' Vee glances at Erica, whose face is all bemused resignation, somewhere between 'not this again' and 'I wish someone would tell me what is going on'. It's a strange look to see on a child. She fidgets on Leonie's lap, realises her grip has loosened, and slides to the floor. She might actually be trying to head for Vee – or, more likely, her camera – but Ursula's arm, still stretched out and pointing Vee to stillness, drops on to Erica's head, pulls her towards her. Erica stands against her mother's body, Ursula's hand more than resting on her shoulder to keep her in place. 'We'll discuss this later.'

'No, we won't,' Leonie says, 'I'm going as soon as the photos are finished. I've better things to do with my day than listen to your bullshit, again.'

Ursula bends to Erica. 'Come on, darling. We don't want to listen to Aunt Leonie's swearing, do we? This is part of why your daddy and I think she's a bad influence.'

'The lady with the camera said a bad word too,' Erica says.

'Woman,' Vee and Leonie correct, in unison. Ursula ignores them.

'Well, we really don't want to listen to bad words.'

Leonie smiles at Erica, and Vee doesn't know what's coming, but she knows it won't be pleasant. 'You don't look much like your daddy, do you, Erica? You should ask him about that sometime. Most children look at least a little bit like their father.'

For a second Vee is sure that Ursula will go for Leonie, slap her at least, and she's damned if she will miss it, hands already raising her camera to her face. But Ursula turns away, propelling Erica in front of her: 'Come on, we can get your dolls' house out.'

Erica isn't going anywhere. 'I want to know how the camera works!'

'Not now,' Ursula says.

Oh, but whether Erica is her mother's daughter or her aunt's daughter, she has their stubbornness. It's like she's grown roots: she's immovable. 'I want to know,' she says, then pointing at Vee, 'she said she'd tell me.'

'Well?' Ursula glares at Vee. Leonie titters. Ursula turns up the glare a notch, switches it to Leonie, who refuses to look away. The tension nests into Vee, making a pain in her temple, another under her heart.

Vee just wants this to end. She bends to Erica. 'It's to do with letting the light in in a controlled way, to make a chemical reaction that makes a photo. When I press the button on top it opens a sort of little door inside, and that lets the light on to the film, and that's what makes the picture.'

Erica looks as though she is framing another question, but Ursula isn't having this go on for a second longer than it has to. 'Now you know,' she says, and then she's moving towards the door, Erica held firmly by the hand. Vee exhales, stretches; her body is full of knots, as though she's spent a day on a job, instead of half an hour in a conservatory on a converted farmhouse in Dorking. She and Leonie look at each other as they listen to the footsteps slamming their way upstairs.

Leonie might be crying; it's the fact that she is trying to hide it that makes Vee hurt. She asks quietly, 'Did it bother you? Giving her away?'

Leonie shakes her head. 'Nope. Babies aren't interesting.'

'The woman she's going to be might be.' Vee raises the camera to her face again. Leonie is gazing out into the garden: rain is starting to spit and spot on the window, the light is a more solid grey than it was. She'll give it another ten minutes and then, if she needs to, she'll put a light reflector on the floor, angle it to bounce the light up to Leonie's face. The skylights should still be enough, though.

Leonie shrugs. 'Well, you opted out of that too, as I recall.'

There aren't many things that stop Vee when she's focused on photographing, but this does; she looks at Leonie over the top of the camera. 'You can't seriously have wanted me to take your baby?'

'The baby. A baby. Not my baby. They're all just – bits of evolutionary necessity. And I'd rather you'd had it than she get brought up in pink ribbons by my fucking sister.'

God. Leonie had been serious in her offer. Vee has wondered about this, sometimes. It's always been hard to tell when Leonie is joking, or testing you, or testing herself. 'You say that now,' Vee says, 'if she was with me I'd never see her. She'd be raised by nannies. That has to be worse.'

Leonie shrugs, non-committal.

Vee has taken the last shot on the reel; she winds it back, facing away from Leonie, clicks the back open and takes the film out. She puts it safely into its container before sliding a fresh film in to the waiting space. Click, then wind on. Click, wind on. She puts the black cassette into her pocket; that's not for the lab, she'll develop it herself. The shots from before Erica came in might be worth using, and if they are, she'll pass them on. Back to work.

Leonie is looking out on to the rain in the garden.

'When I'm back in the States, try to keep an eye out for Erica, will you?'

'Why, aren't you coming back?' Vee hears panic in her voice. Her father's death is a greyscale tint to every thought and sight. She cannot lose the other person she loves most in the world.

There are tears in her eyes and she turns away. But nothing gets past Leonie. Vee hears her exhalation as she gets to her feet, and turns to see her friend waiting, open-armed, to hold her.

When she's cried, Leonie squeezes her again – her body is soft, hot, sweat-and-lavender like always – and sits back down. 'Nothing is forever, Vee. Not you. Not me.'

'I know.' There's knowing in your head and knowing in your being, though.

'So, whatever happens, look out for Erica?'

'Of course.'

'Thank you.'

Leonie is watching the sky, it seems.

Vee drops to her knees, her lens on a level with Leonie's eye-line. The image she captures of her friend is serene: Vee would say statesmanlike, if she dared. She takes another shot, then stands and moves a step away, the viewfinder taking in Leonie's bulk in its dark navy shirt, her cropped hair showing her high forehead, the way her browbone juts. But Leonie doesn't look like Leonie unless she's talking. Unless there's a conversation, this photograph is never going to be anything special. It's certainly not going to be worthy of a cover. More importantly, it's not going to justify the brain in that head, the vision in those eyes. The camera does lie. It's Vee's job to make it.

'My book's coming out next year.'

'Your book?' Leonie's face is perfect when it turns towards her: curiosity, bright attention, a benign sort of rage. Click.

'I told you. In a letter.'

'You didn't.'

Vee is pretty certain she did. 'I was asked to. It's nothing like what you do.'

'No, because mine took me twenty years—'

'You know I didn't mean it like that, Leonie.'

'Oh well that's OK then.'

Click. 'Is it?'

'No. It's not your job to write books! Just like it's not my job to take photos.' Something like pleading sounds in Leonie's words. 'Can't you see?'

'No, I can't.' This is just ridiculous, and Vee doesn't need it. She's shaken enough by seeing the living fact of what had seemed a very hypothetical problem of what to do about Leonie's pregnancy. 'I was never supposed to get out from under, was that it? I was supposed to be your protégé forever?'

Leonie looks genuinely angry. This isn't one of her play-furies, one of her tests. She's moving her face away from the camera every time Vee goes near. Fine. She'll tell the editor that the film was over-exposed when she took the back off the camera, that the winding mechanism had gone wrong. These things happen. This can be The One Time Veronica Moon Didn't Nail It. Or she'll hope there's something from the first roll of film that she can use, and she'll hand the specific negatives over, keep the ones of Erica and Leonie private.

'No,' Leonie says quietly, 'but you were supposed to—'

'What? Come on, tell me.' Looking down on Leonie is a strange feeling, wrong, like looking at the negative of an image you know well.

Leonie looks down. 'You were supposed to care.'

Vee turns away, opens her bag in preparation for nuzzling the camera back in to the protective foam that has made a millimetre-perfect nest for it over the years. She picks up her light meter, tucks it back in its slot in her camera bag, 'You know I care.'

'How do I know that? From when you cancelled your stupid assignments when I needed you? From all those times you called?'

The guilt that has been filling Vee since Stanley died washes up to its high tide mark, threatening to drown her. She goes over to the chair, kneels on the floor, and leans against Leonie's knees. 'I meant to. And I assumed you didn't want to talk about it.' It sounds thin, even to her. She tries harder. 'You've never seemed to need me. Or anyone. And anyway – your book. If anyone lives what they believe, it's you. Motherhood is a construct of the patriarchy, you said, and I knew that you knew you were right.'

'Did you ask?' Leonie might be crying. She's looking away.

'Ask what?'

'If I was OK?'

She's sure she did. But she also feels as though she's being – what's the expression they use now, for when the rules change and you're made to think you're wrong – gaslighted. 'Did you tell me?

If we're getting out from under the patriarchy are we not owning what we're feeling? Telling our truth? Where was yours?'

Leonie wipes at her face; it's not tears, but sweat, on her skin, but her voice has true hurt in it. 'Would you have listened? You could have tried a bit harder.'

'You could have been honest about what you needed,' Vee says. She can hear tears in her own voice.

'Didn't you think it would be hard?'

It's the she-devil and the sea. 'Didn't you think that me thinking it was hard was undermining everything you had taught me about women and motherhood?'

She reaches for her friend's hand. Leonie's skin is clammy. 'You're cold,' she says.

'You were always cold.' Leonie smiles as she says it, so although that ought to hurt it's a comfort, a return to familiar ground. This is how Leonie talks. Vee gets up. Although her body is used to moving into uncomfortable shapes for the sake of a shot, and to staying beyond comfort in squats and stretches, today she's aching. Maybe it's the tension, creeping into the creases in her body, solidifying there.

'You were always impossible to contradict,' Vee replies, 'and anyway, if I was a man, being cold would be good.'

Leonie laughs, and Vee takes her camera out again. She takes a photograph, another, as her friend sits back in her chair, eyes closed, half a smile on her face. She looks like a lazy, self-satisfied cat; the only one who knows where the cream is. The sun has come out; it's moved higher in the sky and beams down through the skylight, so Leonie is lit sharply, brightly, an uncompromising strength in her face. And Vee understands that this is the way to take her friend's photograph: to let the details of her face show, the bags under the eyes and the blotches on her neck, the way her temples shine. Because this is how she would photograph a man. Every line and blemish. On a man, it would be character, not flaw.

'Look at me,' she says, 'like I'm Thatcher.'

Leonie smiles, opens her eyes, then leans forward, a little, her face all fury. 'You owe me, you fucking scarf snatcher.' Click. Leonie will look mad as hell and only they will know what the joke is. Vee grins. 'Now look at me like you're Thatcher.'

Leonie holds up a hand, still smiling. 'Enough's enough, Vee.'

Maybe it's their laughter that brings Erica back to the door; when Vee looks that way, she's standing, quiet and still, taking everything in. She decides to ignore her. Erica can watch, and Vee will claim ignorance if Ursula tries to tick them all off again. She puts a finger to her lips and Erica nods and mirrors the gesture, solemn as death itself.

24 April 2018

A statue of Millicent Fawcett, intellectual, activist, political leader, writer, and suffragist, is unveiled in London. It is the first ever statue of a woman to stand in Parliament Square.

Two days before exhibition opening

The sight of Leonie's face on the poster, here in the street for anyone to look at, has shaken Vee. And she knows she's been overdoing it. She saw the solicitor yesterday. Fen's niece has grown into a formidable woman – not that that is really a surprise. She now heads a firm of solicitors who specialise in working with women, and do a lot of pro-bono work for those who are still being abused by the world. She's the media's go-to person to comment on legal matters relating to women's rights, whether domestic, reproductive or working. A check of a living will, and a change to a dying one, are way below Gloria Wolf's pay grade. But she made time for Vee, like she always makes time for the women who helped her to make a start. That was followed by packing up the darkroom, and the hospital this morning. Now this.

Vee doesn't know if she even wants to see the exhibition, really. But it wouldn't be fair on Erica, who has been so meticulous and conscientious and – well, and kind. Erica deserves her support, and she's going to get it. Vee deserves to be remembered, she knows she does. Erica has done that for her. She's more grateful than she knew she would be.

Just this, then the session with Marja early this evening. And then sleep.

She hopes death will be a sudden switch, like clicking off the bulb in the darkroom and feeling the absence of light everywhere. She does not want a gradual diminishing, the opposite of watching an image emerge when the film is laid in the chemical bath to develop. Foolish to think that she has any choice, though.

There had been an almost giddy frankness to her conversation with Mr Wilding this morning. None of the usual hedging around 'impossible to say' and 'factors at play'. Just straight answers to straight questions. It reminded Vee of the old days, conversations with editors who had two minutes to brief her, handovers to the lab who needed photographs in a hurry and just had to know how fast the film was, how it should be exposed, to get to the truth of the photograph that Vee took.

Yes, it had been all business with her consultant this morning. She'd reported the viciousness of the headaches, the nausea building and her vocabulary and memories being nibbled away at. Maybe. It's not like it was after the surgery in 2007, when Vee was aware of great craters of darkness where her memories and her knowledge used to be, and known that nothing would return them to her. If she hadn't fallen out of love with photography after Leonie died, she would have done it in the aftermath of surgery. She had spent night after night, looking at photographs, sitting with colleagues and old friends from the movement, asking them to tell her the truth that the images swore to. And knowing that, at the moments she pressed the shutter, then wound the film on, she was choosing what to see.

What's happening to her now is of a different order. This is the imperceptible alteration in the twilight that means your first shot might be OK, but the last on the film will be grainy and barely usable. Vee had asked the questions she had brought. They might have been the ones she asked last time.

The straightness of the answers had been comforting, in the way that a clean wound is comforting when you thought it was going to be a ragged cut.

Expect to become more tired, and for your memory to be affected. Know that your judgement is impaired. As for your sight – we can scan you again, but really, you're the best judge.

I don't think it will be more than two months.

Erica is teetering on those boots again. Well, if this is what gets her through the day, so be it. She looks terrible, pale and tired. But when she sees Vee her eyes brighten; instead of waiting she comes out onto the pavement. They look at the poster together, and with Erica next to her, Vee can suddenly see what she sees.

She may, finally, have arrived at wherever she set out to, on that sunny day in Dagenham in June 1968. Some people never get an exhibition. Some people are truly forgotten. And that would be worse, even if there have been times when she thought it would be better.

Erica looks down at her hands. 'Do you want to come in?' she asks. 'I mean – I know you do, that's why you're here. I'm – I'm just nervous.'

Vee nods. 'Lead the way,' she says.

Erica puts her hand to the wall as the movement of the lift begins; she wobbles, a little, and Vee puts out an arm. How good, to steady someone else. 'Are you OK?'

Erica gives a smile-not-smile. 'I'm pregnant.'

'Oh.' Vee knows that she is supposed to be congratulatory, but brain tumour or no, she can see from Erica's face that it's not that simple. 'Well.'

'Exactly,' Erica says, 'I don't know what to think. I haven't even told Marcus. Well, I haven't told anyone. Except you.'

The lift stops, and they step out into the exhibition space. Leonie greets them, her head double life-size on a repeat of the exhibition poster. They stand and look at it for a moment. 'Leonie had an abortion,' Vee says, 'and she was absolutely unapologetic about it.'

She feels Erica nod. 'I know. But I don't want Tom to be an only child, and I might not have a lot more chances.'

'So why aren't you happy?'

Erica shakes her head. 'I don't know. What if I don't love Marcus?' She looks at Vee, and Vee wishes she were not out of her depth, wishes she had something to say that is helpful or at least not unintentionally tactless. Like talking about abortions. Erica's eyes, even tired, are as lovely and as clear as Leonie's were.

'I don't know either, Erica.' Erica seems to understand, though, that Vee would say more, give more, if she could. She puts out a hand and rests it on Vee's arm. The touch almost hurts.

Erica straightens and says, 'I don't want to talk about it. I want to focus on this. So. Here we are, at the beginning.'

Vee sees her Dagenham picture blown up, the newspapers featuring it displayed below. Passes the beauty queens, still weeping, surrounded by photographs of early marches and protests. So many faces she might have known the names for, once. Portraits, of the great and the good, the forgotten who were taking their moment and the women as recognisable now as they were then. She pauses in front of Margaret Thatcher.

Erica pauses too. 'I know it sounds weird,' she says, 'but I love your Thatcher photo.'

'I wish I remembered taking it.'

'Why that one? In particular, I mean?'

Vee smiles. 'Because I think that might be Leonie's scarf around her neck.'

Erica laughs, 'Let's say it's true.' They walk on, quietly. It's strange to be in a gallery empty of other people.

And here, almost at the end, is Leonie Barratt.

Still gone. Still the most important person in her adult life. The print must be three feet by two, smaller than it is on the poster but all the more impactful for that: concentrated Leonie. It's like seeing the *Mona Lisa* in all its thirty-inch-by-twenty-inch glory after all the tea towels and jigsaws. Next to it, the contact sheet. It doesn't exactly clear Vee's name, but at least it doesn't confirm the worst things she was accused of: watching her friend die as though it was a blood-filled horrific spectacle that she stood by and recorded without a second thought. Only the war photographers do that. And are praised for it. Oh, to be a man with a camera.

Vee sits on the bench in front of it, and Erica sits down beside her. 'I heard the story so often, about how you were taking your photographs, and Leonie died, and you kept on taking them instead of helping her, and then you published them.'

'And you believed it?'

'Yes, of course,' Erica says, 'who doesn't believe their mother? But then, as I got older, I realised I'd constructed the memory. What I thought was a memory was a sort of' – she scribbles at her temples with her fingers – 'a sort of cartoon. A child's cartoon. You were all big hands and Leonie was bleeding—'

Vee puts a hand over Erica's. She's not sure which of them is shaking. 'She wasn't bleeding, Erica,' she says. 'There was no blood. You can see. Her heart gave out when she was sitting there.' What a burden for a child.

'I know that now,' Erica says, 'I knew it as soon as I was old enough to think about it properly. And then I looked at

308

the photographs. They weren't – it wasn't obvious that she was dead. I could see how you could be – mistaken.'

'Thank you.' The next headache is coming, overpowering the painkiller in her system. That was quick. She can feel tension marching along her jawbone.

'And then when you let me have the contact sheet,' Erica adds, 'I was surprised by how relieved I was. When I saw the other images.'

Vee nods. When she blew the images from that up and looked at them closely, she thought she could see the frames between which Leonie's heart stopped. And she thought there were two images after death, not one. But she is the only one who knows/knew, really, and without her memories there is no record. During her recovery from brain surgery a decade ago, she had had nothing except the last few images on that film to tell her what happened. And they aren't enough. Photographs on their own don't tell the whole truth of anything.

'I remember your camera was on the floor,' Erica says quietly.

'What?' No. Never.

'When I came in. Before you shouted at me to go. Your camera was on the floor.'

'Are you sure?'

'Yes. I'm sure,' Erica's tone suggests that this is the least important part of this conversation.

But Vee has felt something inside her break. Or mend.

Because she would never, ever have put her camera on the floor. Just like she would never immerse it in water. In her hands, round her neck, over her shoulder, in her camera bag; these were the places her camera would be if she was away from home. Nowhere else.

If the camera was on the floor then she did try to save Leonie. It's as simple as that.

You can't do CPR with a camera swinging round your neck.

You don't put your camera on the floor, ever.

She can almost remember it, now. Taking the portraits, before she knew Leonie was dead. Then, realising the scope of the silence. Only one set of breath: her own. Her voice, crying Leonie's name. The bulk of her friend's body sliding from the chair. Forcing Leonie's jaw open, her small, neat teeth guarding the silent red cave of her mouth.

Lavender. Sweat. Silence emanating from Leonie the way it never had before.

Vee closes her eyes, tighter, tighter, tries to make the memory stay, but it won't.

It leaves something behind, though: certainty. Vee thought she would never have certainty. But here it is.

She chose her friend above her craft, above her standards. That time, at least, she did not let Leonie down.

That pain in her: it's definitely a mending. It's the fibres of her heart knitting together over a place that's been raw for almost a quarter of a century.

Vee takes Erica's hand. 'Thank you,' she says, 'thank you.'

'What for?'

'You don't know what you've given me,' she says.

It's time for Vee to give some peace to Erica, if she can. 'There are things I can tell from looking at the images,' she says.

'What can you tell?' Erica is sitting very still, and the gallery itself is silent, though noises travel up the stairwells, making a city-background hum.

'I can tell that she was relaxed. She would have been talking. I was moving around her; the position of her shoulders doesn't move at all. I'd have had her facing a window, maybe a door open into a garden.' Vee inhales, exhales, wishes the physical pain at least would dissolve. 'I haven't changed the set-up – she's in the same clothes, sitting the same way, against the same background. So I would have been photographing all the time.'

Erica is holding on to the edge of the bench where they are sitting, her gaze fixed on Leonie's image. 'I don't understand what you're saying.'

Vee isn't sure that she does, either. Not completely. But she continues, 'Look at the contact sheet. You can't tell when she – goes. There's no fall. There's no cry. Like you say in your notes, you only really know she's gone when someone tells you. She didn't suffer. You can see it.' The ache is creeping round her face now, jawbone, sinuses, temples, forehead. Over the crown of her skull and down her neck.

Erica nods. Those eyes, round like a child's as she listens. Then, unexpectedly, she smiles. She's not looking at Vee. She's not really now: she's then. 'I remember she was always talking, and always looking. I remember her and my mother talking about me, a lot, because I felt . . .' Erica puts her hand on her stomach, her face twisting, as though something is curdling inside her.

'I think the morning you came, Leonie had said my mother was a bad mother. And my father was complaining about how Leonie never shut up and my mother never stopped complaining about her. And then they had to stop arguing and we had to tidy the house up, because you were coming.' She scratches at her temples again, a gesture that little Tom will no doubt remember one day, look back on as being part of what made his mother what she was.

Tears clump Vee's throat. Pain travels down her spine, up again, reaches her crown.

Erica shakes her head. 'That's all.'

'Look at her, though,' Vee says, even though remembering Leonie, really thinking about her, hurts, 'you can see everything that she was. Clever, thoughtful, and just – just a force. And I think that if I saw that, probably even if I knew she was dead, I wouldn't have been able to help but photograph it. I don't know if it was shock or instinct. But it's what photographers do. Female photographers get . . .' what's the word? 'Monstered for it. Male ones get applauded for being unflinching.' She adds, because she can, now, 'If my camera was on the ground, I know I tried to help.'

Vee pauses. She looks at Erica, who might be crying, but the sparks and flares of light at the edges of her vision have begun, so it's hard to tell. She's not saying anything, though, so Vee continues, 'And if you had come in, of course I would have shouted at you to go. I wouldn't have wanted you to see. One of my aunts made me go to see my mother in her coffin and I never forgave her for it. If you were going to be a child without a mother, you didn't need to see it. So yes, I might have shouted at you. But it would have been to save you from something I didn't think you should see.'

God, this pain. All of it, inside and out. Drugs, then sleep, and if tomorrow never comes, well—

'My mother,' Erica says, and she takes Vee's hand in her own. Vee can feel a shaking in her skin, vibration in her palm, as though every cell of her has become held breath. 'Was Leonie my mother? You just said, you knew what it was to be a child without a mother.' Erica's body is leaning into Vee's, her weight against her shoulder, as though she is a child again, waiting for comfort, for love.

Vee closes her eyes – the lights in her vision don't switch off, just shine brighter against the blessed black – and pulls a breath in, deep. This would be the time. If she was certain. Would Leonie thank her for it, if she was?

She can feel how Erica is waiting.

Now is the time.

She puts a hand to her face, and reaches for the bench with the other, holding tight. Vertigo, or worse, 'I need to get home.' It's like unlatching a door that the wind has been teasing its way around: there's a rush and thud of pain, head, neck, face, spine, and she isn't in this room anymore, isn't anywhere except in this burning darkness at the back of her left eye socket. Please, not her sight. Not yet.

25 April 2018

'I'm sorry I'm late,' Erica says, almost as soon as her key has moved the front door away from its frame, 'I just wanted to walk it one more time, and then I got talking to some of the staff, and it just felt as if I couldn't leave. Once this week is over, I'll be more . . .' she pauses, because she's not sure what the word is. More present? More reliable? More undemanding? Not for the first time, she's glad Vee doesn't see her at home. She bends and unzips her boots, slides them off. Her feet exhale and relax to flatness on the floor. It must be four months since she went to a yoga class. She hangs up her coat, then stretches her arms above her head. She has been hunching over the vitrines, poring over the detail.

There's no sign of Tom but there is the sound of his half-snore, half-breathing coming through the monitor, eerie in the space when Erica has stopped talking.

'It's OK,' Marcus says.

'And when I got out, they were limiting how many people were going down to the tube, so I had to wait. I should have got a bus, really, but by the time I realised how long it was going to take . . .' she couldn't have cared less, really. She was thinking about Vee, Leonie, her mother, three women who made her own history, all either dead or dying. She's tried to tell herself that when Vee described Leonie as her mother, she was just confused. It was no more than another symptom of the tumour. Erica has never had any reason to doubt her parentage. She has a birth certificate that declares in confident type that her mother is Ursula Woodhouse, her father Alec George Woodhouse.

And yet, she cannot leave the idea alone. She stood among the mass of people waiting to get on the tube and she felt – what? Something calmer than confusion, bigger than wondering. Something that, along with the little life nestling in her pelvis, was weighting her world, at the same time as making sense of it.

And why didn't Vee answer? Was it really the headache or was that an excuse? Erica will ask again, and she won't take no for an answer next time.

'Erica.' Marcus walks towards her, and she almost steps back; the shock of her reaction makes her look at him, properly, for the first time since she got home. (The first time today? This week?) He looks tired. He's smiling. He puts his hands on her shoulders, gently, 'Erica, it's OK. I texted you to say to take your time. Tom and I were fine. We talked about global politics. He's got some surprisingly radical views for a twenty-month old.'

She laughs and tilts in towards him, lets the top of his chest take the weight of the front of her shoulders. Her head sits sideways against the base of his throat. 'I didn't see your text. I'm sorry.'

'Don't worry about it. Is everything set? My mum's staying over, for the opening, so we can stay out as late as we like. Or I could book a hotel. But I didn't want to book it without checking with you.' She thinks of the baby she's concealing from him. Whether she has it or not, she needs his understanding, and his support. Otherwise the two of them are as good as done.

She shrugs further into him, feels his arms wrap round her shoulders. 'I don't know,' she says. 'I thought it was good, but now I don't know.'

'You know I'm proud of you, don't you?'

She looks up at him. Before she met Vee, she might have said yes, automatically, but – 'Actually, I don't think I do. I've felt as though you'd rather I hadn't taken it on.'

Marcus sighs, 'I know.'

'What do you know? That I felt that way, or you did?' This exhibition has sharpened Erica's attention to detail, woken her research muscles again. And though she wants to shower, to sleep, she wants her marriage to work, more. Well, that's a relief. There have been times lately when she felt she would have exchanged everything except Tom for twelve hours' sleep.

'Both,' Marcus says, and adds, 'We need to talk, don't we?'

'Yes. We do.' The new life in Erica makes itself known in an urgent desire for cereal with hot milk. There's no point in trying to keep this to herself, and anyway, it's not fair. Marcus isn't her enemy. 'And I've got something important to tell you.'

316

Part 7: Developing

There are things that a competent photographer can do in a darkroom to alter an image. You can crop to show what you want, and exclude what you would prefer the viewer not to see. What you cannot do is get detail from a negative, if the detail isn't there in the first place. Don't be afraid to look closely; examine your subject. Interrogate it.

Veronica Moon, *Women in Photographs* (unpublished)

'Veronica Moon winning the Political Photograph of the Year Award, 1979'

Exhibition Section: Focus on the Photographer

Images of Moon are few and far between. Like many photographers she was, and is, if not exactly camera-shy, then wary of handing over control to another photographer. She'd rather be behind the camera, deciding what is seen.

In this section of the exhibition you will see images of Moon, some of which were taken as self-portraits with a timer on the camera (if you look closely, you'll see that in the full-length self-portraits she has the remote shutter in her right hand). Some are press photographs taken at public appearances, including the awarding of the Political Photograph of the Year Award in December 1979 for the portrait she took of Margaret Thatcher earlier that year. The remainder are from Moon's private collection. Many were taken by Leonie Barratt during the years the two shared a flat in London (1970–1977). It's clear from Moon's expressions in several of these that she was taken unawares.

Photographs on film could not be as easily cropped, filtered or deleted as they are today. When you leave the exhibition, next time you take a photograph, challenge yourself to do what Veronica Moon did:

Spend some time thinking about what you want the image to capture.

Take one photograph.

Accept it.

In 2018:

- A survey finds that ten per cent of girls aged 14–21 have been unable to afford sanitary protection
- Fewer than a third of the UK's most influential jobs are held by women
- Theresa May is Britain's second female prime minister. She and her husband, when interviewed, refer to 'girl jobs' and 'boy jobs'
- In the UK, there are 208 women MPs (thirty-two per cent of the House of Commons) and 206 female peers (twenty-six per cent of the House of Lords)
- There is still a gender pay gap – the gap for women of colour is considerably worse than the gap for white women; research in the US suggests that black women are paid thirty-eight per cent less than white men and twenty-one per cent less than white women
- Three million girls worldwide are at risk of undergoing FGM
- The #MeToo movement has provoked discussion and action about sexual harassment worldwide
- The United Nations stated that, 'No country in the world has successfully eliminated discrimination against women or achieved full equality'

Veroinca Moon's health is worsening, and Leonie Barratt has been dead for nearly thirty-four years.

26 April 2018

Exhibition opening day

'I still can't believe you came! Do you want to come and talk to people?' Erica asks, breathless, as she hurries into the side room where Vee is sitting. 'There are a lot here, you know. I recognise some of them from the photos.'

Vee can't believe she came, either. She was planning to drop off the envelope for Erica later in the week, or ask her to come over. But she was sitting at home an hour ago, thinking about how long she has waited to be have her work recognised, and realised that she did, after all, want to be here. And she had something to say to Erica, as well as something to give her. So what if she had lost her nerve when she arrived, waved at Erica and stepped behind the door marked 'PRIVATE', into an office stacked with boxes of catalogues and the trays the wine glasses were stored in? She can go out into the space later, if she feels up to it. When she's done this.

'Erica, I'm very proud of you,' she says. 'You've done a great job. You've – you've brought me back to life.'

'Thank you,' Erica says, 'Vee, it's been an honour.'

Vee can't trust herself not to cry, so she asks, 'How did the press call go this afternoon?'

'All good, I think' – Erica squishes her eyes shut for a moment – 'I can't think about that now. You're going to stay? Now you're here?'

'I don't know.' On the one hand, it's the last thing she wants to do. On the other hand, there are people coming who she will probably never see again: sisters from the old days, the only people who remember Leonie too. She would like to say good-bye to them.

Erica is done up to the nines, of course, heels and a dress and she's obviously had her hair done. Still, it's her night, and this is how the patriarchy has made Erica thinks a woman looks on a special occasion.

'I'm sure people would love to see you,' and she adds, hurriedly, 'not to make a speech, or anything. Just to be there.'

Vee smiles. 'I might come out in a while.' She's not sure that she will. But she does want to support Erica. She feels as though she should, as though she owes it to Leonie, in some odd way. And maybe, just maybe, she is ready to be proud of what she, Veronica Moon, has achieved, instead of angry at what she lost.

Knowing at last that she did try to save Leonie makes her genuinely happy. If happiness is possible, and if the tumour isn't tricking her. Whatever she thinks she has now is uncertain.

Erica is waiting. 'You should be out there. It's your night.'

Erica sits down, and looks straight into Vee's face. 'I haven't said thank you. I will – out there. But I wanted to say it, now. This exhibition – all you've done for it. It's more than I could have thought possible. And – you've helped me to understand.'

'Understand what?'

'Well, more about the history, of course, but that's – that's' – Erica puts her hand to her temples – 'that's the past.' Would that it were, Vee thinks – the tumour seems to be aligning all of the parts of her life that she still holds, childhood and adulthood and this creeping exhausting death, as though it's all laid out in two dimensions in front of her. Too much flash, no depth of field. 'But talking to you has made me realise things about my own life.'

324

'I'm glad I've been of some use, Erica.'

'I feel as though I've woken up,' Erica says, 'and I feel as though I have choices, again. I haven't felt like that for a long time.'

Vee reaches out a hand, and Erica leans forward and takes it. 'You have choices,' she says, 'and you're allowed to make mistakes. Just make them because you chose the wrong direction, not because you stayed asleep.'

'Yes,' Erica says. 'Yes. Thank you. For everything.'

'If you cry, you'll smudge your mascara.'

Erica smiles, half-laughs. 'Fuck my mascara,' she says, 'I've got better things to think about.'

And for all that there's so little Vee can trust in her mind anymore, she trusts this feeling, the one that is filling her, now, of pride in knowing this woman, of certainty that she is looking at Leonie's daughter. 'Go,' she gets out before she starts to cry, 'go and make the most of this.'

While Erica is out there among the noise, talking to those who remain of Vee's contemporaries, hearing from the people who claim to be influenced by her, Vee sits quietly, in the relative silence of this meeting room, surrounded by boxes filled with exhibition catalogues, and thinks about how, after tonight, she will never, ever speak to anyone that she doesn't absolutely have to speak to, ever again. She'll talk to doctors and to Marja. She will lie with her eyes open, when she's awake, making sure that she can still see. And she will sleep, and she will take painkillers, more and more of them. If her sight goes, she'll take too many. She's already started to squirrel them away, getting prescriptions at every hospital appointment, popping the extras out of their foil and into a jar that she keeps in her bedside drawer. She can find it, and open it, with her eyes closed. She has practised. Because if she can't have her sight, she won't be stoic. She won't endure. She'll reach for silence, through the dark.

When Erica starts to talk, she'll go and stand at the back of the gallery. She might be proud of herself, a little, but she is proud of Erica too, and sure she's done the right thing in leaving all of her papers to her. (She still hasn't opened the boxes, but there are bound to be things in there she can use. Leonie's letters, maybe some manuscripts. She can't face looking, doesn't trust her judgement, either, about what should stay and what should go.)

She's not sure about giving Erica the envelope, yet.

Tik-tik-tik.

The fork against the edge of the champagne flute goes through the sound in the gallery, taking the conversation level from din down to hubbub down to the closest you will ever get to silence at an event like this.

Veronica stands. She will listen to Erica's speech. She will say goodbye to the people she remembers, she will talk to Erica one last time, and then she will go home. And that will be the end of it.

Vee, in the lost place, 1984

IT HAD BEEN SUCH A TINY act of forgetting, and under the circumstances an entirely understandable one. Instead of including a note to the lab with her requirements, as she would have done with a more everyday roll of film, she had decided to call. She had wanted to say that the last five shots on the film were not to be used, to explain why, and to make absolutely sure she was heard, understood.

But she hadn't called. She'd gone home and got into bed. She wasn't tired but she was cold with shock and grief, over-exposed to the world. She needed the dark. She'd dropped into a doze, a terrible half-sleep in which her brain reran the morning: Ursula crying, Erica being ushered away to her room, the sight of Leonie, quiet and clammy. Waking after an hour that felt like seven, she went downstairs and poured herself a glass of rum, and then another. Annabel had been to collect the films that were waiting to go to the lab, and drop off contact sheets for Vee to look at. And Vee was definitely planning to call the lab. She had another drink; she started to get the calls from their friends, as the news started to bleed out into their world, their friends, the women Leonie knew. She didn't call the lab. She couldn't, really, feel any sense of urgency about it. The thought of the world continuing to turn seemed ridiculous to her. And every time she formed the intention to make the call, explain what needed to be done with the film, either the phone rang again, or the thought of having to sound businesslike, make a request as though this was any other film on any other day, felt too impossible. There was no Leonie any more. And there had always been Leonie. This was a new world, harsh, lonely, and impossible to navigate, and Vee found she had no will to try.

The next day, she'd gone to work, because she didn't know what else to do. She'd been photographing a girl band, with permed hair, ripped jeans and tanned stomachs. She caught their excitement, their exhausting happy exuberance, and she wished that she had the words to tell them all the ways they were betraying themselves and all that the generation before them had worked for. This was not what she had hoped for, the night she had photographed tearful beauty queens outside the Café de Paris, the night Leonie hurled flour bombs at Bob Hope. It was a tiring shoot, noisy and shambolic, with the band's manager interrupting and the girls always needing something more, coffee or extra lipgloss. And maybe Vee forgot to make the phone call to the lab, or maybe it wasn't even anything that deliberate, that active. She had just lost the intention to do it, among all the other things she lost with Leonie. Nothing had mattered, in those days. Just groping through to another sleepless night.

Leonie's funeral had been a private family event, which was Ursula-speak for 'no feminists', and so Vee had got together with some of the old crowd, to drink and talk and miss their friend. Then she had gone back to trudging through grief, the plod and ache she remembered so well from the first weeks after her father died. She had seen the path ahead as a slow, sore journey to something like acceptance; she knew she hadn't chosen it, but she had no choice but to keep walking along it.

And then the article about Leonie came out, to coincide with the publication of her book, which had been delayed by a month. It was on the day Vee had a meeting with her publisher about her photography book. She had been so proud of *Women in Photographs*, so excited for the ways it would empower her sisters. But now it seemed unimportant, egotistical, and she could not have cared less.

When she had got home, there were seventeen messages on her answering machine, most of them from journalists wanting a comment. Was it true that she had photographed Leonie Barratt as she died, watched her die, called for help only when it was too late? She'd sat on the floor and cried until she was empty. Then she played the messages again, and cried again. She didn't know how to start. She had never been good with words, and now there were none.

She didn't respond to the messages.

And then came the calls from friends, looking to find the truth, wondering how this could have happened. Surely Vee had not really done what Ursula accused her of, all over the newspapers, to anyone who would listen? Annabel offered to deal with them, but Vee knew it was her job. She made a list of everyone who called that week – forty-three people, in the end – and resolved to spend Saturday afternoon on the phone, explaining, explaining. Sort of explaining, anyway. It was easiest to say that she hadn't known Leonie was dead than to try to articulate the denial and fear that kept her pressing the shutter: the deep sure knowledge that as soon as she stopped taking photographs, she would have to raise her voice, call for help, say the words. And as soon as she did that, Leonie would be gone for sure. It was impossible to explain, to a world not minded to understand – that it seemed that Leonie would not be gone, not really, until Vee called for help and made it so.

Bea, Fen and Kiki had all understood that she would never hurt Leonie. But even with the people she was closest to now Leonie was gone, she couldn't get the words out, couldn't do anything but cry, a day-in day-out leaking of grief and sorrow for Leonie and, yes, sorrow for herself.

And then came Ursula's interview: billed as '*the inside story from Leonie Barratt's real sister*'. In fairness, Vee wasn't the only one who got the hammer. Ursula, had looked sadly into the camera for some sub-David Bailey hack photographer who made her look overtired and over-madeup at the same time. It could have been deliberate, but if so, it was cruel. The journalist had been cruel, too, encouraging Ursula to talk about how the feminist movement had not only robbed her of a sister but robbed Leonie of peace of mind and the happy life she could have had.

'People don't die of a heart attack, grossly overweight and terribly lonely, for no reason,' Ursula was quoted as saying, 'I blame the choices my sister made. And I don't mean overeating. Her so-called friends didn't really support her, and Veronica Moon, who was supposed to be her best friend of all, watched her die for the sake of her own career. My poor sister Leonie was brainwashed by so-called feminists and she paid the price.' The idea of Leonie being brainwashed was, theoretically, laughable, but Vee was empty of laughter. She was angry with Ursula, of course, but with the newspapers too, for encouraging her to leak her grief, to spill her story, to hurt herself, and Vee, and most of all, the memory of Leonie. How terrible for the most important thing about you to be the way you die. It added insult to the injury, so strongly felt by Vee now, that Leonie's brilliance was never appreciated in her lifetime.

Editors called to cancel their commissions with her, just until things blew over, they said, but they never called again. Her wider circle of friends in the movement, too, got colder; or it could be that Vee had never been part of them, never more than a hanger-on. It could have been that, because she wouldn't – couldn't – talk about it, they thought she had something to hide, and the newspaper accounts of Leonie's death were true.

She knew that in some quarters she had never been forgiven for photographing Thatcher, and that because she was successful, she seemed to be a sell-out. For all that Leonie had accused her of betraying her sisters, from time to time, it had been nothing more than provocation, really: a flexing of intellect, a poking at Vee to test that she was really solid, sound, a true sister. And Leonie never once gave her a hard time about earning good money, something Vee had always suspected was behind the hostility of some of the other women she knew in the movement. She had always been scrupulous about donating royalties to the causes she photographed, but that brought no warmth to some earth-mothers' hearts.

Vee's publisher called to say they thought it best to delay publication of her book. She agreed. She tried to care, but she couldn't. She hunkered down over the winter, and when the phone didn't start to ring again, she drove to Scotland in the spring, photographed skies, cliffs, seas, wondered at the beauty of nature but in an intellectual, headbound way. Nothing touched her heart. Her lens didn't capture anything remarkable, or if it did, she couldn't see it. She came home to a still-silent answering machine, rented out her house, and went to Canada for a year; more space, more beauty, more lack of inspiration. First, she stopped taking film to be developed, then she stopped taking photographs at all. Instead she walked, and looked, and breathed deeply. She had money, but it wouldn't see her out. She had twenty, maybe thirty years left to live. She needed to do something.

She went back to Essex – not the place where she grew up, not those streets, not that anyone would know her there. She bought a house, another, turned them into flats, rented them to young women who were trying to set out in life without using marriage as a means to doing so. She charged a rent that was below the market rate; she vetted the applicants herself, looked for the ones who needed a stepping stone. She made money, bought more houses in more places, turned them into flats, and rented them out too. She employed a female manager, and a maintenance team made up of women. When she couldn't find female plumbers and electricians, she set up bursaries to train them. The men she employed she used on an ad-hoc basis; she interviewed them herself, first, was at her frostiest and least compromising. One 'love', one patronising explanation of how water needed to be under pressure to travel upwards, and they were out. She went travelling again. China, this time, then India. She didn't bother to pack a camera.

When she got home after one of these trips, there was a message on the answering machine from Bea. They were going to run courses in photography at the university, she said, as part of their new media degrees. Would Vee be interested in teaching on portraiture and on photojournalism? Could she design and teach a module on the technical side of photography, drawing on her specialism of flash-free images?

Vee's first instinct was to refuse. But then she looked at her diary. It was tiring, to fill her time. She called Bea back. She taught. She wasn't terrible at it, and it wasn't terrible. Five years passed, ten.

The housing market boomed. She had an offer she couldn't refuse for her properties. She was minded to refuse it, all the same – weekends would have to be filled, without the business to keep an eye on – but then the headaches started. That was in 2005. She was lucky, they said, the tumour was operable and treatable. So she was operated on, treated. She gave her solicitor's name as her next of kin. Women in the hospital tried to make friends with her, but she had no appetite for friendship. There was a gap in her memories when she woke from the surgery, as she knew there would be: a space that made her unconfident when she was with people she was supposed to know. She looked through her old photographs. They didn't help. If anything, they made her feel lonelier than ever. A photograph was worth nothing if you couldn't find the emotions that went with it. Sometimes she'd look at an image and feel as though a wind was blowing through her. Mostly, she just felt as though she wasn't a real person anymore: surgery had reduced her to two dimensions.

She found undeveloped films, and developed them, for the sake of something to do. One of them was mainly shots of Leonie and little Erica. Looking at it hurt, every bit as much as it should, and there was something about the child that Vee knew was important. She almost posted it to Ursula, but her instinct told her to put it away, somewhere safe, instead. No one could tell her anything about what happened when Leonie died, because she hadn't told anyone.

And through all of those years, the internet had been making itself known, becoming stronger and faster, and women started to connect with each other in new ways, different ways. Vee had imagined a quiet retirement, gentle travels and quiet enjoyment of art and walking, but people who remembered her found her and contacted her via the agency that licensed her photographs. She had ignored them while she was teaching, but now her time expanded again. She got into the habit of day-to-day living: a walk, reading, galleries or films in the afternoon. She marched. She wrote to her MP when prompted by the Fawcett Society. She didn't think she was unhappy.

She was invited to sponsor this or photograph that or come and join in here. She sponsored, but she didn't show up to anything. Illness (non-specific) was her excuse, for a while, but she got better. She travelled again but she didn't take her camera with her. Everywhere were people with digital cameras; it was The

Future, newly arrived, and Vee ached for the days of light meter and darkroom, judgement and skill. She didn't ache for friends, apart from the one she would never get back. It could have been that the part of her brain that cared about others, wanted to connect, was part of what she lost in the operating theatre with that first tumour. It could have been that it was never that big to begin with. All she was left with was tenderness where she knew the memories of her father's death and Leonie's were.

26 April 2018

Erica

Oh, Erica is proud. She was proud already, and then Vee came, and praised her, and she didn't know how to add it to her bursting heart. As she looks along the space of the gallery, so well prepared and so true to her vision, and sees how many people are crowding round the images, she takes a breath and tells herself she has done a great job. This busy, buzzy space will, over the coming months, show thousands of people what a force Veronica Moon was, how far feminism has come and how much is still to do.

The tapping of the champagne flute, the expectant semi-silence that follows, brings Erica back to tonight. How can it be time for her speech, already? She's nauseous with a sickness that is different to the one she fought this morning, not wanting Marcus to see it, throwing up quietly in the en-suite when he was downstairs unloading the dishwasher. They've had the first conversation about the pregnancy. Both of them were cautious. Neither of them is sure.

It wasn't until Tuesday, after Vee left, that Erica admitted to herself that this is more than a retrospective: it's a memorial. Veronica Moon leaves only photographs. But who will commemorate the person? Who will mourn? Erica can't let herself think this now (if it is her, and not just her hormones, which is more than possible). She has to focus.

Fortunately – something Erica has learned in academia, watching presentations and later giving one or two, at conferences, then lecturing – silence reads as confidence. She takes a sip of water and glances at her notes. They are words, not sentences, because she will look worse if she loses her place and stumbles.

'Good evening, and welcome,' she begins. Marcus had suggested jokingly that she had better not say 'ladies and gentlemen' but actually, he was right. 'We are here, at the opening of this exhibition of the work of Veronica Moon, to celebrate the contribution that she made to second wave feminism in the UK. She recorded it, yes, but she shaped it, by dint of being the success that she was.'

She raises her head and looks around. Vee is standing at the back of the crowd. No one has seen her. She gives Erica the smallest of smiles, the slightest of nods, and Erica wishes she still had a living mother. Breathe, Erica. She looks at her notes.

'The feminist movement in this country has had many stars, many suns, many shining lights. But only one moon.' There's a hum of laughter around the space. Erica tries to make her voice come from her diaphragm, now, not the top of her chest. 'I'm not going to say a lot about the work, because it speaks for itself. But I will talk about the moon.' She wants to look at Vee, but knows that, if she does, everyone will turn to see where she is looking, and Vee won't want that. So she shifts her gaze to the portrait of Leonie, just visible over the heads to the right. Oh, for an eighth of that woman's confidence, a tenth of her ability to speak the truth as she saw it.

'The moon is always with us, although sometimes it is hidden by the light or the shadows of other bodies. The moon shapes the tides and so shapes our experience of the world. The moon is connected, intimately, to the experience of women everywhere.'

This had looked cleverer on paper; the audience looks, if not bored, tolerant at best. Well, Erica is better on paper. That's why she's an academic, and now a curator. She keeps. She holds.

She looks back at her notes. She's written, 're-centring'. She can certainly speak to that. She puts a hand to her belly and breathes.

'When I began this project, it was because I found treasure in my mother's attic. Leonie Barratt's box of clippings and mementos of Veronica Moon's work. Even though this was not, strictly, my specialism, and even though historians must always be wary of the pull of the personal, I could not stop thinking about Veronica Moon, about Leonie Barratt, about all of the other women in the photographs. They deserve to be seen. And heard.

'We have work to do, in this world, in making sure women's voices are heard. One look at the news, or half an hour of TV, remind us that women are still talked over the top of, sidelined, ignored, and oppressed.

'By recognising, remembering and re-centring the women who showed their faces and raised their voices, in the 1960s, 1970s, and 1980s, we can be part of the change the world still needs. Veronica Moon is an example to us all of how to see women in the world: strong, capable, powerful, and equal.'

The applause surprises her; she looks around, smiles, waits for it to stop.

She finds Vee's face at the back of the crowd. 'It's been a pleasure and an honour to curate this exhibition and, in doing so, to spend time with the incomparable, unforgettable Veronica Moon. Thank you.'

Marcus catches her eye across the room, smiles. He looks proud of her. For now, that's enough.

And then she sees Veronica approaching through the crowd. Others notice, and the applause starts up again, warmer than politeness. Vee is wearing a long T-shirt over leggings, both a dark denim-ish grey, and shoes that Erica hasn't seen her in before, a kind of clog, thick-soled, in mustard-coloured leather. No makeup, of course; short hair brushed back as usual, curling behind her ears. Erica has not been able to spot where the scar from Vee's previous surgery is, but she knows it must be at the place where her hair kinks, above her left ear, because that's where her hand goes, when she's anxious, when she's talking about being ill.

Vee makes her way to Erica's side without smiling, without looking left or right. She steps forward, holding the podium with both hands, leaning forward. Erica raises her mobile, takes a photograph of Vee, and then a few of the people watching her. The images won't be anything special, but suddenly she feels the need for her own record, just for her, that she is here, that she is watching this woman at what is almost certain to be her last public appearance. She feels a grim sort of protectiveness; wonders if anyone else in the room sees how frail Vee is, how unwell. It feels that the room holds its breath. Not just the people here, but those in the photographs too.

Vee seems small. She breathes in, out, and then she looks forward and starts to speak.

Vee hasn't really much of an idea of what she wants to say. She wasn't going to say anything at all. Was going to slip away.

But then, listening to Erica, she was hit with the knowledge that this is, without any doubt – she will not think of the shadow of doubt, of the shadow of anything, for fear of inviting darkness behind her eyes – this is her last chance to be heard. She used to think that her photographs were her voice. She used to think it didn't matter if she was misunderstood. And then came Erica.

She looks across at the younger woman – what does it matter if she's madeup to the nines? It's her fine brain that matters. And she feels panic, panic because she has never spoken publicly, because she cannot trust her brain, because Erica has spent months applying herself to the words all around them tonight. The faces turned towards her are full of surprise, expectation, waiting. It would make a great photograph. But she cannot talk. She never could. If she had been able to, she might have saved her name, long ago.

Erica leans forward, and says quietly, 'Tell us what you remember.'

Yes. She can do that.

'This is what I remember,' she begins. Her voice feels thin in her throat and she has a sense of the room leaning in to her. That won't do. She straightens, tightens her hold, begins again.

'This is what I remember. I remember that, in 1968, I was a young woman from Essex who knew what a camera could do, but not a lot else. I had a feeling, though, that I was worth more than the world was telling me I was worth. I could—' Her mouth has too much saliva, from the drugs, and a tang of metal. 'I could taste it. So I went to see what some women at Dagenham were doing to change the world. And, thanks to Leonie Barratt, I joined in.

'This is what I remember about the women's movement. It was a fierce, furious beast, and it was sure that it would win. It didn't compromise and it didn't care. It invited the world to smell its hairy armpits and to mock its dungarees and it didn't matter because women knew we were right.'

'Hell yeah!' shouts one of the sisters, Kiki maybe, or Fen, from the back, and although Vee appreciates it, she can't acknowledge it, can't do anything but keep her eyes on the top of the podium. There's the soft steadiness of Erica's presence to her left. She doesn't look at her; feeling her there is enough.

'This is what I remember about Leonie Barratt. She was the cleverest woman I knew – the cleverest woman any of us knew. We let her down because we didn't see that she was right. If we had listened to her more closely, we might not be where we are now. We might not be living—' Her throat constricts around the 'living', cutting it off at the end, as though to remind Vee that she is barely living at all, or perhaps that she barely has been. Try again, Vee. Not every shot is a winner. 'We might not be living in a world of Me Too and women's reproductive rights being rolled back, if we'd listened to Leonie. We might have closed the gender pay gap by now. We might have men who can look after a baby without the world treating them as though they are superheroes.'

There's applause, sudden and loud, as Vee draws breath. She could swear she smells lavender. Her back aches; her legs are telling her there's not much standing left in them. She doesn't always trust what her body says but this she believes.

'And this is what I remember about the night Leonie Barratt died.'

The room inhales, and Vee looks up, over the heads of those who are waiting to hear what she will say. She looks into the photograph of her friend's face, the cat-got-the-cream laziness in her half-smile. Leonie, who never apologised. Vee never learned what power there was in that. 'I remember – nothing. But there are some things that I know. I know that I would never deliberately do anything to hurt Leonie, and she would never have done anything to hurt me. I know that Leonie Barratt and Veronica

Moon deserve better than being reduced to one image, on one day. I know that for as long as we keep obsessing over the details of how things look, we will never solve the bigger problem of how the world needs to be.'

There's applause, again, loud, again, and although it's meant to show Vee how much support there is for her, for her words, it feels like an attack, each palm meeting palm another brain cell lighting up in agony as it dies.

Erica thinks Vee might be gripping harder at the podium, might be wincing, but it's hard to judge whether the discomfort is at being so publicly on view, or something else. Vee inhales; it's audible from where Erica stands.

She steps forward, and Vee takes her arm. Together they make their way through the crowd, and out.

In the half-dark away from the gallery lights, Vee looks as though she is already a shadow. Erica has seen this greyness on her before, when she's in pain.

'Can I bring you anything?'

There is a tiny shake of the head in response, as though Vee's skull is balanced on her neck, rather than attached to it. Erica notices the blister pack of tablets, the glass of water, on the table.

'Would you like to take some of these tablets now?'

A tiny nod. She pushes two pills from the pack, puts them in Vee's palm, and passes her the glass. Vee swallows the medication with the practised gulp of the long-term patient; Erica takes the glass from her shaking hand, returns it to the table, sits in a chair next to her, and waits. How much did it cost Vee to say those words? How right she is. Whatever Erica does now, about Marcus, the baby, everything, will be different because she met Veronica Moon.

Ten minutes pass, and then Vee opens her eyes, nods to Erica: permission to speak, an acknowledgement that things are better, for the moment.

'You've given me much more than you needed to,' Erica says, as softly as she can to still be heard above the noise and chatter from the party beyond the door. 'And I can see what it's cost you. Why?'

'Because . . .' but there's a pause, and it gets longer, and it's as though Vee isn't even in the room anymore.

Vee

'Because . . .' Because what, though? Because the new tumour was already back? Because her thoughts weren't trustworthy? Because she still thinks she owes Leonie something? Owes this child a mother? (Strange thought.) When she first went to meet Erica, in January, it was only going to be a courtesy: she was going to let her get on with it. She had no intention of getting involved. Something changed.

'You should be proud,' Erica says.

'Everything comes around.'

'But you know you were good?' Erica has the same obstinate tone as Leonie when she's making a point. Vee smiles and it feels as though it comes from somewhere, is a real smile, a feeling that has never changed; she could be sixteen, in the darkroom her dad made for her, watching an image swim to the surface of the paper as it develops.

'I know I was good.'

'Good.'

Vee closes her eyes and then she is aware of Erica leaning towards her, hovering a hand over her arm, not touching it, 'You're shaking, Veronica.'

'I'm tired.'

'Is that all?'

In her head, Vee says: yes, Erica, that's all. Don't fuss. What comes out of her mouth is different, 'I think so. I don't know.'

'You're not usually uncertain.' There's no malice in Erica's tone; it's observation, and it's fair enough. Well, there it is. You reap as you sow. 'You should have seen the way people were looking at your work. Before you came out.'

There was something that Vee needed to say to Erica, to give her; she can't remember what. There's a mushrooming of noise in the gallery, laughter, the gradual raising of voices over other voices so that soon everyone will be shouting over everyone without realising they are doing it. Each notch in volume is a notch of pain.

She needs to remember the thing for Erica. And then she can go home and be done with all of this.

'They love the contact sheets,' Erica continues, with the chattering brightness of a woman at a deathbed: anything but silence. 'I suppose a lot of people don't know what they are. And it's a reminder of old times, for the rest.'

That's what she's been trying to remember. 'In my bag,' Vee says. She cannot open her eyes, now; she hurts, skull and spine, at the very thought of light.

There's the sound of the zip of Vee's bag pulling back. 'What do you need? Do you have more painkillers in here?'

'There's an envelope for you,' Vee says.

It's A4, board-backed, and Vee checked more than once that she had put the right things in it, and that she had put it into her bag. She found an empty mug in the fridge this morning, and has left her key in the front door more than once over the last week. She hears Erica tear at the paper flap; a chair scrapes as she sits. 'What are these?'

'Look,' Vee says. Erica has the power over the images now.

There is a rustling sound. Erica is taking out the two contact sheets. If Vee can't speak of this – and she doesn't dare, in case she is wrong – then the images can.

The first contact sheet is the film of Leonie and Erica on the day Leonie died. Vee hadn't looked at these photographs for years. They had been a shock when she developed them, in her own darkroom, sometime during her recovery from surgery. Her world had lurched and pitched as she watched the images bloom through the liquid in the chemical bath. She saw love, affection, a bond. She saw a mother and daughter. Or, she thought she did. In the photographs, the roundness of Leonie's body made it look as though she was curving herself in, around Erica, an animal with her young. In one image, Erica looked simply, joyously happy; about to laugh, not yet moving, so caught in uncoerced delight. The expression on Leonie's face matches it.

Vee cannot remember taking these, and when she looked at them they didn't seem right. She saw love, but she felt something more complicated. It could be that the ill-feeling was hers, though, and the photograph was true. In another image, the two of them were looking at each other, their faces almost mirror-images. The bridge of Erica's nose was slightly less pronounced than that of Leonie's; Leonie's chin was jowlish and lost to comparison. But the relationship was clear. You might, if you had been told it often enough, believe that you were looking at an aunt and her niece. But if you came to this photograph cold there would be no question that you were looking at a mother and daughter. And a mother and daughter who adored each other, at that.

But Vee has never really trusted the photographs she took on the day Leonie died. Nothing in her other memories of Leonie – nothing in her writing – suggested she could love a child, or would want to. And yet, here is something you could class as evidence that she did.

The second contact sheet is the photographs of Erica and Tom that Vee took at the Greenham Common Peace Garden. Developing them, along with the pictures from the rally, in the darkroom in her hollowed-out, blacked-out attic, she had known that it was likely to be the last time she went through this process of particular chemical magic.

Vee would have been proud of these portraits of Erica, if she was still a photographer. The light, the way the rain in the air diffused it, the paleness and softness of the trees and sky mean that Erica's face is strong and clear against a fading world. In Vee's favourite – she has circled it, like she did in the old days, she couldn't help herself – Erica is looking straight into the camera, eyes dark, hair made lighter than it is in reality by the spring light, mouth ready to ask a question. It is perfectly Erica, and at the same time, perfectly Leonie, despite the changes Erica has chosen to make to her face. In another, she is looking at Tom. It matches the way Erica and Leonie are looking at each other, on the other contact sheet. Displayed side by side, a connection is asking to be made.

The pain is not worsening, but it's changing, a series of tremors flecking at the edges of her consciousness. The noise from the adjacent gallery seems to be fading, as though Vee has become untethered, and is drifting away. Erica is still close, though, sliding the contact sheets over each other: there's a smoothness to the sound of it, and then the pierce of air while Erica inhales. 'Veronica?'

Vee keeps her eyes closed; waits. The world is shrinking. It's too late to wonder whether she has done the right thing. The thing is done.

'Vee? Is this – was Leonie my mother?'

Vee wants to think that Erica knows the answer. That she need do nothing more than provide the evidence.

An unexpected sound: Erica is crying. Vee cannot-cannot-cannot open her eyes. The pain in her head is too much, a domino-effect now of one thing burning out after another, burn-burn-burn. She lifts a hand, hoping – hoping what? That Erica might take it, or at least see it? But Erica is sobbing now, the sounds muffled in a way that suggests her face is in her hands. She won't see anything that Vee is signalling.

So Vee summons her breath. 'What do you think?'

Erica pauses, drags breath into herself. 'Why does it matter what I think? She was or she wasn't.'

'She was and she wasn't,' Vee says. And now, even though there is no new memory, she is finally sure. Ursula did the mothering, but Leonie was the mother.

'What do you mean? Vee? Veronica? Please!' Her eyes will no longer open, but she can feel the closeness of Erica, can imagine her face, touching distance away, with pain and questions and mascara all smudged on her skin.

'Yes,' Veronica says. Some things can only be black and white.

She has never noticed how the catch of a crying breath and the sound of a camera shutter closing are almost the same, a rush and clutch of sound.

And then, there's the darkroom-quiet.

Epilogue

Epilogue

5 February 2019

'Was Norfolk always this far away?' Marcus asks as Erica parks the car near the entrance to the churchyard.

'I know what you mean,' Erica says, stretching back her shoulders and reaching over to tousle Tom's hair, 'do you remember when we used to listen to Radio 4 when we were driving?'

Marcus laughs, 'Yes. And I think there was sometimes silence. Seems unlikely, though.' He takes hold of her hand, kisses it. 'I wouldn't have it any other way, you know.'

'Me neither,' Erica says, though to say that the first three months of baby Leonie's life have been hard work doesn't even come close to describing it.

Vee lasted for a week after being taken ill at the exhibition opening. Erica saw her the day before she died. Vee was in bed, at home, a nurse within earshot. Though Erica had known that she was ill, she wasn't ready for her to be so still, lying tucked under a duvet even though the room was warm, her face a dying grey against the white bedlinen. She'd brought the reviews of the exhibition to show Vee, though she could have recited most of them. 'A thought-provoking triumph', 'a must-see for anyone who cares about the past – and the future – of feminism'. She still couldn't believe it. She'd spent a week doing three things: reading reviews, checking to see how Vee was doing, and looking at the contact sheets of her and Tom, and her and Leonie, and trying to make up her mind that Leonie truly was her birth mother. It had seemed certain, on the night of the exhibition opening; as the days passed, it began to look like more of a stretch of imagination. She's checked her birth certificate, even ordered another copy just to be sure. Marcus said her mother was the one who raised her. She knew she shouldn't even entertain the thought of Leonie as a mother. She's an academic. There was no real evidence. Vee, with her missing memories and her dying brain, was not a reliable witness. And yet, she had not been able to leave the idea alone.

'It's Erica,' she said, taking Vee's hand.

Vee opened one eye, slowly, then the other, turned her head on the pillow, smiled. There was pain, and effort, in the movement; Erica felt an answering ache in her heart, knew it was grief, waiting. She wasn't ready to lose Vee. She had barely found her.

'Do you need anything?'

There was a fraction of a shake. 'My sight's starting to go,' Vee said, as though it was an answer: if I can't see, everything is irrelevant, unwanted.

'Oh.' Tears in Erica's throat stopped her from saying more. And if Vee wasn't crying, she shouldn't be. She wouldn't ask Vee for anything: not comfort, not answers.

Vee nodded, another tiny movement. 'I'm leaving you my papers. I didn't go through them. Leonie used to send me her writing, though. I never threw it away.'

Erica squeezed Vee's hand, and got out a 'Thank you', even though she was almost mute with misery. Ursula's deathbed had been like this, too: not so lucid, not so serene, but every bit as impossible to endure.

Vee closed her eyes. 'Thank you. I didn't think I cared that I was forgotten. But I did.'

And then she seemed to sleep. Erica sat with her until the nurse came quietly up the stairs and touched her on the shoulder, dismissing her.

Erica was not surprised, the next morning, to get the phone call to tell her that Veronica Moon had died, peacefully, in her sleep.

Marcus puts the sling on over his coat and nestles the baby into it; Tom says he wants to walk, because he's too big for the buggy.

'Do you want to do this on your own?' Marcus asks. He already has a hand out to Tom.

'I think so,' Erica says, 'I won't be long.'

'Be as long as you need to be. We'll go and throw sticks in the river,' he says, and then, kissing her on the forehead that's accessible under her hat, 'I'm proud of you. And I love you.'

'Thank you. I love you too.' The moment is warm and sweet enough for her to taste it on her tongue, where it melts the frosted air. The last few months, for all that they have been filled with tiredness and tag-team parenting, may have been her and Marcus's happiest. It was as though Erica inherited some of Veronica's uncompromising spirit with her archive. She told Marcus exactly what she needed; why she was unhappy; what she was afraid of. He listened. He changed his working hours; she signed a contract to edit Leonie's and Vee's unpublished books, to write their linked biographies. (Vee's photography book had been a surprise. Erica can only assume she forgot about the manuscript.) Baby Leonie Sarah was born two days after Erica's thirty-ninth birthday, and she was not easy, not peaceful, not calm. She was loud and determined and Marcus and Erica could not love her more.

They arrive at the gate of the churchyard, where an older woman is just leaving, dead flowers in a basket on her arm. Erica steps back for her to pass through. She smiles at them both, says hello to Tom, and then looks in the sling at the sleeping Leonie.

'Oh, bless,' she says, then, looking up at Marcus, 'Boy or girl?'

Marcus smiles. 'Baby.'

∞

Ursula's funeral would have been the last time Erica was here. Four years. And yesterday, and tomorrow. This place is as timeless as a photograph.

The granite headstone lists Erica's grandparents, then Leonie, then Ursula. The grass around it is short and sparse; the ground, where Erica kneels, pushes cold into her knees.

At Vee's wake, Bea had proposed that there was no one place for Veronica Moon to rest. In the months since, her ashes have been taken, by one of the sisters or another, to the places that were important to her. Fen went to the Colchester grave-yard where Vee's father was buried, Bea to the Peace Garden at Greenham Common; Gloria to the gardens opposite the Royal Albert Hall. And Erica is here.

From her handbag she takes a trowel that looks as though it will be no match for the freezing earth. But she finds a place near the bottom of the gravestone that is already lower than the rest, and she scrapes away until there's a hole the size of her fist. She reaches in her pocket for the envelope Bea gave her, tips the contents into the hole she has made, covers it, and tamps the dry earth down.

Author's Note

The Woman in the Photograph makes me rock back on my heels and laugh because I am so damned proud of it.

This is my fifth published novel, and I am an intelligent, capable, professional woman who knows for a fact that she can write. But there is a part of me that wants to delete that sentence, or make a joke of the fact that I am proud, because—

Because what?

Because even though it's 2019, and women all around us, all around the world, are kicking all kinds of ass in all kinds of ways, owning our power isn't easy. There is still a message, under all of the 'you can be anything' and 'women are amazing' rhetoric, that what women need to do, before anything else, is to be likeable. Likeable is a Trojan horse with flowers woven into her mane; she disguises our fierce and fine capability.

Too often, likeable means: modest, self-effacing, quiet. Expert, yes, but backwards-in-high-heels expert: as though the only way we can display our power, our strength and our cleverness, is by making what we do look easy or pretending our achievements are negligible or answering questions in interviews about juggling work and childcare. Questions that men would never be asked.

Likeable is not okay if it means shucks-it-was-nothing apologetic. Or don't-be-mean-to-me-on-Twitter apologetic. Or feminist-but-oh-my-god-the-calories-in-that apologetic.

I was born in 1971. At school boys did woodwork and girls did cookery, but still my dad taught me how to develop film in his darkroom, and there was never any suggestion that I wouldn't go to university.

As I played with Sindy dolls, women were marching to get girls like me the right to be more than a mother. The feminists of the 1960s and early 1970s gave me the life I have now.

And as I started to work on this book, I wondered what those feminists would think of me: a woman who still does not know how to take a compliment about her work, though I am fine if you say nice things about my hair.

Writing *The Woman in the Photograph* has changed me. It's given me new respect for the women who bellowed and marched and organised, and changed the law. And changed the world. I thought I had educated myself about feminism, but there was so much I didn't know. Spending time in archives and reading the work of women who were uncovering and exploring the things I take for granted was humbling. It's made me determined to be a better feminist myself. It's made me frustrated at how far there is still to go. I'm furious about the ways women are mistreated, and exhausted at the insidious sexism of our day-to-day lives – and I know how sheltered I am from most of it, by dint of being white in the West. I know that makes it easy for me to write this letter: to own my achievement.

The world has changed, but it has not yet changed enough.

We need more unapologetic women. We need them in fiction, and we need them in the world.

I'm proud of *The Woman in the Photograph* and I worked hard on it. I hope it means something to you too.

Stephanie Butland

Acknowledgements

Thank you:

When I was small, I used to 'help' my dad when he took photographs, then I used to 'help' in the darkroom. In the writing of this book my dad was a great help to me (without the inverted commas). Veronica's ability and understanding of her craft come from him, as do the words of her unpublished book.

For expertise, advice, and/or outings: Luke Dodd, Clare Grafik, Shelley Harris, Rebecca Leete, Clare Macintosh, Louise Williams.

You know what for: Carys Bray, Sarah Franklin, Shelley Harris.

For patience, wisdom, and general knocking it out of the park: Oli Munson.

Bonnier: especially Sarah, Katie, Margaret, Clare, Sahina Felice, Imogen, Alex, Kate, James, Nico, Vincent, Angie, Victoria, Jeff, Graham, Sarah and Jennie.

A M Heath: especially Florence, Alexandra, Prema, Mairi and Vickie.

For sharp and intelligent copyediting and proofreading: Genevieve Pegg and Jane Howard.

The unsung heroes of publishing are the bloggers and booksellers who champion the books they love. Thank you.

Kate Beales, Alan Butland, Clare Grafik, Tom Nelson, and Susan Young, my trusted beta-readers.

I've said it before, and I'll say it again, because it's still true: being the family or friend of a writer is not easy. Honourable mentions go to: Alan, Ned, Joy, Auntie Susan, Lou, Jude, Rebecca, Scarlet, Tom, Kym, Donna, Victoria.

This novel has its roots in the faith and creative egging-on of my extraordinary editor, Eli Dryden. She takes everything I do and shows me how to shape it into something better and brighter. I am more glad of her than I know how to say.

Hello!

Thank you for choosing *The Woman in the Photograph*. Although I've always been an avid reader, I don't think it really hit me how many books there are in the world until my first novel was published. SO MANY BOOKS! I'm honoured that you chose mine.

My intention for *The Woman in the Photograph* started with a desire to write a feminist novel about feminism: a novel that was about the feminist movement, but also feminist in approach, centring women and telling their stories in an unapologetic way.

How, though? I've always loved photography, and in 2016, I went to 'The Radical Eye', a photography exhibition at Tate Modern. It was fascinating in many ways, but the thing that caught my eye most was a single, framed negative of a print. The collector (Elton John) had taken the trouble to buy not just the print, but the negative. He owned the image.

That got me thinking about how different photography has become. The power of a photographer to create, and own, an image, was so much greater on film than it is in the digital world, when everyone has a camera in their pocket and can take hundreds of photographs in a day without much thought. As I walked around the gallery, I thought: what if the world chooses to see a photograph in one way, but the photographer knows that something else happened? And it struck me, too, that 'the camera never lies' is, simply, untrue. Especially as the photographer is the one choosing where to point the lens, what to focus on.

So, if I were to write about a female photographer – and if she chronicled an era of the feminist movement – and if there was one image, that suggested a certain truth, but the reality was different . . . that was the first glimmer of *The Woman in the Photograph*. I spent a couple of hours in the exhibition, and then

I walked along the South Bank, and by the end of the afternoon, although I didn't know what exactly the novel would be, I knew I had the beginnings of it.

I'm immensely proud of *The Woman in the Photograph*. The writing of it was absorbing, interesting, and at times difficult, especially as I moved between the 1960s and '70s and the present, and reflected on how, although much has changed for women, it's probably not as much as the feminists of the second wave hoped for. I came out of the writing changed: more fierce, more unapologetic, more likely to call out sexism and inequality when I see it.

I hope you love it, and I hope it speaks to you.

You'll often find me hanging out on Twitter and Instagram if you want to talk books – any books, not just mine! And please tag me in your reviews and chats – I'd love to hear what you think about *The Woman in the Photograph*, and for us to join in the wider conversation about women in the world.

Thank you again for reading *The Woman in the Photograph*.

Be well,

Stephanie xx

P. S. If you would like to keep in touch with my writing life, you can visit **http://www.bit.ly/StephanieButlandClub** and join my Readers' Club. It's free to join, and we won't spam you – we'll get in touch now and again with bookish news and exclusive content. (Small print: Zaffre will keep your data private and confidential, and it will never be passed on to a third party. You can unsubscribe at any time.)

For your Reading Group

For discussion

1. From Women's Lib to #MeToo – in the novel, the fight for women's rights seems as needed in 2019 as it was in the 1960s. Vee appears surprised when she looks at Erica's life to find that despite the victories they won in the last century, today's women still have a lot to protest, a lot to fight for. Do you agree with Vee that equality is still a cause that needs battling for?

2. Has the novel made you more or less likely to think of yourself as a feminist? And why do you think people still find it a controversial term?

3. Has the novel made you think differently about photography?

4. Writing about a different medium always requires skill and invention. How well do you think the author managed to bring the photographs to life with her words? How clearly could you see the key pictures in your mind?

5. If you had to sum up your life in a handful of photographs, which ones would you choose? Is there a moment in your life that you wish had been caught on camera?

6. Vee's views and ideals undergo a dramatic shift in her late teenage years. Can you think of a pinnacle moment in your life which changed your views or beliefs?

7. To what extent does Vee choose her isolation? Which comes first – a solitary nature, or the desire to be a photographer?

8. Could you sympathise with Vee's final photos of Leonie? Were those photos brave, intrusive, accidental or a coping device?

9. Do you think you'd have been friends with Vee or Leonie if you met them in your teens or twenties?

10. Who was your favourite male character in the book and why?

11. Do you think it matters who Erica's mother is?

12. On page 359, the author includes an extensive bibliography covering lots of novels and landmark books on feminism and gender – has *The Woman in the Photograph* inspired you to try any of these? What other books would you recommend for readers who enjoyed this, whether stories of female friendship, novels about Britain in the '60s, '70s, and '80s, or books that explore issues of feminism?

Select bibliography

John Berger: *Understanding a Photograph*
John Berger: *Ways of Seeing*
Susan Sontag: *On Photography*

Chimamanda Ngozi Adichie: *We Should All Be Feminists*
Lisa Appignanesi, Rachel Holmes and Susie Orbach (eds):
    Fifty Shades of Feminism
Jessa Crispin: *Why I Am Not A Feminist*
Simone de Beauvoir: *The Second Sex*
Susan Faludi: *Backlash*
Betty Friedan: *The Feminist Mystique*
Roxane Gay: *Bad Feminist*
Germaine Greer: *The Female Eunuch*
bell hooks: *feminism is for everybody*
Audre Lord: *Sister Outsider*
Kate Millett: *Sexual Politics*
Susan Mitchell: *Icons, Saints and Divas*
Robin Morgan (ed): *Sisterhood is Powerful*
Susie Orbach: *Fat is a Feminist Issue*
Laurie Penny: *Bitch Doctrine*
Camille Paglia: *Free Women, Free Men*
Ann Pettitt: *Walking to Greenham*
Marsha Rowe (ed): *Spare Rib Reader*
Rebecca Solnit: *Men Explain Things to Me*
Victoria Pepe, Rachel Holmes, Amy Annette, Martha Mosse and
    Alice Stride (eds): *I Call Myself A Feminist*

Jessica Valenti: *Sex Object*
Naomi Wolf: *The Beauty Myth*
Virginia Woolf: *A Room of One's Own*

Angela Carter: *The Bloody Chamber*
Marilyn French: *The Women's Room*
Erica Jong: *Fear of Flying*
Sylvia Plath: *The Bell Jar*
Alice Walker: *The Color Purple*
Fay Weldon: *Praxis*